BROKEN
THINGS

Also by
LAUREN OLIVER

Before I Fall
Liesl & Po
The Spindlers
Panic
Vanishing Girls
Replica
Ringer
Curiosity House: The Shrunken Head
Curiosity House: The Screaming Statue
Curiosity House: The Fearsome Firebird

THE DELIRIUM SERIES
Delirium
Pandemonium
Requiem
Delirium Stories: Hana, Annabel, Raven, and Alex

FOR ADULTS
Rooms

BROKEN
THINGS

LAUREN
OLIVER

HARPER
An Imprint of HarperCollinsPublishers

Library of Congress Control Number: 2018933333
ISBN 978-0-06-222413-2 (hardcover)
ISBN 978-0-06-286249-5 (signed edition)
ISBN 978-0-06-287743-7 (international edition)
ISBN 978-0-06-289113-6 (special edition)

Typography by Erin Fitzsimmons
18 19 20 21 22 PC/LSCH 10 9 8 7 6 5 4 3 2 1

First Edition

To MRK

For the stories

Before we were the Monsters of Brickhouse Lane—

before everyone from Connecticut to California knew us by

that tagline, and blogs ran pictures of our faces, and searching

our names led to sites that crashed from all the traffic—

we were just girls, and there were only two of us.

BRYNN

Now

Five years ago, when I had just turned thirteen, I killed my best friend.

I chased her down and cracked her over the head with a rock. Then I dragged her body out of the woods and into a field and arranged it in the center of a circle of stones I'd placed there with my other friend, Mia. Then we knifed her twice in the throat and five times in the chest. Mia was planning to douse her body with gasoline and light her on fire, but something went wrong and we bolted instead.

Here's how everyone knew we were guilty: we had described the crime, more or less, in a fan-fic sequel to the book we were all obsessed with, *The Way into Lovelorn*.

Afterward, Mia and I split up. She went home and spent the evening conked out in front of the TV, without even bothering to clean up the gasoline that had soaked her jean shorts. I was more careful. I did a load of laundry—hauling ass to the local Bubble 'N' Spin, since we didn't have a machine at my house. The police were still able to extract samples of blood from my T-shirt, not Summer's but a bit of animal blood, since we'd previously practiced the knifing ritual on a cat, also found in the field.

Owen Waldmann, Summer's kind-of-maybe boyfriend, disappeared after the murder and didn't return for twenty-four hours, at which point he claimed he didn't know anything about it. He never said where he had gone.

He was lying, obviously. He was the one who orchestrated the whole thing. He was jealous because Summer had been hanging out with older boys, like Jake Ginsky, who was on the high school football team. That was the year Summer started growing up, leaving the rest of us behind, changing the rules.

Maybe we were all a little jealous of her.

I tackled Summer when she tried to run, hit her over the head with a rock, and dragged her back to Mia so that Mia and I could take turns stabbing her. Owen was the one who brought the can of gasoline and the one too stupid to dump the can after we mostly emptied it. It was found, later, just outside his garage, behind his dad's lawn mower.

Owen, Mia, and me, Brynn.

The Monsters of Brickhouse Lane.

The child killers.

That's the story the way everyone tells it, at least, a story repeated so many times, accepted by so many people, it has become fact.

Never mind that the case against Mia and me never even made it out of family court. Try as hard as they could, the cops couldn't make the facts fit. And half the information we told them was illegally obtained, since we'd never even been cautioned. Never mind that Owen was acquitted in criminal court, not guilty, free to pass go.

Never mind, either, that we didn't do it.

In books, secret worlds are accessible by doors or keys or other physical objects. But Lovelorn was not such a world, and appeared at whim and only when it felt like it, with a subtle change like the slow shifting of afternoon to evening.

So it was that one day, three best friends—Audrey, Ashleigh, and Ava—were bored and hot and decided to explore the woods in the back of Ava's house, though in truth there was little to explore that they hadn't already seen.

That day, however, a curious thing happened when they set off into the woods.

—From *The Way into Lovelorn* by Georgia C. Wells, 1963

BRYNN

Now

"Your physicals look fine." Paulie bends over my file, scrubbing her nose with a finger. A big pimple is growing just above her right nostril. "Blood pressure's great, liver looks good. Normal heart rate. I'd say you're in good shape."

"Thanks," I say.

"But the most important thing is how you *feel*." When she leans back, her blouse strains around the buttons. Poor Paulie. The residential director at Four Corners, she always has the dazed look of someone who just got into a fender bender. And she can't dress for hell. It's like she buys clothes for someone else's body— too-tight Lycra blouses or too-big skirts and man shoes. Maybe she Dumpster-dives her whole wardrobe.

Summer used to do that: she got her clothes in bulk from the Salvation Army or just stole them. But she could make anything look good. She'd take an old band T-shirt, extra-large, and turn it into a dress, belting it with a bike chain and pairing it with old Chucks. Garbage fashion, she called it.

She was going to move to New York City and be a model when she turned sixteen, and afterward have her own fashion line. She was going to be a famous actress and write her memoir.

She was going to do so many things.

"I feel good," I say. "Strong."

Paulie adjusts her glasses, a nervous habit. "*Six* rehabs since eighth grade," she says. "I want to believe you're ready for a change."

"Four Corners is different," I say, dodging the question I know she wants to ask. Of all the rehabs I've been to, plus hospital detoxes, sober-living facilities, and halfway houses, Four Corners is the nicest. I have my own room, bigger even than my room at home. There's a pool and a sauna. There's a volleyball court on a bit of scrubby lawn and a flat-screen TV in the media room. Even the food is good—there's a salad bar and smoothies and a cappuccino machine (decaf only; Four Corners doesn't allow caffeine). If it weren't for all the therapy sessions, it would be like staying at a nice hotel.

At least, I think it would be. I've never stayed at a hotel.

"I'm glad to hear it," Paulie says. Her eyes are fish-big, wide and sincere behind her glasses. "I don't want to see you back here in six months."

"You won't," I say, which is kind of true. I'm not going to come back to Four Corners. I'm not leaving at all.

* * *

I like rehab. I like the whole routine of it, the clean rooms and the staff with their identical polo shirts and identically helpful expressions, like well-trained dogs. I like the mottos posted everywhere on construction paper: *let go or be dragged*; *live and let live*; *have an attitude of gratitude*. Life in bite-size portions. Miniature Snickers–sized wisdom.

It turns out that after a first trip to rehab, it's easy to hopscotch. All you have to do is make sure to flunk a pee test right before you're supposed to get out. Then counselors get called in; insurance companies, social workers, and relatives are contacted; and pretty soon you've got yourself an extended stay. Even now that I'm eighteen and can technically leave on my own recognizance, it won't be hard: you'd be amazed at how quickly people rally together when they suspect their patient might have killed someone before she was even menstruating.

I don't like lying, especially to people like Paulie. But I keep the story simple and pretty basic—pills and booze, Oxy I used to steal from my mom—and apart from the actual *I'm an addict* part, I don't have to fake it too much.

My mom *was* on Oxy the last time I was home, since some idiot in an SUV rear-ended her when she was coming home from a late shift at the hospital and fractured her spine in two places.

I get nightmares, panic attacks. I wake up in the night and still, all these years later, think I see the bright burst of a flash outside my window. Sometimes I hear the hiss of an insult, a voice whispering *psycho, devil, killer*. Sometimes it's Summer I see, beautiful Summer with her long blond hair, lying on the ground in the middle of a circle of stones, her face a mass of terror—or maybe peaceful, smiling, because the story she had been writing for so long had at last come true.

That's one thing I don't talk about here, no matter how many times Trish or Paulie or any of the other counselors push. I don't talk about Mia, or Summer, or Owen, or Lovelorn and what happened there, how we believed in it, how it became real.

In rehab, I can be whoever I want. And that means, finally, I don't have to be a monster.

Lovelorn had its own weather, just as it had its own time. Sometimes the girls passed through into Lovelorn at high noon and found that within the quiet hush of the Taralin Woods it was all rose and purple, long shadows and crickets, and that the sun was already kissing the horizon. Just as often, when it was cold and rainy in their world, it was brilliantly sunny in Lovelorn, full of summertime bees and fat mosquitoes. One or another of the girls was always abandoning sweatshirts, scarves, or hats on the other side and being lectured for it later.
—From *The Way into Lovelorn* by Georgia C. Wells

MIA

Now

"Holy mother of funk." Abby, my best friend, holds up a moldering piece of fabric between two white-gloved fingers. "What *is* this?"

Whatever it used to be—a jacket? a blanket? an area rug?—is now black, stiff with years of stains accumulating and drying, and full of holes where it's been chewed up by a procession of insects. And it smells. Even though I'm halfway across the room and separated from Abby by mounds of books and newspapers, lamps and old AC units, and cardboard boxes containing a hundred different never-used, never-unpacked purchases, the kind you order off TV at midnight—blenders and multipurpose knives and Snuggies and even a rotisserie oven—the smell still makes my eyes water.

"Don't ask," I say. "Just bag it."

She shakes her head. "Did your mom stash a dead body in here or something?" she says, and then, realizing what she's said, quickly stuffs the cloth into a lawn-and-leaf bag. "Sorry."

"That's okay," I say. That's one of the things I love about Abby: she forgets. She legitimately fails to remember that when I was twelve, I was accused of murdering my best friend. That the first Google result that pops up when you type in *Mia Ferguson* is an article on a popular parenting blog called "How Do Kids Become Monsters? Who's to Blame?"

Partly, that's because Abby moved here only two years ago. She'd heard about the murder, sure—*everyone's* heard about it—but secondhand is different. To people outside our town, Summer's death was a tragedy, and the fact that three kids were the primary (okay, *only*) suspects, a horror, unimaginable.

But in Twin Lakes it was personal. Five years later, I still can't walk around town without everyone glaring at me or whispering awful things. Once, a few years ago, a woman approached me outside the Knit Kit—I'd been looking at the baskets piled with fleecy, multicolored wool, and the sign in the window, *Make Socks, Not War*—lips puckered as if she were about to kiss me, and spat in my face.

Even my mom is abused whenever she has to go shopping or drop off laundry or go to the post office. I guess everyone blames her for raising a monster. At a certain point, it just became easier to stay inside. Luckily—or maybe unluckily—she has her own online marketing business. Since she can order everything from toilet paper to socks to milk on the internet, she can go six months without ever stepping out the door. When she announced a few days ago that she was going to visit her sister, I nearly had a heart attack. It's the first time she's left the house for more than an hour since the murder.

But then again, she didn't exactly have a choice. After my mom's "collections" started spreading, first onto our back porch, and then onto our front porch, and then into our yard, our neighbors started a campaign to get Mom and me thrown out. Apparently, our very presence was contaminating the neighborhood and single-handedly destroying the chance that our neighbors could ever sell their houses. While the town stopped short of taking legal action against us, they did give us two weeks to clean up or face fines for all sorts of environmental hazards. My mom went to stay with my aunt so she wouldn't be in the way, sobbing every time I tried to throw out a used dinner napkin, and I got stuck sorting through five years' worth of accumulated trash.

"Check this out, Mia." Abby extracts a stack of ragged newspapers from beneath a broken standing lamp. "Now we know what was major news in"—she squints—"2014."

I hoist a box from the floor, feeling a small rush of satisfaction when a bit of the carpet is revealed. I read off the side of the box: "'With the amazing Slice and Dice, kitchen prep is a breeze!'"

"Maybe you should sell that. It's still in the box, right?" Abby climbs to her feet with difficulty, using a TV stand for leverage. Abby is fat and very beautiful. She has light eyes and dark hair, the kind of lips that make people think of kissing, a perfectly straight nose, just slightly upturned.

When she was ten, she started a YouTube channel all about fashion and beauty. By fifteen, she had two million subscribers, sponsorships from major brands, and a flow of bank that meant her family could get out of Garrison, Iowa, and move back to Vermont, where her grandparents lived.

Abby travels to so many Beautycons, vidcons, and fashion weeks, she has to homeschool, which is how she and I ended up together—when she's not traveling—five times a week, four hours a day, listening to Ms. Pinner drone on about everything from narrative techniques in *The Sun Also Rises* to the covalent bond. We meet at Abby's house, three blocks away, for the obvious reason that there is nowhere to sit in my house. There's hardly room to breathe.

The Piles have seen to that. They are ruthless. They breed. They multiply overnight.

"Sure," I say. "If you like your veggies with a side of black mold." I tuck the box beneath my arm and make my way to the front door, sticking to the path carved carefully between the Piles, an endless canyon of belongings—flattened cardboard boxes tied with twine, rolls and rolls of expired grocery store coupons, packing tape and rusted scissors, old sneakers and deflated inner tubes and no-longer-functional lamps—all stuff that my mom, for some reason, thinks it necessary to keep.

Outside, the sky is a weird color. The clouds are a seasick green. We're supposed to have a few bad days of storms—maybe even a

tornado—although nobody really believes that. We don't get tornadoes in Vermont, at least not often, and half the time the news
predicts one it's just to boost ratings.

I heave the box into the Dumpster parked in our driveway. The
Dumpster is the big, industrial kind used for home renovations
and construction projects, and already, after only two days, it's
half-full.

Back inside, Abby is red-faced, coughing, cupping a hand to
her mouth.

"What?" I say. "What is it?"

"I don't know." She chokes out the words, eyes watering. "I
think it's an old pizza or something."

"Leave it," I say quickly, trying to ignore the twin rotor blades
that start going at the bottom of my stomach. "Seriously. The sky
looks like it's about to throw up."

"Are you sure?" Abby obviously feels embarrassed that *I'm*
embarrassed. Which just makes me feel worse, especially since
Abby's not the kind of person who is easily made uncomfortable.
She is the kind of person who, instead of wearing big sweatshirts
or sweatpants and trying to disappear, wears feathered skirts and
multicolored tights and dyes her hair a variety of colors, then
spends four hours staging a photo shoot with her pet Maltese,
Cookie Monster. "We barely made a dent."

This is not entirely true. I can see several bare spots in the carpet. The TV and TV console have been revealed in the living
room. I wonder whether we still have cable. "So?" I force a smile.

"More for us to do tomorrow. Maybe we'll even find a buried treasure."

"Or the lost city of Atlantis," Abby says, peeling off her gloves and depositing them in one of the open trash bags. Before she leaves, she grips my shoulders. "You're sure-sure-sure? I won't find you tomorrow suffocated under a pile of dirty laundry and old newspapers?"

I force a smile. That awful shredding feeling is still there, churning up my insides. But Abby wants to get out. And I don't blame her.

I've been wanting out for as long as I can remember.

"Go," I say, sidestepping her. "Seriously. Before a tornado sucks you somewhere over the rainbow."

She rolls her eyes and gives her stomach a slap. "I'd like to see a tornado try."

"You're beautiful," I call after her as she heads for the door.

"I know," she calls back.

After Abby's gone, I stand there for a minute, inhaling slowly without breathing too deeply. We've opened all the windows—the ones we could get access to, anyway—but still the living room stinks like unwashed upholstery and mold and worse. The curtains, ragged and slick with stains, twist in the wind. It's dark for four o'clock and getting darker every second. But I'm hesitant to turn on one of the overhead lights.

The Piles look bad in the dark, sure. But manageable. Formless and soft and strange. Like I could be in the middle of a weird alien landscape, a place where whole mountain ranges are built of cardboard and copper and rivers of plastic flow softly between them. In the light, there's no way to pretend.

My mom is crazy. She can't get rid of anything. She cries if you try to get her to throw out a catalog, even one she doesn't like. She holds on to matchbooks and sandwich bags, broken garden rakes and empty flowerpots.

Maybe things would have been different if Dad had stayed. She wasn't totally normal back then, but she wasn't totally screwy, either. But Dad didn't stay, and Mom fell apart.

And it's all my fault.

Abby was right: there is a pizza box, and the remains of something that must once have been a pizza (Ms. Pinner would have a field day explaining *that* series of chemical reactions) smushed beneath an old leather ottoman. I work for another few hours and fill another ten leaf bags, dragging them out to the Dumpster one by one. The sky gets wilder by increments, deepening from a queasy green to the color of a bruise.

I stand for a minute on the front porch, inhaling the smell of wet grass. As a little kid I used to stand just this way, watching the other kids wheel around on bikes or pummel a soccer ball across the grass, shrieking with laughter and noise. *Go on and play with them*, my dad would say, irritation pushing his voice into spikes. *Just talk to them, for God's sake. How hard is it to say hi? A couple of words won't kill you.*

I couldn't talk. I knew how, of course, but in public my throat would simply stitch itself up all the way to my mouth, so trying to speak sometimes made me gag instead. I knew even then that my dad was wrong—words could kill you, in a thousand different ways. Words are snares to trip you and ropes to hang you on and whirling storms to confuse you and lead you the wrong way. In fifth grade I even started a list of all the ways words can turn nasty, betray and confuse you.

#1. Questions that aren't true questions. For example, *How are you?* when the only right answer is *fine. #2. Statements that are really questions.* For example, *I see you didn't finish your homework.* I got as far as *#48. Words you can scream into the silence that will never be heard:*

I'm innocent.

As a kid I found a different way to talk. At night I used to sneak outside and practice my ballet routines on the lawn, throw my arms to the sky and leap with bare feet across the grass, spinning and jumping, turning my body into one long shout. *Listen, listen, listen.*

The wind has picked up and whips an old catalog down the street. Maybe we will get a tornado, after all. Maybe a storm will come ripping through the maple trees and old cedar, tossing off branches and cars and even roofs like high school students do with their graduation caps, tear straight down Old Forge Road, and mow through our house, suck up the Piles and the bad memories, turn everything to splinters.

Back inside, I have no choice but to turn on a lamp in the front hall—one of the few standing lamps that hasn't been buried under a mountain of stuff—and maneuver by its light, trying not to knock into anything in the living room. The wind has picked up. Newspapers whistle and plastic bags swirl, tumbleweed-style, across the living room.

The rain comes all at once: a hard, driving rain that batters the screens and bowls them inward, pounds like angry fists against the walls and roof. Thunder rips across the sky, so loud I jump, accidentally dislodging a laundry basket filled with magazines. Two whole Piles go over—an avalanche of *toasterumbrellascanvasrollspaperbackbooks*—tumbling across the strip of carpet we recently cleared.

"Great," I say to nobody.

My mom likes to say that she collects because she doesn't want to forget anything. She once joked that the Piles were like a personal forest: you could read her age in the size of them. And it's true that here, a history of our little two-person family is written: water-warped postcards, now indecipherable, dating from just after my parents' divorce; five-year-old magazines; even one of my science textbooks from seventh grade, the last year I ever spent in public school.

But it's more than that. It's not the story of a family but of a family gone wrong. It's a book told in silences, words suppressed underneath enormous cloth-and-cardboard mountains.

I squat down to keep sifting and discarding. Then I shift a stack of moldering printer paper and my heart stops.

Sitting on a patchy square of carpet is a single paperback book. The cover, speckled with mold, shows the image of three girls holding hands in front of a glowing door carved into a tree. And suddenly, for no reason, my eyes are burning, and I know that this thing, this small, bound set of pages, is the heart of it all: this is the root of the forest, the seed, the reason that for years my mother has been building walls, mountains, turrets of belongings. To hem it in. To keep it down.

As if it's alive, and dangerous, and might someday come roaring back to life.

The book feels simultaneously heavy and hopelessly brittle, as if it might break apart under my touch. The inside cover is still neatly marked in blue pen:

Property of Summer Marks.

And beneath that, in red, because Brynn insisted: *and Mia and Brynn.* Even though Summer never even let us read it unless she was there to read it with us. It was hers: her gift to us, her curse. I have no idea how it ended up in my house. Summer must have left it here.

The last line of handwriting I recognize as my own.

Best friends forever.

For a long time I sit there, dizzy, as everything comes rushing back—the story, the three friends, the landscape of Lovelorn itself. Those days in the woods playing make-believe under a shifting star pattern of leaves and sun. How we'd come home at night, breathless, covered in bug bites and scratches. How things changed that year, began to twist and take different shapes. The things we saw and didn't see. How afterward, no one believed us.

How Lovelorn stopped being a story and became real.

Slowly, carefully, as if moving too fast might release the story from the pages, I begin leafing through the book, noting the dog-eared pages, the passages starred in pink and purple, the paper warped now from moisture and age. I catch quick glimpses of familiar words and passages—*the River of Justice*, *Gregor the Dwarf*, *the Red War*—and am torn between the desire to plunk myself down and start reading, cover to cover, like we must have done eighty times, and to run outside and hurl the book into the Dumpster, or just set it on fire and watch it burn. Amazing how even after all this time, I still have whole passages practically memorized—how I remember what comes after Ashleigh falls down the canyon and gets captured by jealous Nobodies, and what happens after Ava tempts the Shadow by singing to it. How we used to spend hours arguing about the last line and what it might possibly mean, trolling the internet for other Lovelornians, theorizing about why Georgia Wells hadn't finished the book and why it was published anyway.

A sheet of paper is wedged deep into the binding. When I unfold it, a Trident wrapper—Peach + Mango Layers, Summer's favorite gum—flutters to the ground. For a second I can even smell her, the gum and the apple shampoo her foster mother bought in jumbo containers at the ninety-nine-cent store, a shampoo that smelled awful in the bottle but somehow, on Summer, worked.

My heart is all the way in my throat. Maybe I'm expecting an old note, a scribbled message from Summer to one of us; maybe I'm expecting her to reach out from the grave and say *boo*. I don't know whether to be disappointed or relieved when I see it's just an old three-question Life Skills pop quiz that must date from sixth grade. It's covered all over with the teacher's red pen markings and various deductions for wrong answers and misspellings. At the bottom, the teacher has even included a summons. *Come see me after class, please.—Ms. Gray.*

Ms. Gray. I haven't thought about her in forever. She was one of the Earnest Ones and seemed to believe that her subject, Life Skills, would *actually* improve the quality of our lives. Like knowing how to unroll a condom on a banana and identify a uvula on an anatomical chart were going to get us through middle school.

I'm about to replace the failed quiz and toss the book, once and for all, when I get the poky feeling that something isn't right—a discomfort, like a rock in the shoe or a bug bite on the knee, something itchy and impossible to ignore. It doesn't *fit*.

I grab the book and the quiz and make my way out into the hall, where the light is better. The temperature has dropped by at least fifteen degrees, and I shiver when my feet hit the linoleum. Outside, the rain is still pounding away at the windows like it's trying to get in.

Summer was never a good student—she was more interested in *Return to Lovelorn* than she was in doing homework—and her foster father, Mr. Ball, was always threatening to lock her in her room if she didn't bring her grades up. She just didn't *care* about school. Her future was bigger than graduation, bigger than college, way bigger than Twin Lakes.

But she was the writer. She was the talent. She was the one who insisted we meet up at least twice a week to work on *Return to Lovelorn*, the fan fic we were making up together, the sequel that would resolve the awful, baffling, unfinished ending of the original. She would sit cross-legged on Brynn's bed, directing us to change this or that scene, to add in certain details. She would go away for a week and come back with sixty pages, with the three of us as the heroines instead of Ashleigh, Ava, and Audrey; and her chapters were brilliant, detailed, and strange and gorgeous, so good we always begged her to try to get them published.

Here, though, Summer's answers are all screwed up. She switches around common words and misspells stupid things like *their* and *they're*, writes half her letters backward, mistakes words for words that sound similar but mean totally different things.

I get a sudden rush to my head, like a fever coming on all at once. Suddenly I realize: Summer *couldn't* have written those perfect pages of *Return to Lovelorn*.

Which means that there was somebody else.

The day turned brighter and the shadows darker, the trees grew incrementally taller and their leaves turned a very slightly different green, and the girls knew without speaking a word that something tremendously exciting was happening, that they had come to a new place in the woods.

"I don't remember a river," said Audrey, wrinkling her nose as she often did when she was confused.

"Or a sign," said Ava, and she read aloud from the neatly lettered signpost tacked to a tall oak tree. "'Welcome to Lovelorn.'"

"Lovelorn," Audrey said scornfully, because she was often scornful about things she didn't understand. "What on earth is that?"

Ashleigh shook her head. "Should we go back?" she asked doubtfully.

"No way," Ava said. And because Ava was the prettiest one, and also the most opinionated, and the others always did what she said, they went forward instead.

—From *The Way into Lovelorn* by Georgia C. Wells

BRYNN

Now

Friday night is movie night at Four Corners, and after dinner all the girls pile into the media room, half of them already in their pajamas. The DVD collection at Four Corners is pathetic and features exactly two kinds of entertainment: "recovery dramas"— bad TV movies about hard-core addicts getting to rock bottom and then having some epiphany and moving to Costa Rica to find love and do charity work—or the handful of normal features that meet Four Corners' rules against any cursing, depictions of sex, violence, alcohol, or drugs, aka pretty much every single thing that makes a movie worth watching unless you're six years old. The old Tom Hanks movie *Big* makes the cut. So does *Frozen*, supposedly because it celebrates the idea of self-acceptance. But I'm pretty sure it's just because one of our counselors, Trish, loves the music.

Tonight everyone votes to turn on the local news. The big

storm moving through the Northeast is supposed to reach us by midnight, and everyone's freaking out about power outages and the water shutting off and being stranded with no AC for days.

"I didn't even know we had TV," a girl—I think her name is Alyssa—says. She looks kind of like a Muppet. She even has weird orangey skin. Either she really likes tanning beds or she grew up next to a nuclear power plant and is now radioactive.

"Do we have Showtime?" another girl, Monroe, asks. "Or HBO?" Monroe's supposedly in for opiates, like me, but I'm pretty sure she might just be addicted to being the most annoying person alive. Every time she tells a story she has to include a metaphor from some dumb TV show. *I felt the way that Arianna felt on season two of* The Romance Doctors *when she got passed over at the very last minute even though everyone thought she was going to win.*

"Local news only," Jocelyn, one of my favorite counselors, says. She punches at the remote. *Input/Output Error* is blinking on the screen.

"What about ABC?" Monroe asks, with increasing desperation, like this is a life-or-death, stranded-in-the-desert situation and she's asking how much time is left before we have to start eating people. "Or the CW?"

"Local news only, Monroe," Jocelyn repeats, and Monroe slumps back against the sofa.

Jocelyn pushes a few more buttons and the TV blinks into life, showing a reporter clutching a microphone and holding on to the hood of a rain slicker with the other hand. Behind her, trees are bent practically sideways by a hard wind; even as she's standing there, an awning rips off from one of the stores behind her and goes tumbling down the street.

It takes the sound a few seconds to catch up to the visuals. ". . . standing here on Main Street in East Wellington," the reporter is saying, raising her voice to be heard over the wind. "And as you can see from the scene behind me, Tropical Storm Samantha has also arrived. . . ."

East Wellington is where Wade lives. That's only two towns over from Twin Lakes. For some reason, it isn't my mom and sister but Mia who comes to mind: Mia locked up in her big house, listening to the wind batter the shutters. Even though I haven't spoken to her in five years, haven't even seen her from a distance in maybe three, I suddenly wish I could call her and make sure she's okay.

"Tropical storm?" Alyssa reaches for the popcorn. "I thought they were saying hurricane."

"Shhh," another girl hushes her.

"What's the difference?" someone else says.

"*Shhh*." Now several girls speak at once.

". . . Meteorologists are saying that so far wind gusts have reached only forty miles per hour, and so the storm has been downgraded from original reports predicting a historic hurricane," the reporter says. "Still, they warn that the storm is just beginning and is expected to worsen as it meets the cold front coming off the Atlantic. It is still possible that we'll be facing hurricane conditions—record winds, flooding, power loss, and road closures. Basically, a big mess."

The screen cuts to another reporter, this one sitting behind a studio desk and wearing a badly fitting suit, with teeth way too square and white to be real. "Stay safe and stay home, people. . . ."

"There goes visiting day." Rachel makes a face. Rachel is in for depression and mood disorders, a cluster that includes everyone with serious suicidal tendencies—people who've done far more than, say, stick a thumbtack in their arm just to see if it would hurt. (It did.) Rachel has the sharp, sweet face of a squirrel and looks like the kind of girl you'd want to cheat off during a math test—until she rolls up her sleeves and all her old track marks are visible.

"What do you mean?" I say.

She jerks her chin toward the screen. "We're marooned. See? Flood zone number one." Now there's a big map on TV showing different portions of Vermont and how much water they can expect. Addison County is highlighted in a fire-engine shade of red.

"The weather reports always exaggerate," I say quickly. "They're just trying to boost ratings."

Rachel shrugs. "Maybe."

"When's the last time we had a tornado in Vermont?"

"Like, four years ago," she says. "Why do you even care, anyway? No one's coming for you."

Stupidly, hearing the words out loud like that, I get a weird ping in my chest, like a popcorn kernel has gone down the wrong pipe.

"My cousin's coming," I say, which is mostly true. Wade Turner is actually my mom's cousin's son, which makes him once removed or twice baked or whatever you call it. For the past five years, he's run a conspiracy site dedicated to the murder at Brickhouse Lane. He's convinced, for reasons I don't completely understand, that he can find the truth and clear my name. For twenty bucks in gas money—half of what my mom gives me for the month for incidentals, like candy bars and recovery-themed sweatshirts and postcards—he'll drive an hour and a half from East Wellington to Four Corners to drop off bottles of dirty pee. He'd probably do it even if I didn't pay him, just for the chance to grill me on what happened—not that I ever have anything new to say.

Wade is weird as hell, but at least he's *someone*. My mom hasn't visited Four Corners at all, and my older sister—her face narrowed so much it has achieved the look of an exclamation point—came only once, still wearing scrubs, to drop off a stack of magazines I hadn't asked for and tell me that I was disappointing everybody. And my dad has been out of the picture forever, a fact that has never much bothered me but has been used time and again by therapists and bloggers and the state-appointed attorney who argued against my transfer to criminal court to explain everything from my supposed juvenile delinquency to the fact that I don't like math.

My system with Wade is simple. Once every ten days, he makes the seventy-four-mile drive from East Wellington with a bottle of yellow Gatorade rattling around on the floor of his old truck—a bottle that just happens to contains pee he snuck out of the state-sponsored clinic for junkies and drunks where he works during the week. He gets to Four Corners and signs in at the lobby. Then, pretending he's desperate to use the bathroom after the drive, he ducks into the visitors' bathroom and drops the Gatorade bottle in the toilet tank, which only occasionally gets checked for bags of pills or floating vodka bottles.

Later, after Wade and I do our obligatory chat—the most painful part of the whole process, as far as I'm concerned, since I have to pretend to actually be happy to see him and he just sits there with a dopey smile on his face, like a kid in front of a mall Santa Claus—I walk out with him to say goodbye, carrying an empty plastic soda cup from the cafeteria, fitted with a lid and straw. There are always so many people signing in and getting waved through security or blubbering while they talk to the counselors, it's no big deal to use the visitors' bathroom without anyone noticing. The pee goes in the soda cup, and then in the shot-glass-size containers the counselors distribute with my name written in Magic Marker on the label. Just in time to flunk my drug test and land myself a very late checkout.

Maybe I'll get to stay for ninety days this time.

"Thank you, Ellen," the fat guy in the badly fitting suit says, and then puts on his bad-news voice. "In other news, the town of Twin Lakes is preparing to commemorate the fifth anniversary of the tragedy at Brickhouse Lane—"

All the air goes out of the room. Half the girls turn to stare at me. The rest of them go still, as if they're worried the slightest motion will cause an avalanche.

"—in which, on a seemingly normal Tuesday afternoon, thirteen-year-old Summer Marks was viciously murdered." A picture of Summer flashes and my heart closes up, fist-like. She looks so young. She *was* so young: our thirteenth birthdays, only three days apart, had passed two weeks before she was murdered. And yet when I imagine her, and when she comes to me—which she still does, in quick impressions, popping in and out of dreams or running through my memories the way she used to run through the woods, suddenly full of light and suddenly plunged into shadow—she's always my age. Or maybe I'm *her* age, back when she was my everything.

"Suspicion quickly fell on Summer's then-boyfriend and two best friends, who had been obsessed with a little-known and especially violent children's book—"

Please don't show the picture. My lungs feel as if they're being flattened to paper. *Please don't show the picture.*

"Turn it off," one of the counselors says sharply. Jocelyn is looking for the remote on the carpet, where it has become lost in the tangle of legs and blankets and soda cups. And it's too late, anyway. A second later, the picture is on the screen, the infamous picture.

In it, Mia and I are dressed up for Halloween like the Reapers of Lovelorn, wearing black hoodies and lots of eyeliner that Summer pocketed from a local CVS and carrying homemade scythes fashioned from tinfoil and broom handles. And Summer, standing between us, is the Savior: in all white, her blond hair pinned and curled, her lips bloodred and pulled into a smile and a matching circle of red around her neck, too. The news has fuzzed out my face and Mia's as if with a giant eraser, but Summer's face is perfectly clear, grinning and triumphant.

I didn't even want to be a Reaper. I thought we should dress up as the original three—Ava, Ashleigh, and Audrey—but Summer said that would be boring. It was all Summer's idea.

"So wait. Which one is you?" Zoe asks, turning to me. Zoe is new. She got out of the detox unit only a few days ago and since then has done nothing but sit sullenly in group, chewing on the sleeve of her hoodie or staring at the ceiling fan as if it's the most fascinating thing in the universe.

"The remote." The buzz is building among the counselors. Jocelyn is shoving people aside, rolling other girls onto their hips, trying to find the lost remote.

"The case against the two girls was soon dropped, and Summer's boyfriend was ultimately acquitted, due largely to objections by the defense that the investigation had been mishandled." He pauses and lets this sink in for a minute, staring at the camera sadly, as if to say that this, the failure to put us in jail for the rest of our natural lives, is an absolute travesty.

He doesn't say that the cops never even cautioned us before dragging us down to the police station, so nothing we told them would have held up in court. He doesn't say that Owen's defense turned up evidence of insane police incompetence: the DNA sample that supposedly showed his blood intermingled with Summer's at the crime scene had actually been left in the back of a police van for forty-eight hours and was so broken down by heat that it was ruled inadmissible.

"That *is* you, right?" Zoe repeats, now looking hurt by my refusal to acknowledge her.

"Five years later, this small, tight-knit community is still shattered by the incomprehensible horror of this crime, and on Sunday plans to host a memorial to—"

The TV goes blank. Jocelyn has at last found the remote, and she sits there panting, like a dog that's worked too hard to find a bone. There's an electric silence, somehow louder than any sound. Everyone is watching me, or deliberately not watching me, as if they're afraid I'll scream or throw something or maybe just start crying.

Or maybe they're just afraid.

"Well." Trish springs to her feet, false cheerful, clapping her hands. "What's it going to be tonight? Last week there was a vote for *Tangled*—should we watch that?"

No one answers. The room is still laced with tension. I stand up, slightly dizzy, not caring that this will make it worse. No one says anything as I force my way out into the hall, stomping over popcorn kernels and plastic cups, stepping on a girl's hand. She yelps and then goes quickly quiet.

The hall is empty and cool—an AC thrums somewhere in the walls. As soon as I'm alone, my eyes start to burn and blink fast; I'm not even sure why I'm crying. Maybe it was seeing Summer's face on TV—that crazy-beautiful heart-shaped face, all big eyes and thick lashes, smiling like she always had a secret.

The pay phone at the end of the hall is etched with initials of previous patients. The receiver smells like bubble gum, and it's always coated with a thin moisture-film of sweat and lotion. I try to keep it far away from my cheek as I pull out my phone card— sold in the Four Corners store next to racks of stuffed animals and motivational T-shirts—and punch in Wade's number.

He picks up on the first ring.

"It's Brynn," I say, instinctively lowering my voice, even though there's no one in the hall to eavesdrop. "You're still coming tomorrow, right? You're not listening to all this bullshit about a hurricane?"

"Brynn! Hi!" Wade always speaks in exclamation points. "I'm still . . ." His voice fades out and I have to wrench the phone away from my ear as a brief series of cracks and pops explodes through the line.

"What?" I knuckle the phone a little harder. "I can't hear you."

"Sorry!" Another series of cracks, like the sound of someone balling up tinfoil, disturb the line. "The wind's bad already. They say we're going to get maybe three feet of rain. River's supposed to . . ." His voice fades out again.

"Wade," I say. I can still hear him talking, but his words are hopelessly distorted. "Wade, I can't understand you. Just tell me that we're on for tomorrow. Promise me, okay?"

"I can't control the weather, Brynn," he says. Another annoying thing about Wade is that he comes out with deeply obvious statements as if they're major pieces of wisdom.

"Listen." At this point I'm pretty much desperate. I need Wade. I'm not leaving Four Corners. I'm not going back into a world of people who stare at me or, even worse, choose to ignore me altogether—push past me on the sidewalk, refuse to serve me at the diner, look straight through me, as if I don't exist. "Just say you'll be here, okay? I have something I want to tell you. It's important." All bullshit, obviously, and like I said, I'm not a liar by nature. But I've learned to look out for myself. I've had to.

"What kind of something?" His voice turns suspicious—but also hopeful.

"Something I remembered," I say, making it up as I go, trying to keep it vague.

"It's about Summer," I add quickly when he says nothing. "You still want to help me, right?"

There's a long stretch of quiet, disturbed only by the faint pops and buzzes on the line.

"Wade?" I'm gripping the phone so tightly, my knuckles hurt.

"If the roads are open," he says. It sounds like he's talking through a shitty computer speaker. "I'll be there."

I say, "They'll be open." I don't even say goodbye before hanging up.

* * *

The rain gets to us just before lights-out, beating so hard on the roof it sounds like a stampede. Half the girls scream when lightning rips across the sky, and a moment later, the lights flicker.

Monroe finds me just after I've brushed my teeth, planting herself in front of the bathroom door so I have no choice but to stop.

"Hey." She flicks her bangs out of her eyes. "I'm sorry about what happened before. The whole news thing. No one knew what to—" She breaks off, sighing. "Look, *I* think it's cool, okay?"

"You think what's cool?" I say automatically, and then wish I hadn't.

She blinks at me. "That you killed someone."

At Four Corners there's this thing called T.H.I.N.K. Before you speak, you're supposed to make sure that what you have to say is Truthful, Honest, Important, Necessary, and Kind. In principle, it's a nice idea. But principles and practice are very different things.

"You're an idiot," I say. "And you're in my way."

The wind is so loud it keeps me up for hours. It screams like someone lost and desperate in the dark. But finally I do sleep. And for the first time in years, I dream of Lovelorn.

Mia was the nice one, but she was shy. Summer could get anyone to like her, and she wasn't afraid of strangers. And Brynn was always in a fight with someone, although deep down she might have been the softest of them all. (But she'd never admit it.)

—From *Return to Lovelorn* by Summer Marks, Brynn McNally, and Mia Ferguson

BRYNN

Now

"Everything looks good, very good. You're feeling good? Good." Paulie's nerves are obviously shot. It's like her brain is set to repeat. The admin offices flooded during the storm. Even though the water has receded, the carpets are still soaked and will probably need to be pulled up. "I know you're old enough now to sign your own release. I see you never provided us the name of the person coming to pick you up today, but never mind. . . . It's been such a whirlwind. . . ." She manages a faint smile. "No pun intended."

It's Sunday morning, and while I should be relaxing in detox courtesy of Wade's delivery, instead I'm sitting in the cafeteria across from Paulie and a big stack of release papers. The sun is out for the first time since Friday afternoon, and the lawn is tangled with tree branches and garbage blown in from who knows where. Outside, men in identical green T-shirts and thick rubber gloves move across the puddled lawn, sorting through all of it.

I seize onto the idea of a mistake. Maybe I can buy an extra day or two. "Nobody can come," I say, and it's not hard to sound disappointed. Wade really *couldn't* come. Apparently a branch went straight through his windshield. "The storm," I clarify when Paulie looks surprised.

For once, the storm was just as bad as the news predicted. Tornadoes did, in fact, touch down in parts of the county. Half the towns from Middlebury to Whiting are without electricity. Otter Creek flooded and carried away cars and garden sheds and even an eighteenth-century windmill—just swallowed it whole, burped out a few two-by-fours, and *thanks again, see you next time.*

According to the news—ever since the generators kicked in on Saturday morning, we've had the news going in the media room—Twin Lakes got hit hard. I saw footage of the old movie theater missing half its roof and Two Beans & Cream, its windows shattered, its antique coffee grinder half-submerged in water. Telephone lines sparked in the street and water moved sluggishly between parked cars.

When I tried my mom's house phone, I got nothing but a cranked-up beeping in my ear. When I called my sister's cell phone, she practically hung up on me.

"Shit's insane," she said, and I could hear Mom in the background, her voice high-pitched and worried, telling her to mind her language. "Look, I can't talk. The basement's flooded. Mom's freaking out. Stay dry, okay?" And that was that.

Of course, it's also true I never asked either my mom or my sister to pick me up at Four Corners, for the simple reason that I never told them I was leaving. I was never *planning* to leave.

"Oh." Paulie shoves her glasses up her nose with a thumb, frowning. "But what about the young woman out in the lobby?"

I stare at her. "What?"

"She signed in half an hour ago." Paulie shuffles through her set of papers. "Here she is. Audrey Augello. She said she was here to see you. I just assumed she meant to check you out."

For a second my brain blinks out. My first thought is that it must be a joke. One of the other girls got the idea to prank me after seeing the news. But almost immediately, I know that can't be it—the news never mentioned Lovelorn by name or any of its characters. So: someone else, someone who knows, must have tracked me down, hoping to freak me out.

That was a thing we used to do, the three of us. It was a game of ours to pretend to be one of the original girls. Summer, the beautiful one, always the leader, the one who got to say yes or no or stop or go, was Ava; Mia, sweet little Mia with her big eyes, who bit her nails when she was nervous and moved like a ballet dancer, even when we were playing soccer in gym, was Audrey; and I was Ashleigh, the loud one, sarcastic and funny and just a little mean.

We used to use our second names when we wrote notes to each other in school. Mia even had a set of stationery made up online that said *Audrey Augello* at the top in pink, and whenever it was her turn to write a part of the story, she would do it by hand on her special paper. And Summer had a secret email account, lovelorn-ava@me.com. We were supposed to use it for messages about Lovelorn. But then Mr. Ball, Summer's foster father, found out she'd been spotted riding around with Jake Ginsky and his older brother and insisted on having all her passwords and checking her email and Instagram and Snapchat and everything. (Summer was convinced he'd even trained their old cat, Bandit, to spy on her and start yowling when she tried to sneak out.) So we ended up using the secret account, which Mr. Ball never knew about, for everything we wanted to say and didn't want anyone else to know about: Summer's crush on Jake Ginsky and whether Owen Waldmann would grow up to be a serial killer and the fact that Anna Minor had already given a blow job to not one but *two* guys, both of them eighth graders. Crushes and secrets and confessions. Inside jokes and YouTube videos and songs we had to listen to together, singing until our lungs gave out and our voices dried up in our throats.

"Oh, right. Yeah. Audrey." My voice sounds different, tinny and strained. I don't know whether Paulie notices. "I'll go talk to her."

"Don't forget, you'll need to fill out some paperwork," Paulie calls after me as I start for the reception area. Of course. Places like Four Corners aren't built out of brick or concrete but out of forms and authorizations and disclaimers and requests for forms and requests for future requests for forms.

I pass several group rooms, most of them empty, the little

chapel, and the movie room. Someone has left the TV on, still tuned to local news. Reception is at the end of the hall, through a set of swinging doors fitted with the circular kinds of windows you see on ships.

She's sitting on the couch closest to the exit, as if needing to guarantee the possibility of a quick escape. On the news Friday night I was struck by how young Summer looked. But even though I haven't spoken to Mia in five years, since It happened, and even though she's grown and I've grown and her hair isn't in its usual ballerina-style bun, she looks exactly the same: big eyes and a fringe of dark lashes; little upturned nose and a chin so sharp and narrow it looks like you could poke yourself on it.

For a long time, we don't say anything. My heart is going so hard I worry it might just leapfrog out of my throat.

Finally, she speaks. "Hi," she says, and then shuts her mouth quickly, as if biting back other words.

"What are you doing here?" I say. I've imagined seeing Mia again a hundred times. Of course I have. I've imagined seeing Summer, too, imagined she might suddenly come back to life and step into the present, wearing one of the crazy outfits only she could pull off, laughing like the whole thing was just a joke. *Boo. Gotcha. Did you miss me?*

Never did I imagine standing face-to-face with Mia here, at someplace like Four Corners.

I didn't imagine I'd be afraid, either.

"I needed to talk to you." She speaks so quietly I have no choice but to take a step forward just to hear her. Her eyes tick to the woman behind the desk. "In private," she adds.

Maybe Mia's been in rehab too and has just hopscotched to Step #9. (Step #8: We made a list of all persons we had harmed and became willing to make amends to them all; Step #9: We made direct amends to such people wherever possible, except when to do so would injure them or others.) Maybe she wants to say sorry for selling me out to the cops, for wiping out our whole friendship in one go. *I wasn't even there. . . . I left Summer and Brynn alone. . . . I don't know what happened. . . . Ask Brynn. . . .*

But whatever the hell has led her here, to me, after all this time, I'm not buying. I'm not forgiving, either, even if she begs.

"How did you find me?" I ask.

For a second she looks faintly irritated, like the Mia who used to lecture us when Summer and I were supposed to be doing homework and instead were sprawled out on the couch, legs criss-crossed over each other, sharing a computer, competing over who could find the weirdest YouTube clips.

"How do you think?" she said. "Google." When she sees I don't get it, her mouth twists up like she's just taken a shot of something really gross. "Some blogger did a whole 'where are they now' piece for the fifth anniversary."

"No way," I say, and she nods. "That's fucked." For a fraction of a second, we're on the same team again. The Monsters of Brick-house Lane. Bring out your pitchforks and light up the bonfire.

Then she ruins it.

"Look," she says. She lowers her voice again. "I think I might have found something. . . . I know it sounds crazy, after all this time. . . ."

"What are you talking about?" I say.

She avoids looking at me. "Going back." Now she's practically whispering. "We have to go back."

"Go where?" I say, even though I know. Maybe, deep down, I *have* been waiting for this. For her.

I notice she's holding something double-wrapped in a thin grocery bag, like raw chicken she's afraid will contaminate anything it touches. Even before she fully removes the book, I recognize it: the faded green-and-blue cover, the girls huddled together in front of a tree glowing with a secret, as if a burning ember has been placed somewhere between its roots.

She looks at me then, and says only one word.

"Lovelorn."

Mia's favorite thing about Lovelorn was the princesses who lived in high towers and sang sad songs about the princes who were supposed to come rescue them. Brynn's favorite thing was the tournament and the chance to see everyone she hated beheaded.

And Summer's favorite thing was the fact that there were no cats, especially no crabby old tabby cats named Bandit, to pee in her shoes and claw her favorite jeans.

Okay, maybe that wasn't her favorite thing, but it was awesome.

—From *Return to Lovelorn* by Summer Marks, Brynn McNally, and Mia Ferguson

MIA

Now

Brynn loads her duffel bag and slams the trunk—harder than necessary—then climbs into the passenger seat, immediately slumping backward and putting her feet on the dashboard without asking for permission, so her knees are practically at her chest. If Brynn were a dance she'd be something modern, coiled and tight and explosive. A dancer on her knees, but ready to leap, punch, tear down the theater.

#18. Words that want to be screams.

"Are you going to drive?" she says.

Earlier, when Brynn came through the lobby doors, I couldn't believe it was really her—not because of how much she'd changed, but because she looked the same. It was like my idea of her, my memories, had simply doubled and spat her out a few years older, in a different setting, but unmistakably *her*: the wild tangle of dark hair, the heavy jaw, the way she walks almost angrily, with her hands curled into fists.

But now, it's the changes I notice: the fact that she has stopped biting her nails, which used to be chewed nearly raw; the three studs in her left ear, which used to be unpierced; the small tattoo of an infinity symbol on the inside of her right wrist. She catches me staring at it and tugs down her sleeve.

She's a stranger.

Evidence of the storm is everywhere: roads blocked off because of downed trees or power lines, men and women in waders and hard hats redirecting traffic, detours looping us around and back again so I begin to worry we'll just end up back at Four Corners. There are a thousand things I'm dying to ask Brynn, a thousand things I want to tell her, too, but the longer the silence drags on, the harder it is to know how to begin. She keeps her nose practically glued to the window, knees up. When I put on the radio, she immediately punches it off.

Finally, I can't take it anymore. "You could at least say something. I'm not your chauffeur." Too late, I realize I sound like a mom.

"You want me to say something?" She turns to me at last, narrowing her eyes. "Fine. I'll say something. You're out of your mind."

This is so unexpected, I can't immediately find my voice. "What?"

"You're out of your mind," she repeats. "Showing up out of nowhere—talking about Lovelorn." She makes a face, as if the word smells bad. "What were you thinking?"

I almost say: *Excuse me. Didn't I just pick you up from* rehab*?* I almost say: *Which one of us is* really *crazy?* But I don't.

#19. Words that stick spiny in your throat, like artichokes.

I say, "I was thinking you might actually care about what happened that day. I was thinking you might want to help."

"Help what?" She puts her legs down, finally. She's left footprints on the dashboard and doesn't bother to wipe them off. "It doesn't matter what happened that day. Don't you get it? She's dead. Everyone thinks we did it and they'll never stop thinking it and that's the end of that. Move on. Change your name. Get a life."

"Oh, because that's what you did?" In my head, a dancer breaks formation. Rapid frappés, striking the floor. *One two three four five.* "Were you moving on when you landed in rehab? When you landed in *six* rehabs?" The words are out of my mouth before I can regret them.

She mutters something too quietly for me to make out.

"What?" I say.

She exhales, rolling her eyes. "I said yeah, actually. I was." Then she turns back to the window. "It's called survival of the fittest."

"Oh, thanks," I say sarcastically. "And here I thought you slept through seventh-grade science."

She doesn't bother responding.

I'm half-tempted to pull the car over and order her out, see how she likes trekking the last however-many miles home to Twin Lakes through a sludge of mud and garbage. It was craziness to think she would help me, to think she would even care. She hasn't asked me a single thing about Lovelorn, hasn't even asked me what I found, why I drove two hours through a once-in-a-century storm just to talk to her. All she did at Four Corners was stand there, staring at me like I was a smelly stuffed animal she'd ditched in the local Dumpster—like she couldn't imagine how I'd crawled back into her life. "Put that thing away," she'd said, when I'd shown her the book—wincing slightly, as if it pained her. And then: "Look, I don't know what you're doing here, but I'm about five minutes away from splitting. And that makes you my ride, so."

Then nothing. Just ordered me into the car and told me to wait, like I was a limo service she'd hired to be her getaway.

Stupid, stupid, stupid. Somehow I believed that if I could only talk to Brynn, she would make it better—or at least know what to do. I thought the old magic would come back, that special force that bound us together as a unit, that spun the rest of the world off into the distance. Back then, I thought Brynn could handle anything. I truly believed Summer would grow up to be famous.

I truly believed we were special.

But maybe the magic, like Lovelorn, never really existed: just another memory to let go.

As we near Twin Lakes, we have to slow down behind a line of cars waiting to be fed into a single lane. Half the road is blocked off by a police cruiser, and flares fizzle on the road, marking a wide circle around an uprooted tree, roots raised to the sky like the spokes of a gigantic wheel.

We inch into the left lane, following the instructions of a cop, who gestures us forward. I suck in a quick breath when I see the line of low-rent row houses just past Meers Lane, or what's left of them, anyway. Whole porches have collapsed; garbage is scattered across the grass. One of the houses—where Pia, my old babysitter, used to live—has a chunk missing from one of its walls, like a giant has taken a bite out of it. I can see straight through into the living room.

"Holy shit." Brynn sits up a little in her seat. "Isn't that where your babysitter used to live? Pita?"

"Pia," I correct her. But the fact that she remembered—that she remembers—makes me suddenly and stupidly happy. She hasn't totally forgotten.

"Right. Pia." Brynn seems more alert now. She leans forward. Farther toward the historic district—a name I've never understood, since it's where all the newest shops are—9A turns into Main Street, and the sprawl of Laundromats and shingle-sided houses becomes instead a tidy collection of cafés, organic restaurants, jewelry stores, and art galleries. At the intersection of Main and Maple, the exact center of downtown Twin Lakes, Brynn whistles. "Damn. Check out Luigi's. It looks like something exploded."

My heart gives another squeeze. Luigi's is actually now

Flatbreads & Co., and has been since we were in fifth grade. Now the big glass windows that belly out onto the street are gone, shattered by winds. One of the tables has made its way out onto the sidewalk, where it's lying, legs up, like a drowned insect.

"I didn't know it was going to be this bad," I say. Abby told me Twin Lakes got hit hard—*hammered like a frat boy on a Friday* were her exact words—but hearing about the damage is different from seeing it.

"You weren't here?"

"I missed the worst of it," I say. The streetlights at the corner of Main and Maple are down. There's another cop directing traffic, and yet another long line of cars waiting to turn right. This portion of Main Street is completely blocked off, and we have to reroute down Maple and onto King. The parking lot behind Nooks & Books is still flooded. A Prius is just sitting there in a sludge of dirty water. "I left on Saturday afternoon, before the wind really picked up." I don't tell her I spent the night a few miles away from Four Corners, at the Sunshine Motel and Motor Lodge, on sheets that smelled like old cigarettes. I don't tell her it took me hours this morning just to work up the courage to drive those final 3.6 miles.

"I can't believe you drove a car in this." She turns to stare at me. "I can't believe your mom *let* you. Weren't you scared?"

"Yeah, well." I don't answer directly. And of course, she doesn't know that my mom is currently 110 miles away, probably sneaking dinner napkins into her purse and collecting junk mail from

Aunt Jess's house, and that she thinks I spent the whole storm safely tucked away in my bedroom. "It was kind of important."

Brynn's still looking at me sideways, like she's never really seen me before. "We made it all up, you know," she says in a low voice. "There was never a Lovelorn. Not really. We went crazy."

"I know that," I snap.

"Crazy," she repeats, with a funny expression on her face. "And half in love with each other."

"You weren't in love with me," I say. "You were in love with Summer."

I regret the words as soon as they're out of my mouth. *#31. Words like shrapnel: they get inside before they explode.* For a split second, she recoils, as if I've slapped her. I see her spotlighted on a stage, on her knees, a small, coiled ball of fury.

Then she leaps. She's out of the car even before I've stopped moving. I jerk to a stop. The trunk is already open. The bag is in her hand. By the time I get the window down and call her name, she's gone.

MIA

Then

The first time we went to Lovelorn, it was raining.

This was late June, a few weeks after the end of sixth grade, and I shouldn't have been home. I was supposed to be at ballet camp in Saratoga Springs, New York, bunking up with other dance nerds and spending my mornings perfecting my pas de bourrée and trying not to be hungry and generally getting as far as possible from my parents, who had been in a four-month competition to see who could be angrier.

But two weeks earlier, during our stupid end-of-school field day, Noah Lee shoved into me from behind and down I went, hard, on my left ankle. Summer told me afterward that even my fall was dramatic and graceful. Brynn said she wished she'd been filming for YouTube.

So: I had a sprained ankle and no summer plans.

We'd played at Lovelorn plenty of times since September of

sixth grade, when Summer had first moved in with Mr. and Mrs. Ball, a couple with four grown children of their own who had for unknown reasons decided to foster a child late in life—largely, Summer thought, for the cash they got from the government.

Plus Mr. Balls—that's what Summer called him—*needed someone new to order around.*

Brynn and I weren't even friends before Summer came along. Summer had slid suddenly and effortlessly into our orbit, bringing Brynn and me into alignment, like the gravitational center of a very small universe.

We were on the same bus route. Our whole friendship, and everything that happened, can be traced back to that dumb yellow bus that always smelled like the inside of a Cheetos bag. Mr. Haggard, our bus driver, had a weird comb-over and was always singing show tunes and joking that he should have been on Broadway. Brynn liked to say that school was just a big sanity test to see who would crack first, and on that bus, it was easy to believe that.

For years, Brynn and I sat separately in the very back, sometimes leaving a few rows of seats between us, sometimes directly across the aisle from each other, without ever once speaking. And then one day Summer appeared, wearing cutoff shorts and men's suspenders over a flimsy Coca-Cola T-shirt, and she slipped between us—sitting right next to me, legs up, little blond hairs growing over her knees—and started talking to us as if we'd chosen to sit there deliberately and not because it was far away from everybody else. As if we were already friends.

From then on, we were.

Summer was the one who introduced us to the book. She had the whole thing practically memorized. She'd been toting it around from foster home to foster home and always said it was the only thing she owned that truly belonged to her and wasn't borrowed or stolen.

By June we'd played at being the three original girls plenty of times. Sometimes one of us would sub in as a different character—Gregor the Dwarf, or one of the Sad Princesses who lived in the Towers. Brynn loved to play Firth, a centaur thief who'd stolen one of the princesses' hearts and bartered it for his own freedom, only later realizing he'd cursed himself to a loveless life. Summer often switched characters halfway through the game, declaring that she was both Audrey and the nymph conscripted by the Shadow to steal Audrey away, and we never questioned her, because she knew the book better than we did and because she played all the characters so well, really hamming it up and making us believe. That's one of the things I loved about her: she wasn't afraid to look like an idiot.

She wasn't afraid, period.

That day, the day in early summer when Lovelorn turned real, we had to go slower because of my ankle. Summer and Brynn leapt over the creek and then helped me across, and we pretended we'd forded the Black Hart River. We fought through the long field filled with cattails and spider grass, pretending that we were on the road to the dwarfs' village in the Taralin Woods.

Maybe it's just because of what happened next, but I remember feeling then a kind of magic coming to me on the wind. The trees lifted and lowered their great green hands and then fell still. The birds went quiet. Summer and Brynn were already far ahead of me, laughing about something, and I stopped, suddenly struck by the strange wonder of the sky, a sweep of golden sun and dark clouds and the whole world gone quiet as though waiting for something.

Lovelorn, I remember thinking. And even though it made no sense, a thrill went through me, a certainty that made me feel breathless. *This is it. We're really here.*

Then the rain came. It swept in out of nowhere, the way summer storms do, throwing the trees into a frenzy again. Summer's house was the closest, but Mr. Ball didn't like her to have friends over—and besides, the whole place was dark and smelled like old-man breath.

We were soaked within seconds. My jeans felt like they were trying to suck the skin off my thighs.

"The shed!" Summer yelled, reaching out and seizing Brynn's hand. Everything felt so urgent then. "Make for the shed!"

In the spring we'd found an old equipment shed that had at one point belonged to a farmhouse that had been torn down to make room for a whole bunch of double-wides and rent-by-the-week cottages like the kind Summer lived in with the Balls. We'd been to the shed plenty of times, although I was too afraid of spiders to stand inside for more than a few minutes. The shed had a plank floor and smelled like it was rotting. The single window was so coated in dust, even in midday the room was practically pitch-black, and it was piled with rusted tools that looked like parts of human anatomy, arms and fingers and teeth.

Brynn and Summer went dashing off, and I remember seeing the outline of their bras through their T-shirts and being jealous because I had nothing but bug-bite nipples and an occasional achy feeling. I was annoyed, too, because I couldn't keep up and even though I kept shouting for them to wait, they wouldn't. They were always doing things like that—ducking into the bathroom to whisper about something and shutting the door in my face, or raising their eyebrows when I complained that Mr. Anderson was *too hard* and then bursting into laughter. "That's okay, Mia," Summer would say, patting my head as if she were a thousand years older than I was. "You'll understand when you're older."

They disappeared into the shed. By the time I caught up, the door had swung closed again. It was swollen and warped with age and I had trouble getting it open. For a second I thought they were going to leave me outside, in the rain, as a joke. I started pounding on the door and shouting, and finally it swung open.

They hadn't even heard me. They were standing in the middle of the room, water pooling beneath their feet, dripping from their hair and clothing. I remember how quiet it was when I shut the door, and the rain was nothing but a dull drumming on the walls and roof.

The shed was clean swept and smelled like scented vanilla

candles. All the old tools were gone. All the spiderwebs, too.

The walls were papered with old-fashioned floral wallpaper, cream with pretty bouquets of roses, and a green braided area rug muffled the sound of our footsteps. In one corner was a small cot covered with a patterned quilt. Next to it was a wooden bedside table and a battery-powered lantern designed to look like candlelight. The windowpanes had been scrubbed mostly clear, although a few webbed bits of mold remained in the corners. There was even a mason jar filled with tiny wild violets.

And a small wooden sign, looped with cursive writing, nailed above the bed: *Welcome to Lovelorn*.

"Did you do this?" I turned to Summer, even though I knew from her expression that she hadn't.

In the books, the original three were never anything but delighted when Lovelorn appeared, when it began to change things, melting familiar landscapes like butter softening at the edges, kneading it into new shapes: a tree into a tower; the old stone wall into the gremlins' grotto. And later, we would love the clubhouse, the way it had materialized for us in the rain; the warmth of the quilt, which we draped over our shoulders like a communal cape; the lantern with its flickering glow.

But I wasn't delighted, not then. Then, I was scared.

"It's magic," Summer said. She went to the walls and ran her fingers over the wallpaper, as if worried it would dissolve under her fingers. When she turned around again, her eyes were bright. It was the only time I ever saw her close to crying. "It's Lovelorn.

We found Lovelorn."

"Lovelorn doesn't exist." Brynn still hadn't moved. She looked angry, which meant that she, too, was scared. "Admit it, Summer. You planned this. Admit it."

But Summer wasn't listening. "It's Lovelorn," she said. She went spinning through the room, touching everything—the blanket, the cot, the lantern—her voice rising in pitch until she was practically shouting. "It's Lovelorn."

In the bedside table, she found a box of chocolate chip cookies and tore it open with her teeth. They were stale, I remember, and crumbled like caulk between my teeth.

There were probably lots of entrances to Lovelorn, maybe in old cupboards or under beds or in places no one thought to look, like the back of an old storage closet. But the easiest way to get there was through the woods, and so that's where Summer, Brynn, and Mia went the day they decided to see it for themselves.

—From *Return to Lovelorn* by Summer Marks, Brynn McNally, and Mia Ferguson

BRYNN

Now

Mia's words keep cycling through my head as I trudge up Harrison Street, like a song I can't stop hearing.

You were in love with Summer.

In love with Summer.

Summer.

Summer.

Summer.

Part of me wishes I hadn't climbed out of the car. I should have laid into her instead, for getting it all wrong, for always getting it wrong. For being the tagalong, the scared one, the one who told the cops all about Lovelorn.

But another part of me—the small, vicious, dark piece, the little monster squatting somewhere in my brain—knows that she isn't wrong, at least not about this.

Was I in love with Summer?

Was she the first one?

The only *real* one?

There have been others since. I'm a lesbian. Or a *lez*, *dyke*, *rug-muncher*, and *box-bumper*, according to the graffiti that covered my locker in the years after Summer died. Vermont is mostly a liberal state—the principal of Twin Lakes Collective, Mr. Steiger, brings his husband to graduation every year—but that's only so long as the queers stay invisible. Harmless. Nothing to worry about here, all hands accounted for, vaginas and children safe.

I don't know when I knew I was gay, exactly, except that I didn't ever *not* know, either. And in case you're into the idea that sex is like cauliflower and I'll never know for sure unless I've tried it, I *have* tried it. I've been with exactly three girls—like, *really* been with them—and hooked up with a half-dozen others. There's not a whole lot else to do in rehab.

There was Margot, a skinny French-Nigerian girl with a dozen piercings in her face, who'd grown up in Ohio. Her nose ring fell out whenever we kissed. Sasha: Russian, from Brighton Beach, New York, with an accent that always made it sound like she was purring. Ellie, who I stayed with for a few months: she covered her mouth when she laughed and had hair that reminded me of a porcupine's spikes.

But Summer was different. Special. Pure, in a way. Maybe because I couldn't have her—maybe because, back then, I wasn't even sure I wanted to.

Maybe just because I loved her so bad.

Maybe because she broke my heart.

I remember getting caught in a sudden downpour with her on our way back from Lovelorn, alone, in the fall of seventh grade. Summer hadn't wanted to tell Mia, and I was guilty and thrilled all at once. And then back at her house we crowded into her little shower in our underwear and T-shirts, so close together we had no choice but to touch, and her blond hair was all in a tangle and mascara smudged her cheeks and her breath smelled like strawberries and we couldn't stop laughing, taking turns shouldering each other out of the way to get under the water, and every time she touched me it was like someone had turned lights on beneath my skin. And then there was the time she said she was running away from home, and she spent three nights in the clubhouse, and one night she begged me to stay with her, so I did, wrapped in the same sleeping bag, our knees touching, the smell of her sweat filling the whole room and making me feel dizzy. She was a princess. I was going to be her knight.

I was going to protect her.

There was the Kiss. There was what came afterward, the rumors at school, the way people hissed at me when I passed, how none of the girls would change in front of me for gym. How Summer refused to look at me, how seeing her from down the hall made me feel like the witch at the end of *The Wizard of Oz*, like I was dissolving, melting into a sizzling puddle.

But as always, my mind redirects when I get too close to that memory, veering sharply past it, my own little mental detour. Danger ahead.

I backtrack to Main Street, keeping my head down, praying

no one notices me, wishing I had a hat. Luckily, the people who are out are too busy checking for damage or picking up debris. It seems like all this mess should come with a lot of noise—flashing lights, sirens wailing, the growl of equipment—but the emergency has passed and it's weirdly quiet.

Turn left on County Route 15A and a few miles out of town you'll hit Twin Lakes Collective: the elementary and middle schools and, across the street, the high school I never attended because the harassment was too bad. Instead, I turn right. This way leads to cheap subdivisions like the one my mom lives in now—home, I guess, although I've done my best to stay away— all of them carved out of old farm property that got cut up and mixed around like a chicken getting butchered for the fryer. Keep going, and the space between the houses grows, until it's all browns and greens, forests and farms, and little blobs of civilization like the mistakes someone made while painting. Eventually County Route 15A peters out into a one-lane dirt road and winds past roads with names like Apple Orchard Hill and Dandelion Circle, and my old street, Boar Lane. Summer's house was one lane over on Skunk Hill Road. Beyond that: Brickhouse Lane, named for the tumbledown house at the end of the lane scrawled over with graffiti tags and Sharpie initials, a rusted Dodge still raised on cinder blocks out front.

Perkins Road is blocked off by a fire truck. A big pine tree has taken out a power line, and now various workers are milling around, looking bored, like people waiting at the post office.

Across the street, I notice Marcy Davies's front door open. Even though it's too dark to see inside, I'd bet anything she's sitting in a lawn chair in front of the AC, watching the road show. Marcy, the not-so-mysterious "source" quoted in four dozen newspapers who claimed to have known about my psychopathic tendencies since I was a little kid. For years, she told people, I'd tortured frogs for fun and stolen other kids' bicycles; I'd always had a thing for knives and had played war instead of Barbies—despite the fact that we only moved to Perkins a few months *after* Summer died, after Billy Watson, our old neighbor on Boar Lane, said he was acting on a command from God and tried to burn our house down—when I was inside of it. I don't even think Marcy was getting paid for her interviews. She just liked making shit up.

I swing my duffel bag onto my shoulder, like it's a body I'm rescuing from a collapsing building, hoping it will completely conceal my face, and step up onto her lawn to get around the truck.

Right away, a firefighter stops me.

"Hang on." He has acne around his jaw that makes him look twelve. He isn't even wearing his whole uniform—only the overall pants over a thin white T-shirt. "Where do you think you're going?"

"Home," I say. Sweat is running freely down my back.

"Road's closed," he says. "You're going to have to come back later."

I can feel something hard—my cell phone—digging into my neck through the thin cotton duffel. "I can't come back later. I live here." Another firefighter briefly turns to stare. "Look," I say. "I can see my house. See that little gray house over there?" I point because all the houses on Perkins are gray, since they were all built in two years out of the same sad collection of cheap shingles and plywood. "I'll hurry. I won't even go close to the lines."

"Road's closed," the guy repeats. He doesn't even look over his shoulder to see where I'm pointing. "Fire department's orders."

Finally, I lose it. "Are you even old enough to be giving orders?" I say. I know it's stupid to argue, but my mouth and my mind have never exactly been in perfect sync. "Don't you have to ask your daddy or something?"

"Very funny," he says. "If I were you—" He breaks off. Something changes in his face—it's a subtle shift, but instantly, my stomach drops. He knows. "Hey," he says. "I know who you are."

I turn away quickly, forgetting momentarily about Marcy, and in that second I see her, exactly where I thought she would be, revealed by a bit of sunlight slanting into the hallway: her legs, feet encased in grubby sandals; her hands gripping the arms of her chair, and a cigarette smoking between two fingers. She shrieks.

"David!" Her voice carries all the way across the lawn. "David, you'll never guess who's home!"

I start to run, not even caring how ridiculous I look, not caring about the weight of my duffel or the fact that my heart's going club-beat-style in my chest. I don't stop until I've rounded the corner and turned onto Waldmann Lane, where I'm concealed by the thick growth on either side of the road. I drop my duffel, cursing, rolling the pain out of my shoulder. There's a chalky taste in my mouth. Goddamn Marcy. Goddamn prepubescent fireman. Goddamn Twin Lakes.

I remember one time toward the end of the school year in sixth grade, when it was too hot to go to Lovelorn, too hot to do anything but lie across my bed reading magazines and taking quizzes online with the AC on full blast, Summer said her biggest fear was of being forgotten. That's why she was going to be a model and then write and star in her own TV show. If you weren't famous, Summer argued, if no one remembered you, you might as well not have lived at all. I understood her point, even though I'd never wanted to be famous.

But Summer hadn't thought it all out. She didn't realize how much depends on what you're remembered *for*. Sometimes, it's so much better to be forgotten.

All the roads in this part of Twin Lakes were once driveways leading up to farm and manor houses. And Waldmann Lane hasn't grown much since then: it's still a one-lane dirt road rutted with tire tracks and sticky with mud. While the Perkinses of Perkins Road and the Halls of Hall Street and all the other families who used to own the land around here took their money and left decades ago, Waldmann Lane still dead-ends at the ancestral home of Dieter Waldmann, great-grandfather of Owen. As far as I know, the house still belongs to Owen's dad, even though a month after Owen was acquitted, they picked up and went off, supposedly to Europe.

From Owen's house I can cut through the woods and circle back to Perkins Road, a fact the press loved to mention. There was even a theory that Owen was a warlock controlling us all with his mind, and he'd forced my family to move after the crime so he could keep an eye on me. No mention of why Mia got to stay put, and why he'd need me close if he was telegraphing commands directly to my brain.

The mosquitoes are thick and the sun lies in long, heavy slabs, like butter. But as I get to the top of the hill, the day seems to get darker. The trees crowd closer overhead. The Waldmanns haven't been around to make sure the road gets cleared by the county.

And then the house appears, partially obscured by the trees, and I stop.

It's been years since I was up here, and in a flash I know I've been avoiding it. Just like I never go up to Skunk Hill Road, just like I haven't gone into the woods once, just like I stopped reading, too, even though it meant nearly flunking eighth grade.

The house is the same, which is what shocks me—nothing should be allowed to stay the same when so many things are different. I think again of Summer's face on the news report, how young she looked.

Forever thirteen. Forever gone.

I walk a little closer and finally register small differences: weeds have swallowed up the lawn, and at some point the Waldmanns dropped a fence around the entire property, probably to keep people from sneaking up and writing stupid shit on the walls with spray paint, like they used to do at our house. I can't remember whether the fence was put up before Owen got shipped to Woodside Juvenile Rehabilitation Center, or afterward.

I press my face right to the cool metal fence and peer down the length of the driveway, and once again my breath gets punched out of me: an enormous oak tree has collapsed onto what used to be the solarium, where Summer and I smoked our first cigarette behind a potted plant in the fall of seventh grade and then felt like we might puke. Then there's a flash of color through the trees, and suddenly Owen Waldmann rounds the corner of the house, threshing the tall grasses with a stick.

I jerk backward, but it's too late. He sees me.

For a long second, we just stare at each other through the fence.

"Brynn," he says, letting out a long breath. "Hi." He's gotten tall—he must be six-three—and he's filled out a little, although he's still skinny, and with his red hair all wild it looks as if a giant reached down, grabbed him by the scalp, and stretched him out like taffy. His eyes are still the kind of blue-gray that darkens from sunny sky to storm in a second. And the second he sees me, they knot up with clouds.

Owen Waldmann. Owen the warlock. Owen, with the crooked smile and the bad temper and moods that broke like waves on the beach.

Owen Waldmann, the maybe-killer.

Owen Waldmann, who was *maybe* lucky enough to get away with it.

Luck is a funny thing like that. Like a coin whose two sides you can read at once.

At the scene of the crime, the police found Summer draped with Owen's sweater, soaked with blood that might have been Summer's.

Not just her blood: Owen's.

Allegedly. The cops thought the case was so open-and-shut, they failed to properly store the sample, and during the trial the evidence was ruled inadmissible.

"What are you doing here?" I say.

He flinches. "Nice to see you too."

"Answer the question."

The last time I saw Owen was just after the trial, a few months after we moved to Perkins Road, two years after Summer was killed. In that time, there'd been other bad murders in the country, even in the state: in Burlington, a PTA mom kissed her husband goodbye in the morning and straightened up the kitchen and then drowned her newborn child in the sink. In New Hampshire, a twelve-year-old opened fire in a school, killing three people, including the guidance counselor who'd been trying to help him, and on and on and on. When you can't count on anything else, you can count on the news to make you sick.

I remember hearing that Owen had been released from Woodside and that he and his dad were leaving. I hoofed it up the hill from Perkins Road just in time to see the last moving van rumbling down Waldmann Lane, followed by Owen in the passenger seat of his dad's old Mercedes. An old man spat on the hood of the car. A woman kicked the tires and screeched "murderer." I hung back in the trees, overwhelmed by a kind of jealousy that felt like having my guts pulled out through my mouth: he was getting out.

He was maybe, maybe, getting away with it.

Owen shoves a hand through his hair, making it look even wilder. His T-shirt is faded green and imprinted with the image of a cow. He never used to wear color. He had a whole wardrobe of black jeans, black T-shirts, black hoodies. Everyone used to say he would grow up to be a serial killer: he wore a black trench coat and combat boots every day and spent most of his classes doodling violent comic books or sleeping with his head on the desk. Plus, his dad was a drunk. Even worse, he was a rich drunk—he could buy his way out of hitting bottom.

I remember once on the playground in third grade, Elijah Tanner was making fun of Owen for being small and skinny and generally weird, the way kids did back then, and Owen barely even seemed to be listening. Then *boom*. All of a sudden he whipped around and drove a fist straight into Elijah's nose. I'll never forget how much blood came from that little nose—like a spigot had been turned on.

I never understood what Mia saw in him. I never understood what *Summer* did.

Except: she always had to be a part of everything. She always had to be the center. Maybe she had to be the center of that, too.

"I live here, remember?" he says. His voice is faintly accented.

"No, you don't," I say. "You moved."

"I went to school," he corrects me. "I graduated."

Graduated. Jesus. *Graduated* is keg parties and sports trophies and a gift certificate to Bed Bath & Beyond. *Graduated* is proud grandparents and tearful selfies and country songs. I wonder whether Mia graduated this year too. I think I'm still a sophomore, but I'm not totally sure. Mom always said she was reenrolling me as soon as I could prove I could stay sober for more than eight weeks. But so far, thanks to good old cousin Wade and our little arrangement, I haven't had to.

"So what, you're back now?" I don't care if I sound rude. First Mia, and now Owen, all in the same day. The whole point of the past is it's supposed to actually, you know, pass.

Owen just shrugs. "We're selling the house," he says. "To be honest, I'm not sure why we've hung on to it so long. My dad's away on a business trip. I came back to help him get everything in order. But now . . ." He gestures to the tree, still poking its arms up through the wreckage, like a drowning person waving for help. "On the plus side, now you can walk straight from the kitchen into the garden. No need to use a door. I keep telling my dad we should put that in the real estate brochure."

Something hard yanks at my stomach again. I forgot Owen was funny. I forgot so many things, like the way Mia chews the inside of her lip when she's nervous, gnawing on it like a corncob.

I didn't *want* to remember.

"Sucks," I say, and turn away from him, suddenly exhausted.

"Hey!" Owen calls me back. Now he looks hurt, and also surprised, like a middle schooler at a social who was just *sure* his crush was going to ask him to dance. "I haven't seen you—I mean, it's been years. How are you? How have you been?"

This seems like such a stupid question that for a second I just stare at him.

"Oh, I've been great." Apparently he doesn't pick up on my sarcasm, because he starts nodding really fast, like his chin is set to overdrive. "Flipping fantastic. I graduated." I don't know why I lie. It just slips out.

"That's great, Brynn," he says. "That's really great."

"Yup. With honors. And a varsity frigging cheerleading jacket. Now I'm going to Harvard on a full ride. I wrote an essay called 'The Girl Behind the Monster.' It won a prize."

His smile fades.

Now that I'm on a roll, I can't stop. "Every year the town throws me a parade. You should come down next time. There's even popcorn."

He looks so sorry that I almost—*almost*—feel bad. "Things are still shitty, huh?" he says quietly.

"Never stopped," I say.

Once again, he calls out to me when I turn to leave. "Brynn!"

"*What?*" I spin around, no longer even pretending to be friendly.

Owen comes across the lawn slowly, like he's worried I'll startle and run if he gets too close. There's something scary about Owen, even now that he's dressed normally and has *graduated* and has a kind-of-cute accent—something intense and airless, like the pull of a black hole. And the thought comes back to me, as always: just because they couldn't nail him doesn't mean he didn't do it.

"I wanted to ask about . . ." He trails off, looking away, squinting into the sun. "I mean, is Mia still around?"

Just like that, I feel a rush of hatred, strong and dark, like a mudslide. "You know what, Owen?" I say. "Leave Mia alone. Do us a favor, and leave both of us alone."

Then I turn around again and stomp into the woods. This time, he doesn't call me back.

All the dwarfs were crying, but none so hard as Gregor—he would never forget how the three girls had saved his sister from being taken by the Shadow.

"Please come back," he said. "Please don't forget us."

"Of course we'll come back," said Ava stoutly.

"How could we ever forget you?" said Ashleigh loyally.

"We'll always be with you," said Audrey kindly, pointing to her heart. "In here."

"But—what will happen to you?" he cried.

That was, indeed, the question. What would happen to them? What would happen to Lovelorn, to the doors in and out? And yet they had to go home. They had to move forward. Because if not, then

—The controversial last page of *The Way into Lovelorn* by Georgia C. Wells

MIA

Now

"I don't know about this," Abby says, gripping a birch tree around the trunk and sliding backward down into the creek bed. "This feels suspiciously like exercise."

"We're almost there," I tell her. "Besides, the water feels good."

Abby stares skeptically at the creek, which, after the most recent rains, is now pummeling and frothing across a pathway of small rocks, forming little white eddies, and then wiggles awkwardly out of her flip-flops.

"Have you ever noticed," she said, "that people don't feel the need to endorse things that *actually* feel good? Sleep in, it feels good! Finish those nachos, it'll feel good! Only things that cause physical discomfort need the extra advertising dollars."

"Don't be a baby," I say. She wades into the water and squeals.

"See?" I say, when she makes it to the other side of the creek, gripping her flip-flops in one hand, and hauls herself up the bank. "That wasn't so bad."

"Compared to what, the Inquisition?" She swats at a mosquito with a flip-flop. "Most people celebrate the Fourth of July the American way—by sitting on their ass. Where's your sense of patriotism?"

"Fresh out," I say, reaching over to squeeze her shoulder. She grumbles something that sounds a lot like *evil*.

It's Monday morning, ten a.m., and I'm doing something I've never done before, something I swore I would never do: I'm going back to Lovelorn, and I'm taking a stranger with me.

But of course, as Brynn was quick to point out, there is no Lovelorn, and so the rules don't matter. There is no ancient magic, nothing but a big stretch of woods that gobbles up the hills and the houses, and an old supply shed. Still, as Abby and I fight our way up the mud-slicked bank and start across the meadow, I can't help but feel excited. Butterflies zip through the trees and insects chitter.

"So this is where it happened?" Abby breaks the silence. Today she's wearing a short black skirt, thick black-framed glasses, a white T-shirt that says *Save a Horse, Ride a Unicorn*, and a knotted necktie. *Harry Potter–punk*, she calls her style.

"Where what happened?" My voice sounds loud in the thin morning air.

"Where Summer's body was found," Abby says bluntly, the way she would if she were talking to anybody else.

"Not here," I say. "In the long field. I'll show you." Weirdly, I've never actually spoken about the way her body was found—only what came afterward, and where I'd been.

Soon the trees run out at a long, rectangular meadow, a place mysteriously devoid of trees that we named the long field years ago. I point to a line of thick pine trees, through which I can just make out the roof of the old supply shed. "The police think she was killed over there. There was evidence she ran. Someone hit her on the back of the head with a rock. Then she was dragged."

Standing here in the sun, it all seems so surreal, like I'm only narrating a story I once heard. Birds swoop over the field, bright blurs of color, sending their shadows skimming over the grass.

Abby squints at me. "You okay?"

"Yes." I close my eyes for a second and say a quick prayer to Summer, if she's out there, if she's listening. *Tell me*, are the only words that come. *Tell me what happened.*

A bird cackles somewhere in the trees. I open my eyes again.

We keep going. Halfway across the field we come across a circle carved out of the underbrush, as if a giant cookie cutter has removed a portion of the meadow. A large wooden cross is staked in the ground. On it, someone has written in purple marker: *5 years later . . . we will never forget you.* Amazing how many people claimed to love Summer after she died, even people who didn't care at all when she was alive.

Next to the cross is a beautiful flower arrangement, red and white roses interlinked in the pattern of an enormous heart. It must have cost three, four hundred dollars. Curious, I bend down to look at the card. There's no signature, only a quote from the Bible.

I read it out loud. "'Though I walk through the valley of the shadow of death, I will fear no evil. For you are with me.'" I look at Abby. "It's a psalm."

"Hmm." Abby frowns. "I'll stay on the hill of the brightly lit land of happy, thanks."

"The Bible was written, like, two thousand years ago," I say, standing up. "They didn't *do* happy back then."

"Probably because they didn't have Wi-Fi."

We keep going, passing once again into the shadow of the trees. The shed is even smaller than I remember it, but otherwise looks the same, except for a flimsy chain lock cinched like a belt across it. Funny that the shed never got much attention from the police or the press, despite all the time we spent lying on the braided rug, giggling, playing music on our phones, or just talking about nothing. We never knew how to talk about what had happened: how Lovelorn had materialized overnight.

And how it vanished.

A few months before Summer died, Brynn and I went to Lovelorn without her. It must have been right after the spring dance, because neither of us was talking to Summer, and I remember how badly my throat hurt whenever I tried to swallow, as if days of crying had left it bruised. I'd missed four ballet classes in a row—my teacher, Madame Laroche, had even called the house to see if I was sick.

I was. Just not in the way she thought. I'd always thought heartbreak was beautiful, like the adagio in *Swan Lake*: a kind of graceful withering. But this just felt as if I'd been gutted and bled, my insides lifted clean away.

We'd never been to Lovelorn just Brynn and me. I didn't feel like going. But Brynn thought it would be a good idea.

"She can't take everything," she said, seizing my hand and practically hauling me off the bus. I knew she wasn't just angry at me. Something else had happened, something between Brynn and Summer, but I didn't know why or exactly what: only that people had begun to whisper about Brynn liking girls, and several girls had refused to change next to her before gym class. People were saying that Brynn was obsessed with Summer, and that Summer had caught Brynn staring into her window at night. The worst part was that Summer wasn't denying it. "She can't just take everything you want."

It was a raw, cold day, more like March than April. We stomped across the fields in silence, both of us miserable and half-frozen, jackets flapping open, breath steaming in the air. Brynn was first through the door and I'll never forget the way she cried out—half gasping, as if someone had punched her in the stomach.

The wallpaper was gone. The rug, the cot, the blanket, the lantern—gone. The shed had the same whitewashed walls as always, the same rough-hewn plank floors, the same random assortment of dusty farming equipment piled in the corners and tacked to the walls.

It was as if Lovelorn had never existed.

Of course, I know now that it never had.

Still, a small, buried part of me believes. It was there. We *saw* it.

"Check it out." Abby reaches for the lock, showing me that it's actually been snapped, then rehung and stuck together with a disgusting combination of a hair tie and chewing gum. From a distance of even a few feet, you'd never be able to tell it was broken. "Looks like someone beat us to it." Her voice is still cheerful, but I can tell from the way she palms her hands on her skirt that she's nervous.

"Probably some sicko taking pictures for his blog," I say. I've made it this far. No way I'm turning around now.

Tell me. The prayer comes now even without my willing it to. *Tell me what really happened, Summer.*

The door shudders on its hinges when I shove it open. I take a deep breath, like I'm about to submerge, and practically throw myself over the threshold.

I scream when I trip over a body.

Almost immediately, the body, bundled underneath a pile of old clothing, starts to wriggle and move. Now Abby begins shouting "It's alive," like it's some old-school horror film, and then a head emerges from beneath the hood of a sweatshirt.

"Brynn?" I can barely choke out her name.

"What the hell?" She's on her feet in an instant, shaking off the old clothing like a snake molting its skin. But one sock still clings to her sweatshirt, just by her left shoulder. "Are you *following* me?"

"Following you?" I stare at her. She's wearing the same outfit she was wearing yesterday, when she bolted out of my car. A faded hoodie over a T-shirt, jeans with a big hole, right in the crotch, patched with something that looks like a dinner napkin. "Of course not."

"Then why are you here?" When Brynn's really mad, her lips get totally white and very thin, as if they've been zipped together. She jerks her head in Abby's direction. "And who's she?"

Abby raises a hand. "Name's Abby," she says. "Resident sidekick." When Brynn and I just keep glaring at each other, she says, "Old friends, I presume?"

"Can I talk to you outside?" Brynn says to me, practically growling. "Alone?"

She grabs my elbow and pilots me outside, kicking the door closed forcefully, sealing Abby inside. I start to protest, but she cuts me off.

"So what is this, your sick idea of a good time?" she says. "Relive the glory days?"

"Excuse me." I pull away from her. "I'm not the one *sleeping* in the old clubhouse."

"It's a shed," she spits back. "It isn't a clubhouse. It isn't anything." She turns away. "Besides, I didn't have a choice." When she turns back to me, her eyes are practically black. "My mom was in an accident last night. My sister took her to the hospital. They forgot to leave a key for me."

Immediately, my anger lifts. "Oh my God." I reach out to touch her arm and then think better of it. "Is she okay?"

"She'll be fine," she says angrily, as if she's annoyed at me for asking. "Now it's your turn. What the hell are you doing here?"

I count to three this time. "Someone else knew about Lovelorn. Someone else was writing about it. And I want to know who."

She stares at me, openmouthed. It occurs to me for the first time how pretty Brynn is, how pretty she's always been. Even with her hair wild and dirty and tangled down her back, and the crisscross marks from where her cheek has been pressed into something made of corduroy, she's beautiful. Maybe I didn't notice it before because of Summer—when she was around, it was impossible to see anyone else. Like the sun, just drowning all the stars in light, evaporating them.

"You're serious, aren't you?" she says at last.

It's not until then that the hugeness of it hits me—all this time, there was someone else. Someone who knew about Lovelorn, someone who was there in the woods that day, watching. Of course, it seems obvious now. Otherwise there's no way to explain Summer's murder at all. Otherwise the Shadow came to life, and reached out of our story, and took her.

Either that, or Owen did it.

But the police interviewed everyone they could think of, anyone who'd been seen with Summer, spoken to her, had contact with her day-to-day. They talked to her teachers. They had Jake Ginsky into the station three times, even though he had an alibi: he was playing video games with the other freshmen on the varsity football team. They even searched the Balls' house, while Mr.

Ball stood outside screaming curses about police incompetence, wearing knee-high black socks and boxer shorts that made him look just like the child molester everyone whispered he might be.

And they kept coming back to us. To Brynn, Owen, and me.

But what if the answer wasn't in testimony and eyewitness accounts and alibis? What if the answer was in the book all along?

"Let me explain something to you, Mia," Brynn says, in a low voice, like she's talking to a child. "You're barking up the wrong tree, okay? What you're looking for doesn't exist. There was never any clubhouse. There were never any signs from the other-world or strangers who wanted a sacrifice or any of that. We made it all up, every last bit of it. We were bored, we were deviant, we were in love, we were out of our fucking minds—"

"Guys?" Abby pokes her head out the door, and Brynn whirls around, inhaling the remainder of her sentence. "Check this out. I think I found something."

"What if we never went back?" Ava asked one day, when she, Ashleigh, and Audrey were all lying together on the banks of the Black Hart River, watching bees drone around flowers as large as fists. Both Ashleigh and Audrey turned to her in surprise.

"What do you mean?" Ashleigh said.

"Just what I said." Ava reached out to pluck a flower and began removing the petals, one by one. "Why not just stay in Lovelorn?"

—From *The Way into Lovelorn* by Georgia C. Wells

BRYNN

Now

Inside, my duffel bag is open and all my clothing is scattered like guts across the floor. I catch Mia staring at a pair of my underwear—polka dots, a gift from my mom—and shoot her a dirty look.

"Is there a problem?" I say.

She opens her mouth, closes it again, and shakes her head.

I bend down and grab a fistful of clothing, shoving it back into my bag. Screw Mia and her little white sundress and big sunglasses that probably cost a hundred bucks and her kooky-looking tagalong best friend. My back aches from sleeping on the hard floor, and there's a foul taste in my mouth. I need to brush my teeth.

Mia's friend—Abby—is already wading into the junk that has accumulated over the years. She moves aside a large sheet of corrugated metal, barely clearing an old car battery. "You said the cops cleaned out the shed after the murder?"

The way she says *murder* so casually makes me wince. "Pretty much," I say. "They were looking for proof that we'd been holed up doing devil worship and murdering cats."

"Were you?" Abby asks. I scowl at her and she shrugs. "Well, someone's obviously using it again," she says, gesturing to the piles of old crap. "Who does the shed belong to?"

"Nobody," Mia says. She's still standing in the doorway, hugging herself. Her hair is pulled back in a high ponytail, as if all these years she's just been on one long detour on her way back to the ballet studio. "I mean, this land is public. It belongs to the town."

"I'm surprised the town didn't tear it down," Abby says. She turns sideways, squeezing between two big metal grilles, the kind that might come off a Dodge Challenger. "Considering what happened."

"The cops didn't think it was important," Mia says quietly. "They didn't believe us when we told them how the shed had . . . changed. They didn't understand about Lovelorn."

"That's because we made the whole thing up," I say again, for at least the third time in two days.

It was a game we used to play. Not an hour in the police station, and Mia rolled. The cop taking notes in her interview read me back the pages. She told them all about the original Lovelorn book and how angry we were when Summer wanted to stop playing.

But Brynn was the maddest.

I left Brynn alone with her. I don't know what happened next. Ask Brynn.

"Maybe not," Abby says brightly. I stare at her as she leans hard against a massive piece of ancient machinery that looks kind of like an upside-down mushroom. "It's not all farm equipment, you know. It's someone's stuff. Maybe more than one person's stuff. There's an old DVD player in the corner, and a violin case. No violin, though. But there's this." She bends down kind of awkwardly, resting one hand on the wall for balance, and holds up something that looks like a narrow funnel.

"What is that?" I say.

"Mouthpiece," she says. "For some kind of horn. Looks like a double French, but I'm not sure." When I just look at her blankly, she smirks. She's an excellent smirker—she must have practice. "My mom's the band teacher at TLC. And check it out." Abby passes me the mouthpiece, which is surprisingly heavy. A small laminated label, warped with age, has been plastered to its underside.

"'Property of Lillian Harding,'" I read out loud. Then I hand it back. I'm losing patience for this little mystery theater. "So someone's got a hoarding problem. What does it matter?"

"It probably doesn't." Abby has gone back to clearing crap away from the corner. "But this might."

She pulls her cell phone out of her bag, swipes to her flashlight app, and angles it toward the floor. Blocked by several pieces of heavy equipment, that corner of the room is heavily shadowed, but Abby squats so we can see the ragged line of paint near the floor.

And see, too, that in one or two places the wallpaper underneath it—a pattern of rose bouquets—has started to show.

"The corners are always the hardest part," Abby says, grinning.

BRYNN

Then

Two days after Mia's twelfth birthday, in December: a hard freeze on the ground and the snow piled up in drifts above the basement window, blocking out the light. Mia and I were messing around with the balloons, still half-inflated, chucking them at each other, while Summer was sitting at the desk, hunched over an ancient desktop computer that growled whenever you so much as pressed the shift key. She was always online at Mia's house, since her foster parents had put up firewalls to keep her from accessing anything good on YouTube. She'd caught Mr. Ball pulling up her online history, too, and snooping around in her dresser drawers. *Just want to make sure you're staying out of trouble*, he always said, but Summer thought he was a freak who got off on things like that.

"Maybe," I said, tossing a balloon and punching it toward Mia, "she was dictating the pages, and she fell into a manhole and died."

"Or maybe," Mia said, punching it back, "she was sending the manuscript page by page while she was on safari, and she got eaten by a lion right in midsentence."

"What do you think, Summer?" I asked, lobbing the balloon at her. She swatted at it without looking and it bounced off the keyboard. "You think Georgia Wells got swallowed up by a manhole or a lion?"

"What?" She turned around in her swivel chair, frowning, and blinked as if seeing us for the first time. "You guys are *still* talking about the ending?"

Mia and I exchanged a look. It was like asking whether we were still breathing. We were always talking about the ending. It was our favorite pastime, as mindless as checking our phones. *Why, why, why? What happened to the sequel? What could she possibly have been thinking?* Georgia Wells's website, which hadn't been updated in ten years, gave us no answers. The sequel to *The Way into Lovelorn* was, according to the home page, still forthcoming. The author page showed a picture of Georgia smiling into the camera and a two-line bio: *Georgia Wells lives in Portland, Maine, with her three cats and her favorite trees.*

But Georgia Wells was dead by the time we found Lovelorn, the promise of a sequel forgotten. Still, that didn't stop us from scouring the internet, looking for clues, trying to piece together details of her life.

"Got eaten by a lion, dropped in a manhole, flattened by a bus, her brain bled out by leeches—it doesn't matter. You know that, right?" Summer gave us a look like we were both period stains on her underwear. I felt the blood rushing to my face. *Knock, knock, knock*. Beating in my head like an angry fist.

Mia looked hurt, which just made me feel angrier. "Doesn't matter?" she repeated. "It's Lovelorn."

Summer frowned. "We can't play forever," she mumbled, turning back to the computer.

Mia's mouth fell open, as if it had been unhinged. "We—what?"

Summer whirled around again. But she was suddenly furious. "I said we can't play forever," she repeated, and I saw her hands tight and white in her lap, the angry spaces between her knuckles. "People grow up. That's all right, isn't it? For people to grow up? You don't have a problem with that?"

"Don't yell at her," I said quickly, and Summer stared at me for a second.

Then, once again, she turned back to the computer. But I heard her say it one more time.

"Everyone grows up," she whispered. "Everyone."

Ashleigh was the one who first noticed that no one in Lovelorn seemed to be much older than Gregor. When she questioned him about it, he laughingly explained that since the Shadow had arrived, no one had to grow any older than they already were.

Ava, who always wanted to do things older kids could do, wasn't sure she liked the idea of that, but Gregor reassured her.

"It's much better this way," he said. "Change is just another word for disappointment, you know."

—From *The Way into Lovelorn* by Georgia C. Wells

BRYNN

Now

Twenty minutes later we're sitting in Mia's car, AC on. Mia is gripping the wheel tightly, as if trying to guide the car down an icy road, even though we're still parked. Abby has reclined her seat. From the back I can make out the little ski-slope jump of her nose.

"Okay, let me get this straight," I say. "Someone else knew about Lovelorn and decides—what? To mess with us? To make us think we're going crazy?"

"Maybe," Mia says. "Maybe whoever it was—"

"The Shadow," I interrupt her.

This time, she does turn around, releasing the wheel with a small sigh. "What?"

"I'm not going to keep saying 'someone' or 'whoever it is,'" I say. "We might as well name him. He might as well be the Shadow."

"That's so heteronormative," Abby says. Her eyes are closed. "How do you know that a *guy* killed Summer? Why not a girl?"

"Would have to be a guy," I say. "You never met Summer. She was fierce. Could take your eyes out with a penknife. And someone knocked her down and dragged her halfway across the field."

Abby opens her eyes, tilting her head back a little farther to look up at me through her lashes. "A guy, or a strong girl." Then she settles into her original position.

"So, the Shadow," Mia resumes, emphasizing the word and giving me a *does that make you happy* look in the rearview mirror. "Maybe he wanted us to *look* crazy, not just feel crazy. If the cops wouldn't believe us about Lovelorn—which they obviously wouldn't—no way would they believe us when we said we didn't have anything to do with the murder."

"Hmmm." Abby has her eyes closed again, fingers interlaced on her stomach. "Maybe. That's a lot of planning, though. There's another possibility."

"What's that?" I say.

She sits up finally, twisting around in her seat so she can see us both at once. "Maybe he just wanted to play. Like for *real* real."

There's a long moment of silence.

I clear my throat. "Owen knew about Lovelorn," I point out. "He's the only one who—"

Mia cuts me off before I can finish. "Owen never read any of our stuff," she says.

"As far as we know," I correct her. I still haven't told her that I saw Owen yesterday, and that he asked after her. And I'm still not *planning* to tell her. Mia's not exactly up for any Lifetime

Friendship Achievement awards. Besides, it's for her own good. She was always so sure he couldn't have done it, that he *wouldn't* have. But she wasn't there that day he clocked Elijah Tanner in the face and just stood there staring while Elijah howled and blood came out from between his fingers.

I never understood how she could protect him even after he broke her heart. Then again, I protected Summer even after she shattered mine.

"Please." Gone is innocent-wounded-Mia, with her big eyes and trembling lip and constant kitten-up-a-tree act: *I'm a victim too, I just played along, it was never my idea, none of it was my fault.* Now she's all fire and brimstone. "The cops were *desperate* to stick the murder on Owen. So was the prosecutor. If he did it, he'd still be rotting in Woodside. He was acquitted, remember?"

"Maybe because the cops screwed up," I say, even though she has a point.

Hank and Barbara Ball live in one of the cottages: a prefab double-wide souped up with fake siding and a screened-in porch, like all the other backcountry cottages plopped-and-dropped on two-acre parcels back in the 1970s. Even the hummingbird feeder comes standard, I bet. That's the type of rustic crap the summer people go for. I've never even seen a hummingbird around here.

I can't remember visiting Summer at the Balls' house more than a few times, but I recognize the turnoff right away, still marked by a dented mailbox sporting a faded American flag motif. A hand-painted wooden sign tacked to a birch states simply *Balls*.

Abby thinks this is hilarious. "That sign is ambiguous," she says. "What does it mean? Balls for sale? Balls go here? All balls welcome? Free balls?"

"All right, all right, let it go." The whole Balls things would be funny if Hank Ball weren't so damn mean. Mean—and creepy as hell. I remember one time we stopped by just to get *Return to Lovelorn*, and in the middle of a pee I could have sworn I saw an eye staring in at me through the keyhole. Summer swore up and down it hadn't been her, either.

The driveway spits us out through the chokehold of summer blackberry bushes and overgrown pine trees into a narrow clearing where the cottage, looking even sorrier than I remember it, sits among a surf of trash, old furniture, and abandoned car parts.

I remember that Mr. Ball was always fixing something in the front yard—rehabbing a crappy desk no one would buy even new, or fiddling with an ancient grandfather clock he'd bought at a yard sale—but it looks like things have been breaking a little faster than he can keep up with.

An orange cat watches our approach from the porch railing, and I get a bad feeling in my stomach. We shouldn't have come.

But it's too late. Even before Mia cuts the engine, the cat startles off around the house. A second later, Barbara Ball comes out onto the front porch, holding a dish towel, hobbling the way old women do when they've been on their feet all day.

And she is—old, I mean. Older than I remember her. Sadder-looking, too.

"Can I help you girls with . . . ?" She swallows the rest of her sentence just as soon as she recognizes us, and for a long moment no one says a word.

Finally, Abby breaks the silence. "Get any hummingbirds?" she asks, gesturing to the feeder. I glare at her. She gives me a *who, me?* face.

"Mostly squirrels," Mrs. Ball responds, without taking her eyes off Mia and me. She lashes her dish towel around the railing and humps a little closer to us, squinting, like she wants to be sure she hasn't mixed us up for someone else. Or like she's hoping she has. "What are you doing here?"

Mia swallows so hard I can hear it. I bet when she decided to start playing detective, she forgot all about the awkward middle chapters. I let her sweat it out. "My name is Mia Ferguson. And this is Brynn—"

"I know who you are." For someone so old, Barbara Ball sure has some volume in her. "What are you doing here?"

"We were hoping to talk with you and Mr. Ball. . . ."

"You were hoping to talk to us?" She says *talk to* as if it really means *bludgeon*. "What in God's green you want to talk about?"

Mia looks to me for help. But I just shrug. This was her idea. Make a bed, lie in it, blah blah.

"About—about Summer," Mia says.

Mrs. Ball squints again, like she's trying to make us out through a hard fog even though she's no more than a few feet away from us.

"Anything we had to say about that child, we said it a long time ago," Mrs. Ball says. It's strange to hear her describe Summer that way, as a child—she was the leader to all of us, in all things. But of course she was a child. We all were. "I think you should go now."

Mia shoots me a helpless look. And now an old, dark anger starts poking my chest. Unfair. "She was our friend," I blurt out. "She was our best friend, and all we ever wanted was to make things right for her—"

"Let it go, Brynn," Mia says, in a quiet voice.

But it's too late. "—and everyone treats us like we're some kind of disease—"

"Look." Abby cuts me off before I can say something that'll get us booted off the Balls' property for sure, possibly on the wrong side of a rifle. "Mia and Brynn have been doing some spring cleaning. The memorial coming up, and everything. You understand. Good time to let bygones be bygones, turn over a new leaf, et cetera, et cetera."

Mrs. Ball looks at Abby as if registering her for the first time. Her eyes linger on Abby's skirt, on her fake eyelashes and carefully drawn lips. She looks suddenly uncertain. "I'm sorry," she says. "Who are you?"

Abby doesn't even blink. "Abby Bluntich. Abby B, to my fans." She actually says this. Out loud.

"Fans?" Mrs. Ball repeats faintly.

"You might recognize me from Beautycon, or from my YouTube tutorials and my Insta partnership with Howl Cosmetics. . . ."

Mrs. Ball nods dazedly, looking like she's just been hit by the blunt side of a shovel—I doubt she's ever even heard of YouTube.

"Anyway, what Mia and Brynn meant to say is that they turned up some old stuff that might have belonged to Summer. Spring cleaning, remember? Most of it's trash. But if there's anything you want . . ."

It's a brilliant tactic. The Balls are obviously pretty damn late on their spring cleaning.

"What kind of stuff?" Mrs. Ball addresses Abby directly. It's like Mia and I have disappeared entirely.

Abby shrugs, all casual. "There were some old notes, a tube of lip gloss—we trashed that, because *yuck*—and a mouthpiece for some kind of instrument. Summer was in band, wasn't she?"

I can't imagine why it matters: the mouthpiece we found made its way into the shed only recently. But when I shoot her a look, she ignores me.

"When we could convince her to go," Mrs. Ball says. "But she played the drums." And then, a second later: "My husband fixes old instruments, though. He has quite a collection of old horns. She might have . . . borrowed it by accident."

A wind lifts through the trees and touches the back of my neck. Could Mr. Ball have been responsible all along? I can't remember now why the cops never treated him seriously as a suspect. It makes a horrible kind of sense: how he monitored her emails and social media, how he forbade her to date, even rifled through her stuff while she was out of the house—at least, according to Summer.

The eye I saw, peering at me through the keyhole.

"It's okay, Mrs. Ball," Mia says. Surprisingly, her voice is steady. "We knew all about her borrowing. We knew her, remember?"

It's the funniest thing: Mrs. Ball looks at her for a second, her mouth working soundlessly, her body all coiled up with tension. And then, in a split second, she collapses. She lets out a *whoosh* of air, like she's been holding her breath this whole time. Her face loses all its suspicion, all its confusion, all its anger, and cracks open along little fault lines of sadness. She ages another ten years right in front of us.

"Yeah," she says. Even her voice sounds tired. "Yeah. I guess you did." She gestures vaguely in the direction of a footpath through the antique debris that winds around the house. "Hank should be around back in the workshop. You can go on and ask him yourself."

Hank Ball's workshop is nearly the size of the house—and, in contrast to the rest of the property, pristine. Both doors are rolled open to reveal a clean and bright interior, neatly fitted out with circular saws and benches, drafting tables and shelves. One wall is tacked entirely with paper and labeled for tools I've never even heard of.

And one wall is shiny with dozens and dozens of instruments.

Tubas, saxophones, clarinets reflecting sun off their polish: it's like some vertical band dropped their gear before running.

Mr. Ball must be into old clocks, too, because there are plenty of those, including a cuckoo clock frozen with its wooden figurines on parade, like a face stuck with its tongue out. He's straddling a workbench, doing some fiddly operation on a grandfather clock with all its parts exploding everywhere, like a body mid-surgery.

He barely glances up to look at us. "Help you?" is what he says. I might even think he doesn't know who we are. But that's impossible.

Everyone knows who we are—or who they think we are, at least.

Mia takes up Abby's spiel about the spring cleaning and the mouthpiece. I have to hand it to her. She used to be a shit liar. But she's doing a passable job.

Hank just keeps on working. His fingers—stumpy with age and arthritis—move with surprising grace. I try to imagine those fingers holding on to a rock, bashing Summer's head with it. But all I see—all I've ever seen—is a shadow, clinging to her back like some kind of horrible cloak, pouring itself down her throat when she tries to scream.

"Might've come off one of my horns," he says at last. "Doesn't matter now, though, does it? Ain't missed it in five years. You can go on and trash it." He straightens up at last, wiping his hands on his jeans. But he stays seated. "We don't keep nothing she had her hands on around here, anyway. Barbara doesn't like it. Might as well toss it like all the rest. Besides." His eyes are mud brown, nested under enormous eyebrows like insects burrowing for cover. "Can't believe you came all the way out here because of some old junk like that."

And suddenly I remember that moment in the bathroom when I had my pants around my ankles. I remember a creak outside the door and seeing the wink of an eye at the keyhole. *Blue.*

"Did you ever hear Summer mention a Lillian Harding?" I ask. Strangely, the fact that it wasn't him all those years ago—that it must have been Summer, doing it as a joke or to freak me out, or both—makes me want to pin the murder on Mr. Ball even more, not less. I watch closely for his reaction, but he doesn't even blink.

"Never had any girls coming round here for Summer except for you," he says. "Had to run off some of those football boys a few times, though. Summer had gone and turned those boys' heads. They were at each other's throats, fighting over her like she was a trophy. Lost more than a game or two because of it, I bet." He shook his head. "I told her she shouldn't be hanging with older boys like that. What'd she think they wanted from her, anyway? I told her she would get into damn trouble. And look. Look what happened." He speaks with sudden viciousness, and Mia goes tense beside me. I have an old urge to take her hand, to tell her it'll be okay. But Mia's not my responsibility anymore. "She went and got herself killed."

"You're acting like it was her fault," I say. "Like you think she deserved it."

He stands up then. He plants both hands on his workbench and heaves up to his feet. For a second, I'm half-afraid he'll come at me.

But he just limps slowly out into the sunshine. His left foot drags slightly when he walks. Mr. Ball, like his wife, seems to have aged two decades in the past five years.

"Nah, she didn't deserve it," he says, in a softer voice. "It wasn't her fault, neither. She'd had it rough. Her mama pretty much booted her curbside when money ran tight for drugs. And she'd been bounced around some bad places. Some real bad places, with some real bad people."

A memory overwhelms me: Summer, looking up at me calmly, while her cheek reddened with the impact of my fist. It was the first and only time I'd ever hit her. It was the first and only time I'd ever hit anyone.

"But she didn't make it easier on herself, that's for sure," he continues. "Her lying and stealing. Running around with those boys. Jake and Heath and that boy Owen they looked at and God knows who else. Still. We thought if we gave her a stable home . . ."

"Sure," I say, crossing my arms. The cat is still slinking around the shadows, and I don't like the look of it. It reminds me a lot of their old cat, Bandit; Summer hated that cat with a passion. "And spied on her, and looked through her email, and kept her basically on lockdown . . ."

Mia shoots me a look and mutters, "Brynn." But I don't care. Someone killed Summer. Someone dragged her into a stone circle and made her into a sacrifice. And I'm sick of seeing the killer's face only in my dreams, a gaping hole that turns to fog as soon as I wake up.

"She needed rules. She needed structure. She'd been running wild her whole life. Never had anyone give a shit about where she was or who she talked to. You think that's what caring for people is all about? Letting them do whatever they want?" He tilts his head back to look down at me, and I think of how Summer used to do the same thing, even though I was two inches taller. And isn't that, after all, what we did with Summer? Didn't we let her do whatever she wanted—to us, to everyone? "You can think what you want. But we cared for that girl. We would have kept her. We tried to."

The Balls' new cat slinks out into a patch of sunshine and rolls down into the dirt. Watching me. Tail lashing.

"I was up in Burlington the day she died, filling out paperwork for her adoption." This he says so quietly I nearly miss it. "We were going to tell her that night."

No wonder the police never looked at Mr. Ball. I feel like an idiot. Worse. I feel like a zero. I can tell Mia does, too. Her skin is the color of old cheese. Even Abby looks sheepish.

"Sorry for wasting your time." Mia can hardly speak above a whisper. She won't look at me.

"That's all right." Mr. Ball squints at us. Then he says, "You know, I always felt kind of sorry for you two. For what it's worth, I always knew you didn't do it. Not a chance."

My whole body goes airless, like the words have knocked away my breath.

"She really had you wrapped around her finger, didn't she?"

He means both of us, I'm sure, but he's looking straight at me when he says it. "Well. That's just how she was."

For a long, long second, we just stare at each other. Then, finally, he shifts his eyes to Mia.

"Sorry I couldn't help you. But you know what they say about the sleeping dogs." He smiles sadly. "Best to let them lie."

Gregor was the best tour guide Ava, Ashleigh, and Audrey could have asked for. He was extraordinarily proud of Lovelorn and knew its history dating back to the time of the Original Twin Fairies, who had so fought over the world they'd torn it in two and created earth and sky.

"What do those flowers mean?" Audrey pointed to a cottage, in front of which was growing a single white lily. It was the fourth time she had seen such a flower.

"The lily is a mark of respect," he said. "It means that family has produced a Savior—a child, you know, for the Shadow."
—From *The Way into Lovelorn* by Georgia C. Wells

BRYNN

Now

"Whoa." That's the first, and only, thing I can say when Mia opens her front door.

Two pink spots appear in her cheeks. "I told you it was messy," she says, righting a brass candlestick that has coasted, surfer-style, over a wave of loose papers on the foyer table and landed on its side.

"Yeah, but you didn't tell me it was"—seeing Mia's face, I stop myself at the last second from saying *crazy*—"*this* messy," I finish.

When we were younger, I *liked* Mia's house. Loved it, even. The bookshelves had actual books on them, as well as funny wooden statues of chickens wearing clothing and playing guitars. Napkins—real cloth napkins—poked out of drawers. There were little collections of rose quartz just sitting around glowing on windowsills. Half the stuff Mia's family owned I didn't even have a *name* for—it all sounded like stuff that could have come from an old sci-fi movie. *Decanter! Abacus! Trivet! Molecular transporter!* And Mia's mom was always shopping for new things. But this is collecting on crack. This looks like every single item they used to have had seven babies.

"Think of the house as a work in progress," Abby says as we head to the stairs, squeezing down a ribbon of empty space lined on either side by accumulated junk. "By next week, this place is going to look like a Zen temple."

Somehow I doubt it. Even the stairs are piled with crap, although in some places I see evidence that Mia has, in fact, been cleaning, in the form of discolored portions of carpet.

"*And* it's temporary." Mia is still stiff-backed, obviously offended. She won't look at me. "Just for the night, right?"

"Right," I say quickly. That's what I told her: that tomorrow, if my mom isn't out of the hospital, my sister will come for me. That I'll be out of her hair.

The biggest problem with lies? They *breed.* Mia's room, in contrast to the rest of the house, could double as an airport waiting lounge. The carpet is beige and smells like stain remover. Her desk is spotless except for an iPad and a mason jar she's using to hold pens. Her bedspread is pale pink. Her headboard is blocky. There isn't a single shoe, coin, or stray sock on the floor.

But certain things—certain tiny things—haven't changed, like the lace curtains that cut the sunshine into patterns and the parade of scented candles on the bookshelf above Mia's bed. The mug on her bedside table, which says *Reading Is Sexy*, where she keeps her glasses. A lamp in the shape of a ballet dancer.

"What is it now?" When Mia speaks, I realize I've been standing there in the doorway, unmoving, for at least five seconds.

"Nothing." Feeling choked up, I dump my duffel bag on the floor and bend over, pretending to examine the few photos neatly framed and mounted on her wall. Almost every picture is of Mia and Abby, most of them in the same room—which, from the explosive zebra wallpaper, hot-pink curtains, and steampunk posters, I assume is Abby's. Abby and Mia dressed up in feather boas and top hats. Abby and Mia lying together on a bed. Abby and Mia dressed in identical T-shirts. I feel a stab of jealousy—I haven't been that close to anyone in a long time. I haven't even been that close to my *girlfriends*.

In the last picture, taken in front of Mount Independence, a woman with wispy brown hair is sandwiched between them.

"Who's that?" I ask, pointing.

"Oh." Mia looks embarrassed. "That's Ms. Pinner, our tutor." She sits down on the bed. Everything Mia does, every move Mia makes, looks graceful and deliberate. This is not a girl who flops, slouches, slinks, or sprawls. This is a girl who sits, minces, prances, and pivots. I swear, I've never even heard her burp. "Mom tried busing me to St. Mary's, thinking it would help to get away. It didn't. Everyone called me a witch and put old tuna sandwiches in my locker and stuff. I begged her to homeschool me and finally she said yes. Abby and I take classes together, when she's not on the road."

Mia never had to go back to Twin Lakes Collective. Just like Owen, she split. She never had to sit in the same classrooms we'd sat in with Summer, or eat alone in the cafeteria, at the table we'd once sat at together. There was only one good thing about being a supposed killer: people pretty much stayed out of my way. Of course, that meant I had no friends, either. I wonder what Mia would say if she knew I'm not even sure what grade I'm in.

"What's your excuse?" I say, turning to Abby.

She wrestles out a packet of Twizzlers from her bag. "Too famous," she says casually. She tears open the package with her teeth. "The cons really mess with a regular school schedule. Plus I'm always booking photo shoots and stuff."

I stare at her. "I thought models were thin," I say.

"Oh, no. We come in all different sizes, shapes, and colors." She raises her eyebrows. Her hair is dyed in stripes of platinum blond and purple, but her eyebrows are dark brown and perfectly shaped, like little crescent moons. "Just like murderers, I guess."

I tense up. "I'm not a murderer."

"If you say so." Abby shrugs.

I look to Mia for help, but she is on her hands and knees, rooting for something underneath the bed.

Luckily, at that moment, Mia emerges, holding a thick, dust-covered photo album. I recognize it immediately. It's her Nerd Notebook. Mia has been saving every single aced quiz, glowing progress report, successful art project, or A-plus essay since she was in kindergarten. Everything goes in her Nerd Notebook.

Or everything used to. From the dusty look of the cover, it seems she stopped keeping track of all her accomplishments. For some reason, that makes me sad.

"I'm telling you, the answer's in the book," Mia says. "In the book, and in all the stuff we wrote in *Return to Lovelorn*."

"You guys wrote a sequel?" Abby actually sounds impressed. I wonder how much she knows about the original story. Weirdly, I feel another quick twinge of jealousy—Mia's been sharing things with Abby. Mia has someone to share things *with*.

"It was fan fic. Summer was mostly writing it," Mia says, and then immediately corrects herself. "Or—we thought she was. But now I think she had help."

"Right. From the same person who put up that wallpaper. The same person who wanted Lovelorn to be real." Abby frowns, pulling at her bangs, which are straight, curtain-like, fifties-dominatrix style. "From the Shadow."

"The Shadow . . . ," Mia repeats, chewing on her lip, like she does. She twists around in her seat to face me. "You know, you might be onto something. Think about it. Summer was obsessed with the Shadow. That's the whole reason she wanted to write the sequel. To tell the Shadow's story."

"And to fix the ending of Book One," I point out.

"And to fix the ending of Book One," Mia admits.

"Why?" Abby asks. "What's wrong with the ending?"

"What's wrong with the ending is that it *doesn't* end," I say.

"The book cuts off in the middle of a sentence. It's crazy. It's like Wells was writing and someone came and decapitated her."

Mia gives me a look, like, *let's not start that now*. "My point is Summer was afraid of the Shadow. That's why she wanted to do the sacrifice. To give him something that would keep him happy," she explains, turning to Abby. "A kind of gift. She thought it would keep the Shadow away."

When Mia looks at me, the memory of that day rises up suddenly between us: of coming up over the hill into the long field, of seeing Summer clutching what we thought was a rag to her chest, her dress nipping around her knees.

"If someone was frightening her in real life, and she didn't know how else to express it . . . ," Abby trails off.

I'm struggling to think through it all. My brain keeps punt-kicking back the obvious conclusion. Maybe it's all the time I've spent around addicts: I've gotten supergood at denial. *The first step is admitting you have a problem*. "You think her killer was help-ing her write the story," I finally force out, not a question but a statement. "You think they left . . . clues."

"It's possible." Abby thumbs her glasses up her nose. "Authors unconsciously write themselves into their books. They transform familiar places into fictional landscapes. It's the same way when we picture aliens, we imagine they'll look like us. Psychologists call it 'transference.'"

"Thanks, Wikipedia," I say.

"It's not just possible. It's *probable*," Mia says. "Think about it.

We took inspiration from real people all the time. That's how we came up with the Ogre, isn't it? You wanted to write in Mr. Dudley after he busted you for cheating."

"I *wasn't cheating*," I say. "I was telling Kyle Hanning to stop mouth-breathing down my neck."

"Whatever." Mia rolls her eyes. "Someone put that wallpaper up. Someone made the clubhouse. And someone tore it down overnight. We didn't make it up. It was real." She knots her fingers in her lap, and I realize then that she needs it to be true. She needs not just to be innocent, but to know who's guilty, to prove it.

Maybe I need it, too. To move on. To be free.

Here's another little thing they tell you in recovery: *Let go or be dragged.*

"Okay," I say, and Mia exhales, as if she's been holding her breath. "Okay," I repeat. "But if there are clues in the fan fic, what good does that do? You heard what Mr. Ball said. He trashed everything the cops didn't take. It's all gone."

Mia shakes her head. Her eyes flicker. For a second, I think she's going to smile. "Not all of it," she says. She sits cross-legged on the floor, heaves the binder into her lap, and begins to page through it. "Summer never let us keep *Return to Lovelorn*," she explains to Abby. "She always had to be in charge. There was a single copy, a notebook stuffed with a million loose pages, some of them typed up, some of them written out by hand."

"Wow." Abby wrinkles her nose as Mia keeps flipping through warped pages plastered with old pop quizzes and papers marked with lots of stickers. "That's so pre-technology of you."

"The first *Lovelorn* was written by hand in the 1960s," Mia says. "Summer thought it was more authentic. Besides, she had to share a computer with her foster family, and they were always spying on her."

"She even thought they'd trained their cat to read," I say, and then wish I hadn't, because Mia flinches.

She says, more quietly, "She wanted to keep Lovelorn private. She wanted to keep it for us."

"We thought she did, anyway," I correct her. *But Owen knew,* I almost add. *Mia told him everything. He knew we liked to play.* But I don't have to say the words out loud. His name hovers there between us, like a bad smell, like the aftermath of a rude remark. His name is *always* there, threaded into the mystery of what happened, of all the things we still don't know.

Mia shifts away from me. "Anyway, the point is, Summer kept the notebook at all times. If either of us wrote something, we had to give it to Summer for her approval. If she liked it, she'd add it to the notebook."

I take a seat on Mia's bed, ignoring the way Mia frowns at me, like I might contaminate her bedspread. I probably will. I stink. "Summer was obsessive. She thought we might even be able to have it published. It seems stupid now." Mia's comforter is pale pink and patterned with loops and curlicues. Some of the stitching is coming undone, and I pluck at a thread with my fingers, wishing the past was like that—that you could just pull and pull until it unraveled and you could start over.

"It doesn't seem stupid," Abby says. "Lovelorn was all you had."

She's nailed it, of course. Lovelorn *was* all we had. Of the three of us, Mia was the smartest and Summer the prettiest. I was the most outgoing. But we were loners, when it came down to it. The other girls hated Summer, called her a whore, wrote dirty shit on her locker and stole her gym clothes and threw them in the trash, or smeared them with ketchup so it would look like period blood. Mia became so afraid of speaking in public that for years she said not a single word, even when the teacher called on her, and she kept getting sent to the principal for disciplinary problems. She'd been at the same school her whole life and still hardly anyone knew who Mia Ferguson was. Owen Waldmann, resident developing psychopath, was the only person who was ever nice to her, the *only* person who could get her to talk—until Summer came along. She told me once that's why she took up dance in the first place. She didn't know how to speak out loud. It was the only way she could communicate.

And I'd been getting into trouble since the first time I put my fist into Will Harmon's face after he called me backcountry trailer trash, which didn't even make sense because we lived in a house, not a trailer. But he knew we were hard up, and he'd seen my mom on night shifts at the gas station, a job she took before she found a job in admin at the same hospital where my sister is doing her residency now.

In elementary school I was involved in fights almost every year. It's like I couldn't keep my anger from coming out of my fists. And once the boys got too big to scrap with, the anger just took up a permanent squat in my vocal cords, so half the time the shit coming out of my mouth wasn't even stuff I meant to say out loud.

I couldn't help it. When I get angry, it's like someone lights my whole body on fire. Snap, crackle, pop. And then the entire world is burning.

But together, in Lovelorn, we made sense. Summer was the princess, beautiful and misunderstood. Mia was the good one, the sweet sister, the voice of reason and understanding. And I was the swordsman, the knight, proud defender of their honor.

"The February before Summer died, I took some pages." Mia looks away, biting her lip, as if worried I'm going to start lecturing her. "We were fighting about this one scene—"

"What scene?" I can't help but ask.

"The tournament scene," she says. "We were arguing about whether or not Gregor should win in his bout with the giantess. Summer thought the Shadow should be responsible for killing the giantess and saving Gregor's life. But I . . . well, it sounds stupid, but I just wanted to give Gregor a little bit of respect, you know?"

As she speaks, I tumble down a hole, landing all the way back in seventh grade, when we used to sit together in this very room and debate what "Georgia" did and failed to do in Book One, about why she'd screwed up the whole book by ending it the way she did or by *not* ending it, about how to make Book Two even better than the original.

"I guess I was just getting annoyed that Summer always got to decide. Besides, Gregor's one of the best characters," Mia says, turning now to Abby. She looks at me for support.

"True," I say. "Although Firth was always my personal favorite. A centaur," I say, when Abby shoots me a questioning look. "He rides around rallying the whole country to banish the Shadow at the end of Book One."

For the first time all day, Mia smiles at me. Mia has a great smile. It turns her whole face into an invitaion "Firth's great too," she agrees. "Anyway, like I said, I took a few pages. I just wanted to make some edits, and then I was going to return them."

"But you didn't," Abby says.

Mia's smile fades. "I never had a chance. Two days later, Summer told us she didn't want to play anymore. She never went back to Lovelorn again, not with us. Not until that day—"

"What did happen that day?" Abby says, adjusting her glasses again. "I mean, what *really* happened?"

"Oh, come on," I say. "Don't tell me you haven't looked it up."

"I haven't," she says, in a tone so sincere I immediately feel guilty. "Besides, I'm not talking about what shows up online. Haven't you ever heard you can't trust everything you read on the internet?"

"Not today, okay, Abby?" Mia wraps her arms around her knees. She looks suddenly exhausted. "We'll explain some other time."

Abby raises both hands, like, *just trying to help*.

"All right, Mia." I scoot off the bed and join her on the floor. "Let's see what you got."

There are three pages, neatly covered with Summer's handwriting. Instantly, I see exactly what Mia meant about someone else helping Summer. There isn't a single error, not a word crossed out or even changed. It's as if she copied the text from somewhere else. Why did I never see it before?

Abby leans in next to me, and I'm surprised by her sudden closeness, and the fact that she smells like lavender.

"All right, explain," Abby says. "What am I reading? What's all this about an amphitheater?"

"The amphitheater was Summer's idea," I say. "In the first book, we never know where the Shadow comes from. She wanted to explain it. An origin story, kind of. So we made up the amphitheater, where bloody battles take place."

"Summer liked to weave in real people and places," Mia adds. "They were like our inside jokes. So the giantess was really supposed to be Mrs. Marston, our math teacher. We named the giantess Marzipan and gave her a wart and tufts of wiry red hair. Things like that."

"So if the amphitheater is where the Shadow first shows up, and the Shadow is supposed to be Summer's killer, then it's important." Abby reads in silence over my shoulder for a while. "What's up with the sprites?"

This makes me smile. "That's another thing Summer made up,"

I say. "They're this really annoying, dumb race descended from the fairies, and their voices are high-pitched and squeaky."

"When they get excited, they can shatter glass," Mia says. "And they go around cheering on the competitors during tournaments."

Abby looks from Mia to me and back. "Bloody competitions and a group of mindless, squeaky cheerleaders? Sounds like the TLC football stadium to me."

For a minute, I can do nothing but stare at her.

"The football stadium . . . ," Mia says slowly, and smiles again. "You're a genius, Abby."

"Nothing to it, my dear Watson," Abby says with a little flourish.

"Jake Ginsky was on the football team," I say. "He was, like, outfielder or something."

"Outfielder's a baseball term," Mia says.

Leave it to Mia to be nerdy about even non-nerdy things. "Whatever. He was tight ass or rear end or whatever they call it."

"Who's Jake Ginsky?" Abby asks. She's still sitting uncomfortably close to me, so close I can see the sticky wet look of her lips, and I scoot backward, leaning against Mia's bed.

"Jake Ginsky," Mia says. "He went out with Summer for a few months. Supposedly."

"Definitely," I say firmly, remembering that time with Summer in the car, how her eyes swept over me as if I was a stranger.

Mia sighs. "But they broke up in January. Besides, the cops

looked at him. He had an alibi. He was hanging out with some other freshmen on the team."

Something tickles the back of my mind. Something *wrong*.

Abby hauls herself to her feet. "Okay," she says. "Let's go."

"Go where?" Mia blinks up at her.

"The amphitheater," she says, as if it's obvious. "We can sneak around the locker rooms and look beneath the bleachers."

"What do you think we're going to find—bloody handprints?" I say. "We're talking about something that happened five years ago."

"Well, we have to start somewhere, don't we?" Abby crosses her arms. "These are the only pages you have left, right? If Summer left clues about her killer in *Return to Lovelorn*, the amphitheater seems like a place to start. Maybe you'll remember something important. Maybe you'll see something. That's how it works in mysteries, anyway."

"This isn't a mystery," I say. "This is real life."

But Abby's already moving toward the door. "Whatever you say, Nancy Drew."

Ava gaped at him. "Do you mean to say the Shadow steals children?"

"Oh no," Gregor said, obviously horrified. "Never that. The Saviors go willingly. It's a great honor. The Shadow, you see, protects us. The Shadow keeps our harvests plentiful and makes sure our rains are not too heavy or too light. The Shadow keeps us safe from war and starvation. The Shadow has chased away the Reapers so that no one has to grow old. The Shadow has great magic."

"Then I don't understand," Ava said, wrinkling her nose.

Gregor blinked at her. "It's an exchange," he said, as though it were obvious. "One child per harvest."

—From *The Way into Lovelorn* by Georgia C. Wells

MIA

Now

The high school at Twin Lakes Collective is separated from the middle school and elementary school cluster by a long stretch of well-tended soccer and lacrosse fields, a looping ruddy-colored track, and the football stadium, standing like an alien spaceship in the middle of all that rolling green.

When we pull into the parking lot, I'm surprised to find it almost full: I'd forgotten all about the Fourth of July parade.

"Christ," Brynn mutters. "Glitter and glee clubs. Just what we need."

Every year, hundreds of kids aged five to eighteen march next to homemade floats and mascots from various local businesses, from the school all the way down to the gazebo in the park at the corner of Spruce and Main. I'm surprised they didn't cancel it this year. They'll be skirting downed tree branches and sloshing through gutters bloated with rainwater. Then again, what better way to celebrate America's independence? Land of the free, the brave, the stubborn, the stupid.

"Pull around the gym," Abby says. "There are usually extra spaces behind the weight room."

"I don't know," I say. "Maybe this was a bad idea. We could come back tomorrow."

"It's a great idea," Abby says. "No one will even notice us. We'll blend in."

Doubtful. Brynn and I are two of the most hated girls in Twin Lakes.

Up near the cafeteria, dozens of preteen girls wearing identical uniforms twirl batons and practice cartwheels. From somewhere in the distance comes the clamor of instruments tuning up. On a stretch of grass that divides the dumpy Life Skills class trailer from the admin office, a woman is trying to wrestle her screaming son into a costume. I'm not exactly sure what he's supposed to be, but multiple arms give him the look of a patriotic bug.

"So your mom's a teacher here, huh?" Brynn leans forward, resting her elbows on the front seats. She smells like my shampoo. She insisted on showering and changing before we left the house, although she put on the same ratty skinny jeans. At least she changed her shirt. This one is black and says *Godzilla Is Coming* in ominous silver letters. As always, she looks not just effortless, but as if the idea of effort was invented for people far less cool. People like me.

"Uh-huh. Music," Abby says. She's been typing on her phone

and now she looks up. "No luck on Lillian Harding, by the way."

"Who?" Brynn says.

"Lillian Harding. Remember the mouthpiece we found in the shed? I googled Lillian Harding in Twin Lakes, Vermont, and related to the murder. Nothing. It was a long shot, anyway. Stop here."

A forty-person marching band, ages eight to eighty, mills around on the grass in front of the football stadium, near the pic-nic benches, all of them tuning and tootling and drumming to individual rhythms. Brynn covers her ears when we get out of the car.

We start across the grass toward the stadium entrance, avoiding the crowd. Instinctively, I put my head down, like I always do in public, and I notice Brynn tugs her hood up. Only Abby looks unselfconscious, swishing along in her skirt, humming a little, as if the noise the instruments are sending up is actually music. I can't find any rhythm in it. I picture the dancers in my head twitching, having a seizure.

We pass into the stadium, where the noise is, at least, muffled. The grass is brilliant green and neatly clipped. Purple-and-yellow banners, many of them sporting an image of an angry wasp, the TLC mascot, hang, listless, along the stands, or have been driven down by hard winds into the mud.

"Okay." Brynn takes off her sunglasses. "Remind me what we're supposed to be looking for?"

I ignore her. "Purple and yellow," I say, pointing. "In the book,

Gregor's tournament colors are purple and yellow."

"So Summer was writing about the stadium," Brynn says. "We already *knew* that. We wrote about a lot of real places."

We move past rows of empty bleachers. I try to imagine what Summer might have seen here, what might have stuck with her. High school boys, padded and painted, moving in formation. Cheerleaders chanting and stamping, backflipping on the grass. Fans roaring in the bleachers. Does any of it matter? Does any of it relate to what came afterward?

After twenty minutes, Brynn loses patience. "This is stupid," she says. "What are we supposed to be doing, communing with the spirits of cheerleaders past?"

Even Abby has to admit she's right. There is nothing here, no old voices whispering secrets to us. Nothing but the continued squeaks and honks of the woodwinds and a distant shouting as the parade-goers assemble, all those hundreds of people so beautifully fixed in the present, in this day, under the bright sunshine.

"Drums over here. No, on the other side of the picnic bench. Danny, are you listening?"

A woman is trying to herd the marching band into formation and not having very much luck. One of the younger boys is running around with a flute between his legs, laughing maniacally.

"Danny, *stop* that." As the woman turns around to yell, sweeping her frizzy blond hair away from her eyes, I stop. It's our old Life Skills teacher, and—I nearly laugh out loud—she's *still* wearing that awful purple cardigan.

Brynn recognizes her at the same time I do. "Holy shit," she says. "That's Ms. Gray."

Miraculously, she hears her name over the clamor. Or maybe her eyes just land on us. For a fraction of a second she looks shocked. But almost immediately, she comes toward us, with both arms outstretched, although she stops several feet away from us and doesn't move to close the distance.

"I don't believe it," she says. She drops her hands against her thighs with a clapping sound. "I don't believe it. You two."

"You remember us," I say. Stupid, since she obviously does. For some reason I feel shy in front of her. Embarrassed. She actually looks happy to see us.

"Of course I remember you," she says in her gentle voice. Brynn and Summer always used to lose it when she said words like *syphilis* or *diaphragm* in that singsong. "Mia and Brynn . . ." She shakes her head. "What are you doing here?"

I can't think of an excuse. Luckily, Abby jumps in. "We just came to check out the start of the parade." Then: "Um, I think that kid's trying to stick his head *inside* the trombone."

Ms. Gray spins around. "Tyler, *please*," she barks, and then turns around to face us again. "The town was looking for volunteers. I can't think why I said yes." Her eyes are enormous, bug-size behind her glasses. "But tell me—how are you? I've thought about you a lot. I've wondered . . ."

She trails off, leaving the question unspoken.

I've wondered what happened to you.

I've wondered if you survived. And how.

"We're okay." Lying is just another thing that takes practice. Your muscles get used to it over time. "Actually," I say, before I can think about it, or wonder whether it's a good idea, because thinking of Summer—beautiful Summer, a ballerina with her arms up, center stage, light spilling around her in a pool, light pouring from her—makes my chest tight with pain, "we're kind of doing a project. About Summer. Summer Marks."

She flinches when she hears the name, like so many people do here in town. Like it's a curse word. But she recovers quickly enough. "I see," she says, adjusting her glasses. "Is this for the anniversary memorial?"

"Yeah," Brynn jumps in when my voice, seemingly exhausted, simply curls up. It does that still, sometimes. Retreats, withdraws. Peters out. Like it's a living thing with its own moods and appetites. I'd forgotten that yesterday, Twin Lakes had been planning a big five-year-anniversary commemoration of Summer's death. It must have been delayed because of the storm. "Yeah, it's for the anniversary. Kind of like . . . a memory book. We're talking to everyone who knew her." I'm sure Ms. Gray can't tell she's lying, but I can. It's the way she's speaking, kind of breathless, as if she's been running for a while.

Ms. Gray smiles. "Well, I'm not sure I'll be able to tell you anything you don't already know," she says. "You know Summer wasn't with me for very long. Life Skills," she adds, with a little shrug, "is a misnomer. The school sticks the students with me once a week to satisfy a state requirement about sex education. The rest is just fluff."

Brynn and I exchange a look. There's something thrilling about hearing Ms. Gray admit it after all these years—that's exactly what we used to say. *Just give us some condoms and a forty-five-minute free period*, Summer had said during one lesson, so loudly I was sure Ms. Gray had heard.

And again, I feel that knifepoint of sadness thinking of all the things Summer will never hear, see, or know.

"Still," Brynn says. "Is there anything? Anything at all about her you remember?"

"I remember the three of *you* were together all the time. I had to separate you so you wouldn't pass notes in class." Ms. Gray's smile fades. "Summer was a difficult student, in some ways. But very sweet, very *alive*, if you know what I mean."

We do. Of course we do. Summer was twice as alive as other people.

I fumble for a way to find out what I want to know—an explanation for all those red marks on the page, for the fact that Summer seemingly *couldn't* write. "What do you mean by *difficult*? You mean she was having trouble?"

Ms. Gray tilts her head to one side, giving her the look of a bird that has just spotted a crumb. "Can I ask why you want to know?"

I glance over at Brynn. We should have agreed on a story in advance. Now I can't think of a single excuse.

Luckily, Abby comes to the rescue. "We want to celebrate the *real* Summer. The Summer nobody knew. That's the point of the memory book."

"Were you a friend of hers too?" Ms. Gray asks. Abby nods, and I pray Ms. Gray won't know the difference. Apparently she doesn't, because she goes on, "I think I remember more than I would have otherwise, given . . ." She gestures helplessly. "She was very enthusiastic about the things that came easily to her. She loved to talk about the reading we did. And she was a great reader. A very *slow* reader, but she truly loved it. But with other aspects of the class, she struggled."

"Writing," I say, remembering her marked-up quiz and feeling a tickling pressure all along my spine.

Ms. Gray nods, but I can tell we're losing her attention. The marching band is breaking formation again. She keeps casting worried glances over one shoulder. "She was badly dyslexic," she says. "It slowed her reading and made it hard for her to write. She was very, very frustrated. I think she was embarrassed, too. I understand she'd bounced around quite a bit." Ms. Gray shrugs. "Other than that, I never got much of a sense of her. I tried to help her, you know. I gave her extra time on the homework and on our quizzes. I suggested she go speak to her guidance counselor or get help from the Tutoring Center. She refused. She said she wasn't stupid." Ms. Gray spreads her hands. "Well, of course that wasn't what I'd been implying. But afterward she wouldn't listen to me, no matter what I suggested." This time her smile is anemic and barely reaches her eyes. "She was a sweet girl. She tried hard—too hard, in certain ways. She was prone to . . . exaggerating. Not lying, exactly, but making things up. *Colin, get back in line.*" This to a little kid carrying a tuba practically as big as he is.

"What's the difference?" Abby asks, genuinely curious.

Ms. Gray turns back to us, squinting. "I always think of lying as a desire to hide the truth. But with Summer . . . I had the feeling she wanted to *remake* the truth. Just invent a whole new one."

There's a beat of silence. Even though Brynn doesn't say anything, doesn't even look at me, I know we must be thinking the same thing. We understand. We remember. I have the sudden, stupid urge to reach out and grab Brynn's hand, but of course I don't.

Ms. Gray shakes her head. "I'm sorry," she says. "I don't know if that's the kind of thing you were looking for."

"That's okay," I say quickly. "Every little bit helps. Thanks, Ms. Gray."

She makes a face as several flute players begin to compete over who can blow the loudest, shrillest, most obnoxious sound. "Sorry. I should get these monsters up the hill. The parade will be starting any second."

But even as we're turning away, she calls us back.

"You know, Summer did get help eventually," she says slowly, as if she's not really sure she should be speaking and so she's just letting the words fall out on their own. "She found a boy to tutor her. I might not even have remembered except . . . well. I think the idea is that they became close. Very close."

The sun blinks out. I hold my breath. I know what she's going to say. Of course I do.

But Brynn still makes her say it.

"Who?" Brynn asks.

"Owen," she says, almost apologetically. "Owen Waldmann."

Wishes really did come true in Lovelorn. Which could be a good thing or a bad thing, depending on who was doing the wishing.
—From *Return to Lovelorn* by Summer Marks, Brynn McNally, and Mia Ferguson

MIA

Now

Back in the car, Brynn puts her feet up on the center console and leans back, crossing her arms. "Owen," she mutters. "Always Owen."

"Don't," I say.

Abby's tufting her hair using the rearview mirror. "Who's Owen?"

"Owen," Brynn says, "was Summer's *boyfriend*."

"They were never together," I say quickly.

"Mia was in love with him," Brynn continues, as though I haven't even spoken, with infuriating matter-of-factness, as if she's explaining to a child that the sky is blue. "That's why she never wanted to believe he was guilty."

"And Brynn was in love with Summer," I say. My voice is shrill. "That's why Brynn always wanted to believe he *was*." I don't have to turn around to feel Brynn glaring at me. "And in case you've *forgotten*, the cops looked at him. He was suspect *one*." I grip the steering wheel tightly, feeling small starburst explosions of pain and color behind my eyelids—a sure sign of a developing migraine. I breathe deep through my nose, willing away memories of Owen—his lopsided smile and poky elbows and hair the color of new flame and the way he used to call me Macaroni. All the other kids made fun of him, but he didn't even care. He moved through the halls as if he was on a boat, tethered to something bigger and better, a future away from here. "He was arrested and released. They never even charged him."

"Because his dad's rich and the cops screwed up," Brynn says. "They took his *blood* off Summer's clothing."

"That was never proven," I say quickly.

"I'm telling you, he's hiding something. He's been hiding something for years." Now she leans forward. "He has no alibi for the day she was killed. He said he was home sick, but he wasn't. Someone remembered seeing him in town." She shakes her head, making a noise of disgust.

"He wasn't in the woods," I say, this time quieter. My throat goes unexpectedly tight. "I would have seen. I would have—" I stop myself from saying *I would have known*. Of course, that sounds ridiculous, and it's obviously untrue. Except that for years I did have an Owen Waldmann sixth sense, a weird ability to know where he would turn up and when. I could decipher his moods even when he didn't say a word to me. We could reach each other's thoughts just by exchanging a single look.

Owen and I had been friends since second grade, when he was so pale people called him Casper, or Nosebleed because of all the times he had to run out of class with his nose plugged up with tissues, and I was so shy no one called me anything at all. It sounds crazy, but I sometimes wished I had a nickname, even an obnoxious one, because it would mean that I existed, that someone had noticed me.

Owen and I sat next to each other in art class. One day, Mr. Hinckel was teaching us about found art by making us glue random bits of everyday items—Q-tips and cotton balls; crumpled receipts and rubber bands; paper clips and pen caps—to stiff construction paper, and then dye it and decorate it how we wanted. I made a portrait out of dried macaroni. The whole damn class, I sat there gluing macaroni in place, hardly looking up, hardly breathing. I must have looked psychotic. But when the bell rang, I saw Owen was looking at me, smiling. He had a great smile. It was crooked: the right side of his mouth always floated up an extra inch or two.

"Hey, Macaroni," he said. "That's pretty good."

That was it: that's how it started. The next day, when he saw me in the lunchroom, he waved. "Hey, Macaroni. How ya doing?"

Maybe he was being mean. Maybe not. But I loved it. Macaroni gave me something to look forward to. *Macaroni* meant *inside joke*, and *inside joke* meant *friend*.

And we did become friends—slowly, by increments, so that it felt just as easy as standing still. On the weekends or after school

I'd look out the window and see him straddling his bike, peering up from the street toward my window, his face like a pale, upturned moon, and I'd go flying out of the house to meet him. We filmed funny videos and posted them to a private YouTube channel. We played kickball on his front lawn and sprawled out in his father's garden, head to head, picking shapes out of the clouds.

In fifth grade, we found a tree house in the woods behind his house. Owen was having a bad year—he was always fighting with his dad, even then, and at school people started to spread rumors that he carried knives, that he cut up small animals, that he would someday come to class with a bomb in his bag. We outfitted the tree house with flashlights and a sleeping bag, junk food and even a battery-operated fan, so Owen could go there whenever he didn't feel like being at home. One time, we got caught together during a rainstorm. We huddled together in the sleeping bag, practically touching noses.

The kids at school spread new rumors. Owen was a sex maniac. I was a slut. Everyone who saw us together made kissy noises or gross hand gestures, the way kids who are starting to outgrow being kids always do. *When are you going to hit that, Owen? Hey, Mia. Have you and Owen done it yet?* I always pretended to be embarrassed—I *was* embarrassed—but a teeny, tiny part of me was glad. I wasn't invisible anymore. I wasn't alone. I had Owen. Casper, Nosebleed, serial killer in the making. Still: mine. The boy with the big ideas and the crooked smile, the boy I could talk to about everything.

Still, I pretended I never thought about him that way. *Owen? You think I like* Owen? *Ew. Never in a million years.* And Owen never said anything at all, just smiled his lopsided smile and shook his head. We didn't have to say it. We both knew.

Of course we were meant for each other. Of course we would be together someday. Of course he would be my first kiss and I would be his. We were just waiting, letting it unfold, luxuriating in it, like staying in bed on a Sunday knowing there's absolutely no place you have to be.

Then Summer came.

"If you're so convinced Romeo had nothing to do with it," Brynn says, "why don't you go ask him why he acted like such a nutcase afterward?"

"Sure. I'll just head off to London and go around knocking on doors," I snap back. "Can't be that hard in a city of eight million."

I catch Brynn's eyes in the rearview mirror. She's making the funniest expression, as if she's just taken a sip of spoiled milk and is too polite to spit it out.

"What?" I say. "What is it?"

"He's back," she says, after a beat. "I saw him."

"Owen's back," I repeat. As if saying the words aloud will help me understand. Brynn nods. "And you saw him." She nods again. I throw the car into reverse, filled with a desperate urge to move, to go, to drive. Otherwise I'll lose it. "When were you planning to tell me?"

"I just did," she points out.

"After *I* brought it up," I say. I've thought about Owen a thousand times—I've had to try hard not to think about him—but never expected to see him again, or even have the chance. Last I heard he was in boarding school in England. For years, there have been rumors that the Waldmann house is for sale.

Brynn snorts, tossing her bangs out of her eyes, like a horse. "I only saw him yesterday," she says. "Besides, you can't tell me you really want to see him after everything that happened. You're not still in love with him, are you?"

"Of course not," I say quickly, pressing hard on the accelerator so the car leaps forward, and Abby slams back against her seat and shoots me an injured look.

"See?" Brynn says, shrugging, as if it's no big deal and she's been doing me a favor. "I was just protecting you."

I'm so angry that for a second I can't speak. The worst thing about it is that Brynn *did* used to protect me. When I spaced out in the locker room once and Lily Jones accused me of staring at her tits, Brynn piped up, "What tits?" and suddenly everyone was laughing at Lily, not me. When I was sad about my parents' divorce, she'd do funny impressions of anyone she could think of to get me to laugh.

When Summer died, all of that died with her.

Brynn stuck up for me to the cops, sure—she knew I had nothing to do with it—but it was as if she blamed me anyway.

"In case you haven't noticed," I say, "I'm doing fine. I've been doing fine without you for the past five years."

Brynn mutters just loud enough for me to hear, "Doesn't seem like it."

"Excuse me," I say, stepping harder on the gas and barely missing a boy on a skateboard who gives me the finger. "I don't think you're one to judge."

"Hey, Brynn," Abby jumps in before the fight can escalate. "Do you want us to swing by the hospital or something? So you can say hi to your mom?"

Instantly, I feel terrible: I'd completely forgotten about Brynn's mom and her accident. I take a deep breath, imagining my anger as a shadow, imagining it driven away by a spotlight. "Yeah," I say. "I'll drop you anywhere you need to go."

But Brynn only looks furious. "I can't believe you," she says finally, her voice tight as a wire. "I can't believe you would use my mom against me. You would use her to get *rid* of me."

"I'm not trying to get rid of anyone," I say. "I thought—"

"Well, *don't* think," Brynn snaps. "Don't think about my mom, or about me. I can take care of myself," she adds, almost as an afterthought.

"She was just trying to help," Abby says.

Brynn's silent for a second, fiddling with her phone. When she looks up again, her face has gone blank. Not angry, but just completely devoid of expression, as if someone has shuttered her eyes. "You know what, actually?" Her voice, too, is toneless. "Drop me off at Toast. I'll meet my sister there. We're going to visit my mom together."

I try to catch her eye in the rearview mirror, but she won't look at me. "How is your sister?" I ask, instead of all the questions I really want to ask, like *When did you talk to your sister? Why are you pretending to text when your phone is off?*

"Fine," she says, staring out the window. A muscle flexes in her jaw like a heartbeat. "It's like you said. We're all doing just fine."

BRYNN

Now

After Mia drops me off, I track exactly five minutes across the face of an enormous clock behind the juice machine, then duck out of Toast again, before the barista side-eyeing me can harass me about placing an order. For half a second, I feel guilty about ditching out on an imaginary date with my sister to visit my mom in her imaginary hospital room.

That's the problem with lies. They aren't solid. They melt, and seep, and leak into the truth. And sooner or later, everything's just a muddle.

It isn't hard to track down Jake Ginsky's address. That's the promise of a place like Twin Lakes. No one's ever really a stranger. Which means: there's no place to hide.

Ginsky's mom ran an acupuncture and massage therapy business out of a converted room above their garage; I remember because once Summer and I had a fight about it. It was December of seventh grade, and surprisingly warm: I remember we strung Christmas lights on the house in T-shirts that year.

Summer told me Jake had told her he'd give her a massage one day after school, and when I made a joke about whether she'd end up handcuffed to a radiator in the basement, she scowled.

"Jake's not like that," she insisted. "He told me he wants me to be his girlfriend."

"That's what all guys say," I responded.

And she tilted her head back to narrow her eyes at me, just like Hank Ball did. "How would you know?" she said. Then she sighed and stepped closer to me, staring up at me through her lashes now. "I'll make you a deal. I won't go to Jake's. But then you have to give me a massage." And, just to bug me, she made a show of touching her shoulders, rolling her neck, running her fingers along the sharp promise of her clavicle.

"What are you doing?" I wanted to look away. I knew she was just messing with me. But I couldn't. Her T-shirt was old, washed practically transparent, and I could see the dark edge of her bra beneath it.

"Come on," she said, and laughed when I tried to pull away from her. "It's not hard. All you have to do is touch me. . . ."

Katharine Ginsky Massage still operates out of Jake Ginsky's house, and the address is listed right on the website. But it doesn't occur to me until I spot the Volvo with the University of Vermont sticker that Jake Ginsky must have graduated by now. Somehow, in my head, everyone's simply stuck, turning like a car wheel through a slurp of mud.

But I ring the doorbell anyway. It's summertime. And I'm here. Might as well keep pedaling the gas.

Someone's home—I can hear a baseball game going inside. Soon enough I hear footsteps cross to the door, and at the last second I get the urge to bolt.

But it's too late. The door is opening already.

I remember Jake Ginsky as a skinny kid with teeth just a little too long for his mouth and the skulking look of a raccoon you surprise going through your garbage. Five years later, he's practically unrecognizable. It looks like someone's taken an air hose to his mouth and inflated him: six foot four, biceps the size of my thighs, a jaw that looks like a shovel. Even his *beard* is overgrown.

He freezes. For a second he looks like he's thinking about slamming the door shut. "I heard you were in rehab," he says. Then: "What are you doing here?"

His voice is flat. Not hostile, exactly, but definitely not friendly.

"Part of my twelve-step program. I'm on number nine. *Make amends to all those you've wronged*. Heard of it?"

Jake squints like my resolution is all fuzzy. "You're here to apologize to me?"

I shake my head. "Hell no. I'm here so *you* can apologize to *me*."

He lets out a sharp bark of laughter. Maybe he thinks I'm kidding. But after a second, the smile swirls right off his face, bottoming out in a look of disbelief. "Wait—you're serious?"

I let a beat of silence pass so that he knows I am. Then I say,

"Did you kill Summer?" No point in dancing around the dead elephant in the room.

He stares at me. "Do you seriously expect me to answer that question?"

"Yes," I say.

"Then *no*." He looks me up and down. "Did you?"

"Hell no," I say.

"Well, now that we got *that* out of the way," Jake says dryly, "are we done here?"

"No, we're not done." I almost add: *we'll never be done*. "Your alibi was bullshit."

His face closes up, like a pill bug when you poke it. "What are you talking about?"

"You told the cops you were hanging out with the other freshmen on the team. But you weren't, were you?" It was in Mia's car, when we were talking about Owen and where he was that day, that I got to thinking about alibis and what Mr. Ball had said: that Summer was playing a few freshman football players against one another. Maybe she did it deliberately, or maybe not. Either way, she was tearing that team apart. *Those boys were at each other's throats*, he said. *Fighting over her like she was a trophy.*

"We were hanging out, Brynn," he says. But the lie sounds tired by now.

"You weren't," I say. "You weren't even speaking." I watch Jake closely, watch the way his face contracts ever so slightly, like I've reached out and hit him. "When did you decide to lie?"

For a long minute, Jake just stares at me. His eyes are the kind of puppy-dog brown that makes straight girls go puddly. And now I can kind of see why Summer went so crazy for him— even though back then Jake looked a little bit like a wet towel, all stringy and wrung-out-looking, he had the same eyes, the same adopt-me vibe.

Finally he lets out a big huff of air, like he's been holding his breath this whole time. "After we found out she was dead," he says, "I heard the cops wanted to talk to me, and I panicked. It'd been months since we last hooked up—it was Moore right after me, but *that* didn't last. Still, I figured they'd think I was crazy jealous or something."

"Were you?" I ask.

He glares at me. "We hung out, like, eight times. Maybe less. Most of the time we were in a group. Besides, I was home that day. But my mom had clients all afternoon. And my dad didn't get home until late. So I couldn't *prove* I was home."

"Right. So you guys covered for each other." I have to force myself not to feel sorry for him. He probably thought he'd put Summer behind him. He'd left her behind about a hundred pounds of muscle ago. And here I am, like the ghost of Crap-mas Past.

Still, if Jake's alibi was bullshit, it means the other boys' alibis were bullshit, too.

Which means: maybe, *maybe*, we're actually getting some-where.

"It wasn't like it mattered. Everyone knew who did it," he

says. At least he has the grace to look embarrassed. "At least, we thought we knew."

"Right. I forgot." Now it's my turn to be sarcastic. "The Monsters of Brickhouse Lane."

"I'm not talking about you." He frowns like I'm being difficult for no reason. "I meant that guy Waldmann. He's guilty, right?"

"Maybe," I say. I think of surprising Owen yesterday, the way he tugged on his lip with his teeth, the look on his face when he asked about Mia. Like even saying her name was some kind of mortal wound. "I don't know."

Jake frowns again. "Who else *could* it have been?"

"You sound just like the cops," I say. "Just because they couldn't figure out who did it doesn't mean that he did." I don't know why I'm defending Owen—only that guilt isn't supposed to be determined like one of those school superlatives, *Most Likely to Succeed, Most Likely to Bash Girl's Head In with a Rock.*

"I'm sorry," Jake says in a quieter voice. "Really. I am." He manages a smile. "See? You got your apology after all."

"Lucky me," I say. Suddenly, I'm exhausted. I shouldn't have come. Even if we are making progress, so what? It doesn't change what happened. It won't bring Summer back.

And it won't change what she did to us.

"It was stupid of me to lie," Jake says. "It was stupid of all of us. But I guess we were all just in shock. I never in a million years expected things to turn out the way they did. I always figured she'd be the one who got in trouble."

"She *did* get in trouble," I say.

"You know what I mean." Now the smile drops, leaving just his eyes screwed up around a wince. Suddenly, he blurts out, "I was a little scared of her, to be honest."

I must be giving him a look, because he coughs a laugh. "I know. She was, like, half my size. But you know how she was. *Intense.* I hardly knew her. But I saw it. Glimpses of it, anyway. That's all she'd let me see." He takes a deep breath, like he's run out of air. "Am I making any sense?"

"Yes" is all I can say.

"Like sometimes she'd open a door, just for a second, just a crack, and what you saw inside was . . ." He trails off, clears his throat, obviously embarrassed. Now I know he really was afraid of her: he's telling the truth.

"She hurt someone, you know," he calls out when I'm already halfway across the lawn. I turn and see him handling his long limbs like they're part of some old Halloween costume he's embarrassed to be wearing, trying to tuck them into hiding. "At her last foster home. It's why she got moved. She—she burned one of the other kids with a fire poker. Did you know that?"

I shake my head. My throat is too full of feeling to speak. I remember another thing Mr. Ball said about Summer: *She'd been bounced around some bad places. Some real bad places, with some real bad people.*

"One time we were messing around with a box turtle we found on the road. Heath Moore said he was going to keep it as a pet.

Then Dunner said we should make turtle stew. It was a joke, obviously. But then Summer went inside and came out with a kitchen knife."

He looks up at me. Face raw. Open. As if years and years have been cut away. As if he's looking not at me but at that moment, the shock of it, the turtle on the ground.

"I swear to God, I really thought she might kill it." Suddenly, he blinks. Tries a smile again, settles for a quick flash of his teeth. "It sounds crazy now."

"No," I say. "It doesn't."

BRYNN

Then

"You must have loved her." The new cop, Lieutenant Marshall, was a lot nicer than the last one. The last one, Detective Neughter—pronounced New-ter, he told us, like being named after the act of cutting a dog's balls off was a good thing—was pale and mean and smelled like tuna fish.

Lieutenant Marshall smelled clean and minty. His eyes crinkled when he smiled. He had dark hair, just graying at the temples, and kept his hands in his pockets. *Relax*, he seemed to be saying. *Just relax. I'm on your side.*

"She was my best friend," I said. "So, yeah. Pretty much."

He moved around the table, removed a hand from his pocket, and rubbed the back of his neck. He didn't look at me. Not because he was angry—because he knew I didn't do it. I trusted Lieutenant Marshall. "It must have made you mad when she started going out with Owen Waldmann."

"Not mad," I said, but my mother cut me off.

"Don't," she said. "You don't have to say anything, Brynn." Then, to Lieutenant Marshall: "We don't have to be here. Don't try to trick her."

He spread his hands. "If she has nothing to hide, she doesn't have to worry."

If. But I skimmed over that word, *if*, ignored it.

Instead, I started to burn. I started to crackle and sizzle in my seat. My mom didn't understand. She was making me seem guilty when I wasn't—she was making it seem like I had something to be ashamed of. Only Lieutenant Marshall understood. "I wasn't mad," I said, a little louder. "It's just . . ." I trailed off, and Lieutenant Marshall nodded encouragingly.

"That's all right," he said, smiling again. I decided he was exactly what I would want my dad to look like, if I had a dad. "There's nothing to be ashamed of, Brynn. Your feelings are perfectly natural."

I closed my eyes. How to explain it?

I wasn't mad. I was exploded. I was full of tiny shrapnel shells. Torn apart with jealousy. It hurt to breathe. My lungs were rattling with cut glass. I wanted to take Owen's eyes out with a toothpick—not just for me, but for Mia, too. I wanted to go back to the night Summer and I kissed and the miracle happened and then she started to cry and I kept my arms around her while she shook in my bed and her spine knocked against my breastbone and her feet slowly thawed from icicles to skin again. Except this time, I'd make sure to fix whatever had gone wrong. This time, I wouldn't screw it up.

I opened my eyes again.

"I didn't understand" is what I said. Lieutenant Marshall was still nodding. "I didn't understand why I wasn't good enough." I didn't mean to say the last part, but the words just flopped out of my mouth on their own, like dying fish. And my sister, Erin, was staring at me, a look on her face like I was a wild animal, disgusted and frightened and confused all at once. I looked away, fighting the sudden urge to cry. The blinds were only lowered partway and I could see into the station's main room and the clutter of desks and sun slanting through the windows and the dusty water cooler and ancient fax machines. But Mia was gone. She must have gone home.

Why were they keeping me here, then, if Mia got to go home?

For the first time, really, I got a bad feeling, a gnawing suspicion that Lieutenant Marshall was maybe not as nice as he was pretending. That these questions weren't routine. That they weren't just looking for my help so they could find the person who'd done it. Suddenly, it was as if insects were chewing my stomach from the inside.

Lieutenant Marshall was still smiling. He sat down on the edge of the table, crossing his hands in his lap. *Relax*. "You must have been pretty pissed off," he said, "when she started spreading all those rumors about you at school."

"It is a strange phrase, 'falling in love,'" said one of the princesses in the tower. Tears stood out on her cheeks, and even these were pretty, reflecting the blue sky above her. *"It sounds like something you do accidentally, by yourself. But isn't someone else always to blame? They should call it strangling in love. Walloped in love. Knocked-out-of-nowhere in love."*

—From *The Way into Lovelorn* by Georgia C. Wells

MIA

Now

Abby almost—*almost*—lets me off easy. We've made it all the way to her house before she turns to me suddenly and says, "So this *Owen* guy . . ."

I groan. She quirks an eyebrow, giving me her sharp, infuriating *I can solve calc problems faster than you* look. "How come you never told me about him?"

Even thinking his name makes me squeeze the steering wheel a little harder, trying to press the memory of him out through my palms. "I did," I say.

"You told me he *existed*," Abby says. "You never told me you had a thing for him."

Abby is omnisexual. I don't know exactly who she's hooked up with, or when, but from the confident way she's talked about it, it seems there have been boys and girls. Once I asked her where she met all these people, and she just said, *Cons. You should come with me sometime. Cosplay gets everyone going.*

"I don't. I mean, I did." I can't bring myself to say out loud: Owen was a five-year-old crush that never even happened. He was just one more thing I made up. "Can we talk about something else?"

"Don't deflect." Abby waggles a finger in my face. "It's not going to work."

"We were kids," I say. "It was just a stupid crush. It didn't mean anything. We never even . . ." I'm about to say *kissed*, but for some reason the word gets tangled in my throat. And that's not true. Not exactly.

One November afternoon in sixth grade, we got stormed into the tree house. We were lying there in our sleeping bags and I could feel his knee bumping mine every time he moved, and his face was so close I could feel the warm exhalation of his breath, which smelled grassy and fresh, and we'd been laughing about something, and then when we finished laughing Owen leaned forward and before I knew what was happening, our lips were pressed together, so warm and soft and perfect, as if they'd been designed to line up that way.

The weird thing is that after it happened, we didn't even talk about it—just went right on laughing, as if it hadn't happened. But it wasn't a bad thing—it was natural, so natural that we didn't have to speak about it or talk about what it meant. We knew. I remember how I kept my toes curled up, trying to squeeze in all my happiness, trying to preserve it. It was, I knew, the first kiss of hundreds of kisses to follow.

Only it wasn't.

"Never even what?" Abby narrows her eyes at me.

"Forget it," I say, too embarrassed to confess to her, Miss Omnisexual, that that single kiss, chaste and tongueless and in *sixth grade*, was my only one—not counting the time in eighth grade, at St. Mary's, when for a whole glorious month nobody knew who I was, no one had put it together yet. I even got invited to a party and wound up kissing a boy named Steven on a dumpy basement couch, and even though his breath smelled a little like Cheetos and he squeezed my boobs once each, like he was trying to ring a doorbell, I was so happy. He held my hand for the rest of the party and even leaned in to whisper, "Do you want to be my girlfriend?" before I left.

But by Monday his texts had stopped, and when I saw him in the hall he raised two fingers and made the sign of the hex, shrieking, "Don't kill me! Don't kill me! Please!" while the rest of his friends laughed so hard they doubled over.

Abby must sense that she's upset me, because she lets it go. For a while we drive in silence. As always, I feel better after we've left behind the new downtown, with its greedy clutching palm of B and Bs and stores and farm-to-table restaurants, and even better once we've successfully skirted the old downtown and its sprawl of fast-food restaurants and Laundromats and gun stores, once the trees run right up to the road again and all the houses are concealed behind heavy growth.

Abby suddenly speaks up. "What if you don't ever figure out what happened to Summer? What if you never know?"

"What do you mean?" We're driving past Waldmann Lane, and I get the sudden urge to spin the wheel to the right, to gun it straight to Owen's front door, to drive straight back into the past. "I'll just go on like I've been going on. Things will be the same as they always were."

Which is, of course, the whole problem.

After I drop Abby off, I wind up at the bottom of Conifer where it dead-ends at the state park before I realize I must have made a wrong turn on Dell. I've been circling aimlessly, while my thoughts wind me back into the past. I keep thinking of Owen, of him so close, less than a mile away, as if there's a giant elastic stretched between us, threatening to pull me back. But what would I say to him?

What *will* I say to him, if I see him?

What if I do see him?

What if I don't?

I don't notice the unfamiliar car parked in front of my house until I'm nearly on top of it. I get out, already half-annoyed and ready to yell at whatever Chinese food delivery service is trying to tuck flyers under my door, when I see a tall, light-haired boy standing on my porch with his back to me, holding a package under one arm. With his right hand he's shielding his eyes from the glare, trying to peep into my front hallway.

Flooded instantly with anger and shame, I start running across the lawn. "Hey!" I shout. "Hey! What are you—?"

He turns around, obviously startled. Time freezes.

It's him.

Taller—so much taller—and still thin, but muscular now. Broad shoulders, like the kind you'd want to hang on. Shorts low on his hips and a faded navy-blue T-shirt that brings out the color of his eyes. His freckles have faded and his red hair has lightened. Now it's flame shot through with sunshine.

"Oh," he says, and sets down the box he's been carrying. "Oh." Then: "Oh." Like he didn't expect to see me, even though he's standing in front of my house.

"What are you doing here?" I manage to say. My voice sounds like it's coming from the far end of a tunnel.

He's smiling at me, all teeth, so big it looks like a wince.

"Brynn didn't tell you?" he asks. I stay quiet and he goes on, "Tree came down straight through the sunroom. The house is supposed to be going on the market, but now—"

"No. I mean what are you doing here? *Here*, here." My heart is beating so hard in my throat it feels like I've swallowed a moth that's trying to get out. He's different—he's so different. And at the same time he's the same. He still cocks his head all the way to one side when he thinks, as if he's trying to peer under a fence. And though his hair is lighter, it's still cowlicked in the back, and he still reaches up a hand to smooth it down when he's nervous.

But he's muscular and tall and hot. More than that: he looks so normal. You'd never in a million years think of calling this boy Casper, or Nosebleed. You'd never imagine him hiding in a tree house or wearing a long coat he'd found in a rummage sale or talking about the historical probability of alien invasion. It's like someone pressed the old Owen through the same cookie cutter that fires out cheerleaders and football players and people who ride in prom limos.

"I didn't have your cell phone number," he says. Even his voice sounds different—his vowels seem to take forever to pour out of his mouth. "I figured you changed it."

"I did," I say. That was the first thing to go. After we were arrested, someone from school posted my number online. My cell went morning and night, texts and phone calls, some of them from halfway across the country. *U kno u'll burn in hell forever for what you did, right?* The funny thing is we'd been Catholic before the murder—my mom's family is Italian—but afterward, after so many people had told us I'd burn in hell and the devil had taken my soul and even that my mother should try an exorcism, she threw out the Bible she'd had since she was a kid. That was the *last* thing she threw out.

"How have you been?" Owen asks gently. A hot rush of shame floods my cheeks. I get it now. He's here to check up on me. To do his friendly, neighborly duty to the screwed-up girl he left behind.

"Fine," I say firmly, for what must be the tenth time in the past two days. I make for the door and deliberately jangle my keys so he'll get the hint and take off. He doesn't. "Everything's fine." Big mistake: now that I'm on the porch, he's close enough that I can smell him—a clean boy smell that makes my stomach nose-dive to my toes. "Don't you live in England or something?"

"Scotland, actually." *Scotland, actually.* Like it's no big deal. Like Scotland is the next town over. At least that explains the new accent. "I was in school there. Finished in May and now I'm back for the summer. I'm starting at NYU this fall."

I can barely get my fingers to work. I fumble the keys and drop them. "NYU, wow. Congratulations. That's . . . that's . . ." NYU was my school. My plan. My dream. I was going to go to NYU and study dance with a minor in English literature, and on weekends take ballet classes at Steps, where generations of dancers have spent Saturday mornings softening their pointe shoes on the floors.

How is it that Owen—Owen, who hated every class except science, who spent half his time in school with his earbuds in, staring out the window, who sometimes put his head down on the desk and slept through tests—is going to NYU? It's like what happened to Summer barely registered. Like the year he spent at the Woodside Juvenile Rehabilitation Center, waiting for his trial to start, penned up with crazies and criminals and sixteen-year-old drug dealers, didn't affect him at all.

Or actually, it did affect him. It made him better. Shiny and new, like an expensive Christmas present. Brynn and I ended up broken, pieced together in fragments.

And Owen, who was so broken back then, became whole.

And now the boy I used to love is heading off to *my* dream school.

Thankfully, I manage to get the door open, but Owen puts a

hand on my wrist before I can slip inside, and his touch startles me into silence.

"Mia . . ." He's watching me intensely, the same way he used to: as if the rest of the world has disappeared.

I remember then a line from the original *Lovelorn* about the centaur Firth, a line that always reminded me of Owen: *His eyes were as dark and wild as a storm, and big enough to drown in.*

"What?" My heart is beating painfully again, thudding against my ribs.

A look of uncertainty crosses his face, and for a second I see the old Owen—weird, wild, *mine*—float up underneath the surface of Owen 2.0, Shiny Plastic Barbie Owen. It occurs to me that now that he's crossed over into Normalville, he isn't used to girls just staring at him like dairy cows. The girls he knows probably do things like giggle and toss their hair and squeeze up next to him to show off pictures of their Caribbean vacation on their phone.

"Look," he says, "can I come in for a second?"

"No," I say quickly, remembering how I first found him: cupping his hands to the window, peering inside. All my shame comes rushing back. How much could he have seen from outside? I've made pretty good progress on the front hall, but the table is still buried beneath mounds of takeout flyers and unopened mail, and there are several cardboard boxes blocking the closet door. Could he have seen into the dining room? I haven't even started on the dining room. The Piles there are so staggering, so complex in their arrangement, that Abby says my mom should have an honorary architecture degree.

Ten days until Mom comes home. Ten days to tackle the Piles. Ten days to turn back time, to find the truth, to start over.

"Come on, Mia." He's standing way too close to me. It can't be accidental. And now he's smiling all easy and cool, one corner of his mouth hitched as if it's hit an invisible snag. Practiced. That's what his smile is: practiced. I wonder how many times he's used it, how many girls he's practiced on. "Don't pretend you're not a little happy to see me."

"Not really." My voice is high-pitched, shrill as a kettle. I feel a sharp stab of guilt when his smile drops away, but at the same time it's a relief to see a crack, a fissure in Owen 2.0. The words are flying out of my mouth suddenly: "It's a funny coincidence you came back on the fifth anniversary. Just couldn't stay away, could you?"

Owen flinches as if I've hit him. But *I'm* the one who feels as if I've been hit—I'm breathless, shocked by what I've just said.

"What's that supposed to mean?" Owen says.

Now that I've started, it's like the words are vomit—they're making me sick, but still I can't stop. "It just seems weird. Like you came back to *commemorate* it. Like it's something to be proud of." I want to take it all back. But my mind has become a monster, and I can only make it better by finishing, by exploding everything—him and me and whatever there used to be between us. "You know, you never even told us where you went that day.

All this time, and you never told us. So what are you hiding?"

There: I finish, practically gasping, hating myself and hating him even more for forcing me to act this way, for moving away and getting normal, for leaving me behind.

Owen says nothing. He just stares at me, white-faced, and for a second I see the old Owen, the Owen who used to camp for days in his tree house when his dad was blackout drunk, the Owen who used to remind me of an animal in a trap, scared and hurt but still fighting.

He bends down and scoops up the box he was carrying when he first spotted me. He yanks open one of the flaps.

"I came to show you that I still had it," he says, jerking his chin toward the contents of the box—an old cell phone sporting a ridiculous pink cover, a water-warped graphic novel called *Revenge of the Space Nerds*, photo-booth photos of Owen and me making goofy faces at the camera, a pair of rainbow socks—all of them items we selected for our personal time capsule, which we were planning to bury somewhere in the woods just in case the apocalypse came and future civilizations wanted to know about us. Owen claimed he was going to do the burying part, but I guess he never got around to it. "I kept it all these years. But I don't need it anymore."

He practically shoves the package into my arms. His cowlick is sticking straight up, as if it, too, is outraged by my behavior. I'm suddenly crushed by guilt, by my own stupidity. I haven't seen Owen in years, and I managed to ruin everything in the span of five minutes. If being an idiot were an Olympic sport, I would win a gold medal.

"Owen—" I start to call him back even as he's stomping toward his car, but he whirls around and the words simply evaporate. He's *furious*. And something else—another expression is working beneath the anger, a look of hurt so deep it makes me want to curl up and die. It's crazy how someone else's pain can do that, just take the legs out from under you.

"You want to know what I was doing that day, Mia?" He crosses back toward me, and for a second I find myself scared and take a step backward. But he stops when there are several feet of space between us. "You really want to know where I went?"

I do. Of course I do. But at any second I know I'm going to start to cry, and I don't want him to see it. "You don't—you don't have to."

He ignores that. "I was *helping* her." He doesn't have to say he's talking about Summer. That's obvious. "She asked me to do her a favor—she made me swear not to tell anyone, not then, not ever. And I did. It was nothing," he says, in answer to the question he must anticipate. "Trust me. She only asked me because she knew I could hop on a bus and my dad wouldn't even notice. He was almost always drunk back then. I spent half the time in the tree house."

"Why didn't you tell us where you went?" I say.

He shoves a hand through his hair, trying to make his cowlick lie down, which it doesn't. "Like I said, it was nothing important.

Nothing *relevant*. She was just trying to put the past behind her. Besides, I felt sorry for her. The least I could do was keep her secret."

"You felt sorry for her?" I repeat, certain I must have misheard. No one felt sorry for Summer. Summer was the light. Summer was the sparkle and dazzle, the beautiful one, the one all the boys broke their necks trying to follow down the hall. Grown men— dad-age men—slowed their cars to look at her and then, when she stuck her tongue out at them, sped up, red-faced and guilty. And sure, the other girls made fun of her trailer-trash fashion and called her a slut and wrote mean stuff about her in the locker rooms, but they were obviously just jealous.

Summer had power. Over them. Over us. Over everyone.

"I always felt sorry for her." All the anger seems to have gone out of Owen at once. Now he just looks tired, and much closer to the boy I used to know, the Owen who was once mine. Casper the Ghost. Nosebleed. The Trench Coat Terror. But mine. "You and Brynn—you guys were always yourselves, you know? You didn't know how to be anybody *but* you. But Summer . . . It was like she only knew how to play a role. Like she wasn't fully a person, and had to pretend. She would do anything to get people to like her." The stubble on his jaw picks up the light, and I have to put my arms around my stomach and squeeze. He's become so beautiful. "That's how it was with me. She didn't *like* me. Not really. But she didn't know any other way. And I was young. I was *in seventh grade*. And stupid. Nobody had ever liked me before." Now I'm the one who looks away, heat rising to my face, understanding that this is his way of explaining, or apologizing for, what happened between them.

I liked you, I almost say. *I always liked you*. But I don't.

"She was always jealous of you, you know." He's making a funny face, as if the words are physically painful and he has to hold his mouth carefully to avoid getting bruised.

"Of me?" This, too, is shocking. Summer was everything I wasn't: confident and gorgeous and mature and cool. Half the time I'd find Brynn and Summer giggling about something—shaving *down there* or period cramps or getting to third base—I was too clueless to understand. *Nothing, Mia*, they'd say, rolling their eyes in unison; or Summer would pat me on the head, like I was a kid, and say, *Never change*. "Why?"

He half laughs. But there's no humor in it. "Because I was in love with you," he says, just like that, so quickly I nearly miss it.

"What?" I say. I feel as if a fault line has opened up directly beneath my feet, and I'm in danger of dropping. "What did you say?"

But he's already turned around, and this time he doesn't come back.

Although it seemed every person, goblin, giant, and dwarf in Love-lorn had gathered to witness the ceremony, it was utterly silent. Slowly, the elders of the village began to chant. "You are a child of Lovelorn," they said in unison, "to Lovelorn you will be betrothed."

"I go willingly for Lovelorn," Gregoria said next, as she had been instructed, as every Savior before her had responded, her voice a bare squeak.

"Will you do your duty and be saved?" The voices rose up again, thunderous.

Gregoria was now completely white—which, considering the green-ish tint of most dwarfs' skin, was extremely alarming. "I accept what is right for Lovelorn," she recited. "I accept what is right for me."

"We have to stop it," Ashleigh whispered frantically.

But of course, they couldn't.

—From *The Way into Lovelorn* by Georgia C. Wells

BRYNN

Now

"Wow." Wade stares up at Mia's house as if he's a holy pilgrim and this is the site of Jesus's birth. "Wow. So she's lived here all this time?"

"Uh-huh." I get out of the truck, grateful to be on solid ground. Riding around with Wade feels like going sixty miles an hour in a tin can filled with crap. He and Mia's mom could have a junk-off for sure. "Now, remember the deal—"

"I help you, you help me," Wade says, raising his hands, like *I got this, I got this.* Wade is nineteen and a sophomore at a local community college, studying How to Be a Hopeless Nerd or Conspiracy Theories 101 or something—but he dresses like he's fifty in 1972. Today he's rocking green plaid trousers, cowboy boots, and an old work shirt with the name *Bob* stitched over the pocket.

"You help Mia on her little crusade," I clarify, not trusting Wade not to screw this up somehow. "And you help me get back into a sweet little rehab of my own choosing. I'm going to need a heavy-duty meltdown this time."

"Unless we finally figure out what really happened. Then you won't need to go back." The only reason Wade helps me at all is because he thinks I *can't* stay on the outside—not while people still think I killed Summer. Since our old neighbor tried to incinerate me and people on the street still whisper "witch" when I pass, Wade wasn't that hard to convince.

"Yeah, sure. Whatever you say." I barely stop myself from rolling my eyes. Wade is one of those supersmart nerds—he's transferring next year to Boston University, apparently on a full scholarship—who can also be hopelessly dumb. Kind of like Mia.

Wade swipes a hand through his hair, which is long, shaggy, and the color of uncooked spaghetti. "Mia Ferguson's house. I really can't believe it."

"Can you try not to be a total creep for five minutes?" I stalk past him toward the front door, skirting the enormous blue Dumpster.

Wade jogs after me. Loose coins and keys and whatever else he has in his pockets jangle loudly—like a cat bell, to let you know when he's coming.

"Hey." He looks hurt. "I'm doing this for you. I'm on your side. We're family, remember?"

"That doesn't mean you aren't a creep," I say. Deep down, I know he really does think he's helping. But seriously—who gets obsessed with a murder case and spends years blogging about it and theorizing and interviewing people? Creeps, that's who.

Today Mia's face reminds me of an egg: pale and fragile and one hard knock away from total collapse.

"Oh," she says, exhaling. "It's just you."

"Who'd you think it would be?" I ask, but she shakes her head, frowning at Wade.

"Who're you?" she asks. Another sign something's screwy. Mia's far too polite to be so blunt.

"This is my cousin Wade," I jump in, so that Wade doesn't ruin things before we make it inside. In contrast to Mia, he's practically beaming. He could probably power a car battery based on the strength of his smile. "He's cool," I add, which is the opposite of the truth. "He can help us."

"Wade." Wade recovers his voice and steps forward to pump Mia's hand, as if he's a campaigning politician going door to door. "Wade Turner. It is so nice to meet you. You have no idea how long I've been wanting—"

I elbow him sharply in the ribs before he can continue. Already, I can tell that the name means something to Mia. She's frowning at him, puzzled, as if trying to place him. I have no doubt that over the years he's tried to reach out to her—he admitted to me that he had, after I refused to give him her email address, knowing she had likely changed it anyway. But she finally shakes her head, letting it go, and steps backward, gesturing for us to come inside.

"Cool place" is all Wade says on the way upstairs, which is just a sign of his major brain scramble. Mia shoots him a look to make sure he isn't making fun of her, then raises her eyebrows at me. I shrug and focus on dodging the piles of crap everywhere, which remind me of overgrown mushrooms sprouting from the filthy carpet. Still, I can tell Mia's been making progress. The stairs are a little bit cleaner than they were even yesterday.

Mia hangs back, allowing Wade to pass into her room first. She stops me before I can follow.

"How's your mom?" Her eyes are big and dark. I swear Mia's eyes are heart-shaped. Or maybe it's just that you can always see her heart through them. "Did you see her yesterday?"

Instantly I get a bad, squirmy feeling in my stomach, like I've just housed a bunch of really bad Chinese food. Is it possible I am destined to become a terrible person? "She's not doing too well," I say, avoiding her eyes. "Look, I hate to ask, but my sister's crazy busy at the hospital and doesn't want me home alone. . . ."

I trail off. Mia stares at me.

"You want to stay here?" she asks, as if the idea astonishes her.

I cross my arms tightly, try to press the bad feeling down. I don't know why it's so much harder to lie to Mia than it ever was to lie to counselors and hospital admin. "I don't exactly have a lot of options."

That's the understatement of the century. Last night I spent the night camped out behind the bus terminal just so I'd be close to a bathroom and a vending machine, trying to sleep while fireworks thundered across the sky in bright bursts of color. I'm sure Wade would have invited me to crash at his house, but then his mom would have started asking questions, and she would have called *my* mom, and then I might as well say adios to my plans to get the hell out of Twin Lakes. So this morning, I charged my phone at a local coffee shop and promised Wade the scoop of a lifetime. How could he turn down the chance to do what he has always wanted to do—to catch the real Monster of Brickhouse Lane? To play a real-life hero?

Mia recovers quickly. "Of course," she says. A little color has returned to her face. She was always good in a crisis. Good at taking care of other people, smoothing over the fights between Summer and me, making me feel better whenever I'd flunked another test or gotten booted out of gym class for maybe-not-so-accidentally chucking a dodgeball directly at Emma Caraway's head. Mommy Mia, we used to call her. Or Mamma Mia, because she danced. She reaches out and squeezes my arm. "I'm really sorry, Brynn."

"Don't worry about me," I say, pushing past her. In Mia's room, Abby is sprawled out on the bed, half supporting herself on her elbows. The copy of *The Way into Lovelorn* is lying next to her on the bed, facedown to keep her place.

"Who's the creep?" she asks me directly, jerking her chin in Wade's direction.

I shoot Wade a look, like *see?* But he's just circling the room, taking in all the details, like an archaeologist admitted for the first time into King Tut's tomb.

"He's not a real creep," I say. "He just plays one on TV." That makes Abby snort a laugh. "Besides," I say, directing the words to Mia, who's reentered her room and is now watching Wade suspiciously. "He knows everything there is to know about the case. He's been studying it for the past five years. If anyone can help us, he can."

Wade bends down to look at a framed photograph on Mia's desk. Big surprise, Abby's in this one too, mooning at the camera, wearing fake lashes coated with sparkly glitter. "Brynn told me you guys think the answers are in Lovelorn," he says, without straightening up or turning around. "I'm with you. The murder was more than ritualistic. It was narrative. It told a story. And of course the sacrifice wasn't out of line with what we learn in the original book, about the Shadow and how he picks his victims."

"It was almost word for word like what we wrote in our fan fic," I say. That was my big mistake, all those years ago—admitting to the cops that we *had* planned the murder, in a way. We'd written about it. I never thought they'd use that as evidence that I was involved. What kind of idiot writes about a murder she plans on committing and then admits it afterward?

Wade is still turning over items on Mia's desk, rearranging a pile of paper clips, straightening her MacBook and aligning it with the edge of the desk. "Someone either wanted to frame you, or was lost in the same fantasy."

"How do you know all of this?" Mia asks, narrowing her eyes.

"Oh, I know everything there is to know. Timelines, suspects, press and media coverage, autopsy results." Wade puffs out his chest, rooster-style. "I even set up a website to help prove Brynn's innocence when I was fourteen. Comprehensive, detailed, and impartial. That's my motto." He rattles this off like it's printed on a business card. Knowing Wade, it probably is. "Since I started, I've gotten four hundred thousand discrete visitors, and my page impressions number in the—"

"Hold on a second." Mia looks like her eyeballs are about to explode. "Hold on *one second*." She puts a hand to her head, squeezing. "Wade Turner. You're *Wade Turner*, from Findthe-Truth.com?"

"That's me." Wade beams at her. "Brynn's cousin."

"*Second* cousin," I quickly add.

For a second, Mia just stares at him speechlessly. Then she turns to me.

"Brynn," she says, in a voice that sounds like she's piping it through her teeth. "May I see you for a second? *Outside?*"

As soon as we're out in the hall, she practically pounces. Gotta hand it to Mia—for a girl with the build of a ballerina, she's got quite a grip. Suddenly I'm immobilized between a teetering card table and a metal clothes rack hung with winter coats.

"What the hell were you thinking?" she whispers. "Why would you bring that—that—"

"Creep?" I offer helpfully.

"Yes. That *creep* into my house?"

I step around her so she doesn't have me pinned against the wall.

"I told you. Wade's cool." This is about 15 percent accurate. "He's my cousin—"

"*Second* cousin," she says through her teeth.

"And he can help us." This is more than 15 percent accurate, but of course I can't tell her that he'll really be helping *me*. Good old cousin Wade is the Travelocity to my one-way ticket out of here. "Look, Wade wasn't kidding. He knows everything. He's been on a mission to clear my name—to clear our names—for the past five years. Did you know the cops looked at another kid on the football team? Some freshman named Heath Moore. He was all over Summer, too."

"The football players had an alibi," Mia says.

I take a deep breath. "Not exactly."

When I tell her about tracking down Jake Ginsky, her eyes go wide, and for a second she looks just like twelve-year-old Mia, our *tiny dancer.* After I finish speaking, she chews on her lower lip for a bit.

"Heath Moore . . ." She screws up her face around his name. "I don't remember Summer talking about him."

"That's my point. Neither do I." For a second, I remember Summer standing next to me in the shower, water running down the space between her breasts and beading on her eyelashes. *Do you love me?* she'd asked, putting her head on my shoulder, and I wanted so badly to kiss her I couldn't move. I was so terrified. *Will you always love me?*

Of course I loved her. I was *in* love with her.

Prove it.

I shove aside the memory, stomp it down, break it into pieces. That's the only way to keep her from haunting me every day. I have to destroy her.

Mia exhales, a long sigh. "All right," she says. "He stays."

Once again I notice how much sadder she looks even since yesterday. Or not sad, exactly. Hollow. Like someone's taken a straw to her insides. Could it be because of Owen, because I told her he'd come home? But she can't still have a thing for him. Not after five years. Not after what he did to her.

What he and Summer did together.

And here's the worst thing, the deepest, truest, most awful thing about me, the thing that twists me up and makes me just a half person, hobbled and horrible: I was sad when Summer died. Of course I was. She was my best friend.

But a teeny, tiny part of me was glad, too.

Back in the bedroom, Abby and Wade have gotten cozy real fast. She's still lying on the bed, but now she's paging through *The Way into Lovelorn*, and he's sitting on the floor with his long legs splayed out in front of him, occasionally leaning closer to point things out on the page.

"I don't get the whole Shadow thing," Abby's saying when we reenter the room. "What *is* the Shadow?"

"Ah." Wade waggles a finger. In his outfit, he really does look like a deranged professor from the 1970s. "The Shadow is the best—the most interesting—part of Lovelorn. The original book is nothing special."

"Hey," Mia protests automatically.

"It's true." Wade brushes the hair from his eyes and squints at her. "Look, I've read all the big fantasy authors. Tolkien, Martin, Lewis, Rowling—"

"Why does none of this surprise me?" I say.

Wade steamrolls over that one. "I mean, in my BU application I wrote about the role of fantasy in modern life—"

"Wait, wait." Mia stares at Wade, at his weird assortment of thrift-store clothing and his permanently surprised, *I just got out of an underground vault* look. "Your *BU* application?"

He blinks at her. "I'm transferring this fall."

Even Weirdo Cousin Wade has a life. Mia and I exchange a look, and I feel a little rush of sympathy, of understanding. The Last Two Losers in the Northern Hemisphere. But at least Mia has Abby. Besides, she's smart. She'll be okay.

"My point is, Lovelorn isn't special." Now he turns back to Abby, wide-eyed. "It's an amalgamation of all these other fantasy tropes—"

"Speak English," I say.

He takes a deep breath. "It's a mash-up. It's nothing new. And it's kind of an unsuccessful mash-up. Dwarfs and trolls and fairies and ghosts and witches. It's like Wells took all the popular fantasy books and shook them together and poured them onto the page. The only thing she got right was ending the book the way she did, in midsentence." He pauses to let this sink in while Mia looks outraged. "But the Shadow . . . well, the Shadow was new, at least. It was *hers*."

"But what *is* it?" Abby says, struggling to sit up. She catches me staring at her stomach, where a bit of her skin, pale and soft-looking, is revealed, and yanks her shirt down.

"We never really find out in Book One," I say quickly, so she won't think I was checking her out or something. "Georgia hints it's a kind of force that gets concentrated in one person."

"But we do know it's hungry," Mia says. "The Shadow's the reason that Lovelorn stays pretty year-round, why the harvests are abundant, why no one fights wars anymore. He keeps the peace. He keeps people happy. But in exchange . . ." She trails off, glancing at me for help.

It's Wade who jumps in. "The people of Lovelorn have to make a yearly sacrifice to the Shadow. Always a kid. We never see it. We just see the selection process and the kid getting led off into the woods."

"He eats them," Mia says quietly. "The Shadow does. At least, that's what Georgia implies."

"But not in our version," I say.

"No," Mia agrees. "Not in our version."

Abby is quiet, absorbing this. The air in the room feels heavy, charged, the way it does before a bad storm: it's as if the Shadow is real and has extended between us.

"What about Heath Moore?" Mia blurts. Abby raises an eyebrow.

"A freshman," I explain to her. "Wade says he was obsessed with Summer."

"He wrote her, like, a thousand messages on Facebook," Wade says. "Snaps, too. And texts. That's why the cops were interested in him."

"How do you know all this stuff?" Abby asks.

"Persistence," Wade says.

"He means being as annoying as possible to as many people as possible," I say.

Wade waves a hand. "Tomato, tomahto. My stepbrother was a cop in the district for years. So I get special privileges."

"They never charged Heath, though," I point out.

"That doesn't mean he didn't do it," Mia counters. "You're the one who said his alibi is crap." Of course she wants it to be anyone other than Owen, even after what he did to her. I remember that spring dance when everything fell apart—when *we* fell apart. The way Mia stood there, watching Owen and Summer together, unblinking, as if she'd simply forgotten how to move.

She never danced again. She said she'd outgrown it, but I knew the truth. I saw it in that moment—like someone had leaned forward and blown out a flame in her chest. But who knows? Maybe we were always broken. Maybe I was always a liar, and Mia was always weak. Maybe what happened to Summer didn't turn us but only revealed what was already there.

Wade hauls himself to his feet. He's so tall, his head nearly reaches the ceiling. "Did you keep your old yearbooks?" he asks Mia.

Mia stares at him. "We keep our old *everything*," she says. "But finding them . . ." She trails off, shrugging.

"Come on," Wade says. "I'll help."

Half of me suspects he just wants an excuse to poke around in Mia's house—and from the way Mia frowns, maybe she suspects it too. But she lets him follow her, leaving Abby and me alone. The way her skirt is bunched up, I can see her thighs, barely contained by a pair of striped tights, and for some reason I think of highways at night, the pattern of the median flashing by.

"Are you okay?" she asks.

"I'm fine," I say. I don't like the way she's looking at me—like every secret I have is leaking out of my pores—so I go over to the window and pretend to be studying the backyard. There's shit piled even at the bottom of the pool, which has been drained. I remember lying next to Summer on a float the summer before seventh grade, thigh to thigh, the smell of suntan lotion and chlorine, the sun hazy in a hot summer sky, making plans for our first-day-of-school outfits.

"Do you miss her?"

I turn around, mentally drawing down the curtains on that memory.

"Sometimes," I say. "But it was a long time ago. And things got so screwed up. Summer was"—at the last second I stop myself from saying *cruel*—"hard, in her own way."

"I didn't mean Summer," Abby says. "I was talking about Mia."

I hardly know Abby, but already I can tell this is her own special skill: she can reach inside and find the major note and bang on it. I've never asked myself whether I miss Mia, but of course as soon as she says it, I realize I do, I have—since the cops first came to my door, since I first passed Mia sitting on the other side of that shitty airless station, her eyes raw from crying, since Officer Neuter sat me down and said, *Mia said she left you two alone in the woods. Mia said she had nothing to do with it. Mia's trying to get out of trouble. How about you tell me the truth?* And in that moment—in that little room smelling of coffee and stale breath and my mom sitting next to me, crying silently into her fist—I knew I'd lost not one best friend but two.

"People change," I say.

"Have *you* changed?" she asks. In the sunlight, her eyes are like amber hard candies, her skin glowing like there's a flashlight behind her cheeks. Out of nowhere I get the urge to kiss her— maybe just to get her to shut up.

I can't make my voice work, and for a moment we stare at each other in silence. Then her expression changes. She looks suddenly afraid. She sits up, drawing a pillow protectively over her stomach, like she's worried I'm going to lunge at her zombie-style and start chowing down on her flesh. "What? What is it? Why are you looking at me like that?"

"Nothing." I turn away again, blushing so hard my cheeks burn, not sure where that momentary bit of insanity came from.

Luckily, before things can get any weirder, there are footsteps on the stairs—Mia and Wade are back. Mia is hugging our sixth-grade yearbook to her chest, and the sight of it makes my stomach hurt. I don't know what happened to my copy, the one covered all over in Summer's and Mia's handwriting, including a doodle of Mr. Springer, our bio teacher, with a hard-on (courtesy of Summer) and a hand-drawn heart border around a picture of the three of us, taken during Spirit Week (courtesy of Mia).

"It's a miracle," Mia says. Her face is flushed and she's smiling. "There's actually a clear path to the bookshelves. I hardly even remembered we *had* bookshelves."

"Making progress, Mia," Abby says.

I deliberately avoid looking at Abby and sit down next to Mia when she kneels on the carpet. Wade sits next to us, cross-legged, and draws the yearbook into his lap. As he begins paging through it, my stomach does more gymnastics. I see quick flashes of familiar faces, classrooms, photographs—my past stamped down, pressed onto the pages like a butterfly pinned behind glass, preserving some piece of the time *before*.

"Check it out." Wade flips to a photograph of the football team and uncaps a pen with his teeth. He circles a guy with a scowl and long bangs kneeling in the front row.

"Hey," Mia protests.

Wade barely glances up at her. "Don't tell me you were saving this for your grandchildren." He slides the yearbook over to me. "Heath Moore."

I lean forward, squinting. The resolution's not great, but even so, I do recognize him. "Wait a second—he was on our bus route."

"Let me see." Mia snatches the yearbook from me and frowns over his picture. A squirrely guy, always sat up front, hunched down in his seat with earphones plugged deep in his ears whenever Mr. Haggard, the bus driver, started in on his usual rotation of show tunes. *Les Misérables, Into the Woods, Meet Me in St. Louis,* even one of the songs from *Cats.* The only reason I remember him at all is because of the way he used to stare at Summer. *Perv much?* I said to him once. And he smiled and showed off nubby teeth and said, *You would know.*

"Okay," Mia says slowly. "If they met on the bus, he might have known that we hung out in the woods."

"Yeah, but how would he have known about Lovelorn?" Wade says.

"She must have told him." Abby scooches to the edge of the bed, accidentally knocking my back with one of her shins.

I shift away from her. "She wouldn't have," I say automatically.

But the truth is, Summer did a lot of things in that last year I would never have expected. She went out with Jake Ginsky, freshman and resident leech, and started cutting school and smoking pot in the mornings. She made out with Owen Waldmann in the middle of the dance floor at the Spring Fling when she knew Mia had been in love with him for years. She even got wasted a few times, even though she'd always trash-talked her bio mom for being a useless drunk, for never leaving Summer with anything except a dumb name and a single copy of the only book she'd ever read to Summer as a child: *The Way into Lovelorn.*

It was like there were two Summers. Or like Summer was a coin with two different faces. You never knew which one was gonna land.

Wade takes back the yearbook and flips forward a few pages, looping a big circle around Jake Ginsky.

"It wasn't Jake," I say quickly.

"I'm not saying it was. Just hang on." He rifles through some more pages and circles another boy, pictured with a serious-looking camera and a slick of long hair in his eyes. Wade's last target, sandwiched between students dressed identically in blazers, smiles stiffly at the camera. "Heath Moore, Jake Ginsky, James Lee, and Noah Shepherd. The cops looked at all of them. Why? Because all of them, at some point or another, were involved with Summer or wanted to be involved with her."

"What's your point?" No matter how hard I try to push them down, memories keep resurfacing, exploding hot and bright behind my eyelids. Summer looping her arms around Mia and me just after the rumors about her and Jake first started, saying, *You know you're the only ones I really love.*

"My *point* is why? Why Summer? Where did they meet her? Where did they even see her? TLC has three thousand students from kindergarten to twelfth grade. It's not exactly tiny. These boys were all in high school. They couldn't have seen her in the halls—she was in an entirely different building. And other than Heath and Jake, none of the boys had activities in common. Heath was on her bus, fine, but the others weren't. I've checked."

"They seriously let you into BU?" Mia says.

Wade ignores that. "Different friends, hobbies, and habits, all of them in love with the same girl."

"You obviously have a theory," I say. "So just spit it out."

"My stepbrother told me that all the boys used to stay after school Mondays and Wednesdays for extracurriculars," he says. "I think Summer must have too. She might have been meeting someone, or was part of some club she never told you about, and if we can figure out what it was—"

"Owen was tutoring her," I say. Mia glares at me, but I don't care. "Our old Life Skills teacher told us. Maybe Owen and Summer stayed after school together."

Wade is staring at us, openmouthed, obviously devastated that his big important theory has proved to be a complete wash. "But . . . but . . ." He looks back and forth from Mia to me, as if expecting one of us to yell *just kidding.* "That wasn't in any of the reports."

"She must have been embarrassed about it," I say. "That must be why she never told us."

"Why would they stay after *school?*" Mia crosses her arms. When she's angry, she looks sharper, as if someone has chiseled her face into a point. "They could have gone anywhere. His house, her house—"

"Oh yeah, right. Like she would have gone to her house with Mr. Ball skulking around her."

She seizes on his name. "You know, I've been thinking we

should look harder at Mr. Ball. Do we have any proof that he was in Burlington that day, like he told us?"

"You think the cops didn't check?" I ask.

"They didn't check the football players' alibis, did they?" Mia lifts her chin. "He used to *read her emails*. And she was sure he was stealing things from her drawers. Remember how weirdly afraid he was that she'd get pregnant? Like he just loved to picture her having—" She stops herself from saying the word *sex*. Her cheeks go splotchy with color.

"You saw the guy. He's a wreck. You really think he could have tackled Summer?" I shake my head. "Besides, Mr. Ball didn't know about Lovelorn."

"He could have guessed," Mia insists. "He could have read the book—"

"And the fan fic? Nobody knew about it except for us—and Owen."

"Owen didn't do it," Mia says quickly. "It's another dead end." She draws her knees to her chest. "I don't know. Maybe this was stupid. What do we know that the cops don't?"

"Lovelorn," I say. My head hurts. Like someone's kicking my eyeballs from inside my brain. "We know Lovelorn."

"If only we had our book back," Mia says, exhaling so hard her bangs flutter. "The cops must have finished with it by now. The case is cold. They're not even doing anything."

"It's evidence," I say. I don't know much about the law, despite Officer Neuter's *you don't have to answer any of my questions unless you want to* lectures, but I've watched enough TV to understand the basics. "They're not just gonna go out and try and sell Summer's stuff at the Goodwill. Besides—" I break off, seeing Wade's face. "What?" I say. "What is it?"

"The cops don't have *Return to Lovelorn*," he says carefully, as if the words carry a strange flavor.

"What are you talking about?" Mia's voice is sharp. "Of course they do."

"They *never* had it," Wade insists. "It wasn't with the rest of Summer's things. It wasn't at home or in her locker. I know. I asked. I *told* you that," he says, turning to me.

"You didn't," I say automatically. "I would have remembered."

"I did," he insists. "You just don't listen to me." He has a point. I've always thought Wade's ramblings were like elevator music: best to just tune out. Now I'm realizing how wrong I was about him. He really does care. He does want to help.

"But . . ." Mia's voice is weirdly high-pitched, like someone has a fist around her vocal cords. "That's impossible. They knew. They knew all that stuff about the sacrifice scene we wrote. They knew about the three girls and the Shadow and the knife."

Wade frowns. "They knew because you told them."

"No." Mia shakes her head so hard her bangs swish-swish with the movement. "No way. I never told them any of the details. I never . . ." She trails off, inhaling sharply, as her eyes land on me. "Oh my God. No. You didn't."

I feel like I've been locked into a toaster: I'm hot all over, dry and crackling. Now everyone's staring at me. "Hold on," I say. "Just hold on." I'm fumbling back through those old, awful memories—that dingy interview room and Mom sobbing next to me, as if she really thought I'd done it. My sister in the corner, tight-lipped, gray-faced, her eyes closed, like she was willing us all to be a dream. "I only told them because I knew they'd find out eventually. They had the book. They *had* it. How else would they have known about the stuff we were writing? How else would they have known all about Lovelorn?"

Mia squeezes her eyes shut. Now when she speaks, it's in a whisper. "I told them about the original book," she says. "I told them we liked to imagine going to Lovelorn. I thought . . . well, if they had our fan fic, they'd find out anyway, right?"

For a long moment, no one speaks. For once, even Abby has nothing to say, although I can still feel her watching me, this time pityingly. My whole body is pulsating, like I'm being rattled around the belly of a giant snare drum, beating the same word back to me over and over: *stupid, stupid, stupid*. It's so obvious now. How did I not see it? All those times Detective Neuter, and later Lieutenant Marshall, left the room to get sodas, snacks, water for my sister, tissues for my mom . . . all those times, he was just ratting to the other cops so they could wring information out of Mia, and so he could use whatever Mia said to get me all wound up.

They were playing us against each other the whole time.

Mia said she left you and Summer alone in the woods. Mia said she had nothing to do with it. Mia's trying to get out of trouble.

I stand up, suddenly desperate for air, and wrench open the window. The cops don't have *Return to Lovelorn*. They never even *found* it.

"The killer," I blurt out. I turn back from the window. "The killer must have the book. Think about it," I say, when Mia makes a face. "Summer loved that thing. She never even let us take it for the night. So why didn't the cops find it with her stuff?" The more I speak, the more excited I'm getting. "The killer must have known it would lead back to him. So he took it and destroyed it. Burned it, or buried it, or something."

"You think the killer broke into Summer's house to get a bunch of fan fiction?" Abby asks, in a tone of voice that clearly says: *You, Brynn, are a deluded subspecies.*

"Maybe not," I say, matching her tone. "Maybe he convinced Summer to give it to him. Maybe he offered to keep it safe for her."

Strangely, Mia has gone totally white and very rigid, like a plaster model of herself. "Oh my God," she whispers.

"What?" Abby at last turns to Mia, and I'm glad when her eyes are off me.

But it's to me that Mia speaks. Her eyes are huge, anguished, like holes torn in her face. "I think I know where Owen went that day," she says. "I think I know what he was doing."

No one had seen the Shadow since the original three had been to Lovelorn. Gregor's hair was now a wiry gray, since obviously without the Shadow's protection people got old and ugly and died. Some people were even grumbling about it. Things had been different when the Shadow was around. Maybe they'd even been better.

—From *Return to Lovelorn* by Summer Marks, Brynn McNally, and Mia Ferguson

MIA

Now

It feels strange to ride in Wade's truck with Abby next to me, and Brynn fiddling with the radio in the front passenger seat, and Wade tapping a rhythm with his hands against the steering wheel—almost as if we're really friends. Some people, I know, get to live like this all the time: they ride in cars with their friends. They listen to music. They complain about being bored.

If Summer had lived, maybe she'd be sitting next to me instead of Abby. Maybe Owen would be the one driving.

If, if, if. A strange, slender word.

Abby reaches over and takes my hand. "You okay?" she asks. Luckily, Wade's truck is so loud—he seems to be carrying the contents of an entire Best Buy in the back—that I know he and Brynn can't hear.

"I'm okay," I say, and give her hand a squeeze. Thank God for Abby. I haven't told her about seeing Owen yesterday. I haven't told Brynn, either.

Always, the story leads back to Owen. I think again of what he said: *I felt sorry for her.* And: *I was in love with you.*

Could it possibly be true?

Does it matter?

Brynn's right about one thing: he's the only one who knew about Lovelorn. If my hunch is right, he's the only one who *could* have known.

To get to Owen's house we have to pass through town. Main Street is, once again, blocked off by squad cars and barricades. Beyond them, a crowd is clustered at the corner of Spruce, in front of the little gazebo and the bandstand where the parade must have ended yesterday. Several trees have come down and been roped off by the parks department.

Abby presses her nose to the window as we wait at the light to turn onto County Route 15A. "What's going on?" she says. "Why's everyone standing around?"

"I don't know," I say, but then I spot the bunches of white lilies arranged in front of the gazebo steps and the microphone set up for a speaker, and my stomach drops.

Brynn must see them at the same time. "Summer's memorial," she says. Her voice sounds thin and uncertain, like a ribbon beginning to fray.

"Should we stop?" Abby asks.

"No," Brynn and I both say together. Abby looks surprised, but she doesn't argue.

When we drive past Perkins Road, Wade raps a knuckle against the window.

"That's your street, isn't it?" he says to Brynn. She gives a nod. "I remember your old house. I came over once for a barbecue when you were, like, five. I think it might have been your birthday party. Do you remember?"

"No," Brynn says flatly.

"I wore a Batman costume. That was during my superhero phase—luckily, *before* I got really into Green Lantern but *after* Superman—"

"Wade?" Brynn's voice is fake-sweet. "Can you please keep your weirdness to a minimum?"

Wade just shrugs and smiles. I suck in a quick breath when he makes the turn onto Waldmann Lane, navigating around a honeysuckle bush that cascades halfway into the road. How many times did Owen and I make the walk up the hill together, while he used a stick to beat at the grasses at the side of the road and overturn the mushrooms growing between the pulpy leaves, while I let every single word I'd swallowed during the school day come pouring out of me, a sudden release that felt as beautiful and natural as dancing?

Abby whistles when we crest the hill and the house comes into view, an enormous patchwork of stone and wood extensions, additions and modifications tacked on over almost two centuries. There was always something sad about the Waldmanns' house—I'd always thought it must be because Owen's mom died at home, just dropped dead one day from a cancer everyone had thought was in remission—but now it looks worse than sad. It looks broken and wild. The breakfast room, which used to feel like being inside a snow globe, has been completely destroyed. A tree has come down straight through the roof.

"Well," Abby says, "that's one way of redecorating." Brynn snorts.

"You guys stay here," I say quickly when Wade parks. I know, suddenly, that I need to get Owen alone. If he did what I think he did, he's been keeping the secret for years. There must be a reason, and I won't—I can't—believe that he did it. That after the years that had passed, he was guilty after all. "I'll talk to him."

Wade is already halfway out of the car but now slumps back in his seat, obviously disappointed. Brynn twists around to look at me, and for a second something flares deep in her eyes, an expression of care or sympathy or maybe just pity. Then she clicks her seat belt closed again.

The gate—a new gate—is open. A big truck is parked in the driveway: *Krasdale Landscaping + Tree Removal.* I don't see any other cars. Someone is working a saw—the air is shrill with the sound of metal on wood, a sound that makes my teeth feel like they're getting filed. The air smells like running sap. Like heat and rot and insects. Like summer.

I start down the flagstone path, now choked with grass and weeds, toward the front door. One of the landscapers, ropy and muscled, comes around the corner of the house, carrying a chain saw. He shouts to someone out of sight. Then he turns to me.

"Not home," he says, gesturing toward the door with his chain saw.

"Do you know where he went?" I ask, wrapping my arms around my waist, even though it isn't cold. Just creepy to stand in a place that used to be familiar when it now feels so foreign, like standing on the bones of a former self. He shakes his head. "You know when he'll be back?" I ask. He shakes his head again. My phone buzzes in my bag. I turn around, squinting, to see whether Brynn or Abby is gesturing to me, but can't make out anything beyond the glare of the windshield.

Another guy comes around the house, this one reed-thin, shirtless, and the color of raw leather, with a skinny blond mustache and a goatee and lots of bad tattoos. There's an unlit cigarette in his mouth. Maybe backcountry, or one of the cottage kids.

"You need help with something?" His tone isn't exactly welcoming.

"I was just looking for a friend," I say. "I'll come back."

"He had a funeral," he calls out when I'm halfway to the car.

"What?" I turn around.

"No, not a funeral." He's got his cigarette lit, and he exhales a long stream of smoke from his nose, dragon-style. Definitely backcountry. I wonder if he knew Summer. I wonder if he knows me. "A memorial or whatever you call it. There was a girl who died a few years ago. Got axed. Nearly took her head off." When he smiles, he tilts his head back and narrows his eyes, like a cat looking at something it can eat. "Your *friend* is supposed to be the one who did it."

As always when someone mentions the murder, I get a weird

out-of-body feeling, like the moment right before you faint. "She didn't get axed," I say. My voice sounds loud. I'm practically shouting. "She was stabbed. And he didn't do it."

I turn around and practically sprint back to the car.

"No luck?" Brynn says, when I get into the car.

"He's not home." I feel strangely out of breath, as if I've been forced to run a long distance. "He went up to town for the memorial."

"What?" Brynn squawks. "Is he insane? He'll get lynched."

"Come on," Abby says. "It isn't that bad, is it? Not after all this time. We were at the school yesterday and no one bothered us."

"That's because no one *noticed* us." Brynn pivots completely around in her seat to glare. "You live here. You should know how people are."

"I'm antisocial, remember?" Abby says serenely. "I'm a shut-in, like Mia."

"I thought you were famous."

"*Online.*"

Brynn rolls her eyes. "Sorry, Batman. You don't exactly look like you're trying to fly under the radar."

Brynn has a point: today Abby's wearing a polka-dot taffeta skirt with a ruffled hemline, a T-shirt that says *Winning*, chartreuse shoes, and her Harry Potter glasses.

"I think we should go," Wade says.

Brynn rounds on him next. "Oh, yeah, right. That'd go over real well. Sorry, but I'm already full-up on shitty ideas."

"I'm serious." Wade turns around, appealing directly to Abby. "Killers often can't stay away—from the scene of the crime, from the media, from anything having to do with the case. What do you want to bet the killer will be at Summer's memorial?"

"He's right," Abby says. "I watched a whole documentary about it."

I can feel Brynn's eyes on me and I look away. Owen came home after five years, right in time for Summer's memorial. Could it possibly be coincidence?

No. Of course not.

But then I think of his smile and the way he used to chuck my arm and say, *Hey, Macaroni* when we passed in the halls. The afternoons up in the tree house, eating cheddar cheese on graham crackers, which was weird but surprisingly delicious. How he would watch my dance routines, really watch, his chin cupped in his hands, totally interested, no matter how long they were. The kiss.

And I know that *that* Owen, the old Owen, the Owen I always believed in even after he broke my heart, is the only thing I have left. I can't lose it, too.

"That's what everyone will think if *we* show," I say. My voice sounds faint and fuzzy. Like a bad recording of itself. "They'll think we just couldn't stay away."

"We don't even have to get out of the car," Wade says. "We'll just get as close as we can, and we'll watch."

Brynn shakes her head. "No. Mia's right."

"Come on, guys." Wade looks from me to Brynn, then back to me again. "Don't you want to finish this?"

Brynn makes another noise of disgust. When we were kids, Brynn always seemed so much braver than everyone. She was a thousand times braver than I was. I threw up in the bathroom in sixth grade when we had to dissect a worm. She barely blinked. When Hooper Watts called me Mute Mia and told everyone I was too stupid to know how to talk, I proved his point and said absolutely nothing. When he told everyone Brynn had been caught stealing girls' underwear from the gym lockers, she told everyone he'd been paying her to do it so he could add to his collection.

And maybe she is braver. But she's afraid now.

I take a deep breath. "Okay," I say. "Let's go."

Brynn gapes at me. "Have you lost your mind?"

"Maybe," I say, feeling strangely relieved, and strangely free, too. She keeps staring at me, shocked, as if she's never seen me before, and I can't help it: in my head I do a little jump, arms up to the sky, *victory*.

Why did Lovelorn appear to Audrey, Ashleigh, and Ava, when countless other children had wandered the woods and found nothing but toadstools and rotting tree trunks and finches twittering nervously in their roosts?

Maybe because Lovelorn needed them.

Or maybe, maybe, because they needed Lovelorn.

—From *The Way into Lovelorn* by Georgia C. Wells

BRYNN

Now

We can't get any closer to the ceremony than the corner of Carol and Spruce, a full two blocks away from the main action. The cops have set up sawhorses to block off the streets, which are packed anyway with moms and kids in strollers and old men dressed up in starched white shirts and blazers. It would look like Memorial Day, or maybe a block party, except there are no balloons and nobody's smiling. The world's *worst* block party, then.

"I'll be back," Wade says as soon as we park. He hops out of the car and scoots between two sawhorses, pushing his way into the crowd. For a while, I track him moving between people, and then I lose him. Even with the windows down, it's hot. Quiet, too. There's scratchy interference from a speaker up ahead. Someone must be speaking into a microphone, but the sound quality is bad, and I can't make out a single word.

Mia leans forward, resting her elbows on both seat backs. "He could have left the air conditioner on," she says.

"Tell me about it." Abby has pulled her hair away from her neck and makes a show of fanning herself.

I scan the crowd again and find myself half expecting to see Summer. One of her games used to be to pretend she was dead. She'd lie in bed, stiff-backed, eyes open, or float on her stomach in the public pool, hair waving seaweed-style in the water, try to scare the shit out of us. Then she'd suddenly stand, spitting out a mouthful of water. *Gotcha*, she'd say, and put her arms around me, rest the point of her chin on my shoulder. *Would you be sad?* she'd say. *Would you be sad if I died?*

Yeah. I'd be sad.

How sad?

It would be like cutting out my heart with a spoon.

Silly. You'd need a knife for that.

I shake my head, like memories are just flies that keep buzzing around my ear.

"Hey." Mia straightens up. You ever seen a meerkat? That's what Mia looks like when she pays attention. All huge eyes and twitchy nose. "Isn't that Mr. Haggard?"

"Mr. Who?"

"Mr. Haggard," she says impatiently. "Our old bus driver." Then: "It *is* him. Look. Over there, in front of Tweed's. Wearing the funny shoes."

She's right. Mr. Haggard, our weirdo bus driver, who used to get the kids to quiet down by singing as loudly as he could in a voice that sounded like piping a foghorn through a funnel, is standing at the edge of the crowd, wearing a badly fitting suit jacket and old waders. His face is shiny with sweat, and every so often he swipes at his forehead with a balled-up tissue.

Summer was horrible to him. She used to call him Mr. Faggard. She used to make her voice all sweet around her insults, shouting, "Doesn't it hurt to sit on your fat ass all day?" or "You ever gonna move out of your mom's basement, Mr. Faggard?" and expecting Mia and me to snicker on cue. Mia would always turn her face to the window, pretending not to have heard, even though Summer would make fun of her for it later. *What's the matter, Mamma Mia? You got an itch in your panties for Mr. H?*

But I laughed. I always laughed.

"I'll be damned," I say. "He looks the same."

As I'm watching him, wondering whether it would be weird to go up and apologize, wondering whether I even *could*, there's a ripple in the crowd. Like someone's just hurled a stone into the mob and everyone's reacting. Suddenly Owen Waldmann gets spat out and goes stumbling down Carol Street. One guy—two guys—three—sprint after him.

"What the hell?" I say. "Did you see—?" But Mia's out of the car before I can finish. "Mia!"

She's already dodging the sawhorses and disappearing down Carol. I curse and get out of the car. Already, the blob of people has re-formed, filled in all the spaces. The scratchy microphone voice is still blaring in the distance. *Five years ago today . . . a tragedy in our community* . . . Other than that, it's silent. Not a single sneeze, cough, or fart.

I tug my hood a little lower, mumble "Excuse me," and work my way over to Carol, skirting the edge of the crowd.

A few doors up on Carol, Heath Moore has Owen shoved up against the window of Lily's Organic Café and Bakeshop. His two friends remind me of blowfish: hovering just behind Heath, doing their best to puff themselves up and look bigger. One of them has a phone out and he's filming the whole thing. And Mia's just standing there with her fists clenched.

"Stop it," she's saying when I blow past her—but quietly, in a voice barely above a whisper. "Leave him alone." Heath doesn't even glance in her direction.

"You think this is funny?" Heath shoves Owen against the window. Owen doesn't try to fight back, although I bet he could. "You think it's a fucking joke?"

I'm out of breath from the short dash down the street and pull up, panting a little. I snatch the phone from the blowfish who's filming and dance out of his reach before he has a chance to take it back.

Heath Moore whips around, keeping an arm across Owen's chest. "What the hell?" he says. "That's *my* phone."

"My phone now." I pocket it, keeping my voice steady, relaxed. The calm before the fuck-you-up. "So what happened, Heath?" I say. I don't even know why I'm so desperate to defend Owen. "Your mom forget to lock your cage this morning?"

His eyes sludge past me and land on Mia. His face goes through about ten different expressions and settles on the ugliest one.

"Cute," he says. In the five years since Summer died, Heath Moore has thickened out, and not in a good way. "Real cute. The whole band's back together." His dopey friends are just standing there, staring. They must be twins. They've got the same chewed-up look, like someone gnawed on their faces and then regurgitated them just a little wrong. "You've got some balls, showing up here."

"At least one of us has them," I fire back.

"Very funny." Heath's not sure who to go after first. He keeps swiveling around from Owen to me, me to Owen. "It's all a game to you, isn't it? Showing up here, laughing at everyone. Laughing at Summer."

I squeeze my hands into fists and imagine black smoke rising through me, blotting out the memory. "She was our friend," I say. "Our best friend. Just because you decided to perv out on her—"

Heath turns red. "*She* went after *me*."

I barrel right over that one. "—doesn't mean you knew her. It doesn't mean you knew anything about her."

"I knew enough to know what she thought of you." He's lost it now. His voice is carrying, and people at the end of the street have started to look. But no one comes over to investigate. They're like frigging cows, just herded up and watching all the action. "I know what you did to her. You turned her."

"Turned her?" For a second, I have no idea what he's talking about.

"Into one of you," he said. "You turned her gay."

He takes another step toward me and leans in, so I can feel the heat of his breath, a gasoline smell, like maybe he's been drinking. He reaches up with hard bloated fingers and takes my shoulder. "Or maybe you just haven't had the right guy yet. What do you think of that?"

Whoosh. Anger crackles through me. Without thinking, I bring my knee up, hard, between his legs, catch him right in the soft parts. Heath lets out a howl and doubles over, cursing, tears streaming down his face.

One of the Regurgitated Twins comes at me. I'm hot now, ready for a fight. But he's stronger than he looks and shoves me off balance.

"Bitch," he says.

"Don't touch her."

Even as I'm swinging at the guy, Owen comes at him, knocking him in the shoulder to spin him around. Owen swings. His fist connects with a crack. The guy stumbles backward, blood gushing from his nose, a bright tide of it, and I think of that day years ago on the playground, when Owen turned on Elijah Tanner and shut him up with a single punch—but when Owen's eyes meet mine, I see in them something that runs through me like a shock: we're the same. He fights not because he wants to, but because he has no choice. He fights from the corner.

Then the other guy leaps on Owen from behind and brings him to the ground, and now Mia's voice has finally broken free of her throat and she's standing there screaming, "Stop it, stop it, stop it!"

People come flowing down Carol Street, and my whole head feels huge and swollen as a blister, about to explode—they're going to see us, they're going to see us. Just then, I spot Mr. Ball, Summer's foster dad, in the crowd. But the next second, a woman shoves him aside and hurtles past me.

"What on earth—?"

It takes a minute for my brain and eyes to connect: Ms. Gray. Owen and Twin #2 are still grappling on the ground. Ms. Gray just steps in and grabs Twin #2 by the shirt collar, like he's a dog, and hauls him backward. "What is going *on*?"

"They started it," I blurt out.

She gives me a look—*are you serious?*—and I press my lips together, wishing I hadn't said anything. Next to me, Mia's practically hyperventilating, as if she were the one getting clobbered. Her voice has dried up again, just straight up and gone.

"Owen," she says. The word is so quiet I almost miss it.

Owen's still on the ground, holding his eye where Twin #2 must have punched him, a thin dark trickle of blood working out of his left nostril. The rest of the crowd is pressing closer, murmuring, and the whole world feels like a guitar string about to snap, tense and humming—they're going to recognize us, they're going to take us apart leg by leg, slurp up our skin and pick their teeth with our bones—when Ms. Gray gets a hand around Owen's elbow and hauls him to his feet.

"Come on," she says to him. Then she turns to me and grabs my wrist, squeezing so tightly that when I pull away, I see that she's left marks. "Come *on*."

Mia looks like she's about to pass out. I link arms with her and we follow Ms. Gray as she plunges into the crowd, one arm extended to keep people back, one arm around Owen, body-guard-style. The crowd falls away, allowing us to pass, even Mr. Ball, dressed in a bright yellow polo shirt like it's a goddamn golf outing. I don't know how Ms. Gray does it, but maybe that's one of her *life skills*. Like she's a motorboat and we're just bumping along in her wake, no problem, don't mind us. Then we're at the car and, thank God, Wade is there too, pacing next to the car, chewing on a thumbnail.

"What the—?" He does an actual double take when he sees us. "What *happened*?"

"Is he with you?" Ms. Gray still has an arm around Owen.

Wade's eyes go to me.

"Yeah," I say. "Yeah, he's with us."

Ms. Gray opens the back door and helps Owen inside. He's still holding on to his right eye, and he stumbles a little trying to get into the car. Mia hurtles into the backseat after him. Ms. Gray turns back to me. Her eyes go to the crowd behind us—I don't have to turn around to know that they're still watching, still mur-muring. A swarm of hornets sharpening their stingers. *Buzz buzz buzz.* Was that Owen Waldmann? *Buzz buzz buzz.* And the Fergu-son girl, together?

"Go," Ms. Gray says. She looks exhausted. Her eyes are bloodshot and her hair has started to come loose from its bun. She has a carnation pinned to her blazer. "Get out of here."

I want to thank her and apologize all at once, but the words stick in my throat. This must be how Mia feels. "I'm sorry . . . ," I start to say.

"*Go*," she repeats, almost angrily. Then she turns and dodges the sawhorses, plunging back into the crowd and disappearing.

"God." In the car now, everyone quiet and tense, Mia still wheezing out the occasional words like she's forgotten how to speak, Owen letting out the occasional moan when the truck hits a rut, Wade just dying to ask questions and chewing his lip to keep them down, Abby finally breaks the silence. "Seriously, guys. We can't take you *anywhere*."

BRYNN

Then

"What do you think?" Summer's breath was warm and smelled like raspberries. She rolled onto one elbow, and I felt the weight of her breast on my inner arm and drew quickly away, my heart scrabbling spiderlike into my throat. Was it deliberate? Her lips were candy-red and sticky. And in my head they were doing terrible things . . . terrible, beautiful things. . . .

But she was the one who'd flopped onto the bed beside me, who interlinked our feet and suggested, giggling, that we just go out with each other since all the guys at TLC were so lame.

Was that flirting? Was she flirting with me? Would I know?

"Hello? What do you think?" Summer wiggled her phone in front of my face and I forced myself to focus. On the screen: a blurry picture of a guy wearing a slouchy hoodie, skinny jeans, not one but two studded belts, holding a Solo cup and squinting through cigarette smoke. *Zap. Zap. Zap.* I pictured my heart getting buzzed by an electric zapper.

"Who is that?" I said, and Summer was already snatching the phone back.

"No one you know," she said. "He's a freshman."

"A freshman?" I repeated. *Zap zap zap.* Until my brain was jelly.

"He's cute, right?" She tilted the phone, left and right, considering.

"He looks," I said, "like a complete assfart."

Summer laughed and tossed her phone aside. She rolled over again onto her elbow. Her hair tickled my underarm. Her skin was warm, so warm it made me burn where it touched.

"Know what I think?" she said.

"What?"

My heart was frying like an egg, twitching to death under the beam of two bright eyes.

She leaned closer, so her sticky red lips bumped my ear. "I think you're jealous."

Afterward Firth would always tell the story of making off with the princess's heart in his vest pocket, and how he was miles away before its rhythm began to affect him and lull him into a kind of sleepy melancholy. He kept thinking of the princess's face, of her beautiful long hair, of the way the sky was reflected in her tears.

He couldn't have known then that the single act of taking something that wasn't his would prove to be his undoing, and later, especially after ale, he would reminisce about his wasted youth. "That's the thing with hearts," he would say. "They're the trickiest, troubledest things in the world."

—From *The Way into Lovelorn* by Georgia C. Wells

MIA

Now

"Are you sure you're all right?" Finally, the lock in my throat has released. "You don't need to go to the hospital or anything?"

"I'll be fine," Owen says, peeling a hand away from his eye, which is swollen shut. "But I guess my modeling career is over."

We're parking in front of a 7-Eleven on the outskirts of the old downtown. Wade, Abby, and Brynn have left us alone to go find ice for Owen's eye. It's hot in the truck, even with the windows open, but sitting so close to Owen, practically thigh to thigh, leaves me with a desperate shivery feeling. Blood is crusting above his upper lip. He looks so raw and bruised and open, and I want to help him, fix him, take his face and kiss it everywhere.

I want to ask him whether he meant what he said, about loving me.

I want to know why, if that's true, he chose Summer.

Why he lied.

Where he was.

I want so many impossible things.

"Does it hurt?" I ask, instead of saying the ten other things that occur to me. *#24. Feelings are larger than a whole dictionary full of words.* He makes a face. "It's not so bad. He was going for my nose. Good thing his aim was off. I kind of like my nose."

"I do too," I say automatically, and then wish I hadn't. He peels a hand away from his eye and grins, then winces. "What happened back there?"

Owen sighs. "I just wanted to pay my respects, like everybody else," he says. "I'd forgotten how crazy this town can be."

"That's because you left." The words come out as an accusation, and I bite my lip. Words would be less frightening if you could swallow them again, chew them and digest them into nothingness.

But he doesn't seem to notice. "Everything was fine until that pinhead and his friends noticed me." He shakes his head. His hair is extra flame-like today. I have an urge to run my hand through it, and an idea that if I did, I'd get burned. "He told me to leave. I said no." He shrugs. "You basically saw the rest."

Before I can respond, Brynn slides into the car again. "Here. Best first aid 7-Eleven has to offer." She hands Owen a frozen burrito. "Our options were limited," she says before I can object. "But it'll help. I promise. And when it thaws, we'll have a snack. It's black bean veggie."

Owen's laugh quickly transforms to a groan. "Smiling hurts," he says.

"And check it out," Brynn says. She pulls an unfamiliar iPhone from her pocket. "I got Heath's phone. What do you want to bet he's got dick pics on here?"

"*Brynn*. You stole that."

"I reappropriated it," she corrects me. "He shouldn't have been flashing it around, anyway. Relax, Girl Scout," she adds, rolling her eyes. "I'll mail it back to him or something, okay?"

Wade and Abby come out of the 7-Eleven together. Abby's carrying a plastic bag distended with sodas and waters and snacks. Wade has, for some mysterious reason, purchased a flat-topped red visor and a pair of sunglasses.

I feel a sudden hard pull of loneliness.

"You okay?" Owen touches the back of my hand, quickly. Skims it.

"I'm okay." I put my hands between my thighs and squeeze. "I was just thinking about Summer. Missing her, I guess."

He seems as if he wants to say something else. But then Wade slides behind the wheel, and Abby maneuvers into the backseat, both of them still arguing about whether Snickers have caffeine. When Owen slides over to make room for Abby, our knees briefly touch.

"Hey. I guess I should say thank you." He straightens up, still holding the stupid burrito to his eye. "I mean, you guys saved me from death-by-mob."

"Yeah. And now you owe us." Brynn reaches into the backseat, swiping a Kit Kat bar from Abby. She rips off the corner of the package with her teeth. "We came to collect."

Owen's face changes. "What do you mean?"

"Mia didn't tell you?" Brynn says, turning to me now. Her voice is light, but I can tell she's trying to telegraph a warning through her eyes. *Don't fall for him again. Don't be stupid. Don't. Don't.*

"I didn't get to it," I say to her, which falls under *#23: Lying by not saying what you truly mean.* Secretly I know I haven't asked for one reason and one reason only: because I'm afraid of the answer.

"Mia and Brynn are on the hunt for a killer," Abby says, in a movie-announcer voice. She's struggling with a bag of potato chips. She doesn't seem to notice that instantly, everything goes quiet, except for the *crinkle-crinkle* of the bag.

"I thought Brynn thought *I* was the killer," Owen says.

"So convince me otherwise." Brynn shrugs, like they could be talking about any stupid argument, about a movie or a new sandwich place.

Owen turns to me after what seems like forever. "Mia?"

I swallow back the urge to apologize. "You told me you did a favor for Summer." The words come slowly, haltingly, but they come. "You told me you kept her secret because you felt bad."

"I did." Even with one eye covered, Owen's staring at me as if he's mentally shrinking me down to the size of an insect. And I feel like an insect, or like I've swallowed one and now it's trying to scrabble free of my stomach. "I swore not to tell anyone. *Ever.*" He emphasizes the last part deliberately.

"Summer's dead, Owen," Brynn says. There's a hard edge to

her voice. "She doesn't have secrets anymore."

Owen opens his mouth, then closes it again. His face has gone white. He turns to me. "I promised her," he says.

Just like that, the old jealousy comes back: a worming, sick feeling, like a stomach virus. Why did he promise Summer? Why did he protect her?

Why did he kiss her, when he should have kissed me?

I know it isn't fair to blame him. We all protected Summer, for reasons I can't totally explain. That's why Brynn and I never told anyone what really happened that afternoon in the woods, and why we never revealed what Summer was really like. How when she was angry she would swipe me with her nails, or grab me by the shoulders and shake me until my teeth rattled in my head. How once she took scissors to her wrists after Brynn admitted to maybe having a crush on Amy Berkowitz, just sat there drawing long scrapes down her skin until Brynn begged her to stop and started to cry and promised Summer she'd never love anyone more than she loved us—and how Summer laughed afterward, telling Brynn she was a hopeless dyke, and left the scissors on my desk, still crusty with blood.

How she became our everything, our tornado. We were caught up in her force. She turned us around. She made the world spin faster. She blotted out all the other light.

We couldn't escape.

And maybe it's the old influence, the winds still embedded inside, but now I'm the one who wants to destroy. I want to break the old connections. I want to flatten her back into the grave.

I want her to let us go.

Owen's still watching me. *Pleading*, as if he expects me to contradict Brynn.

Instead I say, "It's time, Owen."

Owen lets out a big *whoosh* of air, as if instead of speaking, I'd punched him. He slumps down in the seat, lowering his hand from his eyes, staring down at his lap.

"Okay," he says finally. "Okay," he repeats, and looks up. "I didn't think it was a big deal. She asked me to take away your story—that book you were working on. She made me swear I wouldn't read it, that I wouldn't look at it at all."

Brynn's eyes click to mine for a sharp, electric second. "But you did, didn't you?"

Owen shakes his head. "No way. She brought it to me all packaged up."

"She must have told you about the story before, though." Brynn keeps her voice casual. "Since you were tutoring her and everything."

"*Tutoring* her?" Even with his cheek hopelessly swollen, Owen manages to go bug-eyed. "I never even saw Summer with a book."

You were too busy doing other things, whispers a terrible voice inside my head.

Brynn exhales. "All right, so you never saw *Return to Lovelorn* until Summer gave it to you. Did she say why she wanted it gone?"

Owen shakes his head. "All she told me was the game was over," he said. "She told me that she was ending it for good."

"Why you?" Brynn asks bluntly. "Why didn't she get rid of it herself?"

Owen shrugs. "She knew I'd be able to get to Maine, I guess. That was back when my dad was drunk all the time. He never paid attention."

"Maine?" I echo. "What's in Maine?"

But Brynn's the one who answers. "Georgia Wells," she says. She brings a hand to her mouth, as if the words have left a taste there. "Georgia Wells is in Maine. That's where she's buried."

Owen only nods.

As always, Abby is the one to speak first.

"Good thing we bought snacks," she says. "Who's up for a road trip?"

MIA

Then

"She doesn't like him really," Summer said, that night in April, the night of the dance. Spinning around my bedroom, wearing a tank top she'd stolen from my drawer without asking and a full tulle skirt that fanned around her knees. It was the first time in weeks—maybe months—that we'd seen her this way, happy and bright and ours. Her blond hair glimmering, eyes smoky with makeup I wouldn't have even known how to buy. Falling backward onto my bed, snow-angel-style, next to Brynn. "You don't really like him, do you, Mia? It's just a game. You've never even kissed him."

I do like him, I wanted to say. I wanted to scream. *I like him more than anything. More than dance. More than breathing.*

More—so much more—than I like you.

But I waited too long. I hesitated. The words built up backstage, and I couldn't find them in the darkness, and then I'd waited too long.

Summer laughed.

"See?" she said to Brynn. She took a pillow and hurled it at me. "What a tease. Someone should give that poor boy a break."

What do I remember about the dance? Zigzag red and blue lights, patterns of strobe on the floor, an awful sound system beating its patchy rhythm into the air. Standing with Brynn and Owen and Summer in a group, all of us with hands up, laughing, breathless. Whole. It was as if time had simply rewound. As if the past six weeks—the way Summer had avoided us, the way she'd sneered at Brynn in the cafeteria and said in front of everyone, "Stop drooling, McNally. I'm not into girls, okay?"—had never happened. As if they'd been one long nightmare and we had all woken up.

What else? Letting the music flow through me like a river, forgetting form and structure and point your toes and turn out and spine straight, just letting myself swim in the sound.

And Summer the thread, the connection, the spindle weaving all of us together, beautiful and sharp and deadly.

"Mamma Mia!" She grabbed my hands and spun me around in a circle. My palms were sweating. Hers were dry. "You're going to be famous someday, you know?"

And afterward, when a slow song came on, and Brynn looped an arm around my shoulder and we went, sweaty and still laughing, to get punch from the cafeteria table and whisper about the couples walking stiff-armed, zombielike, through a cheesy rendition of a Taylor Swift song, turning around, suddenly realizing Owen and Summer hadn't followed us.

I spotted them right away, but it took me a moment to understand.

Owen and Summer. Summer and Owen. Summer and Owen.
So close they'd become one, a single figure in the middle of the
gym: the end of the dance, the crescendo, the moment the music
swells, just before the stage goes dark.

Kissing.

And the strangest thing was this: in that moment, all the
music—the bubbly, fizzy vivace, the lazy andante and the yawn-
ing adagio, which for years had lived inside of my bones and blood
and marrow, so that when I danced it wasn't so much moving as
becoming the music—drained straight out of my body. I could *feel*
it happening. The dancers withdrew and retreated into the wings,
and they've stayed there—trapped in the darkness of my mind—
ever since. It was as if for years I'd carried this live, humming
secret inside, a secret rhythm that tugged at me to leap and spin,
bend and turn, and suddenly the secret was revealed and it wasn't
mine anymore and it didn't *matter.*

As if someone had cored me like an apple.

I tried. Believe me, I did try. After weeks of avoiding Madame
Laroche's frantic phone calls, of making excuses to my mom and
dad about why I wouldn't go to class or rehearsal; after Brynn
forced me back to Lovelorn, hoping it would make me feel better,
only to find that Lovelorn, too, had vanished; I put on my tights
and my leotard and my favorite pointe shoes and went back to
Vermont Ballet.

For a week I fumbled through classes, missing turns, hitting my arabesques just a second too late, losing track of where I was in the combinations, while Madame Laroche went from encouraging to furious to silent, tight-lipped, and the other girls began edging away from me, as if losing the ability to dance was a disease and might be contagious.

"What happened?" Madame Laroche pulled me aside after the last class I ever took. "You used to dance from here." She pointed to her heart. "You used to dance like singing. Now I don't know *who* is on that stage."

How could I have told her? How could I have explained? There was no heart left to dance. I had no voice to sing.

Instead, I said, "I know. I'm sorry." *#47. Truths you can never say, because they will strangle you on the way up.*

When I got home, I threw out my pointe shoes. My leotards, too, and my collection of leg warmers. My sewing kit with my lucky purple thread that I used to fix elastic onto my shoes.

And when Summer came up to me, shyly, after a week of barely glancing in my direction, of piloting Owen away whenever he made a move to talk to me—when she giggled and slipped a hand in mine and leaned in, smelling like apple shampoo, to ask, "You're not mad, are you? You know I can't stand it when you're mad at me. You know I'll just *die*."

I said, "No, I'm not mad."

#46. Lies that feel like suffocation.

Here's the real truth. She didn't just steal Owen. She took

dancing too—just evaporated it, like cupping a mouth over a window to fog it and then leaning back to watch it disappear. She took both of the things I loved most in the world.

It was my fault she died. I wanted it. I wished for it.

And then it happened, and I never got the chance to say I was sorry.

Only once did Audrey try to sneak to Lovelorn on her own. Ava was sick, and Ashleigh was grounded, after losing both Christmas mittens (since she couldn't very well explain that they were safe and sound sitting next to Gregor's teapot). Audrey thought she'd pop round and see how Gregor was doing, enjoy an escape from the brittle cold, and retrieve the mittens.

She was therefore stunned when she wandered fruitlessly for hours but couldn't find the entrance to Lovelorn. It had never occurred to her, you see, that all three friends had to be together—that in fact, the magic lived only in their friendship.

—From *The Way into Lovelorn* by Georgia C. Wells

BRYNN

Now

Now that Owen has finally confessed, it's like his mouth is in turbo gear. He won't stop talking. He tells us that Summer came to him that final morning, looking like she'd been up all night. That she'd packed up *Return to Lovelorn* carefully, in plastic and an old metal lockbox he figured she'd stolen from her foster parents. That he'd taken cash from his dad's wallet while his dad was PTFO (passed the fuck out, in rehab terminology) and hoofed it up to town to take a cab from Twin Lakes to Middlebury, and from there hopped a bus.

And the crazy thing is, I believe him.

From Middlebury it's two hundred miles to Portland, Maine, and that's if you're doing a straight shot between them. But taking the bus means you go south all the way to Boston before transferring and backtracking north along the coast to Maine, a trip of six and a half hours one way—longer, for Owen, because at one of the rest stops an off-duty firefighter spotted him, thinking it was weird for a thirteen-year-old to be traveling on his own, and held Owen up so long with questions he missed the bus and had to wait for another.

"Thank God for that guy, though," Owen says. "My lawyer tracked him down just before the case went to trial. It was one of the things that saved me."

"Why didn't you tell anyone?" Mia asks. "You let the police *arrest* you. You went to Woodside. Why didn't you just tell the truth?"

Outside the window, houses blur by. A big smear of white-greenwhitegreen. Wade must be going sixty, seventy miles an hour, screeching around the turns, not even paying attention to his speed. But it was all supposed to be a joke—the Monsters of Brickhouse Lane on the hunt for the truth, putting our demons to rest. A few days of make-believe just so I could get back to Four Corners.

Except that it doesn't feel funny, or like make-believe.

"I did, finally," Owen says. "Most of the truth, anyway. I told the cops I'd had a fight with my dad and was out riding the buses. But they didn't believe me. Not at first."

"Why not?" Abby says. She's been leaning back, eyes closed, and I assumed she was sleeping. Abby, I've decided, reminds me of a cat. A kind of obnoxious, maybe a little full-of-herself cat. Cute, though, in a way. Summer would have hated her. I'm not sure why I think about this, but I do. *Chubby chasing, Brynn?* she would say. *You like some jelly rolls with your doughnut hole?*

"Because we'd lied." Owen's voice sounds all cracked up and dusty, like he's swallowed old asphalt. "The first time the cops came around asking where I'd been, we told him I hadn't gone anywhere. That I'd been home. We didn't know . . . I mean, I'd heard someone had been found in the woods, but I thought it was a hunter or something. Not Summer. Never Summer." He sucks in a breath. "My mom's sister was already making noise about taking me from my dad. We thought that's why the cops showed up—to make sure my dad was okay. That I was okay. He'd had an accident in the winter, you know, just passed out at the wheel, went straight into a tree. . . ."

"I didn't know that," Mia says.

Owen shrugs.

"Anyway, my aunt was threatening to sue for custody if my dad didn't sober up. She said he wasn't fit to be a parent. He wasn't, back then. But I didn't want to leave. I *couldn't*. I thought if I did . . ." He trails off. When I look back at him, he's just sitting there, staring at his hands, half his face like an eggplant you forgot was in your fridge. I can't help but feel sorry for him.

"What?" I say.

He looks up, startled, as if he's forgotten we're all there. "I thought he'd die," he says simply.

And I think of my mom and the way she sits in front of the TV eating green beans from the can, fishing them out with her fingers because she kicked potato chips twenty years ago, and how she always scours the dollar stores for every single Christmas, Halloween, Easter, and Thanksgiving decoration she can find and decks out the house for every holiday—I'm talking fake snow and twinkly lights or giant bunny wall decals or cobwebs on all the bushes outside—and I suddenly feel like the world's biggest nobody. I wonder if she thinks of me at all, if she misses me, or if she and Erin have made a pact never to mention my name, if they're happier with me gone.

How can I go back? How can I *ever* go back?

Owen clears his throat. "Dad thought if the cops knew he'd been passed-out drunk and his thirteen-year-old son had taken the bus all the way to Maine, they'd take me away for sure."

Outside, all the trees have their hands up, waving. *Don't shoot.*

"They came by looking for me around six o'clock," Owen continues. "Must have been right after they found out—after they found *her*. My dad was a wreck. Already drinking again, cops at the door, son missing. He told them I was sick. Bronchitis. Couldn't talk to anyone. They said they'd be back. So when I got home, we agreed on a cover story. He wasn't even *mad*." Owen laughs like he's choking. "I didn't get back until two, three in the morning. I'd stolen sixty bucks and spent it all. And he wasn't angry. He was panicked."

I remember when the tires crunched up the driveway and my mom twitched open the curtain and saw the cops, I thought they must have found out I'd stolen some nail polish and a few packs of gum from a local CVS the week before. Even after what had happened in the woods, even after Summer and the cat and the carving knife, I was worried about that stupid black nail polish. "You still didn't know about Summer?" I ask him.

"Not then. My dad hadn't left the house in two, three days. Wasn't picking up his phone, either. And my phone had died before I even got to Maine. My dad thought his sister-in-law—my aunt, the one who kept threatening to take me to Madison—must have been the one to call the cops. That she was *conspiring* with me. I remember that's the word he used. 'She's *conspiring* to take you away.' He thought that's why I'd been out of the house— because I wanted to get him in trouble. I thought he was going to go after me, hit me or something, but he was too drunk to do more than shout."

Mia lets out a little squeak, like a balloon getting squeezed.

"We agreed on a cover story. I'd been sick, twenty-four-hour virus, hadn't left my room at all. The cops came back the next morning. They were the ones who told me about Summer. Otherwise, I guess I would have found out online. I'm glad the cops told me, actually. Before I could read about it."

In the days after Summer's body was discovered, everyone posted to her Facebook and Instagram profiles—prayers and videos and pictures and poems—even people who'd hated her when she was alive, who said she was a witch or a slut or made fun of her for being in foster care. Then someone found a way to log in *as* Summer. I was in the middle of the Walmart parking lot the first time I saw her name pop up in my feed.

Resting in peace right now. Thanks for all the love.

I stood there, my hands sweating so much I nearly dropped my phone, like I could press her right out of those words.

But over the days, the messages on her wall turned nastier.

Guess this is a lesson . . . all devils go to hell . . .

And: *Maybe the good aren't the only ones who die young . . .*

Until finally someone had the account shut down.

"The cops were nice at first. Just asking questions about how I knew Summer. They'd heard some stuff, I guess, about how Summer and I . . ." He trails off. What happened between Owen and Summer is still a major Danger Zone, obviously, Restricted Access, Hard Hat Area Only. "By the time I knew how serious it was—by the time my dad knew—we'd already told our lie a dozen times. Stupid. Someone had seen me in town on my way to Middlebury. And a cabbie remembered taking me home at two in the morning. Not a lot of thirteen-year-old fares, I guess. Even after I told them the truth, they wouldn't believe me about anything."

"Did you ever find out how your blood ended up on Summer's clothes?" Wade blurts out. I can tell he's been dying to ask this whole time.

"No," he says, looking down at his hands.

"It wasn't," Mia says. "It didn't." When she's really angry, her voice actually gets quieter. Mia's the only person I know who scream-whispers. "The cops screwed up. The sample was contaminated."

"The sample was *inadmissible*," Wade corrects her. "Legally. That doesn't mean it wasn't his blood."

"How many miles do we have left until we get to Maine?" Abby jumps in before Wade can say anything else. I turn around and see the look Mia gives her. *Thank you*, the look says.

And that bad feeling in my stomach worms a half inch deeper.

"One hundred sixty-seven," Wade says cheerfully.

"How about the radio, then?" Mia reaches into the front seat to punch the radio on, and for a long time no one speaks again, even after the music buzzes into static.

Around mile 115 everyone starts to get cranky. It turns out Mia has a bladder the size of a thimble. After the third time she asks to stop, I tell her she should keep an empty Big Gulp between her legs, like truckers do, so we have some hope of making it to Maine.

I forgot Mia has no sense of humor.

We pull off I-89 and into the Old Country Store, which is nothing more than a 7-Eleven with a fancier sign and a gas pump around the back. Owen's frozen-burrito ice pack has thawed—Wade proved he is an alien by actually eating it—and he goes in search of new frozen edibles to serve as an ice pack. Abby wants to re-up on iced tea. Wade claims he is starving. He is, in addition to being an alien, a gigantic garbage compactor that needs to be fed a constant diet of beef jerky and potato chips or it starts to wind down.

Wade, Mia, Owen, and Abby disappear into the Old Country Store together, and I quickly yank my phone out of my bag, relieved I have two bars of service. Out here, on these county roads, you never know. The trees absorb the radio signals, or maybe the crickets battle them midair and drown them out.

My sister's cell phone rings two, three, four times. I'm about to hang up when she answers. There are a few fumbling moments before she speaks. The TV's playing in the background. Something with a laugh track.

"It's you," she says, in a tone I can't read. "What's up?"

The Old Country Store is lit up against the long evening shadows. Window signs buzz the way toward cold Coors Light and night crawlers. "Nothing," I say. "Just calling to check in."

"They let you have your phone back, huh?"

Four Corners confiscates cell phones. Cell phones, computers, personal property other than clothing. And she doesn't know I've left yet. This is one piece of good luck: the storm took out home phone service for two days. The usual aftercare follow-up call must not have gone through. "For good behavior," I lie.

"You think they'll spring you one of these days? How long you been in now? More than thirty days."

"Another few weeks, at least. Forty-five-day program." What's one more lie? At a certain point, maybe they'll start to cancel each other out. Crap on top of more crap. Like subtracting from zero. "How's Mom?" I say before she can ask any more questions.

"She's all right. The same. You want to talk to her?"

"No," I say quickly. "That's all right." But already Erin's pulling the phone away from her ear. TV noises again, the roar of all those people laughing. My mom's voice in the background, muffled, so I can't make out what she's saying. "That's all right," I say, a little louder.

"Christ, no need to shout," Erin says. "Mom says hi." Which means she didn't want to talk to me either. I shouldn't be surprised. I'm *not* surprised.

But still.

"I gotta go. I have group," I say. Wade's jogging back to the car, blowing air out of his cheeks hard, like he's crossing a six-mile track and not a stretch of empty asphalt.

"Don't be a stranger," Erin says.

"Sure." I hang up as Wade heaves himself behind the wheel again.

"I got you a present," he says, and tosses a rabbit's foot in my lap, one of the awful ones, dyed neon pink and dangling from the end of a cheap key chain.

"You know I'm a vegetarian, right?" I pick up the key chain with two fingers, get the glove compartment open, and hook it inside.

"It's good luck," Wade says.

"It's nasty." I try not to think of the poor rabbit, twitching out his guts on the ground for someone else's good luck.

I have a sudden memory of seeing Summer that day in the woods, holding something dark and stiff that at first looked like a blanket. . . .

"What? What's wrong?" Wade's watching me.

"Nothing." I punch down the window, inhale the smell of new sap and gasoline. "Everything. This whole mission. It's *all* wrong." *She'll never let us go*, I almost say, but bite back the words at the last second. I'm not even sure where they came from. "Maybe it's better if we don't know what happened. Maybe it's better if we just forget."

"But you weren't forgetting, were you?" Wade says softly. "That's why all the rehab trips. Isn't that what you told me? It's the place you feel safe."

He's right, of course. I wasn't forgetting. Not even close.

"Why do you care so much?" I turn on Wade.

"What do you mean?" Wade looks legitimately confused. "You're my cousin."

"Our *moms* are cousins," I say. "I saw you maybe twice growing up. And one time you were dressed as Batman. So what's your excuse?"

Wade looks away, bouncing one knee, hands on the wheel, quiet for a bit. "You ever read about the Salem witch trials?"

"Sure," I say. "Back in the 1700s, right?"

"No. Earlier. Massachusetts, 1600s. But there were others like them, here and in Europe. Some places they still have witch hunts, you know, when things start to go wrong."

"Wade." I lean back against the headrest and close my eyes, suddenly exhausted. In my head I see Summer still teasing us to follow her, running deeper into the woods, passing in and out of view. *Tag. You're it.* "What are you talking about?"

"Witches, demons, evil spirits. Look, it's human nature to point fingers. To blame. Hundreds of years ago, whenever something went wrong, the crops failed or a baby died or a ship got lost at sea, people said the devil did it. They looked for reasons because just plain bad luck didn't seem like a good reason at all. Plain bad luck meant no one was looking out for you, there was no one to blame and no one to thank, either. No God." He takes a deep breath. "What happened in Twin Lakes five years ago was a witch hunt. Something terrible happened. No one could understand it. No one *wanted* to understand it. So what did they do? They made up a story. They made up a myth."

An invisible touch of wind makes the hair on my arms stand up. I open my eyes. "The Monsters of Brickhouse Lane."

He nods. "They turned you into demons. Three average, every-day girls. A little lonely, a little ignored. The boy next door. An old book. They made a movie out of you. It was a witch hunt."

Three average, everyday girls. A little lonely, a little ignored. I turn toward the window and swallow down something hard and tight. *No one's ever lonely in Lovelorn.* The line comes back to me, from our fan fic. *No one except the Shadow.* The trees are creeping on the edge of the parking lot, like they're planning to make a sneak attack. For a second, I imagine that maybe Lovelorn's still out there. Maybe it just picked up and moved, found some other lonely girls to welcome.

"The funny thing is," Wade says, "they got it all mixed up."

I turn back to him. "What do you mean?"

His face is pale, like a photographic impression of itself. But here in the half dark, his features are softened and I realize he's not bad-looking. His face has character. Strength. He looks like someone you can trust.

"Someone really did kill Summer," he says quietly. "Someone knocked her out and dragged her into the stones and knifed her seven times. There's a monster out there, Brynn. All this time, there's been a monster out there. And no one's tracking it."

"Except for us," I say.

"Yeah." He sighs. He seems almost sad. "Except for us."

MIA

Then

What I remember: a day in January, dazzling with new snow, the sky like a flat mirror, white with clouds. Brynn and I hadn't wanted to go to Lovelorn that day—it was much too cold, and I had a late dance practice. I was training harder than ever, then, in preparation to audition for the School of American Ballet's summer program, one of the most competitive in the country.

Besides, for a week Summer had been ignoring us, the way she sometimes did, punishing us for God knows what reason (because we'd gone to the movies the day after Christmas without her; because we'd failed to be as miserable on break as she was; because we had families to *share* Christmas with; all of the above), but when Summer came running up to us after school, backpack jogging, cheeks blown red from the wind and blond hair sweeping out from beneath her knit cap, we couldn't say no.

I remember how Brynn lit up, as if Summer was the current,

the electricity, and for the past week she'd just been waiting for someone to plug her in. I knew then that Brynn didn't love me, not half as much as she loved Summer. I was just a shadow substitute, someone to keep her company while she waited for her *real* best friend to come back.

The woods were deep and quiet with snow. Our footsteps plunging through the film of surface ice disturbed crows from their perches, sent them screaming toward the sky.

Summer was in a good mood. She hardly seemed to notice the cold and kept urging us to hurry up, go on, just a little farther— past the shed, past another frozen creek, down into a kind of gully where birch trees stood like ghostly signposts, frightened by some past horror into the same stripped whiteness. This was the prima ballerina Summer, the dazzlingly beautiful one, the one we could never refuse. But there was another Summer, another *thing* inside her, something bent-backed and old, something that crouched in the shadows.

It started snowing. Flurries at first. But soon fat flakes were coming down, as if the whole sky was chipping away slowly, and I was freezing, and I'd had enough.

"I want to go back." I never spoke up, not to Summer.

She and Brynn were floundering ahead. This far in the woods, the sun barely penetrated, and the drifts of old snow were higher, swallowing them all the way to the knee. Summer didn't even glance back. "Just a little farther."

"No," I said. Feeling the word through my whole body, like an earthquake. "Now."

Summer turned around. Her whole face was pink. Her eyes were a blue that reminded me of the creek—sparkling and pretty, until you noticed all the darkness tumbling underneath.

"Since when," she said slowly, "do you get to decide?"

I'd made a mistake. That was how things were with Summer: like crossing a frozen river, just praying the ice would hold you. Then *bam*, suddenly you fell through, you were drowning. "I'm cold," I managed to say.

"I'm cold," she parroted, making her voice sound thin and high and afraid. Then, with a wave of her hand: "All right, go ahead. Go back, then. We don't need you. Come on, Brynn." And she started to walk again.

But Brynn stayed where she was, blinking snow out of her lashes. Summer was several feet away by the time she realized that Brynn hadn't moved. She turned around, exasperated.

"I said *come on*, Brynn."

Brynn licked her lips. They were peeling. The winter had come especially hard that year. It had snowed on Thanksgiving and hadn't stopped snowing. "Mia's right." Her voice echoed in the emptiness. *Nothing alive around for miles.* I remember thinking that. We might as well have been standing in a tomb. "It's freezing. I want to go back."

For a second, Summer just stood there, staring, shocked. And cold gathered in the pit of my stomach and turned my throat to ice. *#35. Things you aren't allowed to say (see: curse words; God's name in vain; the word "Macbeth" whispered in a theater, which brings bad luck to the whole production).* A shadow moved behind her eyes again, something so dark it didn't just obscure the light but swallowed it.

But then she blinked and shrugged and only laughed. "Whatever," she said. "We can go back."

The moment had passed. Brynn exhaled. Her breath hung for a second in the air before dispersing.

As Summer stomped past me, she squeezed my cheek with ice-cold fingers. "How could anyone," she said, "say *no* to this face?"

But she gripped me so hard, it left my jaw aching. We were safe, but not for long.

It was Summer's idea to bring back the tournament.

"I mean, you can't just say you're loyal to Lovelorn," she argued.
"Anyone can say anything. There has to be a way to prove it."
—From *Return to Lovelorn* by Summer Marks, Mia Ferguson,
and Brynn McNally

MIA

Now

It's dark by the time we get to Portland. The downtown is a compact network of tight turns, old houses, and light stretching out of bars and doorways, like elongated golden legs. Owen has fallen asleep; I barely touch his knee and he comes awake. Almost immediately he grimaces, as if the pain has come awake too.

He brings a hand to his face and then, thinking better of it, drops it. Instead he sits forward, elbows on knees, spine hunched gargoyle-style.

"This is it," he says. "Follow the coast a few miles north, you can't miss it. There's a sign. At least, there used to be."

For the past hour we've been silent, stilled by the slowly descending dark, like people being drowned by increments. We used to talk about going to Portland to visit Georgia Wells's old house. One of Brynn's favorite theories about the ending was that it *wasn't* an ending—that Georgia had written extra pages but for whatever reason had been forced to conceal them.

Now we're here to fix a different kind of ending. I know I should be grateful that at last we know the truth about Owen and where he was that day, and that even Brynn seems to accept it.

But I can't. I just feel afraid. Suddenly, this seems like a very bad idea.

I press my nose to the window as we pass out of the city, trying to make out silhouettes in the dark, but all I can see is the glitter-eyed image of my own reflection. A few miles out along the coast the headlights pick up a sign pointing the way to the Wells House.

"Turn right here," Owen says, and Wade does, the light skittering off a badly kept dirt path. Trees crowd either side of the lane, ghastly trees with distorted limbs and squat, knobby trunks, trees with leaves like spiked fronds, trees I've never seen in my life.

The lane ends at a gravel parking lot, empty of cars. Wade's headlights seize on a sign that says *Welcome to the Georgia C. Wells House* and another that says *Absolutely No Smoking!* Wade cuts the engine and we all climb out. After being in the car for so long, I'm surprised by how warm it is. The air is sticky and heavy with the sounds of tree frogs and crickets.

A flagstone path cuts from the lot to the main house, only partially visible in the dark, and half-concealed behind more of those Frankenstein trees with scissored leaves and squat trunks. It's a small Cape Cod house, gray or brown—hard to tell in the dark— with a weather vane on the roof, pointed toward the ocean. We're all so still. For once, even Abby has nothing to say.

I feel suddenly overwhelmed. This is where *Lovelorn* was written. In a way, this is where it all started.

Is that why Summer made Owen take our pages here? Because she wanted them to lie where they had been born? Like a person killed at war, shipped overseas to be buried in his hometown?

"I don't get it." Brynn crosses her arms. In the moonlight, she looks very pale. "It's like a museum or something?"

"A nature center," Owen says. "She donated the house after she died."

"I didn't think that anyone remembered her," I say. I'm surprised to feel my eyes burning, and I look down, blinking quickly. The gravel under my feet throws back the moon, sheer white, practically blinding. The book, I knew, was old long before Summer got her hands on it. It was written when Summer's grandmother was a girl and had been passed down to Summer's mom. *It's the only book that dumb-ass* could *read*, Summer used to say, spitting on the ground to make a point about what she thought of the mom who'd shoved Summer into foster care when she got tired of pretending to be a parent.

And sure, we found some other fan sites about Lovelorn—Lovelornians, the communities called themselves—most of them dedicated to that famous ending and why on earth she would have been allowed to publish a book that wasn't finished. Some people said she'd gone crazy. Others said she'd had a heart attack. Still others speculated that it was a code, a secret message about a sequel they were sure she was still planning to write. But most of the sites had gone inactive after her death. I guess no one was going to wait around for a ghost to finish a sentence.

"Not as a writer," Wade pipes up. Brynn looks exasperated. "She was a famous environmentalist. An arborist, too. Trees," he clarifies, when Brynn shoots him a look. "She has over two hundred species of trees on her land. She asked to be buried here, on her own property."

Owen is transformed by shadows into a stranger. The wind lifts the hairs on the back of my neck. "Summer didn't tell me what to do when I got here. Just that she thought *Return to Lovelorn* should go home."

Even though it isn't cold, I wrap my arms around my waist. Feel the ribs and the space between them. Body, tissue, blood, bone. All of it so easily damaged.

"What *did* you do?" Brynn's voice is loud in the silence.

Owen doesn't seem to have heard. He's already starting across the gravel, toward a second path, this one winding not toward the house but into a thick copse of trees, these with leaves that look almost jointed, like fingers.

"Come on," he says. "She's back here."

We go single file down a path that winds deep into the trees. It feels like maneuvering through the dark of a backstage, surrounded on both sides by the rustle of tall curtains. Brynn and Abby hold their cell phones like torches, lighting up the sweep of vaulted branches; the ribbed undersides of leaves crowding overhead; the ghost-white look of the grass and the occasional placard staked in the ground, reminding visitors not to litter or stating the scientific name of the various species of trees. *Magnolia stellata*. *Acer griseum*. Names like magic spells, like songs written in a different language.

And as we walk, a strange feeling comes back to me. A change—in the air, in the texture of the dark—and a rhythm that emerges from the nonsense pattern of cricket song and the faint susurration of the leaves in the wind. *Lovelorn*, it says. *Lovelorn*.

My lungs ache as though with cold. Every breath feels thin and dangerous. And then, just as I'm about to say *go back*, Owen says, "Here it is," and the trees relax their grip on the land, leaving us on a long, open stretch of lawn that runs down toward the beach. I hadn't realized how close we were to the water: a silver-flecked expanse disrupted by a strip of dark and rangy islands.

There are a half-dozen picnic tables set up near the tree line and a stone seawall dividing the grass from the beach. A stone angel, darkened by weather, stands guard over the lawn. Even before we cross the lawn and Wade crouches to light up the inscription at its base, I know that this is it: Georgia C. Wells's final resting place.

Wade reads:

"The kiss of the sun for pardon,
The song of the birds for mirth,
One is nearer God's Heart in a garden
Than anywhere else on earth."

"Dorothy Frances Gurney," he finishes.

For a minute we just stand there, looking out over the water. The ocean is calm tonight and crawls soundlessly over the gravel on the beach. The moon cuts itself into tiny slivers on the waves.

"Not a bad place to be dead," Abby says. "You know, relatively speaking."

Owen hoists himself up onto the stone wall. For a second he stands there, silhouetted, his hair silvered by the moon, and I think that he too could be an angel—wingless, bound to earth. Then, without a word, he drops.

We all crowd forward to the wall, leaning over to see the way the land abruptly drops away, as if someone has just excavated it with a giant scoop.

This side of the seawall is six, maybe eight feet tall. In places it has been shored up with netting. Owen has landed between the rocks that go tumbling down toward the beach, splintering slowly into smaller and smaller bits until they're sucked into the waves to become sand.

"What are you doing?" Brynn whispers, even though there's no one around to hear us. But it feels wrong to shout over somebody's grave. I remember how Summer used to tell us to hold our breath when the bus went past the Episcopal church on Carol and its narrow yard, brown with churned-up mud and patchy grass and the accidental look of its crooked graves. She said that the dead were always angry and the sound of breathing infuriated them with jealousy, that they would come for us in our sleep if we weren't careful. And now she's buried there among the other tumbledown gravestones, in a cheap casket her foster parents picked out, cinched and stitched and stuffed into clothing she would have hated.

Another vengeful spirit. Another soldier for the angry dead.

Owen doesn't answer. He's still picking his way between the rocks, some as large as golf carts, moving parallel to the seawall. For a moment he disappears in the shadows. Then he reappears, pedaling up one side of an enormous rock, keeping low and using his hands for purchase, until he reaches a surface beaten flat by the wind and can stand.

"Owen!" Brynn tries again to get his attention, but he ignores her.

Now he's feeling along the seawall, like a blind person trying to get his bearings in a new room, working his fingers through the bright orange netting that's doing its best to girdle the wall in place. In places whole chunks of the wall are missing, gap-toothed black spaces crusted with lichen and moss. Other portions of the wall have been recently rebuilt. The stone is newer, a flat gray that reflects the moon. I wonder how many years it will take before the wind and the ocean swallow the whole thing.

Owen has gotten an arm through the netting. From here, it looks like the wall has his arm to the elbow and is sucking on him like a bone. Slowly, as he works it, one of the larger stones shimmies outward. A final grunt, and then he crouches, freeing something from beneath the tight foot of the netting. With his shoulder, he shoves the stone back into place.

Then he drops down to the beach and darts toward us through the shadows, tucking the plastic-wrapped object under his arm like a football. He has to find a new way up to us. The rocks, knuckled against one another, form a rudimentary staircase. Even so, he has a hard time getting back over the wall.

"Here." He passes up a small box, straitjacketed in plastic and duct tape, before heaving himself over the wall, teetering for a second on his stomach with his legs still dangling over the beach before Wade gives him a hand. He sits up, breathing hard, his face sheened with sweat, his black eye worse than ever. "Go ahead," he says. "Open it."

I kneel in the grass. The plastic is wet and slicked with dirt. A beetle tracks ponderously across its surface. I flick it into the grass. My fingers are clumsy and I realize they're shaking.

"Let me." Brynn shoves me aside. We've all gone quiet. Even the wind has disappeared. There's no sound at all but the tape protesting as she pries it loose, revealing the lockbox, the secret that Owen spent five years protecting. Even Brynn hesitates before she thumbs the latches loose.

Inside, the pages have been rolled and bent to fit the box. They are, miraculously, dry. For a second, I imagine they still smell faintly of apple shampoo. Brynn loosens the whole bundle of them—dozens and dozens of pages—smoothing them out on a thigh.

Under the moonlight, the title page plays tricks with the eye and seems itself to be glowing.

Return to Lovelorn, it says.

Summer was walking alone in the arena because her friends were lame and ditched her. The tournament was over. When no one was around, the arena seemed much bigger. Like a big, empty eggshell. There were still massive bloodstains everywhere in the dirt.

And then she heard a voice. A whisper, really.

"Don't be afraid."

She spun around, totally freaked, because obviously whenever someone tells you not to be afraid, well . . . it never works. For a second she didn't see anyone. Then she saw a flicker, and she blinked, and she saw a shadow like a single brush of dark paint.

"I'm not going to hurt you," the Shadow said. It was smaller than Summer expected. Friendlier, too.

—From *Return to Lovelorn* by Summer Marks

BRYNN

Now

"Coffee," I say, shoving my mug across the floor toward Mia. "More coffee. I would get up myself," I add when she shoots me a look, "but that seems tiring."

"There is no more coffee," she says, pointedly taking a sip of her decaf green tea. *Decaf.* The single worst word in the English language. "You went through the last of it."

"Coffee!" I say again, pounding a fist on the floor. "Coffee!"

Owen sighs, climbs to his feet, and stretches. Mia pretends not to be looking at the waistband of his boxers, which is briefly visible, and I look at *her* so she knows she's been busted. "I'll make a run to 7-Eleven," he says. "I could use some coffee myself. Or some rocket fuel."

It's nearly three a.m., an hour since we made it back to Vermont and set up camp in Owen's living room. That's what it feels like—like we should be reviewing military strategy or staging a coup on a foreign dictator. Papers litter the floor and surfaces, pinned in place by random objects: a picture frame, an iPhone, a pair of cheap sunglasses. Well-thumbed stacks sport new Post-it notes. Owen's been staring at the same few pages for the last hour, and Abby's been making notes in a spiral notebook. Wade has been counting how often the Shadow shows up. Mia's been trying to organize pages based on who wrote what, a nearly impossible task, since half of it is a jumble of all our ideas combined. I've been working on getting the world's worst headache, reading through pages of material Summer wrote—or at least, we *thought* she wrote—and never showed us, all of it signed with only her name. Cups and mugs everywhere, an empty bottle of soda, overturned, balled-up napkins and the powdered dregs of chips in an empty bowl.

Wade stands up too, releasing a mini avalanche of crumbs. "I'll come along for the ride," he says. "I could use a break."

"I'll come too." Mia gets quickly to her feet, deliberately avoiding my eyes. Stupid. It's obvious she's still half in love with Owen. Every time they're close, she freezes, as if he's an electric fence and she's worried about getting zapped.

That's the thing about hearts. They don't get put back together, not really. They just get patched. But the damage is still there.

"Stay," I tell her, thumping the floor. "Let the boys have a joy-ride."

"I want some air," she says, still not looking at me. Stubborn. *Mulish.* Or like a pony, all skinny arms and legs and jutting lip, determined to have her way.

That's the thing I always admired about Mia. Mute little Mia. I never heard her say a word until Summer moved to town. She talked to Owen, sure, but since Owen was such a nutter butter back then, I stayed well clear of him, too. And Mia was so shy she would burn up if you even looked at her the wrong way.

But deep down, I always suspected she was the strongest of any of us. Like in the way she stood up to Summer. The way she refused to laugh when Summer started in on Mr. Haggard for being gay or a pervert. Summer turned me to string, tangled me up. I forgave her everything, did everything for her, twisted and twisted trying to turn her into something she could never be. But Mia would stand there, arms crossed, staring at the ground and frowning slightly, even when Summer laid into her or played nice, trying to get Mia back on her side. Eventually Mia would give in, sure, but not like I did. I could tell it made Summer nervous, too, that you could never really know what Mia was thinking, that she had her own ideas.

It was the same with Owen. Mia had something that was hers, and she just held on to it, even though everyone said Owen was a freak and would wind up becoming a criminal. But Mia was so loyal, and Summer didn't get it, couldn't get it.

So Summer had to take it away.

"Don't worry," Owen says. "We'll make sure she doesn't run away."

"Whatever you say." I don't like looking at Owen's stupid

swollen eggplant eye because then I start to feel sorry for him. Even if he didn't kill Summer, he nearly killed Mia. That's what heartbreak feels like: a little death. "We'll hold down the fort."

Everything in Owen's house is oversize: the rooms, the furniture, even the sounds, which echo in the emptiness. Footsteps are mini explosions. The front door wheezes open again and closes with a *whoompf.* Funny how much quieter it is once the others are gone, even though we haven't been talking. Too quiet. It makes me miss the weird crammed corners of my house, the way the furniture looks like people leaning in to each other at a party, trying to tell secrets.

I can even hear the noise of Abby's pen across the paper. *Scratch scratch.* I mentally track the distance between us. One, two, three, four, five feet. A lot of sleek polished wood, like a golden tongue. I imagine for no reason crawling over and sitting right down next to her.

"You're staring at me," she says.

"No, I'm not." Quickly, I pretend to be studying the table behind her instead.

She looks down again, continues making chicken-scratch notes. "Go on," she adds after a beat. "I know what you were thinking. So just say it."

Now I do stare at her. "What are you talking about?"

"You want to ask me why I'm so fat, right?" she says—casually, like it doesn't matter. "You want to know why I don't even try and change."

She's dead wrong. I wasn't going to ask. Not even close.

I was going to say I like the way she rolls her lips toward her nose when she's distracted.

I was going to say I like her bangs and how they look like someone cut them by lining them up to a ruler.

But there's no way I'm saying either of those things out loud. I didn't even mean to think them. So I say nothing.

"My body wants to be fat," she continues impatiently, as if we're mid-argument already and she's cutting me off. "Why bother hating something you can't change?"

"That's stupid," I say automatically. "You can change. Everyone can change."

"Really?" She gives me a flat-out *you're an idiot* stare. "Like you can change who you are? Like you can stop being so scared?"

That makes the anger click on, a little flame in my chest. "I'm not *scared*," I say. "I'm not scared of anything."

She gives me the look again. "Uh-huh. That's why the drugs and the drinking. That's why the rehab. Because you're so good at facing up to reality. Because you're *so brave*." She shakes her head. "You're scared. You're hiding."

This brings the flame a little higher, a little hotter, so I can feel it burning behind my cheeks. She's right, of course. Maybe not about the drugs or drinking, but about why I've stayed in rehab, why I've been desperate to go back, why I've been avoiding my mom and sister, too. "Well, you're scared too," I fire back. "You're hiding too."

"Hiding?" She snorts, gesturing to her outfit: the taffeta skirt, the crazy shoes. "I don't think so."

"Sure you are." I'm picking up steam now. "You hide behind your weirdo outfits and your makeup tutorials and your loud-mouth everything. So no one will have to look at you. So no one will have to *see* you."

I don't even plan on saying the words until they're out of my mouth. Abby blinks, as if I've spit on her, and I know then that I'm right. Abruptly, the flame goes out with a little fizzle and I'm left swallowing the taste of ash. I want to apologize, but I'm not sure how.

The worst is that she doesn't get angry. She studies her hands in her lap—plump, heart-shaped, and soft, with nails the color of watermelon. I think of kissing them one by one and then shove the image out of my mind. She's not even my type. She's not even a *lesbian*, as far as I know.

"I don't know how to be anything else," Abby says, looking up at me again. "I've never been anything but too fat. Ever."

It isn't any of my exes that come to mind but Summer, Summer hovering somewhere around the ceiling, maybe exhaled by the pages, her blond hair transformed by the lights into an angel's halo, but her lips curled back into a sneer. *Chubby chaser. Freak parade. Dyke.*

"You're not too fat," I say. My voice sounds overloud. Like I'm shouting.

And maybe I am, partly. Shouting at Summer to shut up. To

leave me alone. To leave *Abby* alone.

She isn't yours to break, Summer.

"You don't have to say that." Abby cracks a smile.

"I'm serious," I say. What's shocking is that in that moment, I realize I am. "You aren't *too* anything. You're just fine. You're . . . good."

Long seconds of silence. Summer, wherever she is, holds her breath. Finally, Abby smiles.

"Wow," she says. "I guess you're not a total bitch after all."

I roll my eyes. Just like that, all the awkwardness between us is gone. "Stop. I'm blushing."

"Hey, check it out." She scoots over to me, closing the *onetwothreefourfive* feet of distance. Leaning forward so our shoulders touch and I get a nice shivery feeling. Like eating ice cream with a really cold spoon. She flips open her notebook and shows me what she's been working on: a two-columned list, with *Return to Lovelorn* characters and places in the left-hand column. The right-hand column is mostly empty, except that she's written *football stadium* next to *arena* and *Mrs. Marston* next to the giantess Marzipan.

"What is it?" I ask.

"I want to keep track of all the real people you guys wrote about," she says. "The real places, too. Maybe we'll see a pattern."

"Some of the characters we didn't make up," I say. "Some of them we took from the first book." I point to Gregor, the thief, and Arandelle, the fairy, and she crosses them off her list.

"What about Brenn, the fierce knight who takes off everyone's heads in the tournament?" She looks up. All smirk and smile. Lashes midnight-black and lips a vivid bloodred. "Sounds like someone I know."

"Brenn was my idea," I admit. "Summer wouldn't let my character enter the tournament, since we were supposed to be in the stands cheering Gregor on. So we wrote in Brenn instead."

"And the kiss she demands from Summer after she decapitates the troll?"

I look away. "That was Summer's idea. Kind of a joke."

"Were you guys . . . ?" Abby licks her lips. Her tongue is pink, small, catlike. "I mean, was she your . . . ?"

"Girlfriend?" I say, and she nods, obviously relieved she doesn't have to say it out loud. "No. She wasn't even gay. She just liked to mess with me."

And then, before I can stop it, I remember the time she came in through the window after she and Jake Ginsky broke up in February, her clothes smelling like cold, her skin like a freezer burn. How she climbed into bed with me but wouldn't stop shivering, even when I squeezed her so tight I wondered how she could keep breathing. How she lay there gasping and snotting all over my pillow while her back drummed a hard rhythm on my chest. How we took off our clothes down to our underwear. For body heat, she said. And how she turned to me just as I was starting to drift off. . . .

Do you love me, Brynn?

So much.

Show me. Show me.

That was more than just messing with me. Or so I thought.

I kissed her.

And for a single, time-stopping moment, her tongue slid into my mouth, warm and needy, like something alive and desperately searching. But almost as quickly, she jerked backward with a sharp quick gasp that to me sounded like glass breaking.

Her smile then was just like a blade. I ran straight up against it; I felt everything it cut apart.

She smiled like someone dying, to prove she didn't care.

She smiled like *I* was the one who'd killed her.

And afterward I couldn't walk down the halls without girls hissing at me and calling me *dyke*, and even Summer began to avoid me, pivoting in a new direction when she saw me coming toward her. I knew she must have told everyone, and all the time the memory of her smile was still embedded in my stomach like shrapnel. I felt its pain in every one of my breaths.

"But you are." Abby's still giving me that look I can't figure out.

"I am what?" We're close, I realize. So close I can see three freckles fading like old stars on the bridge of her nose. So close I can smell her, a fresh smell, like grass after it rains.

The tongue again. Pink. Electric. "Gay."

"Guilty," I say. I pull away, widening the distance between us, realizing I'm thinking about that tongue. Wondering whether she'd feel soft to kiss. "Don't worry. I'm not going to attack you."

"That's all right," she says quickly. "I mean, I'm gay too. Or—bi. At least, I think I am."

"What do you mean, you think?" She looks like she feels soft. Cloudlike.

"I've never kissed a girl before. Don't tell Mia," she adds quickly. Her cheeks flush. "I told her I'd hooked up with a girl at Boston Comic-Con last year because . . . because, well, I've always *wanted* to, and there was this one girl in a Wonder Woman costume, and when I saw her, it was just like . . ."

"Magic," I finish for her, and she nods.

She looks so naked—scared, too, like a little kid. Like she's waiting for me to punish her. And in that moment I wonder if maybe Lovelorn wasn't so special after all. Maybe everyone has a make-believe place. Make-believe worlds where they play make-believe people.

And without thinking any more about it or wondering whether it's right or really fucking stupid, I lean in and kiss her.

I was right. She does feel soft. Her lips taste like Coca-Cola. I can feel the heaviness of her breasts against mine, and I lean into her, suddenly all lit up, zing, Christmas lights and candy stores, suddenly want to roll her on top of me and feel the weight of her legs and stomach and skin, the heat of her. But just as quickly, she pulls away with a little "Oh," bringing a hand to her lips, as though I've bit her.

"Why—why did you do that?" she asks me.

"Because I wanted to," I say.

She stares at me for a half second. Now she's the one who leans in first. Her tongue is quick and light. She's not used to doing it. But the way she smells, the way she brings her palm up to touch my face once, as if to make sure I'm real, unhooks something deep in my chest—something that's been locked up for a long time.

Then Summer hisses back into my head.

What are you doing? she whispers, and then Abby jerks away and I realize Summer has spoken in my voice, through me. I'm the one who said it.

"What are you doing?"

And Abby's looking at me like I just puked in her mouth, and that's what I feel like, like I just threw up something dark and old, and it's too late to take it back, too late to do anything but let it all come up.

"What am I . . . ?" The way she looks at me, Christ, she looks just like an animal. Like that poor crow we came across in Lovelorn, all those years ago, like she's just begging me to save her, to make it stop. "You kissed me. I thought we were . . ."

I stand up, feeling like I'm going to be sick. Seeing that bird again, choking on the feel of feathers, Summer's voice ringing out across an empty space of snow. It's Lovelorn. It doesn't want to let us go.

"I'm sorry," I say. Because that's what you do. You drown it, you strangle it, you make the pain stop any way you can. "It was a mistake. I shouldn't have." She's still looking at me, those big blue eyes, fringed with lashes, that face all pinks and softness, all promise. I don't even know what I'm saying anymore, or why I'm saying it. Words that speak for you. Ghosts that speak through you. "I'm really sorry."

I'm out of the house and into the summer heat before she has the chance to respond, before I have to see her react.

MIA

Then

The second time the police asked for us, they made sure that Brynn and I didn't see each other. This time, they sat me in an airless office between my mom and dad, who were fighting. They'd been fighting for days.

#45. Words too hurtful to repeat.

I told you that girl was bad news.

Maybe if you were ever home . . .

Maybe if you didn't make home so intolerable . . .

Your daughter . . .

Your fault . . . .

And at the same time my voice had evaporated. Every word felt like a physical effort, like having to stick an arm down my throat and draw something up that had already been digested.

Answer him, Mia.

Answer the questions, Mia.

Outside the police station, through the thin walls, I could hear the voices of the people who'd gathered. Dozens of people, crowding the entrance, some of them weeping, although I couldn't understand why. They didn't know Summer, hadn't loved her. So what was their loss? Why the signs and the anger, a hiss that followed me the moment I got out of the car?

Monster. Monster. Monster.

#30. Words that burrow like insects in the ear, that nest and wait to eat you from the inside out.

My dad put an arm around me in the parking lot, just like he kept an arm around me here, in the little room with a fan rustling stacks of paper and a table ringed with old stains. Squeezing my shoulders, hard, as if he could squeeze my voice out of me.

For God's sake, Mia, just answer the goddamn question. Tell him. Tell him that you had nothing to do with it.

Outside: a heavy mist, alive with voices. *Monster. Monster.*

Ask Brynn, was all I could say. My throat was a long deep hole and it was collapsing, and soon everything, all the words I had ever said, would be buried. How could I explain? My voice was drying up. *Ask Brynn.*

The problem with fairy tales isn't that they don't exist. It's that they do exist, but only for some people.

—From *Return to Lovelorn* by Summer Marks

MIA

Now

If there's a good time to say *I love you, I have always loved you, let's start over*, it isn't between aisles two and three of the local 7-Eleven, bleached by the high fluorescents, with legions of squat cans of instant Hormel chili serving as witnesses. Or in front of the night clerk with so much metal in her face she looks as if she got accidentally mauled by barbed wire. Or in the car with Wade Turner, who insists on rolling down all the windows "to keep us awake," despite the fact that we've just bought jumbo coffees and chocolate-chip cookie dough for extra sugar highs, flooding the car with darkness and the roar of wind.

Three minutes. That's all I need. Maybe less. And yet Owen and I haven't had a single minute alone. He hasn't *tried* for a single minute alone with me.

Was he lying when he said he always loved me? Or did he mean past tense, loved but now no longer love?

#12. Words that mean multiple and different things. Always loved, meaning *still do*; always *loved*, meaning *used to*.

Owen's house looks strange with just the living room light burning, like a bit of dark matter anchored by a single star. Wade hops out of the car first, but Owen takes a second to fumble with his seat belt. Wade is halfway to the porch by the time Owen starts after him.

Now, I think. Now that I know he didn't do it. Now that even Brynn knows. This shouldn't matter, but it does: on some level, deep down, I realize I've been waiting for Owen's side of the story, for this final proof.

Now. Quickly. In the time it takes to do four *grands jetés*, to take four giant leaps into the air across the studio floor.

"Owen?" I reach out and put a hand on his elbow.

"Hmm?" He turns around, looking almost surprised, as if he's forgotten I'm there.

The tree frogs and crickets are turning the air to liquid sound, and when I open my mouth, I suddenly feel like I'm drowning.

"Listen." My voice is a whisper. "About what you said the other day—"

Just then the front door flies open and Abby stands there, transformed by the light behind her into a bell-skirted stranger.

"Is Brynn with you?" she calls out.

Owen turns away from me. Poof. The moment is gone. "What do you mean? I thought she was with you."

The grass is cool against my bare ankles as I follow Owen

across the lawn. I deliberately avoid the flagstones, stepping hard on the soft earth, a miniature revenge. Then, feeling stupid and childish, I step onto the path again. Abby edges backward to let us in. I can tell something has upset her. She has a good poker face, but not good enough.

"She ran out," Abby says. "I thought she was just taking a walk. . . ."

"She ran out?" I repeat. Abby nods mutely, avoiding my eyes. Now we're all packed into the front hall: me, Wade, Abby, and Owen. On one side, the living room, papers blown around like brittle leaves. Our past, scattered and dissected. On the other side, rooms dark and mostly empty of furniture, the whistle of wind through the destroyed remnants of Owen's sunroom. That's our past too: rooms full of darkness, things we didn't understand, wind blowing through shattered spaces. "I don't get it."

"There's nothing to *get*," Abby says, crossing her arms. Then I know she's hiding something. "She just went out for a bit. I thought she'd be back by now. That's all."

"I'll go look for her," I say quickly.

"Want company?" Wade asks, and I shake my head.

Owen doesn't even offer.

If Brynn had started down Waldmann Lane, we would have seen her on our way back from town. It's a one-lane road with nowhere to hide, unless she'd hurtled last-minute into the nest of trees. So I loop around the house to the backyard, thinking she might have needed a break. But she isn't there, either. A heavy blue tarp, still scattered with old leaves, covers the long-empty pool.

Where could she have gone?

I circle around to the front of the house again, deciding that we must have missed her. The gate whines open and my shoes crunch on a scattering of pebbles. The moon is slivered short of full. Crazy to be wandering around after midnight, just because, making everybody worry.

But maybe she needed a break from Lovelorn. From Summer. From the sizzle and hiss of old words. When Owen pulled up that box from where it had been entombed, when I saw it lashed all over with tape, I had the strangest feeling that it hadn't been hidden to keep it safe—but to keep us safe from it.

Witches, they called us. *Demons*. On a night like tonight all silvery and still, with nothing but a cratered moon and the trees knotted together as though for warmth and comfort, it's easy to believe that monsters exist. That there are witches hunched over cauldrons and people possessed by vengeful spirits and vampires crying out for blood.

Just outside Owen's gates is a wooded area where the underbrush has been trampled and the low-hanging branches snapped or twisted back, forming a kind of hollow. Only then do I remember that Brynn's family moved after the murder. Her house is on Perkins, which runs parallel to Waldmann. Could she have gone home?

I push into the trees, ducking to avoid getting smacked in the face by the branches of an old fir tree. The chitter of insects in the trees grows louder here, as if they're protesting my interference. Now I see that there's a pretty clear path cutting down the hill through the underbrush. I can see the glimmer of lights on what must be Brynn's street, from here no more than a few distant halos, hovering beyond the trees. She *must* have gone this way.

Burn them. There was a whole tumblr dedicated to the murder and to the idea that Brynn, Summer, and I had been witches, and Owen the warlock who helped control us all. I remember coming across it during that awful month when people drove by my house just to take pictures, when Mom and I woke every day and found our stoop covered by the sheen of egg yolk or our trees toilet-papered or our mailbox pitched over in the grass. When Mom started ordering our groceries online and stopped going to the gym and started stacking up cardboard boxes in the kitchen "just in case."

Burn them, someone had posted. *That's what they used to do with witches. Build a bonfire and throw them in to roast.*

Then we heard that Brynn's next-door neighbor had tossed a Molotov cocktail into her kitchen. The fire went through the house like it was paper. Brynn barely made it out. Even though she hadn't spoken to me since the day Summer died, I tried calling her a dozen times, but her phone was always off. And then it was disconnected.

I fish my phone from my bag for light before remembering it's been dead for hours, and instead go carefully, arms outstretched, sliding a little on the muddy path and swatting at the spiderwebs that reach out to ensnare me. There's something claustrophobic about these woods and the trees all hemmed close together in this narrow spit of undeveloped land, and I'm relieved when I break free of the last entanglement of growth and end up on a road lined up and down with cheap cottage housing stacked side by side.

Immediately, I spot her: fifty feet from me, standing absolutely still in front of a house that looks like all the others next to it. There's something unearthly about her stillness. As if she *can't* move. Her face is touched with a shifting pattern of blue light.

I start toward her and am about to call out, when the window becomes visible and in it I see Brynn's mother stand up to turn off the television. She's wearing a bathrobe. I see her face only briefly before the blue light dies in the window and on Brynn's face. But Brynn's mother is supposed to be in the hospital.

"Brynn?"

She turns quickly. For a second I see nothing on her face but pain. Then, almost immediately, she looks furious.

"What the hell are you doing?" she says.

"I don't understand," I say. "You told me your mom was in the hospital."

"Keep your voice down, okay?" Brynn glares at me as if I'm the one who's done something wrong.

"You *lied*," I say. A word that doesn't sound half as bad as it is. To lie, to deceive, to cheat, to trick. To recline on a soft bed. #12 again. "All this time, your mom was fine. You could have gone home. You didn't have to sleep in the shed—"

"God. Just keep your voice down, all right?"

"You didn't have to stay with me—"

The rest of the sentence turns hard and catches in my throat. Suddenly I can't breathe.

The answer is so obvious. Why did she agree to help, after she told me at first I was crazy? Why did she go to the shed and then make up a huge lie about her mom? Could she have known I'd invite her back to my house? She's been looking for something—evidence, something she wrote for Summer or Summer wrote for her. She hasn't been helping me find the truth.

She's been trying to cover it up.

Run, Mia, she'd said. *Run*. And I did. I didn't stop, not even when I heard screaming.

Brynn—wild, ferocious Brynn, Brynn and her big mouth, all curled-up anger and leaps and explosion, Brynn with a fist hard like a boy's—killed Summer. And I've been too stupid, too stubborn, to believe it.

"You." Now, when I've never been so scared in my life, my voice is strong. Steady. Pouring over the words. "You killed her. It was you all along."

"Oh my God, are you for real?" Brynn rolls her eyes. "Look, I can explain, okay? Just not here." She grabs my wrist and I yank away. She stares at me. "Wait—you're not serious, are you?"

Before I can answer, a lamp clicks on in the living room, lighting up Brynn's mom, face pressed to the window, eyes creviced at the corners, squinting to see outside.

"Shit." This time Brynn gets a hand around my arm and pulls me into a crouch, so we're concealed behind a straggly line of bushes. An old plastic Easter egg is half-embedded in the dirt. "Shit," she says again.

"What are you——?"

"*Shhh*. Come on."

"I'm not going anywhere until you——"

But she's already hauling me back to my feet, and like it or not, I have no choice but to follow, have never had a choice. We shoot across the street, bent practically double, and push into the trees just as the porch light comes on and Brynn's mom steps out onto the stoop, hugging her bathrobe closed, peering out over the now empty street. Brynn takes a step backward even though we're sheltered by the trees and the shadows, wincing as a branch snaps beneath her weight. But soon her mom returns inside and the porch and living room lights go off in succession.

Brynn exhales. "That was close."

At last, she releases me. I whip around to face her, rubbing my wrist even though it doesn't really hurt. Still, she's left half-moon marks in my skin. "Explain," I say. *"Now."*

"Come on, Mia." She doesn't sound guilty. Not even a little bit. Just angry and tired. "Cut the shit. You can't *really* think I killed Summer."

The words sound ridiculous when she says them. That brief

sense of certainty—the truth like an electric pulse reaching out to zap me—is gone. Brynn's a lot of things, at least half of them bad, but she's not a killer. I remember how upset she was years ago when we stumbled on those poor crows, two of them skewered as if for a barbecue roast, the last one bleeding out slowly in the snow. While my lunch came up in my throat she kneeled down in her jeans and scooped the poor thing into her arms, went running with it toward the road as if there was anything she could do, any help she could give it there. It died in her arms and she wouldn't believe it was beyond rescue. She insisted on finding a shoebox so we could bury it.

Still, she lied.

"I don't know *what* I think," I say.

She stares at me for another long moment. Then she turns around and starts beating her way up the hill, back toward Owen's house, thwacking through the trees and sending down a patter of moisture from their leaves.

I hurry to keep up. "I want the truth, Brynn."

"You wouldn't understand." She deliberately lets a branch rebound so I have to duck to avoid getting swatted in the face.

"Try me." The slope is steeper than it seemed on the way down. Brynn must have walked this path plenty of times. She's moving quickly, confidently through the dark, leaping over stones that knock at my shins, pinballing from tree to tree for momentum. I hit a slick of rotting leaves and my ankle turns, and I grab hold of the back of Brynn's shirt at the last second to keep from going down. She turns around with a little cry of surprise. "What are you hiding?"

She looks away. Sharp nose, sharp cheeks, sharp chin. Brynn is the most knifelike person I've ever known. "I'm not an addict," she says finally, after such a long pause I was sure she wouldn't answer.

"What?" This, of all things, was not what I expected her to say.

She turns back to me, almost impatient. "I'm not addicted to anything. Not pills. Not alcohol. I don't even like the *taste* of alcohol. The last time I had a beer it made me sick. I don't know how people drink that stuff."

I stare at her. "I don't understand," I say finally, and the crickets say it with me, sending up a fierce swell of protest.

She makes a little noise of impatience. "When I was in eighth grade, I got drunk with some kids from Middlebury and took some of my mom's sleeping pills when I got home. I wasn't trying to kill myself," she says quickly, before I can ask. "I was just tired. School was hell. I begged my mom to move away, but she wouldn't. We couldn't. She didn't have a car that winter, and she needed to be able to get to work on foot. I started taking the bus into Middlebury after school just to have a break. I met some older kids, potheads, and they were the ones who got me drunk. Lost my virginity that way too." She smiles, but it's the worst smile I've ever seen: hollow, as if it's been excavated from her face.

"Brynn." I want to say more—I want to hug her—but I feel paralyzed.

"It's okay." She takes a step backward, as if anticipating I might try to hug her. "You wanted the truth, so I'm telling you the truth. I took pills and puked and my sister found out and freaked and got me into rehab. I was so mad at first. But then . . . I started liking it."

I stay quiet now, hardly breathing.

"I was in for forty-five days. I finished eighth grade in rehab. Took a few tests, sent in my answers, got a see you later, okay to pass Go. The program recommended me for a special high school, an alternative program, you know. Freaks and geeks and burnouts and losers. But that was good. It meant I didn't have to go to TLC. A special car came to pick me up at my house and everything." She shrugs. "But I still had to be *me*. I still had to go home. My mom and sister can hardly look at me, you know," she says in a rush. "They can hardly stand to be in the same *room* as me. It's like everything that's happened, every single thing that's gone wrong, is my fault. They like it when I'm away. I think sometimes they wish I'd just go away permanently. Don't say it isn't true," she adds flatly, before I can. "I'm giving you facts. My mom and I used to have this weekend tradition, whenever she wasn't working. We'd sit on the couch and watch all the soaps she'd missed during the week. We'd try to guess what would happen before it did. But suddenly she got too busy. She had stuff to do around the house. She was too fat and shouldn't be sitting around. Excuses. I'd hear the soaps going at night, you know, when she thought I was asleep." She looks away, biting her lip.

As if one pain can be traded for another. "I had a girlfriend freshman year at Walkabout—that was the name of the alternative school—and her mom was a doctor. I stole some samples from the medicine cabinet when I was over one time and flashed them around at school. Walkabout had a zero-tolerance policy. Back to rehab I went. And then, sophomore year, when I was out again, I started hanging around with Wade. He'd been bugging me since the murders, you know. Thought he could help. Thought we could clear my name together. I guess he's always had a bit of a superhero complex."

"Batman," I say.

"Batman," she says, nodding. "Wade has a part-time job working in a clinic for fuckups. Real fuckups. Not pretenders like me. Sixteen-year-old heroin addicts, that kind of thing. He helps me . . . fake it. So I can stay in the system. Bounce around." Brynn stares at me, tense, chin up, as if daring me to ask how.

But I'm not sure I want to know. So I just say, "Why?"

She hugs herself, bringing her shoulders to her ears. "He knows I like it," she says shortly. "He knows I feel safe there. Plus—"

"What?"

"I think he just needed a friend," she says. "We're family, sure, kind of, but . . . friends are different, aren't they?"

Now the crickets and the tree frogs and all the tiny stirrings and windings of the invisible insects in the dark have gone still. Hushed and silent.

"That's why he's here," I say. I'm fumbling, struggling to piece together the facts, but as soon as I see Brynn's face, I know I'm right. "That's why he's helping. You made a deal with him."

She shakes her head. "It started off that way. But now . . ." She trails off. "I don't know. I don't know what to think anymore."

Under the vaulted canopy of trees, I have the feeling of being in a church. And I have the craziest idea that Summer was the sacrifice, that she had to die so that the four of us, these broken people, could find each other. A Bible quote comes back to me, from years and years ago, before my dad left, when we still went to church. *I desire mercy, not sacrifice.*

"Why did you lie about your mom?" I ask Brynn, and the trees let out a shushing sound.

Brynn looks down at the ground. "I didn't tell my mom I was coming home. I wasn't planning to come home, but . . . well, everything got messed up. But that first day, after you picked me up, I went by the house—" She abruptly stops, sucking in a breath, as if she's been hit by an invisible force.

"What?" I touch her once on the elbow. Feel the ridge of her bone beneath my fingers. *Mercy.* "What is it?"

When she speaks again, her voice is very quiet. "It's stupid," she says. "My mom and sister were sitting on the couch. Feet up on the coffee table, matching slippers, bowl of popcorn. They were watching *Days* together. That was always my mom's favorite soap. 'The most bang for your buck and tears for your time,' she always said. They looked so happy." Her voice breaks and I realize she's trying not to cry.

I want to hug her and tell her it's okay, she's going to be okay, we all are, but I don't know that. How can I know? How can I promise? Terrible things happen every day.

Then she clears her throat and I know she's gotten control of herself again. "I couldn't interrupt. I started walking. I didn't know where I was going until I was in backcountry. Didn't know what I would do. But then I remembered the shed and knew at least I'd have a place to crash until I figured it out. It was weird being there," she says, in a different tone. "Spooky. Like . . . someone was watching. Like *she* was watching. In the middle of the night I woke up and . . . I swear I saw her face in the window. Just for a second. Those big eyes, her hair. Guilt, probably. Or I was dreaming."

"I'm sorry, Brynn" is all I say. *Sorry* is one of the worst words of all: it hardly ever means what you want it to.

"That's all right," she says. Another thing people say and hardly ever mean.

"No, it's not." Suddenly I'm overwhelmed by the stupidity, the *futility* of it all. Brynn and I were Summer's best friends. We fell in love with a story. We fell in love with an idea. And for that we've been punished again and again. Where's our forgiveness? Where's mercy for us? "You have to go home."

"I don't *have* to do anything," she says. Sharp again.

"You can't be homeless forever."

"Thanks for the advice." She stares at me for a long second, her face striped in shadow, her eyes unreadable. Then she looks away, shaking her head. "Forget it," she says. "I knew I shouldn't have told you. I knew you wouldn't get it."

"That's not fair," I say. "I do get it." And then, as she starts to turn away, anger makes a leap in my chest. "You're not the only one who's been hurt."

She turns back around to face me. "Poor baby," she says. "You want to start a club or something? Want to be treasurer and get a trophy?"

"Stop it. You know that's not what I meant."

Moonlight catches Brynn's teeth and makes them flash, like a predator's. "I'm sick of your poor-me act, okay? I'm not buying it."

"I don't know what you're talking about."

"Sure you do." Brynn has lost it plenty of times in front of me, but never like this. Never *at* me. The woods seem to be shrieking along with her. "You sold me out."

"What?" I nearly choke on the word.

"To the cops. You sold me out." In the dark, she looks like a stranger, or like a wild spirit, something not of this world. Flashing teeth and eyes striped with dark and wild hair. "'Ask Brynn,'" she mimics. "'Brynn will tell you. I don't know anything. I wasn't even there.'" She's shaking, and in an instant I know that this, her anger, what she thinks I did, is the reason she stopped picking up my calls, never texted back, dropped stonelike straight out of my life. "They wouldn't believe me about anything. You had them *convinced* it was my fault."

I remember sitting in the musty room, armpits tickly with sweat, my mouth desert-dry despite the Coke they'd given me. My dad glaring at me, losing control, not quite shouting but almost.

"I never meant to get you in trouble." *Tell them, Mia. Just tell them the truth.* And me: trying to haul the words up from some sandpit where they'd gotten stuck, through layers of stone and sediment, shaking with the effort. *Ask Brynn*, I said. *Ask Brynn.*

"Oh yeah? What did you mean, then?"

"I didn't want to say the wrong thing." She turns away from me again and now it's my turn to grab her wrist, to force her to stay and listen. "You made me *lie* for you, Brynn. You made me swear I wouldn't tell what happened—"

"I didn't do it for me." We're so close I can *feel* the words as she shouts them. Stab, stab, stab. Like she's hitting me instead. "I did it for her, don't you get it? So no one would know. I was *protecting* her, I—"

"Brynn? Mia?" Owen's voice comes to us from the street. I drop Brynn's arm and she steps backward quickly. My heart is racing, as if I've been running.

"Mia?" Owen's voice is closer now.

"Here." Brynn brings a hand up to her eyes as she turns away, and I feel a hard jab of guilt. Was she crying? But when we make it onto the street and her face is revealed in the moonlight, she looks calm, almost blank. As if someone has taken an eraser and wiped away not just her anger but every feeling.

Owen looks like a matchstick on fire. His hair shoots toward the sky. He's practically crackling with excitement. "There you are," he says. "Come on."

"What?" I say. "What is it?"

He's already started back toward the house. He barely turns around to answer. "It's Abby," he says. "She found something."

BRYNN

Then

The snow was coming hard on a slant, and somehow we got turned around. We'd been in the woods a hundred times, walking through the same trees, making our landmarks of stumps and depressions, clumps of briar and places where ancient walls had tumbled into piles, but with the snow so fast and pure white and all the ground caked over, we'd gotten lost.

You heard stories growing up in Vermont. Stories of people run aground in their cars in wintertime: people who wandered out of their cars and got lost in the whiteness. Stories of people frozen to death because of being in woods just like these, unprepared, cocky, no way back, the sweat built up on their bodies turning them into icicles. Stupid. We couldn't be a quarter mile from Brickhouse Lane, but the more we walked, the less we recognized. Blank spaces, all whited out by snow. Like they were getting erased with it. Like we were getting erased, too.

"You're doing it deliberately," I said to Summer. I was only a few notches on the belt down from panic. "Take us back." She'd been leading us in circles—I was sure of it. To punish us for wanting to go home.

"I'm not. I swear I'm not." The tip of Summer's nose was patchy, white and red. The first sign of frostbite. And I knew from the way she said it that she was telling the truth—but that just made me more scared. Mia was crying but without making any noise. Tears and snot ran down to her mouth. And not a sound in the world but the soundlessness of snow, swallowing up our footsteps, swallowing all of us.

"We're lost." When Mia finally gave voice to it, I turned around quickly, as if she'd cursed.

"We aren't lost," I said. Snow dribbled from my hair. Ice made crusts of my eyelashes. "We just have to keep going."

There was nothing to do but go on, into the white, hoping we'd see something we recognized. Snow stung like cigarette burns on our cheeks. The snow stretched time into stillness. Mia cried her throat raw, but Summer was surprisingly quiet, her face turned up to the sky, like she expected direction to come from there.

And then the trees fell back like ranks of soldiers on retreat, and we saw we'd somehow looped around to the south side of the long field, missing the shed by at least a few hundred yards. We were less than five minutes from Summer's house. Mia shouted with relief, and I remember I almost cried, too. But even my eyeballs were cold. The tears froze and wouldn't fall. Only Summer was still quiet, still staring at the sky flaking into snow and the landscape all blurry with white, like there were secrets there we could never guess.

And when halfway across the field we found the crows—two of them frozen, long dead, mounted together on the same stick, like the bloody flag of an ancient warrior warning others not to trespass, and one of them fluttering out its last breaths, drowning in snow, a pellet ribbed deep in its flesh—she stood there shaking her head, almost smiling.

"It's Lovelorn," she said, even as I took up that poor bird, that poor dumb innocent crow, and Mia turned away to retch between her fingers. "Don't you see? Lovelorn doesn't want to let us go."

Summer, Brynn, and Mia made a pact that they would never tell anyone else about Lovelorn. It would be their secret. Secrets are like glue. They bind.

—From *Return to Lovelorn* by Summer Marks, Brynn McNally, and Mia Ferguson

BRYNN

Now

After the smash-heat of outside, Owen's house feels overbright and empty, like a museum. Abby has moved to an ottoman. Mia and Owen sit on opposite ends of the leather couch, leaving a whole cushion between them. She has her hands pressed to her thighs, like she's trying to convince them not to run her straight out of there. I've chosen a chair across the room, stiff-backed and uncomfortable, and possibly only meant for show.

Only Wade looks comfortable. His long legs are stretched out in front of him and he's taken off his shoes, revealing mismatched socks, one of them red with Christmas penguins. Every so often he slurps loudly from his coffee.

"When we first started talking about who killed Summer, Brynn suggested we call him the Shadow." Abby's voice rebounds off every empty wall. "From the beginning, it seemed like the right symbol of her killer. Why?" She starts ticking items off on her fingers. "One. Summer was obsessed with the Shadow. Two.

She began to think she was actually in danger from him. That was the point of that day in the woods, right? She wanted to make a sacrifice to him?" She glances at Mia for confirmation.

"Right," I say instead, trying to force her to look at me. She does, but only for a second. Her face hitches—a look of embarrassment—like she's accidentally looked at someone peeing.

She turns to Wade. "In the original *Lovelorn*, the Shadow is mentioned *how* many times?"

"Fifty-two," Wade says. Then, as if it isn't obvious: "I've counted."

"In *Return to Lovelorn*, the Shadow gets over *one hundred* mentions in a single chapter." She pauses to let that sink in. "So let's assume we were right all along. The Shadow is the murderer. The Shadow wrote himself into the story, just like you guys wrote yourselves into it." She looks around, as if expecting us to contradict her. "There should be clues. Details about who he was in real life. The way the Giantess Marzipan—your math teacher—has a wart above her right eyebrow. That was real, right?"

"It used to turn red when she was mad." I'm thinking that'll at least get a laugh, but instead she frowns and looks down at her notepad.

"There's the dwarf Hinckel, who smells like sour cheese. There's a pixie named Laureli with a voice so shrill she can't be near glassware."

Mia hugs her knees to her chest. "I don't remember writing any of that."

"Summer, or whoever was helping her write, must have added

it in without telling us," I say quietly. Then something occurs to me. "Laura Donovan. Had to be. Remember her laugh?"

"Like a fire alarm." Mia cracks a small smile.

"There's a psychotic dwarf named Joshua," Abby goes on, "who gets flattened by a wagon wheel and dies horribly—"

Finally, something I remember. "That was my character," I say. "Josh Duhelm. Four foot seven of straight crazy. He used to put chewed-up gum on my seat."

"But the Shadow is never described," Mia puts in. "We took it from the first book. It's just . . . a shadow."

"Wrong." This is it: Abby's big reveal. This is what she's been waiting to tell us. For a second I hold my breath, and Mia holds her breath, and even the lampshades look tense. "In *Return to Lovelorn*, Summer visits the Shadow seven times, mostly on her own. Wade helped me look for statements that don't show up anywhere in the first book. Backstory. Made-up information about where the Shadow came from and where it lives now and how it spends its days. But what if it wasn't made up?" She pauses again and then nudges Wade with a toe. "Maestro?"

He flips open a laptop and reads. "Okay, here's the list we made."

1. *"Will you sing again?" the Shadow asked. "I've always loved music. I used to teach music, before."*

2. *"Who made you this way?" Summer asked.*
   "Everyone and no one," the Shadow said. "In my city, there's a

giant door in the shape of an arch, and I went through one side
a regular person and came out this way."

3. *"Sometimes I spend whole days going in circles," the Shadow*
   said. "Street to street. Following the same old route. Just hop-
   ing something new happens. But nothing ever does. That's the
   trouble with being a shadow. No one notices. No one cares."

4. *"I once lived in the desert," the Shadow told her. "There was a*
   kind of cactus there that can survive without any water. If only
   people could survive like that—totally alone. But they can't.
   Not even shadows can."

5. *Summer knew the Shadow's biggest secret: the Shadow was*
   lonely, horribly lonely, and just liked having someone to talk to
   and be with. But she also knew she couldn't tell anyone, because
   no one would understand. The Shadow was completely different
   than people thought—no one would ever know the truth.

Wade finishes reading, and there's a beat of silence. My brain
keeps stalling and turning over, like an engine in the cold. Abby
sits there watching us expectantly. Correction: watching Owen
and Mia expectantly. I'm a no-fly zone.

Stupid. Why did I kiss her? And why did I have to screw it up
afterward?

"Okay, so what are we saying?" Sometimes I think the whole

point of talking out loud is to shut the inside voices down. "The Shadow—the killer—likes music and maybe even taught it. That's point number one. He comes from a city. Point number two."

"He walks around town when he's bored," Owen jumps in. "Point number three."

I frown. "That could be *anyone*."

"He used to live in a desert," Wade adds. "Don't forget that."

"It's still not a lot to go on," I say.

"It's more than we knew before," Abby says.

"Sure, but it doesn't actually get us anywhere." Owen slumps backward on the couch. His hair loses steam too, and falls over one eye.

"Read number two again," Mia puts in, before we can keep fighting. The way she's sitting, ramrod straight, like she's a split second away from leaping into a ballet routine, makes me think she's heard something specific. Even her voice sounds like it wants to leap—like she's keeping down some excitement. "About the city."

Wade repeats the bit about the city and the arch, and this time I hear it too.

"A city with an arch," I say slowly. "St. Louis?"

"St. Louis," Mia repeats. And then, unexpectedly, she begins to sing: "*Meet me in St. Louis, meet me at the fair...*"

All of a sudden I feel like I've been punted in the stomach. "Holy shit." My throat burns with the taste of acid. Too much coffee. Too much. "Mr. Haggard."

"Mr. *Who*?" Abby and Wade say together.

Mia turns to them. "Haggard." Now the excitement has broken through. She practically squeaks the words instead of saying them. "Our bus driver. He used to sing to us every day. Show tunes, you know. *Les Misérables* and stuff. But one of his favorites was *Meet Me in St. Louis*."

"He *sang*," I say. "Maybe he plays piano, too."

"Did he seem lonely?" Wade asks.

"Of course he's lonely," I say. "He's a bus driver."

"That's mean," Owen says, but I ignore him.

Mr. Haggard. I close my eyes, remembering the sheen of his scalp through thinning hair, the way he used to grin when he saw us. "All aboard," he would say, and give a toot of an invisible horn. Like we were still first graders. His sad pit-stained shirts and the way he gargled out the same songs as he rumbled off to school. . . . I open my eyes again. "He was at Summer's memorial," I say, remembering now how I spotted him in the crowd, standing there in a badly fitting suit. Did he look guilty? "He came to watch."

"Half the town came," Owen points out.

"Read number three again," Mia says to Wade, and he does, obediently. "Street to street? That could be a bus route."

"That's a stretch," Owen says, and Mia turns to look at him—mouth screwed up, like she's preparing to spit.

"Why are you protecting him?" Mia says.

"I'm not protecting him," Owen says. "We're talking about *murder*. We have to be sure."

I try to imagine Mr. Haggard stomping through the woods, taking a rock to the back of Summer's head, dragging her across the long field, and can't. And Summer was horrible to Mr. Haggard. Was that all for show? Did she secretly meet with him to work on *Return to Lovelorn*? I can't picture it. Why would she open up to him, of all people?

Still: it's the only lead we've got.

Abby's consulting the list again. "What about the desert? Did he ever live in the desert?"

"There's only one way to find out," I say, and everyone turns to me now, even Abby, light winking from her glasses. I take a deep breath. "We ask."

Summer was nervous as she waited in the arena for the Shadow to appear again. Why had she agreed to come? Why hadn't she at least told Brynn and Mia? But she knew why: because they would have told her it was a bad idea.

Maybe, she thought, the Shadow wouldn't show. But even as she thought it, she heard a light step behind her and turned around quickly.

"You're scared," the Shadow said. "Don't be scared."

"I've heard stories about you," Summer said, tossing her hair so as to look unconcerned. But the Shadow was right. She was scared. "You steal children. You take them away underground to eat them."

"That's not true," the Shadow said. "I only take them to keep them safe. So they won't grow old and ugly. So they can stay children forever."

—From *Return to Lovelorn* by Summer Marks

MIA

Now

"Morning, sunshine."

I wake from a dream that breaks up immediately and leaves me with only the sense of someone shouting. Brynn is standing in front of me, hazy in the sun beaming in through the windows.

I sit up, jittery from the dream I can't remember. "What time is it?"

"Ten," Owen answers from the hall. A second later he appears, showered and clean-looking, his hair curled wetly, in a faded red T-shirt that says *London*. The black eye seems to have grown overnight, bleeding down into his cheek. I don't know why people call it a black eye. This one is plum-colored. "Sorry. Brynn thought you'd want coffee."

When I bring a hand to my cheek, I can feel the spiderweb impressions of faint lines from the couch.

"Where's Abby?" I ask. I don't remember falling asleep last

night—only that Wade and Brynn were arguing about whether or not Haggard could have possibly known about Lovelorn, whether he could really have been the one helping Summer do the writing, and I decided to close my eyes just for a few minutes, and then I wasn't on a couch at all, but on a boat. At some point, I thought Owen was beside me—I thought he touched my hair and whispered—but that must have been part of the dream.

"Wade must have dropped her at home on his way to work," Brynn says. "They were gone when I got up. She probably didn't want to wake you up," Brynn adds quickly, because she must see that I'm hurt. Brynn looks good—alert, dark hair bundled up in a messy ponytail, fashionably rumpled, as if sleeping on the floor in other people's houses with a sweatshirt for a pillow is part of her strategy for success. She passes me a Styrofoam cup of coffee, too sugared, pale with cream. "Gotta caffeinate," she says. "Today we nail Haggard."

"Today?" I nearly spit out my coffee. "You want to talk to him *today*?"

"What's the point in waiting?" she says.

I look to Owen—old habit, from back when I could count on him to agree with me, when I could read what he was thinking by the way he squinted his eyes, by the smallest twitch in his lips; when we didn't *have* to speak, because we just understood—but he sighs, dragging a hand through his hair. "She's right," he says, and only in his voice do I hear how tired he is. "I just want this to be over. Finally."

And then what? I nearly say. Then Owen goes off to my dream school, and the Waldmann house is sold, and I lose him forever—beautiful, bright, matchstick Owen, full of crackle and life. Then Brynn does whatever Brynn is going to do, and Abby and I are still stuck here, in Twin Lakes, and no one will hail us or call us heroes. And that's it, the end of the story: curtains down, dancers gone home, a theater sticky with spilled soda and old trash.

Then I will still be as lonely as ever. Lonelier, maybe. Because this time, there will be no chance that someday Owen will come home and we'll get to start over.

In the bathroom mirror I barely recognize myself. I look spidery and thin and old. My eyes are sinking into two hollows. I wonder what Summer would look like now, had she lived—all that blond hair and skin like a new peach. I find a single half-used tube of toothpaste in an otherwise empty drawer and use my finger to clean my teeth, then finger-comb my hair back into a bun.

What will we say to Mr. Haggard?

Do you remember a girl named Summer Marks? Stupid. Of course he does. Everyone does. And he was at her memorial.

Mr. Haggard, we know what you did to Summer.

Mr. Haggard, tell us what you know about Lovelorn.

I whisper the words very quietly in the bathroom. There, they sound silly and harmless. Musical, even. #44. *Words mean different things to different people, at different times, in different places.*

Through the window I see a dark car—the limousine type that service airports—nose through the gates and disappear from view. A second later Brynn pounds on the bathroom door.

"Mia," she whispers.

"What?" I say, opening the door. She looks as panicked as I've ever seen her. "What is it?"

But then, from the front hall, a man calls, "Owen? You home?" The voice is instantly familiar, even after all these years.

Mr. Waldmann is back.

Brynn edges behind me into the front hall, as if she expects Owen's dad to start shooting at her and wants to use me for cover. Mr. Waldmann is almost unrecognizable. I remember him mostly as a disembodied voice—a voice slurring from behind a locked door to be quiet, go outside. He wasn't fat back then, exactly, but he was soft. Blurry. Chin folding into neck into chest into rolls of stomach. Even his eyes were blurry and seemed never to be able to focus on one thing without sliding over to something else.

But Mr. Waldmann now is all sharp corners and edges: close-cropped hair, thin, a jaw like Owen's, perfectly defined. Even in his jeans, wearing a blazer over a T-shirt, he looks like the kind of person who's used to being listened to. Something old and damaged has, in the past five years, seemingly been fixed.

"Dad." Owen is frozen in the living room doorway, trying to block the mess from view.

"Jesus." Mr. Waldmann takes in Owen's black eye. "What happened?"

"It's nothing," Owen says quickly. "Just a stupid fight."

"You look terrible," Mr. Waldmann says, and then looks at

Brynn and me, squinting a confused smile in our direction. "Hello."

Brynn looks like someone trying to swallow a live eel. I try to say hello, but all that comes out is the final syllable. "Oh."

"You weren't supposed to be home until Friday," Owen says.

"Business closed early. I wanted to surprise you. Hopped a red-eye from LA." Mr. Waldmann looks increasingly confused as he turns back to us. "And you are . . . ?"

Owen shoves his hands in his pockets and kicks at nothing, making a scuffing noise on the floor. "Dad, Mia and Brynn. You remember Mia." He won't look at me, and it occurs to me that he's embarrassed. Blood beats a hard rhythm in my head. *One two three four one two three four.*

"Mia. Of course. Mia. And Brynn." But this time when Mr. Waldmann tries to smile, he only winces. "Wow. How wonderful. I had no idea you were all still in touch." He turns to Owen, leaving the question unspoken: *Why?*

"It's been kind of like our reunion tour," Brynn blurts out. "But we're just wrapping up."

Mr. Waldmann's attention moves to the living room—the mess of papers, coffee-ringed Styrofoam cups, empty chip bowls. "What happened here?" he says. "There another storm I didn't hear about?"

I shove past Owen and start snatching up pages, one by one—some of them brittle, like old leaves, some of them damp as though imprinted by sweaty palms. I shuffle them carelessly into a pile, ignoring the echoes of an old fear: they'll be out of order now, we'll never be able to sort them, Summer will be so angry.

"Homework," is the first thing I can think of to say, which is why I'm always so careful, why I weigh words in my mouth before I speak them. The first thing that comes out is often so wrong.

"Homework?" Mr. Waldmann sounds almost amused. Almost. But the strain is obvious in his expression. "In July?"

"Summer school." More lies, more words I haven't chosen, as though they're just staging a riot. For a second I catch Owen watching me with the strangest look on his face—as if I'm some-one he's never seen before. "Owen agreed to help out, because of NYU and everything."

That doesn't even make sense, but Mr. Waldmann nods. "Okay," he says. "Okay." Then: "Owen, can I see you for a sec-ond? Alone?"

This is it: the end of the line. *Get them out*, Mr. Waldmann will say, and Owen will be nice about it, give us an excuse, and shut the door in our faces. We dragged him into this. He didn't want any of it.

All he did was kiss her in front of half the school and break my heart.

"I was just about to drive Brynn and Mia home," Owen says, already going for the door. Goodbye, thanks for coming, please don't crowd the exits.

"Nice to see you, girls," Mr. Waldmann says, but it's not hard to figure out what he really means: *Nice to see you* leaving.

*　　*　　*

Owen's car is stifling hot. The AC does nothing but flood hot air at us. I roll down the window, worried I'm going to be sick. I'll lose my chance to talk to Owen unless I do it now. But I won't do it. Of course I won't. Not here at ten forty-five a.m. in a sweat-sticky car, not anywhere, never.

"I'm not going home," Brynn says as Owen reverses onto the lawn to turn around. "I'm going with Mia." She hasn't asked me, of course, but I'm too tired to argue.

"Neither of you is going home," Owen says. For a second he looks just like the old Owen: stubborn, explosive, unpredictable. The boy who lived half the time out of his tree house and wore a bulky flea-market trench coat everyone said he would someday conceal a gun inside and spent half of class gazing out the window, doodling shapes in his notebook. Brilliant and strange and mine. "Not yet, anyway. We owe Mr. Haggard a visit, remember?"

BRYNN

Then

"Nice skirt, Mia," Summer said, bumping Mia on the shoulder with a hip before she slumped into the seat next to me, even though for more than a month she'd been avoiding us entirely, turning down different hallways when she spotted me from a distance, refusing to answer any of my texts. In the cafeteria she'd practically shoved me when I put an arm on her shoulder. *Stop drooling, McNally. I'm not into girls, okay?* Furious, practically spitting, as if *I* were the one who ruined everything, who'd told about what had happened between us the night she climbed into my bed. It was April—a raw day, when the rain couldn't decide whether to come down or not and so just hovered in the air, making trouble. "Trying to give Mr. Haggard a view of your prime real estate?"

"Shut up," Mia hissed. "He'll hear you."

"So what if he does? Hey, Haggard. My friend Mia wants to know if you think she's pretty—?"

"I said shut up," Mia said.

We were stopped at a light. Haggard twisted around in his seat, bracing himself with one arm on the steering wheel.

"What's the trouble back there, girls?" Mr. Haggard's voice sounded like it was rumbling out of a foghorn.

"Nothing," Summer called back sweetly. "We were just saying how cute you look in your new jacket. . . ."

I elbowed her. She rolled her eyes.

"Just giving him some excitement," she said. "Look at him. He probably can't even see past his stomach to his dick."

"Can you not?" Mia made a face. Mia hated every word associated with sex, but *dick*, *pussy*, and *lube* were among her least favorites. I knew because in the fall of seventh grade—back before Summer had turned on us, back when we were all best friends—we made a list during a sleepover and took turns reading them out loud to make Mia squeal.

"Speaking of special occasions." I was trying to keep things light, like I hadn't been dying to talk to her, like every time she'd glared at me and looked away hadn't gouged me full of holes. "Any reason you're gracing us with your presence?"

"Couldn't get another ride," Summer said, shrugging. Gouge. Gouge. "Besides," she said after a minute, in a different voice. "I wanted to talk about the spring dance. We're still going together, aren't we? The three of us and Owen?" She reached for my hand and squeezed, and my heart squeezed too.

Once again, I forgave her. Forgave her for telling everyone I was in love with her. Forgave her for taking my deepest secret, my truest thing, my love for her, and turning it into a joke.

"You still want to go with us?" Mia's face was suspicious, but also hopeful, happy.

We just didn't work without Summer.

"Uh-huh." She unwrapped a piece of gum carefully. Her nails were painted yellow and chipping. "I might need your help with something soon, too. It's about Lovelorn," she added casually, almost as an afterthought.

"I thought we weren't playing anymore," I said.

She looked up at me, eyes wide and sky-blue, eyes to fall into. "Who said it was a game?"

The problem with the Chasm of Wish wasn't so much what it contained. Wishes weren't in themselves dangerous, and many Lovelornians had lost years, decades even, swimming in the river at its bottom, buoyed up by wishes, enfolded in the happy visions of everything they'd ever wanted.

Which, of course, was the problem: not getting in, but getting out.

—From *The Way into Lovelorn* by Georgia C. Wells

BRYNN

Now

We pull Mr. Haggard's address easily from whitepages.com: he lives on Bones Road in Eastwich, a speck of a town twenty minutes away. While Owen drives, Mia tries googling Mr. Haggard to find out more about him. There are only a handful of results: Mr. Haggard at a church picnic; Mr. Haggard manning a booth at the local Christmas bazaar; Mr. Haggard smiling with his arm around a skinny kid in front of a YMCA, where he apparently coaches basketball.

"That proves it," I say. "Church and Christmas and coaching. That's like the trifecta for pedophilia."

"Or he's a really nice guy who just likes kids," Mia says.

"Or he's pretending to be a nice guy who likes kids sweaty and worked up."

"That's gross, Brynn."

"I'm not the pedophile. Besides, this was your big idea."

"I know." Mia turns to face the window. "It's just . . ."

"Just what?" Owen asks, so quietly I barely hear him over the rush of the AC.

"It feels different, during the day. Harder to believe."

She's right. In the middle of the night and amped up on coffee, Haggard seemed inevitable. The nice dumpy bus driver, silently sporting a hard-on for Summer, maybe earning her trust, offering to help her out with homework, turning on her one day when she wouldn't give him what he wanted.

Now, with houses flashing by behind neat-trimmed hedges and packs of kids riding bikes in the road, wind turbines up on the hill waving slowly, it's hard to believe that anything bad could ever happen or has ever happened. It strikes me that maybe that's the reason for it all—the nicely mowed lawns and hedges and houses painted fresh every few years. We build and build to keep the knowledge down that someday it will fall apart.

Bones Road is not what I expected. No old graveyards and headstones like splintered fingernails, no stormy-looking manor houses, no run-down farms with goats glaring at us from behind barbed wire. It looks kind of like my street, actually, with a bunch of pretty ranch houses set on identical tracts of land, lots of American flags and mailboxes in the shapes of animals and lawns littered with plastic kids' toys. Mr. Haggard's house is painted a cheerful yellow. There's a big SUV in the driveway.

Owen parks down the street, as if he's afraid Mr. Haggard might make a run for it if he so much as catches sight of the car. For a few seconds we just sit there after he cuts the engine, letting the heat creep back in. Doubts are still waggling their fingers at me.

"What's the game plan?" I ask. "We need a cover story. I mean, we can't just barge in and ask him if he killed Summer."

"Follow my lead," Owen says, like he's the hero in a bad cop movie and we're about to bust a terrorist ring.

Outside, the sun is doing its best to turn the pavement to butter. In the distance, kids are laughing and splashing, and the air smells like barbecue. I haven't had anything to eat since we fueled up on gas station chips last night, and I'm starving. For a quick second I wish I lived here, on Bones Road, in one of these tidy houses. I wish a mom and dad were busy grilling up lunch while I went splashing through a sprinkler. But like my mom always said, *Wishes are like lotto tickets—they never pay out.*

An old, frayed welcome mat on the front stoop reads *There's No Place Like Home.* Owen jabs the doorbell, and musical notes echo through the house. Standing there gives me the uncomfortable feeling of being a little kid on Halloween, waiting for someone to swing open the door. *Trick or treat.* I count four, five, six seconds.

"What if he's not home?" Mia whispers.

"Someone's home," Owen says. "The car's in the driveway."

"But—" Mia starts to protest, but quickly falls silent. Footsteps patter toward us. He is home, after all.

But it's not Mr. Haggard who swings open the door.

It's a little girl. A girl maybe eleven or twelve, wearing a bathing suit and hot-pink short shorts, with a cloud of blond hair and sky-blue eyes, just like Summer's.

For a second we all just stand there, gaping at her, three fish hooked through the lip. She rests one foot on the inside of her opposite knee, stork-style.

"Who are you?" she asks.

"Who are *you*?" I finally manage to say. But before she can answer, more footsteps—a brown-haired woman appears behind her and draws the little girl back. She's bouncing a blond-haired boy on her hip. His face is coated with what looks like strawberry jam.

"What did I tell you about answering the door?" she says to the girl, and the girl spins away from her, squealing, and disappears down the hall. The woman rolls her eyes and pushes hair from her forehead with the back of her hand. "Can I help you?"

It hits me: we must have gotten the wrong house. Owen must think so too, because he says, "We were looking for Mr. Haggard. Do you know where—?"

But she cuts him off. "You're not selling anything, are you? No Bible subscriptions or anything?"

Owen shakes his head. "It's for . . . a project." His voice sounds like it's being squeezed through a tube of toothpaste.

She waves us inside. The boy on her hip is sucking on his fingers, staring. "Come on. Everyone's out back. Quickest way is through the kitchen." She's already heading down the hall and we have no choice now but to follow her. The house is small and messy in the best way. Kids' toys and fuzzy blankets, TV showing a baseball game and a teenage boy who doesn't acknowledge us watching it with his elbows crooked to his knees, kitchen exploding with platters of food: potato salad, macaroni salad, hamburger meat, hot dog buns. I look at Mia and she shakes her head, as confused as I am.

A sliding glass door leads from the kitchen to the backyard. Kids are running around a wading pool, and the fence is decorated with balloons. There must be forty people out there, adults and kids, and a grill sending thick smoke into the air.

Whatever Mr. Haggard is, he isn't lonely.

The woman pushes open the sliding door. "Dad!" she calls. "Visitors!" She turns back to us with an apologetic look. "Sorry. It's nuts today."

"We can come back." Owen's face has gone practically as red as his hair, and I know he must feel just as bad as I do. Mia is staring straight ahead with an expression on her face like she's just seen her pet bunny electrocuted.

"No, no. It's no trouble. Here he is now," she says, and it's too late: Mr. Haggard is squeezing in sideways through the door, one hand on his stomach, looking like Santa Frigging Claus, and we're here to assassinate him, and sorry, kids, there goes Christmas.

"Hello," he says. His eyes are twinkling. Actually twinkling. Between the twinkle and the long beard, he really does look like Father Christmas. "What can I do you for?"

The woman—his daughter—has slipped back into the yard. I see a picnic table stacked with birthday presents, a little girl wearing a princess tiara.

"This obviously isn't a good time," Owen says quickly. Mia lets out a whistling sound, like a punctured balloon.

Mr. Haggard waves a hand. "My youngest grandkid turns six today. Wanted to dress me up as a princess and been running me ragged all day. I'm glad for a little break." He fumbles a pair of glasses out of his front pocket. Great. Now he looks *exactly* like Santa. Then again, Old St. Nick has all those elves running around doing work for no pay, so he's got some dirty little secrets of his own. "Now let me see. You all are too old for Girl Scout cookies. Not to mention I don't think *this* one fits the bill. Specially not with that shiner. Ouch." He jerks his head at Owen and grins. "So let me think. You all raising money for the school debate team or something?"

There's a long, horrible beat of silence. I picture the roof collapsing, the kitchen exploding, an earthquake tossing us all into the air.

"Actually"—Owen's voice cracks and he clears his throat—"we're volunteers from the Vermont Transportation Authority—"

Mr. Haggard plugs a finger in his ear and rubs. "The what now?"

But Owen just keeps talking, raising his voice a little, as if he can drown out any of Haggard's objections. "To administer a quick survey about the public school bus systems as compared to private systems—"

"Oh boy." He heaves himself onto one of the kitchen stools, still smiling. "Sounds heavy."

Owen finally runs out of breath and stands there, half gasping. "Just a few questions," he adds. "About your experience, and your bus route, and what the kids are like."

"Were," Haggard says. "I retired last year."

"Okay," Owen says. "What the kids *were* like."

Haggard turns his smile on me. I feel like an ant underneath a magnifying glass. "Well, why don't you just ask these girls? Bet you remember the old bus route just fine."

"You—you remember us," I stutter.

His smile finally goes dim. "'Course I do. You were my three musketeers. You two and the other girl, Summer. Terrible what happened to her." It's clear from the way he says it that he doesn't think we had anything to do with it.

I try to beam to Owen and Mia that we should get the hell out of here and leave Haggard and his grandkids in peace.

Apparently Mia doesn't get the message, because she blurts out, "Mr. Haggard, we're sorry. We haven't been honest. We're not here for a survey. We're here about Summer. We're trying to find out what really happened to her."

Forget the earthquake. Here's to hoping a renegade tiara whizzes in through the doors to decapitate all three of us.

"I see." Haggard scratches his head through the thinning slick of his hair. "Well, I'm not sure whether I can be much help. . . ."

"You—you remember her, though?" If I'm going to hell anyway, I might as well make sure I've good and earned it.

"Sure. I remember all my kids. Drove a bus for forty years and knew that route like the back of my hand."

"Did you grow up in Vermont?" Owen asks, and I know he must be thinking of St. Louis.

"Born and bred," Haggard says. He gives his stomach a thwack. "They make us bigger out here, huh?" But his smile fades again. "She was trouble, that one. Tell you that. Had a mean streak." Then, as though he remembers who he's talking to, he stands up. "But you probably knew that, huh? I felt sorry for her."

Mia shoots Owen a look I don't have time to puzzle out. "How come?" I say.

"She seemed lonely," he says. "Even when she was with her friends, with you two, she seemed lonely. Lost, you know?"

Lonely. Lost. The words remind me of the passages we pulled about the Shadow. Was Summer the Shadow all along? I never thought of Summer as lonely, not once. But then I remember the night she climbed in through my window, the way her ribs looked, standing out in the moonlight, her tears running into my mouth even as we kissed.

Nobody loves me, she said, over and over again. Her chest spasmed against my palms, like she was dying. *Nobody, nobody, nobody.*

Were we wrong about everything? Maybe there was no mysterious Shadow in real life, no one who got close to her and started feeding her stories. Maybe she did write the pages herself. Maybe some psycho met her in the woods and just seized his chance.

A little boy comes tumbling into the kitchen, knees grass-stained and face all scrunched up and red, wailing. He holds out his arms.

"Grandpa," he says. "Grandpa, Grandpa."

"What's the matter, Gregg?" Haggard places a wrinkled hand on the kid's head. I give it a last shot and try to picture that hand wrapped around a knife, bringing a blade down into Summer's chest and neck, over and over. But my brain just burps and goes quiet.

The woman who let us into the house is a second behind Gregg, drawing him away. "Oh, you're fine. Gregg, *honestly*. It was just a little tumble. And you know Grandpa can't pick you up." But she picks him up and plants a kiss on his forehead before rolling her eyes at us and hauling him back outside.

"Slipped disc," Haggard says to us, placing a hand on his back and making an *oh boy, that's age* face. "Used to volunteer with the EMT. Had a bad fall when my own kids were barely out of diapers. Can't barely lift a shovel in wintertime." He shakes his head.

That's that. Whoever killed Summer also had to drag her. Mr. Haggard can't even pick up a toddler.

"We're sorry for barging in on you like this, Mr. Haggard." Owen's still glowing red as a hot pepper. He's put two and two together, too. "We're sorry for wasting your time."

"It's no trouble." For a second, he looks like he's about to say more. Then I find a name for his expression: pity. He feels sorry for us. "I hope you all find what you're looking for."

But as we make our way back into the heat, leaving the noise of shouting kids and laughter behind, just another summer Wednesday, trees bursting like the joy is coming out through their branches, I know that we won't.

Firth had one special skill besides thievery, and that was this: people listened to him. He rode from town to town, from vale to glen, from hermit hovel to the princesses' towers, and everywhere he stopped and delivered the same message:

"We've had it wrong, my friends. We've said one must die so that others might live. But everyone must die. It is the natural way. The only way. Age comes and takes us. Sickness knocks on our door. Death is blind and picks at random. Everyone must die. Only then can everyone live, too. Only then can we banish the Shadow from these lands."

—From *The Way into Lovelorn* by Georgia C. Wells

MIA

Now

We don't speak on the drive back to Twin Lakes. Owen's knuckles stand out on the steering wheel, as if he's afraid it might spin out from his grip. Brynn sits, head back, staring at nothing.

Once, when I was five or six, my mom drove an hour and a half to Burlington to take me to a local production of *The Nutcracker*. I was wearing my best dress—green velvet, with a crinoline skirt and lace at the collar—thick wool stockings, shiny leather boots that laced to my ankle. On the way there, it started to snow, light flakes that winked on the way down and melted side by side against the window.

When we arrived, there were no women in long silk dresses, no ushers in flat caps passing out brochures, no crush of perfume and conversation. Just some teens out of uniform sweeping up crumbs from the aisles, and the stage naked and bare under the lights. My mom had gotten the start time wrong. The show was a matinee.

The worst part of the whole thing wasn't even the disappointment but how angry I was at my mom. We went across the street to a little diner and she bought me a tuna melt and a chocolate sundae and I refused to eat them. Driving home while the headlights sucked snow into the grille, I imagined setting out into the woods all alone until the silence took me.

That's just how I feel now: we came too late. It's been too long.

Summer should have spoken to us sooner. She should have *led* us.

I'm furious at her all over again.

Owen has to wheel up on the lawn to avoid hitting the Dumpster in my driveway. Even before he's fully stopped, Brynn rockets out of the car without saying thank you.

"Construction?" Owen asks.

"What?" Suddenly, Owen and I are alone. Except I can no longer remember why I thought, even for a second, that we might repair something, stitch it back together. Owen, too, was probably fiction.

"The Dumpster. You guys doing construction?" He leans forward, squinting up at the house.

"Yes," I lie quickly. I let myself imagine it's true: that we're building instead of taking things apart.

"I'm sorry, Mia," Owen says. "I know you thought—I mean, I know it was important to you—"

"We were wrong about Mr. Haggard, okay?" I say before he can finish. "That doesn't mean we were wrong about everything." I seize onto this idea, haul myself forward word by word. "*Someone* was helping Summer write *Lovelorn*. Someone left clues behind. Maybe he was *hoping* to get caught. . . ."

Owen rubs his eyes. For a second he looks much older. "Mia . . ."

"Nothing else makes sense." I keep going because I can't stand to hear him contradict me. In my chest, a bubble swells and swells, threatening to burst. "Whoever killed her knew all about the sacrifice. He knew about the woods and the shed and all of it."

"Mia . . ."

But I can't let him finish. "We can talk to Mr. Ball again. Or we look at Heath Moore. We know his alibi's bullshit now." I'm babbling, desperate. "*You* heard Brynn. She took his phone. I bet there's a ton of creepy stuff on it. There's something wrong with him. And Summer was with him, right, before she—well, before you." I still can't say it. "She might have told him about Lovelorn, she probably did, she could never keep her mouth shut—"

"No. Mia, *no*." Owen twists around in his seat to face me, and the swollen thing in my chest explodes, flooding me with cold. "The clues don't *lead* anywhere. It's all make-believe—don't you get it? It's *still* make-believe." He looks like someone I barely know—new hard planes of his face, new mouth stretched thinly in a line, not my Owen, the brilliant wild boy, a boy meant to leap and spin alone in a spotlight, not a scrap of him left. "I'm sorry."

Hot pinpricks behind my eyes mean I'm going to cry. I look down at my lap, at my hands squeezed into fists. "You're sorry," I repeat, and Owen flinches, as if he thought the conversation was over and he's surprised to find me still sitting there. "You're *sorry*." I press down the tears under the weight of an anger that comes tingling through my whole body, waking me up. "You left. You got out. You're going to NYU next year, for God's sake. NYU. That was *my* school."

"Seriously?" Owen frowns. "We always talked about going to NYU."

"I always talked about it. *I* did." My voice sounds foreign to me—cold and hard and ringing. "And you come back here with your cute little car and your fake British accent—"

"Hey." Owen looks hurt, and when he looks hurt he looks, momentarily, like the old him.

But it's too late, I can't stop now. "We've been buried here, don't you understand? We're *suffocating*. And you think you can make it better by saying you're sorry? You don't care about helping, you don't care—" I break off before I can say *about me*. The tears are back now, elbowing me hard in the throat, making a break for it. I take a deep breath. "How dare you show up after all this time and pretend? You're the one playing make-believe. You—you told me you loved me. But you don't. You couldn't." I didn't mean to say it, but there it is. Words are like a virus—there's no telling what kind of damage they'll do once they're out.

Owen stares at me, and I'm so busy trying not to cry it takes me a minute to realize he's looking at me with pity. "I did, Mia," he says quietly.

Did. Past tense. As in, *no longer*.

I make it out of the car without crying. Without saying good-bye, either, even though that's what I mean.

MIA

Then

I was walking with Owen in the fall of sixth grade, arguing about whether or not AI would eventually spell the destruction of the human race (him: yes, thankfully; me: no, never) and dodging caterpillars plopping out of the trees onto the road like gigantic furry acorns—there were hundreds and hundreds of caterpillars that year, something about the reduction of the native population of bats—when all of a sudden Owen broke off midsentence.

"Uh-oh," he said.

I didn't even have time to say *what?* By the time I looked at him he was standing calmly, head tilted back, cupping a hand to his nose while blood flowed through his fingers, so bright red it looked like paint.

"It's okay," he said thickly, while I squealed. "It happens all the time."

But I was already shaking off my sweatshirt—not caring that

it was my favorite, not caring that my mother would kill me, not thinking of anything but Owen and all that blood, his *insides*, flowing out in front of me—and pressing it balled up to his face, saying, "It's okay, it's okay," even though I was the one who was afraid, standing there until my sweatshirt was damp with butter-fly patterns of blood.

Audrey, Ava, and Ashleigh stood, shivering in the sudden wind, and watched Gregoria disappearing with the Shadow into the woods. At a certain point, it looked as if the Shadow bent to whisper something to her. Then they were simply gone.

—From *The Way into Lovelorn* by Georgia C. Wells

MIA

Now

"You okay?" Brynn asks. I'm going to have to dig up my old list of all the ways that words can turn to lies, make some amendments to it. I don't bother answering.

Inside, the smell of mold and wet and rotting cardboard is worse than ever. Or maybe it's just that *everything's* worse. I grab an armful of stuff from the side table, including a framed picture of me dressed as Odette in my dance school production of *Swan Lake*, grinning at the camera, dressed in tulle and pointe shoes and a frosty tiara, and turn right back around, stalk across the driveway, and heave it all up into the Dumpster. *Goodbye.* Another armful—mail and a carved figurine of a rooster and a dozen loose keys in a basket and an orchid in its clay pot, miraculously blooming despite the chaos—and outside I throw it in a long arc, like a longshoreman tossing catches of fish. Not until I grab the side table itself does Brynn say something.

"Are you sure . . . ?" she starts, but trails off when I give her a look. Brynn and I should never have stopped being friends. We must be the two most screwed-up people in Twin Lakes. Maybe in all of Vermont.

When the side table goes into the Dumpster, it splinters. Two crooked legs stick up over the lip, like an iron cockroach trying to claw its way to safety. The Dumpster's nearly full already. And suddenly it hits me how hopeless it all is: the house is still swollen with trash. Like a dead body bloated with gases. Even from outside I can see the Piles shouldering up against the downstairs windows, the curtains going black with slime. I haven't made a dent. The tears come, all at once, like a stampede, and I stand there crying in front of the stupid Dumpster with my house coming down behind me.

I don't know how long I've been standing there when I notice a cop car: swimming slowly, sharklike, down the street. It stops just next to the driveway. I turn away, swiping at my eyes and cheeks. But when the cop climbs out, long-legged and narrow-faced, like a praying mantis, he heads straight for me.

"Hello," he says, all toothy smile, pretending not to notice I've just been sobbing alone on my front lawn. "You must be Mia Ferguson."

"Can I help you?" I say, crossing my arms. He looks familiar, but I can't figure out why.

"I'm looking for Brynn McNally," he says. "Seen her recently?"

What's she done now? I almost ask. Luckily, my throat chooses the right time to close up.

But a second later Brynn bursts out of the door—like she does, like even air is a major barrier—maybe just because she's sick of being inside with the smell, and the cop says, "Ah," like he's just solved a math problem.

Brynn freezes. "What is this?" she says. "Who are you?"

"Afternoon," he says. I imagine the swish-swish of curtains opening across the street, neighbors peering out, wondering what we've done now, whether we're finally going to get it. "Was hoping we could have a little chat. Name's Officer Moore." He pauses, like the name should mean something.

And then it does: Moore. As in Heath Moore. Brynn must make the connection at the same time. She looks furious.

"You're Heath's older brother," she says.

"Cousin," he corrects. His cheeks are round like a baby's, and swallow his eyes when he smiles. "Sorry to bother you ladies," he says, hitching his belt higher, like we're in a cowboy movie. "I'm here about a missing phone?"

In sixth-grade history we studied the fall of Rome. We charted all the factors that led to the collapse of one of the most powerful empires of all time. Corruption. Religious tension. Gluttony. Bad leadership. Little arms pinwheeling out from the central fact: over a hundred years, from superpower to sad little collection of city-states.

But no one ever tells you that sometimes disasters can't be

predicted. They don't throw shadows of warning over you. They don't roll like snowballs. They come like avalanches all at once to bury you.

Look at Pompeii, a city singed to ash in a single day. Or the way a first frost slices the heads off everything but the sturdiest flowers.

Look at the human heart. Think about the difference between alive and not. One second that little fist is going and going, squeezing out more time. And then it just quits. One beat to the next. Second to second.

One. Sound and noise and motion. Two. Another thump. Three.

Nothing.

Fifteen minutes later, Brynn is sitting in the front seat of the cop car, looking like a prisoner. Heath Moore, apparently too afraid to confront one of the Monsters of Brickhouse Lane himself, sent his cousin to do the dirty work. Officer Moore went directly to Brynn's house, where he informed Brynn's very confused mother that her daughter had stolen a phone during an altercation at Summer Marks's memorial.

Brynn's mother insisted she was at Four Corners. Four Corners insisted that Brynn had been signed out several days ago by an Audrey Augello. Officer Moore, no doubt thrilled that his missing-phone case had turned into a missing-girl case and sensing the opportunity to do something other than throw teenage boys in the drunk tank for the night, tracked Brynn down to my house after learning we'd been seen together.

And now Brynn is going home.

I'm still standing on the front lawn. The sun is high above us, like a ball lobbed up in the blue, and I feel just like I used to during curtain call, with all the stage lights bright and blinding and the applause already waning—an urge to laugh, or scream, or keep dancing, anything to keep the silence from coming.

When Officer Moore starts his engine, Brynn finally looks at me. For a second her face is blank, closed up like a fist. Then she brings a hand up and I think she's going to try and say something. Instead she presses her palm flat on the glass. I bring my hand up too, just hold it there, even as the squad car pulls away and Brynn drops her hand, leaving a ghost imprint on the glass, even after they're gone and the noise of the engine has faded.

Across the street, the curtains twitch. Someone is definitely watching. Just because, I take a bow.

"Show's over," I say out loud, even though no one's around to hear me.

Inside, I stand in the dimness of the front hall, squinting at the Piles, trying to imagine them as something beautiful and natural, stone formations or ancient gods. But it doesn't work this time. I see only trash, rot, mold webbing through the whole house. Maybe I'll never even go to college. Maybe I'll stay here forever, slowly yellowing like one of the old newspapers my mom refuses to throw away, or turning gray as the walls are now.

Owen's voice is still echoing in my head. *I did. I did. I did.*

Strangely, the urge to cry has vanished. The urge to clean, too. It's too late anyway. There's no point. There was never any point.

"Sorry, Summer," I say into the empty hall. Something rustles in another room. A mouse, probably. I close my eyes and imagine I can hear the amplified chewing of termites in the wood.

I must have been crazy to think that Owen would ever want me now. Grown-up Owen with his cute little accent and his Boy Scout look, off to NYU and girls with pixie-cut hair and J.Crew smiles, girls with vacation homes in Cape Cod and the Hamptons, girls who aren't all jumbled up and split apart. Maybe my mom hasn't been collecting all this time but *re*flecting. Mirroring our chaos. The chaos inside.

There's a sudden pounding on the front door. Brynn. Maybe she left something. Maybe she catapulted out of the cop car and came running back. For a second, I even hope she did.

Instead my dad is on the front porch, waxy-faced, sweating.

"Mia." He says my name as if it's an explosion. "Mia. Oh my God."

"Dad." Then I remember that the door is open—just a crack, not enough for him to enter, not enough for him to see—and I try to slip outside. But he has his hand on the door, and he stops me.

"Where have you been?" He looks like he hasn't slept. His hair is sticking straight up, as if a giant has grabbed him by the roots and tried to lift him off his feet. "I was this close to calling the police—tried you at least twenty times—phone went straight to voice mail—"

"My phone was dead. That's all," I say.

But he just keeps talking, leapfrogging over half his words so I can hardly piece together what he's saying.

"—came by last night—house was dark—been calling for two days—phone off—"

"I'm sorry, Dad. I—I wasn't feeling good. But I'm fine now," I quickly add. I'm worried he's about to have a heart attack: a vein is standing out in his forehead, throbbing as if it, too, is very upset.

Finally my dad runs out of anger—or out of air—and stands there panting, the vein still beating a little rhythm in his forehead. "Well, Jesus, Mia. Open the door. I've been terrified—your mother and I both—"

"You called Mom?" All this time I've been talking to my dad through a narrow gap in the door and angling my body so he can't see inside. Now I slip onto the porch, closing the door firmly behind me. No way am I letting Dad inside. Dad's never been inside, not since he left.

"Of course I called your mother. She's on her way home from Jess's house now." Dad frowns, and looks a little more like my dad, the stern podiatrist—I'm pretty sure that even as a kid he liked to dress up in suits and diagnose people with acute tendonitis. His eyes go from me to the door and back again. "Come on," he says, in a normal tone. "Let's go inside. I could use a glass of water."

"No!" I cry as he reaches for the door handle. Instinctively, I flatten myself against the door, keeping it shut.

My dad's fingers are wrapped around the door handle. "Mia," he says, in a low voice—someone who didn't know him might think he was being casual—"what are you hiding?"

"I'm not hiding anything." But suddenly the tears are back. Traitors. They always come at the worst moment. "Please," I say. "Please."

"I am going to open this door, Mia." Now my father's voice is barely more than a whisper. "I am going to open it in three seconds, do you understand me? One . . . two . . ."

I step away, hugging myself, choking on a sob that rolls up from my stomach.

"Three."

For a long second, he doesn't even go inside. He stands there, frozen, as if he's fighting the urge to run. Then he lifts a hand to his mouth—slowly, slowly, afraid to move, afraid to touch anything. "Oh my God," he says.

"I'm sorry." I bend over and put my hands on my knees, sobbing in gasps. I don't know what I'm sorry for, exactly—my mom, because I didn't protect her; my dad, because I couldn't stop it. "I'm sorry," I say again.

He barely seems to hear me. "Oh my God." A few feet inside and his foot squelches on something sticky. He flinches. Another step. *Crackle, crackle.* Old magazines snap underfoot. Even from outside I can make out the Piles, pointing like fingers toward a heaven that doesn't exist, and all I can think is how mad he's going to be, and how mad Mom's going to be, and how I've messed up everything, even things that were messed up from the beginning. And I can barely breathe, I'm crying so hard: a broken girl with a broken heart living in a broken house.

"Mia." Then my dad turns around to face me, and I'm shocked to see not anger but a look as if someone just tore his heart out through his chest. I've never seen my dad cry, not once, not even at his own mother's funeral—but now he's crying, fully, without even bothering to wipe his face. Then he's rocketing out onto the porch again and has picked me up like I'm still a little kid, so my feet lift off the ground and his arms are crushing my ribs and I'm so startled that I completely forget to be sad.

"It's okay, Dad," I say, even as he cries in big, long gulps. We've switched roles. Now he's the one apologizing.

"I'm sorry, baby," he keeps saying, over and over. "I'm so sorry. I'm so sorry. I'm so sorry."

There was no denying it. No understanding it, either.

The fact was this: the Shadow was getting stronger again.

—From *Return to Lovelorn* by Summer Marks, Brynn McNally, and Mia Ferguson

BRYNN

Now

Wednesday morning, July 20, two weeks after Heath Moore's cousin dragged me home, attempt number 1,024 to reach Abby, fifth ring . . .

Sixth ring . . .

Voice mail.

"Hey, this is Abby. If you're getting this message, it probably means I'm screening your calls. . . ."

I thumb out of the call just as my sister practically kicks in the door, still dressed in her scrubs, hair swept back into a ponytail and eyes raccooned with tiredness.

She fists the door closed. "Fucking thing's swollen," she says, which is my-sister-speak for *Hi! How are you! Nice to see you!* But she comes and thumps down next to me on the couch, kicking up her feet on the coffee table, nudging aside Mom's laptop. A school brochure slithers to the carpet, wedged with Post-it notes. Ever since I got home, Mom's been writing away to every single alternative high school program on the East Coast. *Not even an addict*, she just kept saying when I told her, shaking her head, as if she almost wished I was. *Really, Brynn. Well, I guess it's about time you finish up school, then.*

Erin fishes a Coke from her bag, pops open the tab, and takes a long swig.

"How was work?" I ask. She's been working doubles all summer, sometimes as many as forty-eight hours on shift, and then two days off when she crawls into bed.

"Same as usual. Lots of old people." Erin always talks this way, like she doesn't give a shit, but I know that's a lie. She's busted ass to get through medical school, taken out tens of thousands of dollars in loans, and she still takes money out of her paycheck to buy gifts for her favorite patients. "Saw your friend Mia again," she says through another slurp of soda.

"She's not my friend," I say quickly, and I'm surprised that it hurts. Stupid. We spend four days playing Scooby-Doo and now I feel lonely because the game's over.

I've spoken to Mia only once since Moore brought me home. Went up to town for coffee and I ran into her at Toast. She was dressed like she always dresses, in neat little shorts that looked like they'd been pressed and her hair in a bun and a polo shirt, but she looked more relaxed somehow—less like she was moving with a yardstick up her you-know-what. She told me she was spending more time at her dad's while her mom got help from counselors at North Presbyterian Hospital, where my sister is doing her residency. Apparently a whole team of people are treating her house for black mold spores and other nasty shit her father was afraid would ruin her lungs.

"Have you spoken to Owen?" I asked her, and her face got closed again and she shook her head. And then, because I couldn't help it, I asked, "How's Abby?"

Mia made a face. "Hanging out with Wade a lot. Can you believe it?"

"*Star Wars* fandom," I said. "What can you do?" That made her laugh, but it was a forced laugh, like wincing.

I never thought there'd be a day when I'd actually *miss* Wade. Half the time I text Wade now, he's with Abby. I nearly spilled everything to Mia then, standing in front of Toast with my iced coffee sweating through my fingers—about Abby, and how mean I was. How stupid I was. How I actually kinda like her.

How over and over I've replayed the kiss in my head.

But then a woman walked by, tugging her child across the street and shooting us a dirty look, like we were contagious, and I remembered who we were, that it didn't matter, that the only thing that bonds us now is Summer's ghost. And Mia's dad pulled up in his sparkly Land Rover and tooted the horn, and she lifted a hand and was gone.

I check my phone out of habit, thinking maybe, by some miracle, I'll find a missed call from Abby. In the past two weeks I've tried locking my phone in a drawer for hours, shoving my mom's ancient TV, as big as a mini-fridge, in front of it to keep me from checking. I've thought about driving to her house. I even wrote her a letter—an actual letter, on paper—before tearing it into pieces and flushing it down the toilet.

"You know, I've been talking with Mom about moving." Erin says this like she says everything else, like the words just rolled out of her mouth without her paying attention. I stare at her.

"Out of Twin Lakes?" I say.

"We're thinking Middlebury." She shrugs. "I could help Mom out with the moving costs. We're looking to get her a car, too, so she'd be able to commute to work. Things might be better . . ." She doesn't finish her sentence, but I know what she's about to say: *Things might be better for you.*

All I've ever wanted was to get out of Twin Lakes. But now the idea makes me feel like someone's placed my insides on blend. "When?" I ask, and she shrugs again.

"Soon as we figure out your school," she says. "Soon as we figure out the money stuff." She reaches over and musses my hair, like I'm still a kid. "You could start over, Brynn. We could all start over."

"Yeah," I say. "Okay."

Her smiles are always so quick they look like they're being chased away. She yawns big, covering her mouth with the back of her hand. "I'm going to bed." She stands up, handing me her Coke. "Want the rest of this?"

"Sure," I say, and take it, even though it's warm. A second later and I'm alone, listening to the chugging of the window AC, the sun through the windows still making my neck sweat.

We could all start over.

A nice idea. Except that it's never that easy. Is it?

I remember how Summer looked the day we found those sad little crows, one of them still struggling in the snow, its feathers stiff and clotted with blood. *It's Lovelorn*, she said. *It doesn't want to let us go.*

And how we found her that day in the woods, holding on to that poor cat . . . the way she turned to us as if she hardly recognized us.

Here's the problem with starting over: Summer won't let us. She doesn't want to let us go, either.

Summer, Mia, and Brynn no longer had a choice: if they didn't give the Shadow something to feast on, its hunger would only grow. That day they set out for Lovelorn in silence, and each of them carried a special item. Mia had a pocketful of pebbles she'd scooped out from her driveway, to use for marking the circle. Brynn had a matchbook. And Summer carried the knife.

—From *Return to Lovelorn* by Summer Marks, Brynn McNally, and Mia Ferguson

BRYNN

Then

June 29 was a perfect day. It wasn't raining. There were no storm clouds. The trees weren't whispering to one another but stood high and quiet with their arms to a blue sky. The bees clustered fat and drowsy in the fields, and birds pecked at their reflections in the creek. It wasn't a day for nightmares or scary stories or shadows.

It wasn't a day for Summer to die.

Meet me in Lovelorn, she texted that morning. *It's time.*

At first we thought the whole thing was a joke. That's what I told myself over and over, what I tried to tell the cops. A joke, or just part of Summer's storytelling, her way of making things real. We didn't really think there would be a sacrifice. We didn't really think she was in danger.

Then why did you go at all? the cops asked.

Because she needed us. Because we missed her. Because it was Lovelorn.

You just said you didn't think Lovelorn was real.

We knew it was a story. But the story was also coming true.

So did you believe, or didn't you believe?

That was the question I could never truly answer. The truth was both, and the truth was neither. Like that old idea of a cat in a box with the lid on it, alive and dead at the same time until you look. We believed in Lovelorn and we knew it was just a story. We knew there was no Shadow and we knew that Summer needed us. We loved her and we hated her and she understood us and she scared us.

Alive and dead. I've thought about that a lot: when we saw Summer standing in the long field, shading her eyes with a hand to look at us, clutching something—a rug, or a stuffed animal—with her other, that she was both, that somehow what was about to happen to her was already built into that moment, buried in it, like a clock counting down to an explosion.

That's what I thought the cat was, at first. A rug. A stuffed animal. Not real. None of it could be real.

"You came," was all Summer said. In the week since school had ended, we hadn't seen her. I hadn't spoken to her at all since the last day of school, when, passing me in the hall, she'd suddenly doubled back and seized my hand. *I'm going to need you soon*, she'd whispered, pressing herself so close to me that a group of eighth-grade boys had pointed and started to laugh. By then the rumors had been everywhere for months: that I hid in the toilet stalls and spied on the other girls changing; that I'd invited Summer to sleep over and then slipped into her bed when she was sleeping.

Summer looked small that day in the field, in a white dress and cowboy boots, both too big for her. Scared, too. There was a stain at the hem of her dress. Cat puke, I later realized. "I didn't know if you would," she said, and as we got closer I saw that her face looked bruised and purplish, like she'd been crying.

Then Mia stopped and let out a sound like a kicked dog. "What—what is that?"

That was the thing Summer was holding, the sad, ragged bundle of fur. Except that when she kneeled I saw it wasn't a *that* at all, but an animal, a live animal or half-live animal: the helpless staring eyes, the twitchy tail now stilled, the mouth coated in vomit and foam. Bandit: the Balls' cat. Barely breathing, letting out faint wheezes, hissing noises like an old radiator.

My whole body went dead with shock. I couldn't move. My tongue felt like a slug, swollen and useless. Mia's whimpers were coming faster now. She sounded like a squeaky toy getting stepped on again and again.

"What'd you do?" I managed to say.

Summer was busy placing rocks. Bandit was stretched out on his side, stomach heaving, obviously in pain, and Summer was putting rocks in a circle, and she may have been crying before, but now she was totally calm.

"Are you going to help?" she said. "Or are you just going to stand there and watch?"

"What'd you do?" I was surprised to hear that I was shouting.

"We have to save him," Mia whispered. Her color was all

wrong—her skin had a sick algae glow to it, and I remember thinking this must be a dream, it must be. "He's in *pain*."

Summer looked up and frowned. "It's just a cat," she said. She actually sounded annoyed. Like we were the ones being unreasonable.

Mia moved like someone was tugging on all her limbs at different times. Jerk-jerk-jerk. Like a puppet. She was inside the circle on her knees in the dirt with the cat. "Shhh." She was lifting her hand, trying to touch him, trying to help. "Shhh. It's okay. It's going to be okay." Crying so hard she was sucking in her own snot.

"It's not going to be okay, Mia." Summer was still frowning. She was done with the rocks and started in with the gasoline. She must have stolen a can from her foster dad's garage. "The cat's going to die. That's the whole point." A little gasoline ended up on Mia's jean shorts, and Summer giggled. "Oops."

"What'd you *do*?" I took two steps forward and I was standing in the circle and I shoved her hard. She fell backward, landing in the dirt, releasing the can of gas. *Glug-glug-glug.* It disappeared into the dirt.

"Jesus Christ." Now she was the one shouting at me. "What do you think a sacrifice *is*? I mixed some rat poison into its food. The stupid thing was too dumb not to eat it."

I hit her. All of a sudden, I was burning hot and explosive, and I wound up and balled up my fist and clocked her. I'd been in fights plenty of times before, but I'd never punched anyone, and I'll never forget the sick, spongy way her skin felt and the crack of her cheekbone under my knuckles. Mia screamed. But Summer drew in a quick breath, sharp, like she'd been startled. She wasn't even mad. She just looked at me, tired, patient, like she was waiting for my anger to run out.

And I knew then that she'd been hit before, plenty of times, and acid burned up from my stomach and into my mouth.

"Are you going to help me?" she said again, in a quieter voice, and stood up. Then I saw she was holding a knife, a long knife with a sharp blade like the kind used for carving turkeys on Thanksgiving, separating flesh from bone.

"It's just a game," I whispered. Even my mouth tasted like ash. I could hardly speak, could hardly breathe, felt like I was choking.

She shook her head. "It was never a game," she said quietly. "That's what I've been trying to tell you. This is the only way." She looked sorry. In a lower voice, she added, "There has to be blood."

She looked down to the cat, still shuddering out his life, and to Mia, bent over, trying to whisper him back to health, her long thin neck exposed, stalk-like; her shoulders bare in her tank top, heaving.

I saw: pale skin, life thrumming through her veins.

I saw: Summer with a knife. Summer saying, *I'm sorry.*

I couldn't think straight.

"Mia," I said. And thank God she listened to me. Mia always listened to me. "Run."

"When it comes to the heart, there is no right and wrong," the *Shadow told Summer. "Only what it needs to keep beating."*
—From *Return to Lovelorn* by Summer Marks

MIA

Now

"You sure you don't want company?" Abby slides her sunglasses—purple, heart-shaped—down her nose to look at me. "I've always thought I'd make an excellent grave robber."

"I'm not *robbing* a grave," I say. "I'm making one."

"Offer rescinded. Sounds dirty."

When I climb out of the car, a chorus of birds starts competing to be heard. A rabbit darts out from beneath the carriage of the old rusted Dodge and scampers off behind the tumbledown brick cottage for which the street was named. I stand for a second inhaling the smell of pine and earth, the way the shadows shift as the wind turns the leaves in the sun.

August is the saddest month: nothing so perfect can possibly last forever.

For the past few weeks, Abby's been spending most of her time with Wade. Whenever I see her, she either brings him along or just spends the whole time quoting him. For a while, I thought she must have a crush on him, but when I teased her about it, she looked almost pained.

"No," she said. "Not him." But she wouldn't say anything more.

So fine. Abby has a secret crush and a new best friend, and every time she forgets to invite me to hang out it feels like I'm trying to digest a pointe shoe. But that's okay. People grow up and grow apart and get new friends.

Normal people do, anyway. I can't even hold on to my old ones.

From the trunk I get a shovel—one of the few useful things we've managed to salvage so far from the endless flow of garbage bleeding out of our house—Georgia C. Wells's *The Way into Lovelorn*, and all the pages of *Return to Lovelorn*, crammed into a single shoebox, and start for the woods.

"What do they call this?" Abby shouts after me. "Behavioral therapy?"

I turn around and manage a smile. "Closure," I say.

I take the creek easily in one bound, zigzagging up the dry bank with the shovel jogging on my shoulder. Only a few feet into the woods, my phone dings a text—Abby, *last chance for company*—and then, a second later, a picture message from my mom. At first I don't understand what I'm looking at and have to stop, squinting over my screen, to make out the splotch of curdled green color in the screen.

Can you believe I found my carpet? she has written, and then I realize that they must be tackling her bedroom, by far the worst room in the house.

Proud of you, I write back, and return my phone to my back pocket.

Ever since Dad found out about Mom and her condition, we've had an army of therapists and professional organizers storm the house, helping my mom deal with more than five years of accumulated disaster. I always thought her hoarding started after Summer died, after Dad left, but it turns out I was wrong. For months before they separated, Dad said, he would come home to find she'd stolen rolls of toilet paper from public bathrooms or stuffed his bedside table drawers with used matchsticks and restaurant flyers. It was part of the reason they began fighting so much: she told him that she held on to stuff because she was unhappy and their marriage left her feeling empty.

So. It's not my fault. It was never my fault.

Now Mom goes to see a psychiatrist at North Presbyterian Hospital on Thursdays and we have family sessions every other week, too, with a Dr. Leblanc, who looks exactly like the lion from *The Wizard of Oz*. Mom has been calling me and texting me more than ever since I started staying at my dad's, as if in the absence of all her stuff it's me she has to hold on to most tightly.

But she's making progress. We all are. That's why the shovel: I figure if she can put the past to rest, so can I.

I head straight for the long field, through buzzy clouds of gnats that disperse like smoke in front of me. Something tugs at me, a residual fear, a sense of being watched—*Lovelorn*—but I ignore it. Dr. Leblanc says that hoarding happens when the brain mixes up signals, confuses trash for treasure, makes things meaningful that don't have any meaning at all. Maybe it's the same for the bad memories we carry, for associations overlaid onto a place or a book or an old story.

In the field the grasses are nearly waist high and riotous, fighting back as I start pushing toward the place where Summer was killed, scything with my shovel. I'm surprised to see that her memorial is still tended. Around the cross, someone has trimmed the grass and must be refreshing the flowers: a bouquet of purple carnations, Summer's favorite, lies next to it. I feel uneasy without knowing why—then I realize it's the circle of trimmed grass, which is almost perfectly proportioned to the circle of stones Summer had set up for the sacrifice that day.

That day. Sometimes I think I can still smell that poor cat, like sick and sweat and gasoline, can still feel its heartbeat slow and sluggish under my fingers. I don't know why we never told the cops the truth about the cat. It would have been so easy to say: Summer did it. Maybe because the truth was too terrible. Maybe because I still blamed myself for running, for not doing anything more to help.

That's the whole point of stories: they stand in for the things too horrible to name.

I start digging. Since the storm there hasn't been an inch of rain, and the dirt is dry-packed, dusty. After only a few minutes I'm sweating. But I manage a hole just large enough to fit the shoebox, and bury it, tamping down the dirt with my foot, releasing a thin mist of red dust. I feel as if I should say a word or a prayer, but I can't think of one. The makeshift grave looks bare and sorry, like an exposed eyeball in the middle of the grass, and I reach for the bouquet, thinking it might serve as a headstone. Goodbye, Lovelorn. Goodbye, Summer.

When I move the bouquet, a small handwritten note slips from it: a psalm. *Though I walk through the valley of the shadow of death, I will fear no evil.* The wind passes over my arm like a phantom finger, lifts the hairs on my neck.

It's the psalm that was attached to the last arrangement, too. Could it be from the same person? Purple carnations were Summer's favorite flowers. Whoever placed them here must have known her—must have known her *well*.

I stand up, and the ground seesaws a little. The bad feeling is back, not a minor note but a full-on chorus, coupled now with the sense that I'm missing or forgetting something.

Though I walk through the valley of the shadow of death . . .

Through the valley of the Shadow . . .

The Shadow.

Even though I haven't moved, I feel breathless. Someone was wearing a carnation at Summer's memorial—I noticed it then but didn't make the connection I should have. Who was it?

I close my eyes, trying to call up my memories of that day, but all I see is the crack of Jake's fist against Owen's face, and Brynn shouting, the way the crowd started flowing down toward us like a multicolored tide. People pressing us from all sides, whispers building, and then through the crowd, our savior, one hand outstretched, eyes huge behind her glasses—

A twig cracks in the woods behind me. A footstep.

I spin around, swallowing a scream.

Ms. Gray doesn't look surprised to see me. She just looks tired. "Hello," she says.

MIA

Then

Brynn said to run and so I ran—hurtling through the trees, my heart trying to scream out of my throat, going so loud it overwhelmed the distant sounds of shouting and that scream, that one long terrible scream (praying for it to be Summer, and not Brynn). When I finally stopped it was because I was back on the road, back on the safety of the road, and a car was bearing down on me, driver leaning on his horn—a driver who later told the police about the girl who'd hurtled out from Brickhouse Lane in front of his car, a girl wild-eyed and crying, less than a quarter mile from where Summer would later be found by an off-duty firefighter who'd been fishing all afternoon in a nearby creek, her neck crusty with blood, her blue eyes reflecting the slow drift of the clouds.

"It's over, isn't it?" Audrey said, panting, staring at the place where the Shadow had curled and shriveled into nothing, leaving a patch of bare dirt instead. "It's really and truly over."

Ashleigh put an arm around her. "Let's hope so," she said.

—From *The Way into Lovelorn* by Georgia C. Wells

BRYNN

Now

Heath Moore's house is disappointingly normal, considering it contains a lizard-disguised-as-a-human. Maybe I was expecting it to be molting. At least a *Beware the Sub-Intelligent, Over-Testosteroned Teenage Boy* sign or two. But it's just a house, just a normal street, basketball hoop in the driveway and no signs of the subspecies lurking inside.

Heath answers the door, thank God. Not surprising, given that it's a Tuesday, his parents probably work, and he is a slug who does nothing but suction the life and goodness out of the world, but still. A good sign.

For a second he just stands there gaping at me, so I can see his fat tongue.

"I'm here to talk about Summer," I say, which makes him shut his mouth real quick. I don't wait for him to invite me in—I'd be waiting awhile—and push past him into the house. Weird that such a nice house could birth such a nasty little toad sprocket. In the living room, a dog that looks like an oversize fur ball is yapping in a dog bed next to a coffee table cluttered with family photos.

He watches me sullenly, keeping a good eight feet between us, hands stuffed deep in his pockets. Not so brave now that he doesn't have the two Frankenstein twins as backup. "I don't have anything to say to you." He lifts his chin. "And I had an alibi, you know."

"No, you didn't. Jake told me you guys were just covering for each other. Relax," I add when he starts to protest. "I don't think you *did* it. Pulling off a murder requires more than one active brain cell."

He wets his lower lip with that obese tongue. "So what do you want to talk about?"

I take a deep breath. "I want to know what she told you and Jake," I say, and since he keeps staring at me with that dumb expression on his face, I say, "About *me*. About . . . liking girls."

What I really want to know is whether she told them about what happened between us the night she came in through my window: that final, sacred thing, the way she jerked backward after we kissed, the terrible way she smiled at me. All I know is that days afterward the story that I was a *massive lesbian*—like you could be a miniature one—was everywhere, and some of the girls wouldn't change near me in the locker room, and Summer was treating me like I had a contagious disease, one of the ones that makes blood come out through your pores.

Jake and Summer broke up, and now I know that afterward she started hanging out with Heath. Back then, Summer wouldn't talk to me, wouldn't even look at me. I remember trying to get close to her in the lunch line and she just spun around, furious, as if I'd hit her. *Stop drooling, McNally. I'm not into girls, okay?* The weirdest thing about it was how angry she was—practically hysterical—as if *I'd* hurt *her*. As if I'd been the one to give up her secret.

Everyone laughed. I remember how it felt like someone had taken a baseball bat and just plain knocked out my stomach, swung my insides up to the ceiling, made a path out of the cafeteria with my lungs. And yet all this time, I've been holding on to the idea that despite everything, Summer loved me. That she cared. That it mattered if I kept her secrets, kept her safe, kept everyone from knowing what happened that day in the woods.

Here's the thing: Summer was the one who made me into a monster. And she's the one who has to change me back.

When Heath thinks, smoke might as well come out of his ears. You can actually see his brain sizzling. "Seems kinda late to be worrying about your reputation. Everyone already knows you're a dyke, McNally."

"Sure. Just like everyone knows you're a virgin," I say, which makes him scowl. Shot in the dark, but looks like I was right. Good. The little scuzzbucket should just marry his right hand and be done with it. "What did she tell you?"

"She didn't *tell* me anything," he grumbles. "It wasn't some big secret. Even the teachers knew."

My stomach seizes. "What are you talking about?"

He shrugs. "That's how I heard in the first place," he said. "My teacher said she was proud of me. For being *open-minded*. You know . . . for hanging out so much with a girl who . . ." He trails off. For a split second, he looks embarrassed.

"A girl who what?" Now my brain is the one that feels like it's grinding along, struggling to make sense of everything.

He rolls his eyes. "A girl who *liked other girls*," he says. "And then I started thinking it was weird, how much time you guys used to spend together. And Summer got pissy when I made fun of her about it." He crosses his arms, all wounded and defensive. As if the fact that I'm gay is a direct strike to his ego, like I'm just trying to embarrass him. "That's why I'm saying I kind of already suspected. And when Ms. Gray pulled me aside—"

"Ms. Gray?" Suddenly I feel like I've been hit with a Taser. There's a buzzy pain in my head.

"Yeah, my English teacher." Heath gives me a weird look, probably because I practically shouted her name.

"Your . . . ?" My voice dies somewhere in the back of my throat. I shake my head. "Ms. Gray taught Life Skills."

Heath shrugs. "Our English teacher was out on maternity leave, and Ms. Gray subbed in," he said. "She'd taught English before." He squints at me. "What? What is it?"

Obviously it has never occurred to him how weird it is—how completely and totally screwy—for a teacher to say that kind of thing. At Four Corners the counselors aren't even allowed to hug you anymore, unless there are two additional witnesses there to swear you gave permission.

Besides, how did Ms. Gray even know?

I turn away, feeling sick. My mind is hopscotching through memories, GIF-style. Ms. Gray in the crowd at Summer's memorial, a carnation pinned to her shitty black dress. Eyes raw like she'd been crying. Ms. Gray directing us back to Owen. Ms. Gray volunteering to help out with all those little kids at the parade, the *band* kids . . .

I used to teach music, before.

"Oh my God," I say out loud. It's so obvious. I can't believe I didn't see it before.

Ms. Gray is the Shadow. All along, she's been living here, floating along, drifting through normal life. But she did it. She took a rock to the back of Summer's head. She dragged her across the field and arranged her in the circle of rocks. She stabbed her seven times, so the dirt was sticky with her blood and cops arriving on the scene had to be counseled afterward, said it looked like a massacre.

All along, it was her.

"Are you okay?" Heath asks me, and I realize I've just been standing there, frozen, freezing.

"No," I say. I burst out of the door. I'm running without knowing where.

Mia. Somewhere in the trees the birds are screaming. I have to find Mia.

BRYNN

Then

"Put the knife down, Summer."

But Summer was still staring after Mia, watching her run, shaking her head. "I wasn't going to hurt her," she said. For a moment she looked irritated, as if I'd bought her Diet Coke instead of regular from the vending machine. But then she kneeled down by the cat and looked up at me. "Are you going to help?"

Panic was like a physical force, like a hand around my throat. "What are you going to do?"

"The Shadow needs blood," Summer said impatiently. "Come on. Help me. We have to do it together."

The smell of gasoline and cat puke was turning my insides. That poor mangled creature was still alive, still breathing. It would be a mercy to kill it now—but I couldn't. I wouldn't.

"No," I whispered.

Summer stood up again. She was a few inches shorter than I

was, but in that moment she seemed huge, godlike, blazing with fury. "You said you loved me," she said.

"I do," I said. "I did."

"Prove it." She took a step forward. She was only an inch away from me, as close as she had been that night in my room, the magic night of skin and fingertips and her bones small and sharp digging into mine as if sending me a secret message. "Prove it." Now she was shouting. "Prove it."

She drew her arm back, her hand still fisted up around the knife, and maybe I felt rooted, cemented to the ground by fear, by the certainty that she was going to kill me, and I grabbed her wrist and was still holding on to her as she twisted down to her knees and drove the knife down straight through the cat's neck.

It screamed as it was dying. It was the worst sound I've ever heard, a sound that has no parallels, no comparison on earth. Like the sound of hell opening. All the birds poured out of the trees as if they couldn't be witness to it. And Summer just sat there, shaking, eyes closed, her hands around the knife handle. I stumbled backward, sick, wanting to scream too. But the scream was trapped there, and as it passed through me, it hollowed me out.

"The Shadow hears," she whispered.

"It's just a story," I said. I was surprised to hear that now I was the one shouting. "We made it up."

"Shhh," she said, as if she hadn't heard. "The Shadow's coming."

"You're on your own," I said: the last words I ever said to her. When I left to throw up in the woods she was still sitting there, head bowed, as if she was praying. And for a moment I felt something pass—something dark and lonely and cold, something that made my breath hurt in my chest—and in that second, I believed too, believed that the Shadow was real, believed that it was coming for its blood.

Summer was actually kinda pissed the Shadow was turning out to be not so evil. She'd had a whole plan to drive the Shadow off and be a hero so that her friends would love her again.

They had to love her again. Everyone loves a hero, right?

—*Return to Lovelorn* by Summer Marks

MIA

Now

Ms. Gray says, "You come here too, then?"

She moves out of the shadow of the woods. I barely have time to slip the note into my pocket. She's sweating. Her hair is loose and there's a burr clinging to one shoulder of her tank top.

My arms and legs feel bloated and useless, and I remember once in fifth grade, at rehearsal for *Swan Lake*, being seized by a sudden dizziness in the studio, a sense that my whole body was floating apart. Madame Laroche caught me just before I fell out of a double pirouette. It turned out later that I had a fever—I was in bed for two weeks with pneumonia.

That's exactly how I feel now: like my body is betraying me. I want to run but I can't. I want to scream but I can't.

I tighten my grip on the shovel as she comes toward me. If anything happens, I'll swing right into her head, and I'll run. But even as I think it I know I can't, that I'd never be able to.

Ms. Gray stops next to me and looks down at the bouquet of flowers, now displaced, at the cross and the churned-up earth. My breath catches in my throat—if she sees that the note is gone, she'll know I took it, she'll know I know—but she doesn't say anything. She doesn't ask me about the shovel, either. She seems hardly to be seeing at all. Her face is strangely closed, like a painted-over door. For a long time, she says nothing.

Then she looks up at me. "I come here, you know, to pay my respects. I was very fond of Summer."

That horrible coiled feeling in my stomach unwinds just a little. For a minute I even think I must be wrong—Ms. Gray couldn't possibly have killed Summer. Why would she?

"Me too" is all I say, and she smiles. It's the saddest smile ever.

"She was a very special girl." Ms. Gray turns to stare out over the field. There's another long moment of quiet. "It's so beautiful here, isn't it? I've always liked it." Then: "I can understand why it happened here."

"Why what happened here?" The wind hisses through the grass. I take a breath and decide to risk it. "Lovelorn?"

She doesn't react to hearing the name. She doesn't say *What's Lovelorn?* or look confused. And when she turns back to face me, I get a feeling like diving deep in winter water, getting the breath punched out of your chest by the cold, a feeling of drowning. Her eyes are like two long holes, like pits filled with nothing but air.

And suddenly I remember turning around that day and seeing Summer holding a long knife, watching me with the strangest look on her face. As if she wanted to tell me something she knew I wouldn't like.

Run, Mia. I hear Brynn's voice in my head now, but I can't move.

"The murder," Ms. Gray says.

I try to say *It was you* and *Why?* and *How could you?* But as usual, when I need it the most my throat curls up on itself like a fern, leaving the words trapped in the darkness.

And then, for the second time in my life, Brynn saves me: my phone starts ringing. The noise hauls me back into the present—the tinny ringtone climbing over the sound of the wind and the birds. Ms. Gray blinks and takes a step backward, as if a spell has been broken, and all of a sudden she looks normal again. Good old Ms. Gray. The woman who showed us how to do CPR using a waxen-faced dummy.

"My friend." I press silence on the ringer, but almost immediately Brynn calls again. "She's waiting for me in the car."

"Oh" is all Ms. Gray says. For a split second she looks so sad I almost feel sorry for her. But then I remember what she's done.

"I should go," I say. My phone lights up for the third time. I start walking, fighting the urge to sprint, acutely aware of the fact that she's still watching me, feeling as if she has one long finger pressed to the base of my spine, making me feel stiff-backed and clumsy. Before I reach the trees I have the sudden impression of silent footsteps—I picture an arm outstretched, a hand raised to strike—and I whip around, swallowing a shout.

But Ms. Gray hasn't moved. She's still standing next to the little wooden cross, still watching me from a distance, face twisted up as if she's trying to puzzle out the answer to a riddle.

This time I don't care about how it looks. When I turn around again, I run.

I barely have time to say hello before Brynn is talking in a rush.

"It was Ms. Gray," she says. "Ms. Gray killed Summer. She must have been—I don't know—obsessed with her or something. It makes sense she was helping her write *Lovelorn*. She was the one who said Summer needed a tutor, it would have been easy enough for her to volunteer. . . ."

"I know," I say, and Brynn inhales sharply. Abby's driving like a maniac, bumping down Brickhouse Lane, raising galloping shapes of dust, as if we're in a high-speed chase. Only when we're back on Hillsborough Road, heading up to town, does she slow down. "I just saw her."

"You saw Ms. Gray?" Brynn sounds like she's speaking with a whistle stuck in her throat.

"Yeah. I went back to bury *Lovelorn*."

"You—*what*?"

"Look, we need to talk. In person." The enormity of it hits me: Ms. Gray, a murderer. Will anyone believe us? What happens now? More police stations, more interviews, more cops looking at us in disbelief. More whispers and gossip. Even the idea of it is exhausting. "Where are you?"

"On my way back from Heath Moore's house," she says. "I hoofed it."

Now it's my turn to squeak. "You—what?"

"Like you said, we need to talk." She makes a noise of disgust. "Can't be at my house, though. My mom's off work today."

"Can't be at mine," I say. "My house is under siege."

"Owen," Brynn says firmly. And still the name makes little sparks light up in my chest. I stamp them down just as quickly. "Owen has to know too. It's only right. We need to tell him."

She's right, of course—even if I have absolutely no desire to see him ever again, not after what he said. Maybe it's unfair to resent a person for not loving you back. Then again, it's unfair that feeling doesn't always flow two ways.

But this is bigger than me. And it's bigger than losing Owen.

"We'll pick you up," I say. I turn to Abby but she starts shaking her head frantically, mouthing *no, no, no.* She looks completely panicked—eyes rolling like a spooked horse's, sweat standing out on her forehead—even more panicked than when I first hurtled into the car and told her to *move.* But I ignore her. "Stay where you are."

No one knew what happened to the children taken as sacrifices by the Shadow. There were many stories: rumors that the Shadow took them to an underground palace and lavished expensive presents on them; suspicions that the Shadow used them as slaves; hints that the Shadow was the only one of its kind, and that the children went afterward to a subterranean city vaster even than its counterpart on earth.

Only one thing was certain: none of the children was ever again seen alive.

—From *The Way into Lovelorn* by Georgia C. Wells

BRYNN

Now

There's a *For Sale* sign staked to the grass in front of Owen's house. The workers have made quick business of the sunroom. The tree has been removed and the glass repaired, although there's still a roofing truck parked in the driveway.

Maybe our luck has finally changed: Owen, not his father, comes to the door. For a second he just stands there, looking like someone who got a mouthful of salt water instead of soda. Then he splutters, "Mia. Hi. Hey." As if Abby and I aren't even there.

"It's Ms. Gray," Mia says breathlessly. "She killed Summer."

"What?"

Abby pushes her way inside first. She hasn't looked at me once since I got in the car, hasn't mentioned all the calls and texts she's been ignoring, is still acting like I'm a giant wart and the best course of action is to pretend I don't exist. But what am I supposed to say? *Hey, Abby, I know we're about to nail a teacher for the murder that got pinned on me, but in the meantime can I just say I really* did *mean to kiss you?*

The living room where we spent our sleepless night poring over *Return to Lovelorn* is all boxed up, furniture wrapped in plastic like it's been swaddled in giant condoms. Instead we go to the kitchen, which is brighter and warmer and still shows signs of life—keys and mail scattered across the kitchen counter, crumpled receipts, a phone charging next to the toaster, still unpacked.

Mia tells Owen about the note and the bouquet of flowers, and I tell him what I found out from Heath Moore. Five minutes into the story the front door opens and closes with a bang and then Wade careens around the corner, panting, his shirt half-tucked into his pants as if he hauled them up while using the bathroom.

"What'd I miss?" he says between gulps of air. Then, grinning at me: "Hey, cuz."

There's a long beat of shocked silence. Abby shrugs. "I called him," she says, by way of explanation.

So we have to start over again. All this time, Owen is frowning, hunched over his phone, like he's only partly paying attention. And then I get this awful bunched-up feeling: he doesn't buy it. And if he doesn't buy it, the cops never will.

Owen shakes his head. "Check it out." He shoves his phone across the counter, as if it's something poisonous that's been clinging to his hand. "She lived in St. Louis. The city with the arch."

There are dozens of results for Evelyn Gray in St. Louis, including pictures that clearly show Ms. Gray but younger: smiling

awkwardly into the camera with her arm around a little girl carrying a big trombone, or arms raised, conducting a band of kids
dressed identically in red jackets.

*Evelyn Gray, volunteer conductor of the Youth Music Society of
Armstrong Grammar School in St. Louis . . .*

*Evelyn Gray, who graduated valedictorian from her high school
in Tucson, Arizona, before attending Washington University St.
Louis . . .*

*Evelyn Gray, pictured here helping the women's extramural
volleyball team spike their way to victory . . .*

"She was an athlete," Mia says, pointing to an image of Evelyn
Gray midair, body contorted like a giant comma. "So we know
she's strong."

*Evelyn Gray, pictured here with first-chair student Lillian
Harding . . .*

"Music," Wade finishes triumphantly. "That was clue number
three in *Return to Lovelorn*. She taught music."

"And she lived in Arizona. The desert. That was clue number
one," Owen says.

"Oh my God." Abby has gone green. "Lillian Harding. I

know that name." For the first time since we kissed, she looks at me directly, and my heart does a sickening flop, like a wet rag slapping in my chest. "Remember that day we found you in the shed? There was a mouthpiece buried there with all that junk. It belonged to Lillian Harding. I googled her to see if there was a connection."

"You googled Lillian Harding in Vermont," Mia points out.

There's an awful moment of silence. Owen reaches for his phone. A second later he stiffens.

"'Lillian Harding of St. Louis,'" he reads quietly, "'ten, disappeared on her way home from school on December 2 . . .'"

"Oh my God." Abby turns away, and I have the urge to put my arms around her, to bury my mouth into the soft skin of her neck and tell her it will all be okay, even though of course it won't. It's already too late for that.

"There's more," Owen says. It's so quiet in the moment before he begins reading again I can hear the *tick-tick-tick* of the old-school hanging clock. Wade no longer looks happy. Even he looks like he might puke on his boots. "'The body of Lillian Harding, who disappeared on her way home from school on December 2, was found just after New Year's Day by an ice fisherman in the Mississippi River, where she'd apparently drowned—'" Owen breaks off. He looks like he's about to be sick. "Jesus. She's quoted."

"What do you mean?" I ask. I feel like I did the first—and only—time I took pills. Like my brain has been wrapped in a thick blanket.

"I mean they interviewed her. Listen. "'Lillian was a wonderful girl, and everyone loved her'" said Evelyn Gray, who gave Lillian lessons in French horn and has for two years been the conductor of the neighborhood youth orchestra. . . . "I'll miss her very much."'" He abruptly stops reading and wipes his mouth with a hand, as if the words have left a bad taste behind. "Christ."

"She killed Summer," I say. My voice sounds overloud in the silence. "What do you want to bet she killed Lillian too?"

"And kept the mouthpiece like a—what? Like a trophy?" Abby's face is white.

"It's pretty common for murderers to keep something that belonged to their victims," Wade says. But even he looks sick. "It's a way of reliving the connection." I look at him and he shrugs, all bony shoulders and elbows. "I've read about it."

"Holy shit. I *saw* her." This occurs to me only as I'm saying it out loud. "The night I spent in the shed—she was there. I woke up and thought Summer was looking at me. All that blond hair . . . I was half-asleep," I say quickly, because now Abby is staring at me as if she's never seen me before. "But it was her."

Owen stands up and then immediately sits down again. "We need to tell the police," he says. "We need to tell *someone*."

"No." Mia practically shouts the word, and everyone jumps. She's gripping the countertop like she's holding herself in place. "No," she says, a little quieter. "Not yet. I want to talk to her first. I want to know why."

"It won't change anything," Owen says. "Besides, she'll probably deny it."

"I don't think so." It's rare for Mia to sound so certain about anything, and for a second I wish that Summer were here to see how little mousy mute Mia grew up: gorgeous and tall and determined. "I think she *wants* to tell. I think it's killing her. That's why she goes back to the long field all the time. That's why she dropped all those clues into the sequel. And that's why she kept Lillian's mouthpiece, I bet. It's not a trophy. It's a way of keeping Lillian alive. Of keeping their connection alive."

Owen's house suddenly feels very cold. "That's sick," I say.

Mia looks at me pityingly, and for the first time in our friendship I feel like the naive one, the girl who just doesn't get it. "Ms. Gray made Lovelorn for us," she says. "She made it come true. She must have thought she was doing us a favor. She must have loved Summer, in a way."

"That's fucking sick," I say again, but I'm surprised that the words come out all tangled and my eyes are itchy as hell and suddenly I'm crying.

For a long second, no one moves. I can't remember the last time I cried. Mia looks as if I've just morphed into a nuclear bomb, like any motion might detonate me and exterminate life on the entire planet.

And then, miraculously, Abby comes to me.

"Hey." She barely touches me, but already I feel a thousand times better. And I don't care about the fact that everyone's staring at us, watching as I lean into her and put my head on her shoulder and inhale. "Hey. It's going to be okay."

I swipe my nose with my forearm. "I know," I say. Because I know she's forgiven me, and so it will be.

"We'll all go," Wade announces, nearly toppling one of the kitchen stools as he moves for the door. "We'll all talk to her."

"No," Mia says again, and for the second time we all stare.

She looks at me and then Owen, then back to me again. Her eyes are very dark.

"She was ours to start with," she says. I know she means Summer. "This is ours to finish."

"Think about it," the Shadow told Summer. "The world you know is evil. People kill one another. They grow old and die. Love turns to hate and friendships to poison.

"But here, with me, you'll be safe forever."

—From *Return to Lovelorn* by Summer Marks

MIA

Now

"It seems so obvious now," Brynn says. We're parked halfway down the street from Ms. Gray's house: a small shingled cabin on Briar Lane, not even a half mile from the woods where Summer was killed. Parked in the driveway is a maroon, rust-eaten Honda. Something about the house seems sad and remote and sympathetic, like a girl standing at a party too afraid to venture away from the corner, even though the lawn is well cared for and there are even flower boxes in the window—carnations, I see, and feel another twist of nausea. Then I realize it's the curtains, which are all drawn, as if she doesn't want any interaction with the outside world. "Why didn't we suspect Ms. Gray? Why didn't the *police* suspect?"

"Because . . ." I fumble for words to explain it. I remember Ms. Gray plowing through a lecture on contraception while Todd Manger made a jerk-off motion behind her, Ms. Gray talking about organic versus engineered produce, Ms. Gray teaching us the signs of cardiac arrest and how to clear food from a blocked air passage. So helpful, so kind, so *convincing*. Of course I see now how easy it would have been for her to persuade Summer to accept extracurricular help, to earn her trust, to make Summer feel special. "She isn't someone we thought much about, is she? She was just *there*. Like wallpaper. Besides, we were thinking the Shadow had to be a guy," I say. "Even though Summer never said it was. And Georgia Wells doesn't either."

"Heteronormative," Abby says, with one of her eyebrow quirks. "I told you." But I can tell she's nervous, and so can Brynn, I guess, because she reaches out to squeeze Abby's knee.

Abby and Wade have insisted on driving with us, although they've agreed to stay in the car while Brynn, Owen, and I talk to Ms. Gray.

"I guess it's now or never, right?" Brynn says, looking as though she wishes it would be never. But she climbs out of the car.

Abby grabs me before I can follow her. "Anything happens," she says, "I'm calling the cops." It's rare to see Abby so worried, and it almost makes me smile.

Almost.

"Nothing will happen," I say, half to convince myself, and then I step out onto the street and slam the door. The knot in my chest makes it hard to breathe.

This is It. The Grand Finale. Except I haven't practiced, don't know the moves, have to fumble through it.

The leaves are starting to crisp in the August heat. The sky is like the white of an eyeball: like something that should be paying attention but isn't.

There is nothing at all remarkable about Ms. Gray's house, nothing that says psychotic murderer or manipulative crazy person. There is nothing about the house that says anything, and this, I realize, is the secondary reason it seems so sad: it is a house that anyone in anyplace could live in, a house that has remained featureless and indistinct.

We go up the flagstone path in a line: Brynn first, then Owen, head down, as if moving against a strong wind. Then me. Even though nothing moves, no curtain so much as twitches, as we get closer I have the distinct sense that someone in the house is waiting for us, watching us approach.

Just before we get to the front porch, Owen wheels around to face me.

"Listen," he says, in a low, urgent voice. And I do not love him anymore, because he does not love me, but my heart throws itself into the sky. "Listen," he repeats. His upper lip is beaded with sweat and even this looks right on him, like his skin is just crystallizing. "I want you to understand something. I'm leaving, okay? I'm leaving Twin Lakes. I'm not coming back. I hate it here. This place—" He breaks off and looks away.

"Why are you telling me this?" I ask. I do not love him because he does not love me, and people don't have the right to break your heart over and over and over.

Brynn has reached the front porch now.

"Just listen, okay?" He grabs my shoulders before I can move past him, and I know, I *know* that something huge is happening, the kind of thing that takes worlds apart and remakes them. Hurricanes and tornadoes and boys with blue eyes. "I applied to NYU—I wanted to go there—partly because . . ."

"Because why?" I manage to say.

"I thought you might come too," he says, in barely a whisper. "I thought if you did, it would be a sign. That we were meant to start over. That we were meant."

"But—" It doesn't make sense. And yet I know he's telling the truth. I believe. "You told me you didn't love me anymore."

"I learned to stop," he says, and his voice breaks, and my heart explodes against the sky in cinders and ashes. Fireworks. "I made myself. I had to."

"Owen." I take a breath. "I still—" But before I can finish, before I can say *love you*, the front door opens with a whine and Brynn freezes where she is, hand outstretched to knock.

"Oh." Ms. Gray looks almost relieved. As if she's been standing there, waiting for us, all this time. "I thought you would come."

Inside the house it's dim and sticky-hot, although several window units are regurgitating air. Maybe that's why she keeps the lights off and the curtains closed: a single lamp pushes feeble yellow light through a graying lampshade.

The house looks just as featureless inside as out. It's very clean, and the wood floors are bare. The furniture is all the do-it-yourself kind made out of painted plywood and cheap plastic. There are no pictures on the walls except for a framed painting of two yellow-haired cherubs cavorting in a sky of puffy pink clouds that looks as if it belongs in a bad diner or a dentist's office.

In the living room, Ms. Gray invites us to sit on a couch uphol-stered in itchy beige. She sits across from us in a fake-leather armchair so stiffly resistant it squeaks under her weight. Possibly no one has ever sat there before.

"Would you like something to drink?" Her tone is pleasant. She interlaces her fingers on her lap. The woman who taught me the meaning of the word *spermicide*. God. "I don't keep soda in the house. But I have lemonade. And water, of course."

"We're fine," Brynn says quickly.

"All right," she says. "Well, if you change your mind . . ."

"Ms. Gray." Owen's mouth sounds dry. He's sitting very straight, palms to thighs, and I press my knee hard into his. For boundaries and safety and comfort. "You said you thought we would come. What did you mean?"

Ms. Gray tilts her head, birdlike. She says in a measured voice, "It's about Summer, isn't it? I thought you would come about Summer."

I'm surprised that I'm the one who answers. Always in the strangest moments I find I have a voice. "Yeah," I say. "It's about Summer."

Ms. Gray looks away, toward a window curtained off, reflecting nothing. "I knew," she says. "When you said you were doing a project for her memorial, I knew. Why would you need to talk to me? You were her best friends. You were more than that." She looks at Owen and for a brief second her whole face peels back— and beneath it is an expression of such jealousy, such need, that my stomach goes watery and loose and I almost run like I did all those years ago. But then her face closes again and she looks like the same old Ms. Gray. "I knew then," she says, and she looks down at her hands. "But I guess in some ways I've been waiting."

"Is that why you didn't leave Twin Lakes?" Brynn asks.

"I liked to be close to her," she says quietly.

"Tell us what happened," Owen says. He still hasn't moved— maybe he can't move—but he's gotten it together, doesn't seem anxious or angry anymore. "When did it start?"

Ms. Gray looks away again. "You have to understand," she says after a long pause. "I loved Summer. I saw myself in her. I was raised in the system, too, bounced between homes—" She breaks off. Then: "You don't understand, can't understand what it's like. I was never loved by anyone, I don't think. I was never even liked, really. If you're lucky, you're tolerated. And then you're supposed to be grateful. Have you ever had a dream where you've tried to run and can't? Tried to yell and can't? That's what it's like. Like . . ." She trails off.

"Like being a shadow," I say, and she smiles a nice normal teacher smile, like I got the right answer on a quiz.

"Summer was having trouble in school. The reading and

writing especially. I offered to help." She glances at me sideways, and I think of her telling us so casually at TLC that Owen was tutoring Summer. Still clinging to her lies. Still trying to protect herself. The hatred blooming inside me feels toxic, like one of those red tides that stifles everything alive.

"What a sweet little setup," Brynn says. "You knew she wouldn't tell anyone. She'd be too embarrassed."

"No," Ms. Gray says quickly, turning to Brynn. "I didn't plan it. I swear. She told me about Lovelorn, and how she'd always wanted to write a sequel. But she was shy, you know, about her writing. I just offered to help."

"Bullshit," Owen says. Still calm, still casual, not the wildfire boy who moved but a boy I don't know, a boy I really, really want to know. Not memory and story but fact and now and real. "You thought it would be easy to put the blame on us."

"You're not listening." Ms. Gray looks upset for the first time. "I'm telling you—I didn't mean for it to happen. I didn't *want* it to happen."

"You took the gas can," Owen says. "You left it behind my house."

Ms. Gray touches a hand to her forehead, and for a second I think she's going to cross herself, but she lets the hand drop. "That was afterward," she says. "I didn't know what to do. And I figured that's where she'd gotten them. You were the only thing she could talk about, in the end. Owen, Owen, Owen. She knew you didn't really care about her, you know. She knew there was someone else." Her eyes slide to mine and I have to look away. "Besides, she had your sweater. She'd forgotten it at my house the day before. We'd had a fight. . . ."

Why? I want to ask. *Why was she in your house at all, removing her sweater, removing any of her clothing?* But I can't bear to hear the answer said aloud.

"My sweater?" Owen repeats.

Brynn shakes her head. "She wasn't wearing a sweater."

"I put it over her," Ms. Gray said. "It was ugly. Dark brown and stained. But it was better than nothing. I was worried, you know, that she'd be cold at night." She says this matter-of-factly, as if there's nothing weird at all about stabbing someone seven times and then worrying about how cold she'll be.

Owen closes his eyes. "The blood," he says, and then opens his eyes again. "The blood on the sweater. You remember how bad my nosebleeds were. She must have taken a sweater without asking. No wonder the DNA was a match. She was wearing *my* sweater."

Ms. Gray leans forward, patient but also emphatic, making a point. She teaches kids. That's what occurs to me. She still teaches kids every day. The sick thing is she's really good at it. "Summer loved Lovelorn. You have no idea—none of you have any idea— what she'd already been through. You *couldn't* know. She didn't want you to feel sorry for her. I was the same way. Lovelorn was her escape." Ms. Gray's eyes are so bright that for a second it's like seeing Summer's ghost there. *C'mon, guys. Lovelorn calls.* "It was her safe place."

"It was a story." Now Brynn speaks up, and Ms. Gray turns to her, frowning. "It was a story and she wanted it to end."

Ms. Gray shakes her head. "She started changing. Cutting school. Smoking pot. I heard rumors about what she was getting into. After what I'd done for her—"

"You cleaned up the shed," I say.

"I did it for her," she says. "For all of you. To make Lovelorn real."

"You killed those birds, too," Brynn says, and she brings a finger to the dark tattoo on her wrist, maybe unconsciously. "You killed them and stuck them on a stake and left them where you knew we would find them."

Those birds: frozen stiff with blood, beaks to the sky, one of them still flapping out its last life. We'd had lasagna for lunch that day, and I remember how it tasted coming up, the vivid orange in the snow.

And suddenly I have another memory—something I must have forgotten—of a time when Ryan Castro thought it would be funny to try to make me talk by spitting on me in the hall, to get me to fight back. This was before Summer and I were even friends—she was still the new girl with boobs who dressed weird—but she walked straight up to him and put an elbow to his neck and said, *I'll kill you*. And afterward she told everyone I didn't talk only because I didn't talk to idiots.

This is the problem with words and even stories: there is never one truth. Summer was awful. We hated her. And she was magical, too, and it was our job to protect her, and we failed.

"It was just a warning," Ms. Gray says. "She shouldn't have been doing what she was doing—it wasn't right. It wasn't good for her. I was protecting her."

"You were hurting her," I say. And this I know, too. I understand it instinctively, without *wanting* to understand it, without wanting to think about it. "She trusted you, and you hurt her." Who knows how it started—little touches on the knee, long hugs, a kiss on the forehead. And Summer, beautiful, crazy, screwed-up Summer, who once sat in my room with an old pair of scissors over her wrist, saying *swear, swear you love me*—who didn't know what love looked like unless it was hurt, too—she might have believed it. She *would* have believed it, like Brynn believed that she couldn't come home and my mom believed she could rebuild her life shoebox by coupon by envelope and I believed in an Owen who didn't exist.

Did Summer know the difference anymore, at the end, between what was real and what wasn't? I remember how she looked on that final day, when we came over the hill and saw her in the long field: like an angel who'd been pinned to the ground only temporarily, like someone not meant to stay. She believed by then, really and truly. In the book, in the Shadow, in the sacrifice.

Or maybe even that story was better than what was really happening, what she didn't know how to stop.

"I loved her," Ms. Gray says quietly. "I want you to know that. I loved her more than anything."

Brynn is shaking a little when she stands. "You didn't love her," she says. "You don't even know what that word means."

"You're wrong," Ms. Gray says. She looks strangely small, collapsed inside her clothing. "That's why I did it. She was trying to leave me. She was so confused. That's what we were fighting about, the day before she died." Not: the day before I killed her. The day before she died. As if it was all an accident. As if Summer ran against the knife herself, all seven times. "When she didn't answer my call, I set out to find her. I knew she must have gone to Lovelorn. But when I saw what she was doing . . ." Her voice breaks, and for a moment she looks close to tears. "The knife and the gas can and that cat. The Sacrifice meant to keep away the Shadow. Meant to keep *me* away. She was—she was scared of me." She shakes her head, as if still this idea makes no sense to her. "*Scared* of me. I just wanted her to stop running. I wanted her to listen. And then I thought . . ." She squints, like someone trying to puzzle out how to explain a math problem. "She was so troubled, you know. She wouldn't have ended up well. I thought she could stay in Lovelorn."

When Owen stands, he puts a hand on my back to draw me up with him. I'm glad. I can't even feel my legs anymore. I'm filled with the strangest sense of relief and loss, like finally giving up on something you were reaching for.

"We're going to have to go to the police, Ms. Gray," Owen says, very politely and formally. And then: "Please wait for them to come. It's the right thing to do."

Again she squints up at us. She has a face that you'd forget five minutes after looking at it. Is that why we didn't see?

"I won't go anywhere." She spreads her hands. "Like I said, I've been waiting . . . and I've accepted what's right, anyway."

We shouldn't leave, I know. We should call the police and sit and wait and make sure she doesn't go anywhere. But we need out. Out, out, out: into air, out of the heat, away from Ms. Gray and the story of love that looks like bleeding.

But I turn around before we get to the door because suddenly I get it, I see all of it—all of Summer, all of who she was and who she was trying to be and who she could have become; but also, for the first time ever, I understand Lovelorn and why Georgia Wells ended the book the way that she did. That broken sentence we puzzled over, all of our theories about sudden shock or writers' block or sequels to come, they were all wrong: she was leaving the story unfinished because that's the point of stories and their power: that the endings are still unfolding.

"She was a kid," I say, and the words seem to come from someone and somewhere else. "She was troubled. But you don't know what would have happened to her and what she would have been. How can you know? You took her story away. You ended it before she had a chance."

"I saved her," Ms. Gray whispers.

"That's just *your* story," I say, and push out into the sunshine where I can breathe again.

BRYNN

Now

Here is how it ends: halfway back to the car a whispery voice in the back of my head speaks up—a voice telling me there's something I've forgotten, something Ms. Gray said.

"Oh my God." I stop. All at once I know what Ms. Gray meant when she said she had accepted what was right.

Mia and Owen have been walking close together, heads bowed, like people on their way back from a funeral. They both turn around together.

"What?" Mia says. Her eyes are scrubby from crying.

"*Lovelorn*," I say. Not just words—a message. A secret code. "It's a quote from *Lovelorn*. It's what the sacrifices say, just before the Shadow takes them."

Mia shakes her head. "What do you mean?"

But I'm already sprinting back, the pavement walloping the soles of my shoes, knees ringing, because even though she deserves it and a part of me wishes for it, I am not a broken thing after all, and not a monster, and so my instinct is to run—and I'm almost there, I almost reach the door, and my heart is beating so hard that when the gun goes off I almost, almost don't hear it.

Audrey, Ava, and Ashleigh were much older by the time they found Lovelorn again, and by then they'd been dreaming of returning for a long time.

They walked into the woods, hands interlinked, though it had been years and years since they'd seen each other, waiting for the magic feeling, the spine-tingly anticipation, waiting for the world to shimmer and change. But after a while they had to admit there was nothing left in the woods but the woods.

"What happened?" Audrey asked. "Where did Lovelorn go?"

Ava checked the time. "I have to go," she said. "I'm having dinner with my family."

Ashleigh agreed. "We can come back and look again tomorrow."

But tomorrow came and they didn't come back, and the tomorrow after that, too. They never did go back in those woods and look again, partly because they knew they'd be disappointed, but also because they were busy now, with lives and friends and families of their own, and it just didn't seem so important anymore. Gregor the Dwarf had told them once before that there was magic in all different kinds of things, and maybe that's what he meant.

—From the final chapter of *End of Lovelorn* by Brynn McNally and Mia Ferguson

MIA

Now

When people talk about New York City, they usually talk about the size of it: the height of the buildings and the endless rivers of people flowing in narrow channels between them, the way I used to have to squeeze through the Piles before the Piles were vanquished. But what really strikes me is the *sound*—a constant hum of traffic and footsteps and phones ringing and kids squealing and someone, always, cursing at someone else. Even here, standing in the middle of Washington Square Park, there's the rattle of skateboards on pavement and a college boy playing guitar with his friends and protesters chanting about inequality.

Since I arrived in New York yesterday, it's like my voice is in a rush to join all the other voices, all the other sounds: I haven't talked so freely or so much in my whole life. Somehow, it feels so much easier to speak when everyone else is fighting to be heard, too.

I love it.

"So?" Dad looks like he stepped out of an ad for Urban Tourism. He has a camera looped around his neck and a fanny pack—an actual fanny pack—around his waist. Every time we've gone on the subway he keeps a hand around his wallet. *Never know in these big cities*, he keeps saying, as if he's hoping he can subtly persuade me to go to college in southern Vermont. "What do you think?"

"I like it," I say carefully. And then: "You know what, actually? I love it."

To his credit, Dad manages to avoid looking totally freaked out. He pats my shoulder awkwardly. "I'm glad, honey." Then: "And I'm sure if I just sell my house, car, and business—"

"Ha-ha. Very funny."

"And you take a job at the Seaport slinging tuna—"

"*Dad*. You're thinking of Seattle."

"We might have enough money for the first semester of tuition." But he's smiling, and a second later he draws me into a hug. "I'm proud of you, honey," he says, into the top of my head, which for him is a major, huge confession of love.

"I know, Dad." As I pull away, my heart stops: he's here. Even though we've been texting or talking or messaging almost every day, seeing him is different: Owen, coming toward us, beaming, his hair longer and wilder than ever and his cowlick straight in the air like an exclamation point. The strangest and most beautiful boy in the city. Maybe in the world.

"Mr. Ferguson," he says, out of breath, as if he's been running.

He barely looks at my dad when they shake hands. He's just staring at me, grinning. "Mia."

"Owen." Since August, when I last saw him, he's grown another inch. He's wearing a navy-blue scarf and a jacket with leather patches at the elbows and he looks older, somehow, like he's filling space differently, like he belongs.

This is something I understand now. This is the miracle—of other people, of the whole world, of the mystery of it. That things change. That people grow. That stories can be rewritten over and over, demons recast as heroes, and tragedies as grace. That Owen can never be mine, not really, and that is a good thing, because it means I can truly love him. That love often looks a lot like letting go.

The real crime is always in the endings. Georgia Wells knew that.

If Summer had lived, she might have learned that too.

"Nine o'clock," Dad says, giving Owen a stern mind-your-manners look he must have been holding on to for the past seventeen years. Then he turns to me. "You can find your way back to the hotel?"

"Yes, Dad," I say.

"I'll get her back safely," Owen says, still with that smile that could power half a city block. Funny that as a kid he wore so much black. He's all color now, all sparkle, like a rainbow in boy form.

"Nine o'clock," my father repeats, adding in a finger waggle. "Love you, Mia."

"Love you too, Dad," I say. Thanks to our sessions with Dr. Leblanc, it's all love all the time. It was as if for five years we were locked in the same holding pattern, circling around the things we wanted to say. But when Ms. Gray committed suicide, we had permission to land.

"So?" Owen doesn't hold my hand, but we walk so close he might as well be touching me. And I think of a lift: held by him, weightless, soaring. "Where do you want to go?"

"I promised I'd get Abby a souvenir," I say. "Ugliest one I could find. I should get something for Brynn, too."

Owen and I walk together down to Canal Street, and he tells me about his courses and his professors and the boy who lives on Owen's floor who runs an illegal gambling den from his room. He tells me about New York and how it opens like an origami figure, showing more dimensions every day, more hidden restaurants and art galleries, more tucked-away stores and more people, always more people, all of them with stories.

In Chinatown I find a horrible T-shirt for Abby with actual working lightbulbs sewn across the chest. For Brynn I pick out a black sweatshirt with a headbanging skunk on the front. I give Owen the updates because he asks: Brynn is enrolled in a special school and gets extra help from Ms. Pinner, who still homeschools Abby; she's picked up volleyball and has proven unsurprisingly skilled at spiking the ball at other players' heads. Wade and I went together to a game one time he was home from BU on break, and we both agreed: Brynn was born to hit things.

I've gone back to St. Mary's, just for the year, because I was told it would help my chances of getting into NYU. The first few weeks were bad. Not bad like the first time—now, since the news of Ms. Gray got out, and the police found proof on her computer, pictures, emails—we've gotten famous again. But this time as the victims—victims of small-town prejudice, cruel injustice, police incompetence, you name it. Before, everyone acted as if I had a contagious disease. Now people want to be my friend just to *prove* something.

But after a few weeks, when it turned out I didn't have much to say about what happened this summer or five years ago, when it turned out I was kind of quiet and nerdy and not very interesting, most people just started ignoring me.

For dinner, Owen takes me to an amazing underground pizza restaurant with some of his friends. It's so loud everyone has to yell to be heard, and I amaze myself by yelling, too. Occasionally, Owen leans in to tell me about the people at the table.

"That's Ragner—the one I was telling you about—he grew up on a legit commune in upstate New York because his parents were protesting the modern emphasis on consumerism—but they got tired of it and now his dad owns a hedge fund—

"That's Kayla. Crazy story. She was actually *homeless* for two years and studied by flashlight in the back of a car she was living in—

"Mark's the one on my floor who runs a poker den—"

And I sit there, smiling, loving the feel of him so close. He was right: all these people, these hundreds of thousands of people, have *stories*. Fascinating, ever-unwinding stories. I am just one of them.

And I am still midsentence.

After dinner, Owen walks me to Union Square, where my dad and I are staying. The day was warm, especially for November. But with the sun gone, the wind is cold and smells bitingly of winter. Still, the whole city is lit up, humming, alive with energy and motion.

"So? What do you think?" Owen unconsciously parrots the question my dad asked me earlier.

Even though I know exactly what he's asking, I pretend to misunderstand. "About the pizza?" I say. "Very good. You were right. *Much* better than in Vermont."

He waves impatiently. "About NYU. About the city."

I hesitate. I love it. Of course I love it. And being here means maybe being with Owen, truly being with him.

But it also means that I might find myself lonely and with a broken heart in a big city.

"It's high on the list," I say cautiously, avoiding his eyes. We've arrived at the hotel far too soon. I barely remember the walk. We may as well have flown. "But I'm looking at Bard too. They have a good program in dance education . . . and it's a little closer to home. And then there's Bryn Mawr—"

"Mia?" Owen cuts me off.

When I look at him, he's smiling again. And it's amazing that the whole city, all its eight million people and countless cars and bars, just falls away in that moment, vaporizes into air.

"What?" I say.

"You're full of shit." He says it like it's the nicest thing he could ever say. And then his smile fades. He looks away, biting his lip. "Listen. I really want to kiss you. Like, *really* really. But I know—I mean, you're in Vermont, and you don't even know what you're going to do next year, and I'm here, and I don't want to do anything to—"

This time, I cut him off. I take his face in my hands and turn it toward me and stretch up on tiptoes to kiss him.

Picture a dance so perfect, it looks like flying.

And here's the thing: I don't know what it means, or where it will lead, or whether it will lead anywhere.

But I kiss him anyway. Because if not, then

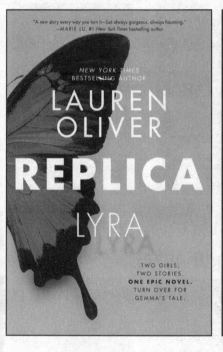
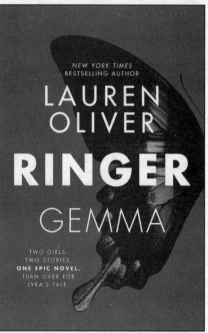

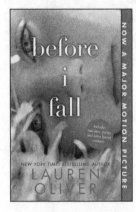
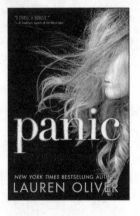
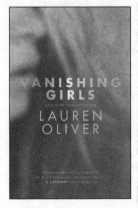